The Kiev Killings

The Kiev Killings

by G.K. George

ILLUSTRATIONS by

George O. Linabury

NEW ACADEMIA PUBLISHING SCARITH

Washington, DC

Library of Congress Control Number: 2011930384
ISBN 978-0-9832451-9-3 paperback (alk. paper)

 An imprint of new Academia Publishing
P.O. Box 27420, Washington, DC 20038-7420

 NEW ACADEMIA PUBLISHING   www.newacademia.com
info@newacademia.com

To Marsha and Mary

ACKNOWLEDGEMENTS

My happy debts are to a number of people who helped greatly in improving the style and narrative continuity of the book and in correcting historical errors. Gerry Smith gave the book its title and provided a detailed and discerning criticism worthy of a true *literaturoved*. I followed all of Carole Avins' valuable suggestions, most importantly on the need for a suitable epilogue. Ezra Mendelsohn saved me from errors concerning Yiddish language and Jewish culture. Alexei Miller performed a similar service for the Russian and Ukrainian side of things. My thanks to Nicholas Breyfogle for his careful reading of the manuscript. I'm grateful to my cousin, George, for his fine illustrations. Special thanks to Marsha Siefert for bearing with V.V. for so long, rescuing me from looming technical disasters and being always there for me. This book is dedicated to her and to the memory of Mary Linabury.

Prologue

An unnatural light etched the silhouette of the *Bet Hamidrash*, the House of Study, against the night sky. Low lying clouds drifting across the Dniepr pierced the red glow over the city. Cries and shouts could be heard at great distances, sounds that did not seem to come from human voices. Podol, the Jewish quarter of Kiev, was burning. Jews were fleeing the city with whatever they could carry, some having lost everything except the clothes on their backs. Less

Fleeing Podol

than a month had elapsed since March 1881 when terrorists of the People's Will movement had assassinated Tsar Alexander II. Now a different kind of terror was spreading through Ukraine, the terror of a pogrom unleashed against the Jews blamed by men driven by fear and hatred over the death of the emancipator of the serfs.

Across the street from the side entrance of the prayer house two youths pressed themselves against a high wooden fence, peering anxiously through a broken slat. Tall with broad shoulders and remarkably similar sharp features, they were dressed in the same shapeless jackets and old linen trousers. Their shoes were worn down at the heels and covered with dried mud, as if they had been tramping for hours in the soft earth of the hills and ravines of the city. The casual passer by might have taken them for twins. But there were no casual passers by that night, and they were not related. The tie that bound them was not blood, but friendship—and a mission.

Later they could not recall how long they had been waiting. They could feel the tension in their legs, and their shoulders began to ache. But they were afraid to move, to reveal their position. First they heard the sound of a door creaking shut, then a shuffling in the shadows of the entrance to the *Bet Hamidrash*.

"David!" It was just a whisper.

"Quiet, Aaron."

David slipped his hand into his jacket pocket to reassure himself. Over the past few days this had grown into a nervous habit. Now, it felt good, the lead pipe, cold and rough-grained with a sharp edge that had already torn a gash in the lining. He kept worrying it might get caught in the frayed threads of cloth if he had to pull it out in a hurry. That's when he would need it most, he thought, and wondered whether he would have the nerve to use it to strike down a human being. He nudged Aaron who shifted his weight onto the balls of his feet, causing the bulky revolver tucked in his jacket to rub against his side. The sensation made him feel slightly nauseous. It was an old German model; he had already forgotten the name of the manufacturer. Only three cartridges left in the cylinder. Earlier in the day when he had practiced shooting, the gun had misfired twice. Suppose it happened again? He reminded himself that he was supposed to squeeze the trigger, as if coaxing the bullets out of the barrel. That's what they had said. The image seemed absurd. "You have to get close to your target," they told him. "You're sure to miss at more than a few paces." But what did they know about six guns beyond what they had read in the cowboy novels of Karl May.

The short, stocky figure of an older man slowly descended the stairs of the *Bet Hamidrash*, pausing as he reached the street level, glancing left and right as if uncertain where the greater danger lay. He was wrapped in a long coat or cape that dragged along the ground. David and Aaron watched until they saw a familiar gesture—a fist raised to the glowing sky—then they nodded to one another and touched fingers. They allowed him a head start of fifty meters or so, and fell in behind him. Although they knew where he was going, they kept him in sight all along Shchekavits Street until he reached an archway leading to a darkened courtyard. There were no lights in the house at the end of the passage. They were surprised, though later they realized that this should have served as a warning. They paused, and stationed themselves behind a large chestnut tree directly across the street, watching the man enter the passage. Suddenly, he stopped short, his hands flew to his head, and he rushed forward as if in a frenzy. He disappeared into the gloom. For a fraction of a moment they hesitated before stepping into the quiet, darkened street. There was no traffic and most of the street lamps had been smashed.

"Did you see him? Like a crazy man." Aaron immediately felt he had said something stupid.

"Something's wrong," said David. What else do you say, he reflected later on, when you sense that the world around you is breaking up?

"Let's go, Aaron!" They were running now, hands jammed into their jacket pockets. They plunged into the passage. The courtyard was deserted. The windows of all the other houses were shuttered. By the faint light of the stars they could see that the doorway in front of them gaped like a black hole.

"The door, it's gone!" cried David. A muffled sound, perhaps a shot. Several more followed in rapid succession. David would never forget the sound of Aaron's cry, "No, no!" The door was hanging on its hinges; the side window had been smashed. They stumbled across the threshold and groped their way down the corridor. The darkness was impenetrable. An acrid odor stung their nostrils. Aaron recognized it from the day before, just after he had fired his revolver for the first time.

"The candles in the bureau, quick!"

Aaron fumbled in the drawer. "Found them! But where are the matches?"

"Top drawer right. Here let me get them." As David gently pushed his friend aside, his foot brushed against a soft object. He sank to one knee and reached out with a shaking hand. Later he could not remember why he was so certain that the Rabbi was dead. He had not taken his pulse, listened for his breathing, or done any of the things a lay person might do to check. He just knew it, was all he could say. Then a spasm seized him, and he retched from the pit of his stomach, holding on to the edge of the bureau, unable to answer Aaron's pleading voice repeating again and again "What's happening, David? What have they done?"

Chapter One

Detective Inspector Vasiliev of the Moscow police was alone in his office, standing behind his desk, and holding the order of the Cross of St. Stanislav in the palm of his hand.

"A pretty trinket," he muttered to himself, "but I'll never get to wear it." He remembered thinking the same thing when the Minister of Interior had pinned the medal on his tunic. His old friend Ivan, known to everyone as the Iron Colonel, had pulled strings to get him the decoration.

"After all," Vasiliev could hear Ivan saying, "you came close to saving the life of the Tsar. Damn near got yourself killed in the process. And you caught the swine who planned it."

Vasiliev had felt nothing at all—no elation, no bitterness. "Coming close wasn't good enough," he had replied. "Besides, no one can ever know who the swine were. They were too important."

There was no need to say more, not to Ivan. He understood better than anyone what would happen if the story got out. The terrorists of the People's Will could not have assassinated Tsar Alexander II without inside help. But only a few people knew it. There were two traitors, a high-ranking officer of the Gendarmes and a personal advisor to the heir to the throne, Alexander Alexandrovich, who had become the new Tsar. The bereaved son, now Alexander III, hadn't a clue. If the truth got out, he would have to live under the shadow of patricide. His reign would have been over before it began. Something similar had happened before in Russia. At the turn of the century, Alexander I had been involved in the murder of his father, Paul. Vasiliev thought about it. Things had changed since then. The conspirators who had killed Paul were nobles. It had been a court *coup d'état,* and it was hushed up. At that time there were no press lords eager to sniff out a scandal, no large educated public to lap it up. But society had changed since the reforms of the eighteen sixties. If the press got wind of a conspiracy implicating trusted officials of the police and the Tsar's entourage, the news could shake the empire.

Standing on the steps of the Ministry, Vasiliev had shared his thoughts with Ivan. "Imagine the rumors, the suspicion, the accusations, Ivan. Out of such stuff revolutions are made." They had turned up the *karakul* collars of their greatcoats to protect them from the raw April wind blowing off the Neva. Vasiliev had almost felt sorry for Ivan struggling to hold the high moral ground.

"Some day…"

Vasiliev had cut him short. "Let's leave your 'some day' to the historians. The Stanislav goes into the desk drawer."

Now he was back in Moscow, and the drawer was open in front of him. He dropped the medal into it, closed it and turned the key. He rubbed his left side, as he must have done a dozen times a day now. The pain had subsided. But taking a deep breath would call it up soon enough. Some small fragments of the bomb that had killed the Tsar were still embedded in his flesh. The doctor assured him they would work their way out over time. "So," he had responded, "I'll be finding shrapnel in my bedclothes for the next ten years. To hell with that."

A soft knock interrupted his thoughts. It would be Serov.

"A message from Petersburg, beggin' your pardon, Vasili Vasilievich."

"Serov, you know you only beg my pardon when official business shows its ugly mug."

Serov looked shocked. He had been begging Vasiliev's pardon ever since they were children wrestling in the dust of the village street. He never thought about why he did it. Maybe it was just to remind himself that he had begun life as a serf, the property of Vasiliev's father. Or maybe he had learned it from his young friend, Vasya. That's what he called Vasili when they were kids together. He also used to beg the pardon of the village elders, just to tease them, with the same mocking words. The trouble was, Serov reflected, that these days just saying it without thinking would no longer be possible. Just as it was no longer possible to call Vasili Vasilievich 'Vasya'. Something had happened to turn those plain words upside down. He decided to avoid the issue for the time being, and turned to the samovar.

"A strong tea, then?" He had already guessed what was needed from Vasiliev's furrowed brow.

Vasiliev glanced at the message, impatiently flicked the paper with his forefinger, and tossed it on the desk.

"Another summons from Ivan. Bless him and forgive him his sins. He doesn't know what to do with us any more. No one does. Just this morning the chief hinted that a long leave might be best for me. A long leave abroad! Imagine! The chief who has never gone further west than Tver. It's too absurd!"

Vasiliev crossed to the window, his eyes trailing a few lazy snowflakes, the sign of an early spring squall. There was a light accumulation on the rooftops and the grass verges along the Tverskaya Boulevard. It would be a heavy snowfall, but it would melt quickly, leaving traffic mired and the constables splashing around in a sea of mud.

"Now, Ivan wants to send us off to Kiev."

"There are worse places than the Mother of Russian cities." Serov snapped his mouth shut before 'beggin' your pardon' escaped his lips. This was going to be more difficult than he thought.

"Not right now there aren't."

"You mean the disorders."

"Disorders? What's this, Serov? You're beginning to sound like some Petersburg bureaucrat. They're beating up the Jews and wrecking their shops. It's a full scale pogrom!"

Serov passed him a cup and saucer. He observed Vasiliev's expression and decided everything was going to go badly that day.

"Sergeant?"

Serov stared at the cup and saucer as though they were mortal enemies.

"The duty officer collected all the tea-glass holders, said they had to be polished, so they gave us these instead."

"For God's sake! Don't they have anything better to do, like polishing doorknobs?"

Serov winced. He hated to see Vasiliev irritated. It was not like him. There, he was stroking his side again. Serov gave a short cough.

"Yes, yes. I know when I'm behaving like an old woman. All right, Ivan wants me, which means us, to leave at once. An official mission to Kiev. He wants to start an inquiry. Wants to know the reason for the pogroms. It seems that the Tsar is upset that law and order are breaking down. Fine, it worries me as well. But why me — us? I — we're detectives not students of society. The reason, my dear fellow, is to get us involved in a messy business that can only end badly."

"But the Iron Colonel wouldn't..."

"No, not on his own. But read the message — here, where it begins: 'My instructions are etc. etc.' 'My instructions' means it's not his idea. He has to be careful. He might have written 'You are instructed etc.' More ambivalent, but dear old soul he wanted us to know that he's had an order from above, and he's just the messenger boy. And then he adds, 'Coming to Moscow to brief you.' At least he'll give us the full story. So let's drink our tea from saucers, watch the snow pile up on Tverskaya, and see what the files can tell us about Russia's long love affair with pogroms."

Serov sighed as his sipped his tea. He knew he was in for a history lesson. Vasiliev was already rummaging in his files. Serov leaned over to read the handwritten label on the thickest one. *Sectarian crimes. The Jews. Newspaper clippings*. Vasiliev slammed down another one labeled *Official Reports*, raising a small cloud of dust. The labels were neatly printed. Vasiliev placed his hands palms down on both files. "Did you know, Sergeant, that the first pogrom took place in Odessa in 1821?"

Serov assumed the stance of parade rest, his fingers laced behind his back. "No, Vasili Vasilievich, I did not." Since he knew nothing at all that had happened in 1821 it seemed like a safe answer.

"And then another in 1849. In both cases the Jews were beaten because they failed to doff their hats when an Orthodox Christian procession passed by." Vasiliev opened the first file. "Then ten years later, again in Odessa. Look at this. An article in the *Odessa Messenger* for April 21; a quarrel among children during Holy Week touched off a riot. Foreign sailors joined in—God knows what for—and the Jewish quarter was sacked. A few wounded, one man killed."

Serov thought for a moment. "What were our boys doin'?"

"The Odessa police birched everyone in sight, it seems. But things got worse the next time, in 1871. See how it seems to happen every ten years, and now 1881, once again."

"Ten years is long enough to forget a birching, but not long enough to stop hatin' Jews."

"Very profound, Sergeant. Give us some more tea will you? This is thirsty work. Now let's go back to '71. Kotsebu was Governor-General. A local man, good family, you know, but he had trouble controlling the riots. It looks as though Russians and the *Malorusy*—Little Russians—were involved for the first time. It was the Greeks who had been the *pogromchiki* up to then. So, I stand corrected. Our countrymen are not in love with pogroms; they learn to like it from others."

Vasiliev took his cup without looking, poured some tea into his saucer, and sipped it noisily. He turned another page, allowing a few drops to spill. Shaking them clear, he continued reading. "'Officials counted eight fatalities from individuals who drank themselves to death with stolen liquor.' So much for the lofty ideals of the defenders of the faith."

"They always say the price of vodka is too high."

Vasiliev looked up, but Serov had raised his saucer to cover his expression.

"A bad joke, Serov. Really shameful!" Serov shrugged.

Vasiliev picked up another folder from the official file. "It seems there are some decent souls in Piter who were upset that there weren't enough police on the streets. But it isn't clear who was responsible. No investigation, no reprimands. It's always the same. We never seem to have enough people to run the country."

"Could be the people who are runnin' it…well, I've no right to criticize my superiors."

"Does anyone have the right these days? We ought to be careful, Serov. We are wading into deep waters. Pretty soon we'll be in over our heads. That's not a comfortable position. Let's have a look at the timetables. Then I'm going to send you off to the station for tickets. D'you know Kiev? No? Neither do I, not really. I passed through on my way to the Danube front in '77. A beautiful setting, on hills like Rome, though it hardly looks like an imperial city. Not as old either, though it was founded in the ninth century. Imagine what Russia would be like if the Mongols hadn't destroyed it. That let the Poles in, and they held the city for three centuries. So Kiev has been ours again for only the past two hundred years. If things had been different, we would be southerners instead of freezing half the year in Moscow or Piter. But aside from a little history, I don't know much about the place."

Vasiliev tapped his fingers on the open file.

"We need some help or else the locals will lead us by the nose. Ivan is arriving tomorrow, but I'm not sure I'll like his recommendations. I'll listen. I'll argue, but then I'll give in. Why does Ivan always get around my best arguments?"

"Beggin'..." Serov quickly corrected himself. "Your conscience. He goes right for it."

"*You* never appeal to my conscience, Sergeant. That's why we always get along. So, Ivan will convince me. I'll resent it. And then? We'll remain friends. But this time I can't just depend on what he tells me. I need another line into Kiev. You know what that means. After Ivan a visit to Papa, the source of all knowledge."

Serov nodded. "Bow to your father for me and tell him I remain his humble servant."

Chapter Two

The St. Petersburg-Moscow express glided into the Belorus Station precisely at 6:00 on a cold spring evening in late April. Ivan was surprised to see Vasiliev on the platform. "You might lose your way," Vasiliev said, "It's been so long since you visited us in Moscow."

"You look fit, a bit pale though. How's the side—still giving you trouble?"

Ivan had aged years over the past few months, thought Vasiliev. He had not been injured by the blast that killed the Tsar, but Vasiliev knew Ivan had been no less deeply wounded by the shock and sense of failure.

"I've reserved a private room at the Strelnya. They'll be happy to see you too."

They climbed into a waiting droshky and sped off.

"These are sad days in Piter," Ivan began. "The moderates are on the way out. General Loris-Melikov hasn't much time left at the Ministry of Interior. Gone are the days when we could call him the 'Dictator of the Heart!' The press has been hounding him. Our new Tsar, Alexander Alexandrovich, treats him with distant respect. But, you understand, it is distant. You exposed Prince Bagration for the scoundrel he was. But there are others who are crowding in to take his place. I fear for Russia."

"And when have you and I not feared for Russia?" observed Vasiliev as the droshky drew up to the Strelnya Restaurant. The place always looked to Vasiliev like an illuminated ice palace with its glass windows and glass roof.

A porter covered with gold braid helped them out of the droshky and bowed them into the crowded, stuffy and noisy restaurant. A trio of young Hungarian string players was working its way through a medley of Viennese waltzes. The manager greeted them effusively, and led them to a private room. "M*essieurs, du champagne, avec mes compliments.*"

"The moderates seem to still be in control here," said Vasiliev as they seated themselves.

"So our rules still hold? No business until after the third course?" This was the part of the meal with Ivan that Vasiliev enjoyed the most. They discussed the entire menu. Each dish seemed to call forth memories of another anecdote, a love affair, a duel.

They ordered the oyster *velouté* and poached salmon. "Shall we stay with the Moët? What about the sweet?"

"I'm swearing off the charlottes. Incipient gout. Let's just have a few *baisers*."

"All right, Ivan—meringue kisses to honor our fleeting youth."

When the table was cleared Vasiliev offered cigars, and they sat quietly for some time until Ivan, always the first to break the perfect silence, blew a last puff of smoke toward the ceiling.

"So why send you to Kiev when the whole Ukraine is ablaze? It's not just the pogroms we're worried about, though that takes first place. The city is a hot bed of conspiracies—or so we're led to believe. It's still a Russian city, but that's changing. The Poles have lost a lot of their political influence. But remember—we are coming up on the twentieth anniversary of the '63 rising. The Poles may be quiet for the moment, but everyone knows that realism is not a Polish virtue. The university students have revived their Union, and plenty of Poles were arrested in the student demonstrations a few years ago. The *szlachta* have their Nobles' Club in Kiev. They seem to be more interested now in making money than revolutions. But, the emigration is still active. Wasn't there a Polish Legion fighting with the Turks against us in '77?"

Vasiliev knew a rhetorical question when he heard one, especially from Ivan. He nodded. "You don't think the local Poles were involved in the pogroms do you?"

"No, no. It was the work of our Russian brethren. Perhaps Little Russians as well. But that raises another question. Were the riots set off by the revolutionaries?"

"That sounds unlikely."

"Eliminate the impossible, and what remains, however improbable, must be true. Isn't that an aphorism of the learned Inspector Vasiliev?"

"As a matter of fact, no. I believe that turn of phrase belongs to a well-known but over-rated English detective. In any case it does not apply here."

Ivan looked offended. "Why not?"

"Because I don't yet know all the impossibilities."

"All right. The People's Will are still around. The central organization is broken. But a few small groups have survived. We think there are a number of Jews who remain in the leadership. Kiev tells us they may have sparked the riots in order to create disorder, expose the weakness of the authorities."

"That seems far-fetched."

"It was far-fetched for the revolutionaries to preach socialism to the peasants a few years ago. 'Going to the people' they called it. Well, we know how that ended. A farce. This time they may be trying the same tactic in the cities."

"What's the evidence for that? As I remember the mad summer of '74, the Gendarmes rounded up a few deluded students. Got a few of the poor devils to talk. What did they call themselves? *Derevenchiki*? That was it–'villagers'. Have there been any confessions like that this time? I mean from the urban revolutionaries."

"Not so far. But one of the reasons I'm sending you is to find out whether there are any grounds for the theory."

"I'm not sure I like my reputation as the expert on revolutionaries."

"Listen, Vasya—we know the Gendarmes'll try to pin the riots on the revolutionaries if they can. So we need a neutral observer."

Vasiliev thought of many clever replies, but he repressed them all.

"So, where was I? Yes—Poles, revolutionaries, Gendarmes and now Little Russians."

"I think they prefer to be called Ukrainians."

"No matter. Ukrainian, if you like! Peasants are moving into the city, a steady stream of them. A few Little...er, *Ukrainian* intellectuals have got some odd ideas about their dialect being a separate

language. Now, I admit it was a mistake to forbid them to publish in this dialect. Just stirs them up. But Petersburg worries about
some of the hot heads. They want to turn the language issue into a
political movement. It's been years, decades in fact, since the government broke up the Cyril and Methodius Society. Of course, they
were only a handful of intellectuals. But there are signs that something like it, but bigger, may be in the works."

"So—Poles, Russians, Ukrainians and Jews. Quite a rich brew.
And you expect me to sort all this out?"

"Vasya, I know that you tend to be skeptical about conspiracies."

"Not exactly. As a detective I am used to dealing with conspiracies—small ones, like somebody who's planning to kill somebody.
Sure, the People's Will is a revolutionary conspiracy. But don't we
think alike, you and I? Piter sees conspiracies everywhere, and in
so doing it creates them."

"Agreed. I'm just trying to give you an idea of what is going on
in the chanceries. We want to head off a wholesale reaction, don't
we? Then we've got to separate the real conspiracies from the imaginary ones."

"Who else are they sending? I can't be the only one."

"Count Kutaisov, Pavel Ippolitovich. D'you know him? He was
governor at Nizhny Novgorod. He'll be going as the Tsar's personal
emissary."

"Then his report will be gospel. Mine can only be heretical, especially if it conflicts with his."

Ivan knew Vasiliev would be touchy on this point. He was prepared, he thought, to deal with it.

"Vasya, don't be difficult. I'm not asking you to be a sacrificial
lamb again. Your report will remain confidential, locked up in my
safe. I will use your information to counter Kutaisov if it becomes
necessary. But I won't quote you. I'll just use the facts you dig up.
And you won't mind if I use some of your theories too? No glory
for you, but no great risk either. Who knows—you may end up
seeing things much the same way as Kutaisov. Unfortunately, I
haven't got a fix on the man yet. I'll keep you informed."

"You still have the same code?"

"Yes. Oh, one more thing—as if you need to be warned. The

Governor-General, as you may know, is Alexander Romanovich Drenteln. Since he is coming off his appointment as Chief of Gendarmes he's been in Odessa, and now he's in Kiev. He knows the region well. He has many friends in Piter. He's a formidable man with a reputation as an anti-Semite. But apparently he conducted himself well during the riots. You'll have to keep on his good side if you want any cooperation at the local level."

Vasiliev ground out the butt of his cigar. "A brandy?" he offered.

"I think not. I'll just finish the champagne."

"Once more into the breach, dear friend." Ivan raised his glass. *"Morituri te salutant!"*

Chapter Three

The next morning Vasiliev rode out alone to the small estate near Kuskovo where his father, Count Vorontsov, was spending the spring. An unusual stretch of sunny days had all but dried out the highway, leaving a few patches of mud in the shadows of the stands of pine and birch. The trees along the verge were no longer thickly massed, as they had been in his youth, but broken up into isolated clumps. Each time he passed this way Vasiliev noticed how rapidly the forest was retreating, giving way to open fields. In the distance he could hear the ringing of axes. For some reason this had a depressing effect on him.

There was still little traffic at this time of year. Occasionally, a mail coach passed him; more rarely, a troika heading out of Moscow, bound for a country house that had been closed up for the winter. As the familiar landmarks came into view he was overcome by memories. A flock of crows wheeling overhead reminded him that it was here at Kuskovo that he had first learned to shoot. On his fourteenth birthday his father had presented him with an English rifle embossed in silver, a reward for his skill as a marksman. He had polished it endlessly, never allowing the servants to touch it. But he never took it to the village, and so never showed it to his mother, for whom shooting was a useless diversion, a game for nobles. "If you want a fowl," she would say, "I'll kill one of those plump hens out there in the yard. It just takes one stroke of an ax, and I never miss! And Uncle Sergei can trap a pheasant or a duck with his nets. No need to make all that noise banging away." Then she would bring her lovely face close to him. "Never mind, Vasya, you are just fated to live in two worlds."

It was as she said, he thought. He lived in two worlds. Walking the few kilometers from the manor house to the village was like falling back in time. His father's daily life followed the formal customs of eighteenth century court life, although the Count had been only three years old in 1796, when Catherine the Great died. He disliked the romantics. Victor Hugo was an abomination. Even Pushkin at times strayed too far from the classic rules, though God forbid that anyone else should say so. Well, he was right about Hugo. And the village? A Russia that had changed little since a hundred years before Catherine came to the throne. The peasants spoke of her in hushed tones, as if she were still alive—not that she had ever done anything for them.

It was in the village that he had first met Serov, strong and tall even when he was ten years old, still a serf but not yet bent or broken by the system. Vasiliev chuckled when he remembered how Serov had wrestled him to the ground, not knowing he was the son of the lord and master. An illegitimate son, but even so. How could he have known? As soon as Vasiliev crossed an invisible line somewhere half-way on the path from the manor house to the village, he went through his ritual of changing himself over. He shed the polite manners diligently instilled in him by his Scottish nanny and drove every French verb out of his head. How that would have distressed, his tutor, the proper Monsieur Lepis! He would always manage to find some excuse or other and escape their surveillance for an afternoon with a great sense of freedom. The servants loved him too much to betray him. He knew his father would never hear about it. As for the villagers, they must have guessed who he was, but they pretended otherwise. He was the son of Vera Alexandrovna and an absent father. No one asked questions. Yes, he had often reflected, they must have known. How else to explain the commotion when Serov had knocked him down that first time? Besides, everyone in the village surely had noticed the small signs of favor that eased his mother's harsh life. They could only have come from a rich protector. But the villagers let Vasya play his part until they began in their quiet way to take over his education.

Vasiliev had never been ashamed of his mother, only of his father for not having followed the example of Count Sheremetev, who had married a serf girl and made her his Countess. But his mother did not yearn for a different life, one where she could not freely "wield an ax." Was she only teasing him? He didn't think so.

He rode on, looking for the track to the village that branched off to the right. The enormous pine came into view, still defying the woodsmen. The peasants believed the demon, who was said to live in its branches, protected it all these years. Or were the other rumors right? Had his father given orders the day his mother died that it should never be cut down? Vasiliev glanced down the track. Had he involuntarily signaled his mount to slow the pace? He urged her forward. Only Serov's old mother was in the village to remind him of happier days; nothing else for him.

Soon after, the manor house appeared behind its screen of birches. The Count called his little estate *Nettles*. Was it because he enjoyed irritating his neighbors, who had opposed the abolition of the serfs? Or was it because he disliked sentimentalism of any sort? Vasiliev had never asked him.

When he entered his father's study, Count Vorontsov was pacing, a crumpled newspaper in his hand. Always restless, thought Vasiliev. He allowed Vasiliev to kiss his cheek, then held him at arms' length squeezing his shoulders. It was always the same, this moment of scrutiny. Vasiliev was impeccably turned out in his dark blue dress uniform. Oleg, the old servant, had brushed the dust off his trousers and even gone down on one knee to polish his boots before he let Vasiliev into the master's presence.

"The wound?"

"Healing well, but don't embrace me too hard."

"I never have!" The old man smiled grimly. He glanced at Vasiliev's tunic.

"And the Stanislav?"

"It raises too many questions."

"Exposing traitors is an honorable task."

"That depends on their rank, like everything else in this country."

The Count nodded his assent. Vasiliev called him a radical Tory, but never to his face. Vorontsov hated the Gendarmes. He called them the secret police. But he believed the Tsar was God's anointed and could do no wrong.

"Sit down and tell me what is going on with these riots," he slapped the newspaper so violently that the pages tore from top to bottom.

"Hard to say at this distance. The Ministry is putting it out that the attacks were spontaneous."

"Spontaneous or not, the government did nothing to stop them."

"That's a different matter."

"Not really. The police have a duty to keep order, not to stand by while it breaks down."

"That is what brings me here."

"They are trying to involve you?"

"Ivan wants someone he can trust."

"You'll be going to Kiev?"

"I'll start there, but the riots have been widespread: Berdichev, Odessa, you know."

"They seem to enjoy placing you in impossible situations."

"They probably believe I have inherited the skill to get out of them."

"None of your filial pieties, my boy! Besides *my* battlefields were straightforward propositions. At least I knew who my enemy was."

"Perhaps I'll win another Stanislav."

"Did I really raise you as a cynic?"

"No, more like a Voltairean."

"Come eat something. Marina has prepared your favorite dishes."

They dined alone. When the dinner service had been cleared and coffee had been served, Count Vorontsov gripped both ends of the table, a sure sign to Vasiliev that he was about to make a solemn pronouncement.

"The Davidovs have returned from Como." This was not what Vasiliev had expected. He had no desire to see Irina's parents. What would he say to them? 'I'm terribly sorry that your daughter has been sentenced to ten years of exile in Siberia?' He did not want to discuss the matter with his father either. How could he explain that the daughter of the Count's old army friend had turned out to be a revolutionary? Vasiliev did not understand it himself. He stared into his coffee cup; no tealeaves to read, he thought grimly. Instead, images went flashing through his head, until they stopped at the gates to the central prison for deportees in Moscow. For one insane moment he had been ready to accompany Irina to Siberia. Since then, he had wondered many times what inspired the idea. Had it been the example of the wives of the Decembrists who had joined their husbands in a life of exile? He remembered how Pushkin's lines had resounded in his head as the warden and he marched down the prison corridor.

"Deep in the Siberian mine…"

And yet he had never before declared his love for her. How strange it was! They had been standing together in the prisoners' reception room, with a score of women, staring at them, he in his starched uniform, Irina her hair already shorn, in the gray smock of a prisoner. Even the revolutionaries had not insisted that she cut her hair for the movement. He remembered trying to explain everything to her, but it came out in a jumble. And she kept repeating. "No Vasya, none of your romantic impulses! If you want to save me, work for a pardon. I committed no crime. They did not even give me a trial, just administrative exile. Prove to them the injustice. The Tsar owes you something, doesn't he?" Then the warden came back, apologizing.

"Vasili Vasilievich, it's my neck if they know I let you in here. Please, you must go now." Vasiliev would always remember it as the worst day of his life.

"So, the Davidovs have returned." He kept his voice steady. He said nothing more. They went out to the veranda to smoke cigars and watch the sun set. There was no need to make conversation. They had reached that point in their lives, Vasiliev reflected, where old quarrels had lost their power to stir them and old wrongs had been forgiven. He would always regret and resent his father's failure to marry his mother, and his father would always regret his son's having become a detective and not a Guards officer.

The Count broke a long silence. "Who do you know in Kiev?"

"Ivan will probably give me a few names."

"I think you need someone there with old ties." Vasiliev smiled to himself. He had not wanted to ask for a favor directly, knowing his father would get around to it in the end. He made a non-committal sound. They watched the peasants coming in from the hayfields in twos and threes, shuffling along in their plaited bast shoes, bowing to the two figures on the veranda just as they had in the days of serfdom twenty years ago.

"The peasants are beginning to ask for their passports now. The temporary obligation period is over. They want to earn money in the towns." The Count sighed. "I worry. Who will harvest the grain next fall?"

"Surely they won't all leave."

It was suddenly cool. The Count did not move, nor did he order candles to be brought. His face was in deep shadow before he began to speak again.

"Maria Alexandrovna, the wife of the Governor-General, Drenteln." Vasiliev recognized the huskiness in the voice; it did not come from the dampness settling around them. Would there be nothing more?

"You know Drenteln, of course."

"I ran across him once during the Danube campaign. I know his reputation."

"Do you? I don't like the type; he enjoyed running the Gendarmes, remember. He did not improve after that Pole—what was his name?"

"Mirsky."

"Yes, Mirsky—took a shot at him. So he added Poles to his dislike of Jews. But, *attention*! He may be hard, but he's fair, to give him his due. Still, he'll probably not be favorably disposed toward you. You had better make a discreet approach to Maria Alexandrovna." The Count fell silent. After a few minutes it seemed to Vasiliev he might say something else. Instead, the Count rose, touched his son lightly on the shoulder and bade him good night.

Vasiliev left early the next morning. He was already in the saddle when the Count grasped his bridle. "You know I am leaving you *Nettles*. It's the only one of my properties that isn't heavily mortgaged. The others will have to be sold to pay off my debts, ancient debts. Everyone will be astonished. They expect you to become a rich man. You don't mind do you?" He released the bridle without waiting for an answer. "God speed."

Chapter Four

Vasiliev had begun reading the lead article in the *Messenger of Europe* three times, but each time he lost the thread of the argument before he reached the end of the first page. He had dismissed his body-servant early in the evening to visit a sick relative, and it was the cook's free day. Being alone in the house normally gave him a great deal of pleasure. He put aside the journal and tried revising his essay on Pushkin in the Caucasus. But that didn't help. He kept re-reading the same words without making sense of them. It was always this way after he visited his father. But this time it seemed worse. He kept going over their meeting in his mind, inventing ways he might have broken through the barrier. It was all stupid and senseless, this endless fencing they engaged in; it was all feints and no lunges. He had piled up so many metaphors, trying to explain it to himself. But they remained mere metaphors. At times he felt a powerful current of feeling for his father, and then before he had the chance to express it, the Count switched it off. And saving that bit about *Nettles* to the last!

He suddenly became aware of a pounding at the door. It must have been going on for some time; it had reached a crescendo. He went to the window and parted the heavy velvet curtains. There was no carriage to be seen, no horse tied to the hitching post. He took a revolver out of his desk, slipped it in the pocket of his dressing gown, and walked downstairs into the dimly lit reception hall. Ivan had warned him that some fanatic in the Gendarmes might be insane enough to seek revenge. They all knew he had exposed Colonel Van der Fleet as one of the conspirators in the plot to assassinate the Tsar. What had been Ivan's exact words? "Some diehards believe your accusations were pure fantasy, just your way of discrediting the entire force. They know how your father despises them. They think you've inherited his feelings." Vasiliev had dismissed the idea as unlikely, but took a few precautions in the weeks after the assassination. Now more than a month had gone by without incident. "Unlikely," he muttered again as he extinguished the gas lamp in the hall, threw open the door, and stepped to one side.

The figure standing on the threshold was bundled up as if it were the depths of winter. His coat—or was it a cape?—was long and shapeless, covering all but the tips of his boots. He wore a strange-looking cap that was pulled down to cover his forehead and ears. The overall effect was comical rather than threatening, or so it seemed to Vasiliev.

"I am sorry to disturb you, Inspector Vasiliev, but it is a matter of some urgency." The voice was deep and mellifluous; it sounded to Vasiliev like a singer's voice, a *basso profondo*. The accent was unmistakable too. Vasiliev immediately guessed the man was a cantor.

Vasiliev peered into the empty street as he waved the man inside. He looked on with astonishment as the man peeled off layer after layer of clothing, letting each piece fall to the floor around him. It was like witnessing the unwrapping of a mummy. Vasiliev felt mildly amused by the man's apparent complete lack of any decorum, but then he realized he was witnessing an act of exquisite delicacy. It must have been obvious that there were no servants around to take his cloak and shawls, soiled and malodorous from what must have been a long journey. He shrank from handing them to his host. Vasiliev had to smile his crooked smile.

"You find my garb outlandish?" He stood fully revealed in his long kaftan, luxurious beard, side curls, and skullcap.

"Not at all! Just an ingenious disguise for a Jewish patriarch who has come from the south. You probably lack the proper documents to enter Moscow. I am Vasili Vasilievich and you?"

"So the detective is already at work detecting. I am Ezra Ben-Zion. Yes, I am from the south and have no legitimate business that brings me here, outside the Pale of Settlement. A journey by wagon

without stops to bathe, except the occasional stream to cleanse my
hands for ritual purposes, allows the body free reign to manufac-
ture its most pungent odors. You must forgive me."

"Forgiveness is not mine to give."

"Ah, yes! They said you were a learned man with a sense of
humor."

"You must be tired and probably hungry as well. As you see,
my servants have deserted me. But I can find something for you to
eat." Vasiliev had noticed that the man's hands were trembling as
soon as he flung off his last wrap. Was it sickness or fear?

The man's face broke into a smile. "I do not think you run a kosher kitchen, Inspector. Water will do." During the rest of the evening Vasiliev kept glancing at the small delicately-modeled hands
laced with prominent veins. The trembling did not cease, but it was
clear that this man could not be easily frightened, at least not for
his own life.

"They are murdering us," were his first words after he was
seated in Vasiliev's study and had swallowed a large glass of water.

Vasiliev nodded. "We have heard about it."

"No, I am not speaking of the pogroms." He held out his glass.
"Please."

He drank deeply and set the glass down carefully on the table
next to him. For a moment he seemed distracted.

"Perhaps you could find a beginning to your story?" Vasiliev
said.

The man smiled again. "I like your way of putting things. Yes,
a beginning, but surely you do not mean the destruction of the Second Temple?"

Vasiliev was getting to like him.

"Let me begin rather in the middle, for I do not know the beginning of this story, and we are counting on you to write the end. Is
this too cryptic? You must forgive an old student of the Kabbala for
his obscure utterances."

Ezra Ben-Zion paused again, but shook his head when Vasiliev
reached for the water pitcher. "No, Inspector, I fear I cannot drown
my sorrows. You see, they really are murdering us," he repeated.
"Who is they and who is us, you ask? When I think of them, I only
see men shod in black boots, with indistinct faces, a peaked cap

above and a dirty neckerchief below. *They* are shadows; *we* are etched too clearly for our own good. They are Orthodox Christians and we are Orthodox Jews. A terrible symmetry isn't it? They are members of a secret organization. They call themselves the Holy Brotherhood. You must forgive me if I offend you, but the word 'holy' always frightens me when men use it to describe themselves or their mission. An old prejudice with us. It goes back to the Crusades. But I am wandering, a fault my daughter reproaches me for, but she is, alas, not here to perform her filial duties."

Vasiliev sat quietly waiting for the story to move beyond its beginning or middle.

Ezra Ben-Zion fixed Vasiliev with his dark eyes. "You do not ask questions like a policeman. You are patient, not a virtue we associate with the police. But this does not surprise me. We know your reputation for tolerance, which cannot be said of our fellow men, police or not."

Vasiliev nodded to encourage him. He had the feeling Ezra Ben-Zion was trying to delay telling his story as long as possible. The man raised his eyes to the ceiling for the first time.

"I come from Kiev. We Jews have lived there at peace with our neighbors for centuries. Of course, the old men tell of better days under the Poles. But our memories do not go back that far. Most of us live in the Podol district, but we are not confined there. There is no ghetto in Kiev. But for many Jews, life in Kiev is precarious. We need special permission to live there, though the city is officially within the Pale of Settlement. But the police are active in rounding up those who lack the proper documents. Still, until now, there has been little violence between Jews and Christians. But now life has become an ordeal for us.

"At the height of the pogroms our Rabbi was killed in his home. All murder is evil; this one bears the sign of the devil. But wait, you must understand that his family was not touched by the hand of the assassin; his home was not looted or burned." He compressed his lips, but was unable to suppress a small sob.

He leaned forward grasping hold of his knees. "Inspector, the Rabbi was shot in the face six times, forming the sign of a Latin cross." He was hurrying his words now. "The first bullet struck the center of the forehead; the second tore away the nose; the third smashed into the teeth, the fourth struck the chin. They were aligned in a perfect vertical." Ezra Ben-Zion's traced the path of the bullets on his own face, his finger pausing at the entry point of each wound. "The horizontal bar of the cross was completed by shooting out both eyes." He shuddered as he closed his eyelids and touched them gently.

Vasiliev felt a dull throbbing in his chest. He did not recall ever having heard anything like this. Mutilations caused by the blows of an ax delivered in a rage; yes, these were horrible. But never, he reflected, this kind of disciplined savagery.

"What are you telling me, Ezra Ben-Zion? That this was a ritual murder, the work of a Christian fanatic?"

"In the past only we have been accused of ritual murders, the blood libel. Is this murder revenge for our imaginary crimes? You understand now why we see the devil in this business. The typical *pogromchik* may be a thug, but he is not diabolical."

"You reported this to the local police?" Vasiliev thought he already knew the answer.

"We hesitated to distract them. They seemed preoccupied with observing the mob smashing store windows."

"That was a mistake. Even if they did nothing to investigate, they would have to have filled out a report. I must be frank with you. Concealing a crime is also a criminal act."

Ezra Ben-Zion stared at him in astonishment.

"If you do not obey the laws, the laws will not work for you." Vasiliev realized how fatuous that must have sounded to this man. "What do you want from me," he added quickly.

"We understand you are shortly leaving for Kiev."

"You are well informed."

"Oh yes, we are well informed, but we are also powerless to employ such knowledge in our own interests."

"You want me to investigate the murder…"

"And to prevent others."

"…although you must know Kiev is a bit outside my jurisdiction." He could not help adding, "And since there is no official record of the crime, it will not do you much good if I solve it."

"We assume your instructions give you broad powers."

"And they count on my discretion."

"In the past your discretion has not hampered you from pursuing the truth and rendering justice."

Vasiliev saw no point in prolonging the Socratic dialogue.

"I must think about this."

"We ask nothing more. We know your conscience will convince you to take up our cause. No amount of persuasion by me or anyone else can match its power. We have a tradition that every hundred years one just man is born. Perhaps you share that belief? When you arrive in Kiev, one of our people will come to you for your answer and provide you with whatever poor resources we can command."

Ezra Ben-Zion rose and bowed to Vasiliev. He passed into the hall, where he wound himself up in his odd assortment of wraps, bowed again, and left without speaking another word.

How they all love to appeal to my conscience, Vasiliev reflected as he closed the door to the street. He vaguely remembered the tradition of the just man, the *lamed vovnik*. At his death God had to warm him between his thumb and finger, so cold was he. Of course, the *lamed vovnik* was a Jew. But a righteous man could be a Christian. Would he too need to be warmed by the touch of God?

Chapter Five

Vasiliev sat across from Serov in their first class compartment. The train was carrying them on the new line from Moscow to Kiev. A chessboard was between them. Serov had won the toss and elected white. He opened with a Ruy Lopez defense.

"Always the same, Sergeant. Don't you get tired of Ruy Lopez?"

"I'll not beg your pardon, Vasili Vasilievich, though this is the right time for it. Just remind you of what you told me when you began to teach me the game. 'When one plays chess, Serov,' you said, 'one does not engage in conversation. One plays chess.'"

Vasiliev shook his head and advanced his pawn.

Serov's mother had warned him, he recalled, that he should never beat Vasiliev at anything. "Show him your strength, but you must in the end allow him to win." They had argued many times about this. He had insisted that Vasiliev would not respect him if he thought Serov was not giving his all, playing games or not playing *the* game. He thought he was clever to put it that way. "So, if it's respect you are looking for," she would say, "then go elsewhere. I'm telling you he'll resent it; he has been bred to be a master." And then the argument had gone the same way; he remembered every word.

"The village has taught him something else."

"What to be our equal? Never, impossible!"

"To be a friend, then."

"A strange kind of friendship, a peasant and a count's son."

"But his mother…she came from the village. He's half peasant himself." And so it had gone. Serov decided to compromise. He would lose four out of five times, whether it was shooting, wrestling or chess. But the fifth time he would get his revenge. As he moved out his knights, he thought. This is the fifth time.

It was a hard fought game. Serov almost let him get away with a draw but suppressed his feelings of generosity. "Check and mate!"

Vasiliev accepted his defeat without comment. This was not his usual way, thought Serov. He liked to analyze his mistakes; 'it was the twentieth move. I shouldn't have taken your knight.' That's what he would have said if he'd been thinking about the game. But he just folded up the board, put away the pieces without a word, and sat back staring out the window of the compartment. Serov saw all the signs of a black cloud descending on him. It was all about Irina, he knew for certain. Vasiliev hadn't confided in him after returning from his visit to the prison. But Serov found out what had happened there. He had his own sources. Since then he had waited for Vasiliev to break his silence. Not tonight he wouldn't, Serov concluded.

Vasiliev pulled out a book of verse, but after a few minutes he put it down. The train had come to a halt at the last station before Kiev. Serov watched his brow furrow. Vasiliev seemed to be making up his mind.

"I have to warn you about something, Serov. I might get myself involved in a messy business. You should know about it before I try to drag you into it. You have the right to stay out of it. I'm serious. It could get us cashiered."

Serov was about to say something clever. He thought about replying that a messy business was always an interesting one. But he never got the chance to say so.

A commotion had broken out in the corridor. There were loud voices, and something heavy banged against the outside partition of their compartment. They both stood up at the same time and turned toward the door. Vasiliev stepped forward and wrenched it open. Two men were facing one another across a pile of baggage. The conductor stood behind one of them, his hands raised in a classic pose of helpless supplication. The man who was gesticulating had the look of a typical Russian merchant, complete with glossy hair parted down the middle, a full beard, and an ample paunch. He threw open his heavy bearskin coat, revealing a blouse embroidered in the old Russian style. It seemed to Vasiliev like a rather theatrical gesture of defiance. When he shouted, his ample beard moved around as if it had a life of its own. But Vasiliev noticed that this was only an impression caused by the curious way the man moved his chin, as though his jaws were only weakly attached to his skull. His booming voice carried the accents of a man from the central provinces, perhaps Orel or Kursk.

"*Pan* Szymanski, I must insist that you precede me," he was saying before he glanced in Vasiliev's direction. His chin managed to stop moving about long enough for him to smile. He bowed deeply from the waist and on the way back to an upright position announced, "First Guild merchant Lev Ivanovich Lopatkin at your service." He then whirled to address the conductor. "Thank you, uncle, but you see, we are well protected now." He pressed a small coin into the man's hand. The conductor shrugged and backed down the corridor.

The other man inclined his head, which seemed to Vasiliev to be abnormally thin, as if it had been compressed from childhood between two boards. He wore an old fashion cloak with a worn velvet collar over an elegantly cut, if threadbare, linen suit. A silver stickpin impaled a dark cravat tied in a double knot at his throat. His face was deeply lined, and his thin hair had receded from a noble forehead.

"Jan Szymanski," he said.

"Baron Szymanski, man of property, a Polish gentleman of the old school," the merchant bellowed; he seemed incapable of speaking in a normal voice. His arms opened expansively again, as if appealing to Vasiliev. "Please forgive me, Your Honor, for causing this disturbance. But the fact of the matter is that we are dealing here with a matter of precedence, you see. The Baron precedes the merchant, no?"

"A matter of politeness." Szymanski's high tenor voice articulated the Russian syllables precisely, but with a slight Polish accent.

For a moment Vasiliev thought he had stumbled onto the stage of an amateur theatrical group.

"So you gentlemen are acquainted?" he asked.

Szymanski opened his mouth, but the merchant was too quick for him.

"Acquainted, you ask!" He summoned up a rumbling sound that Vasiliev assumed was laughter.

"Why I've been buying grain from *Pan* Szymanski's estates in Podolia for ten years. Let me assure you it is the highest quality, no admixtures, pure gold, not a *zolotnik* of chaff. Brodsky's mill accepts it without question. The flour goes straight to Petersburg. Who knows perhaps to the kitchens of His Imperial Majesty, Alexander Alexandrovich."

"Do you always have this much trouble getting through a door together?"

"Capital, Your Honor! What do you think, Baron, should we allow this splendid officer to decide the matter?"

Vasiliev decided to play Solomon. He invited the merchant to be the first to step into the compartment and the Baron to have the first choice of a seat. Szymanski placed himself by the window, facing Vasiliev. The merchant gave Serov a dismissive glance as he sat down across from him.

"May I ask whether you are going to Kiev? Perhaps to help repress the disorders? Shameful business, this beating of the Jews, don't you agree, Baron? You must understand, the Baron has an excellent Jewish overseer, honest as the day — well, you know the expression. But still, you have to admit that the Jews brought it on themselves. It's one thing to manage an estate, work the peasants hard but treat them fair. Another thing to swindle them out of their money."

"I think you are confused, my dear Lev Ivanovich," the Pole pinched the crease in his trouser as he crossed his legs. "The Jews in Kiev are not swindlers. And it is they who are being attacked."

"Ah, my dear Baron, you think you Poles civilized the Jews when you owned Kiev. But we kicked you out of there two hundred years ago, remember?"

"True, but we were always more tolerant toward the Jews than you Russians or your Little Russian brothers."

"You see how he torments me," the merchant shouted, turning to Vasiliev. "Yet I continue to buy his grain and make him rich." He gurgled again.

"So, Baron, then tell us why you think the pogroms have broken out," asked Vasiliev.

"It's a complex business—" Szymanski paused, glanced at Vasiliev's shoulder tabs and added quickly—"Major. The Russians have only permitted a few Jews to enter Kiev, even though the city is technically in the Pale of Settlement."

"A few, he says, a few!" the merchant's voice shook the window pane.

Szymanski sighed.

"All right, my apologies, Baron, but I will demand my turn—and before long, too."

"Please continue, Baron," Vasiliev smiled his crooked smile.

"I say a few because there are many who enter illegally. Then, one fine day, the governor or the chief of police decides there are too many Jews in Kiev. The order is given to round them up and expel them. This is not done quietly. The people witness the disorders. What do they conclude? That the Jews have committed some crime or other. Perhaps that they are guilty of cheating in the bazaar. A small incident occurs, and people blame the Jews. 'So we'll help the police' they say. And they too pitch in to drive out the Jews. Only their methods are more brutal." Szymanski paused and gave a slight cough. "Now, it's your turn, Lev Ivanovich."

"You take my breath away, Baron," the merchant cried out. Serov was tempted to remark that he saw no evidence of this. Instead, he got up and left the compartment. He heard the merchant's voice all the way down the corridor to the conductor's station.

"Does your passenger always act this way?" Serov asked the conductor as he ordered a samovar to be prepared.

"Lev Ivanovich, it must be said, has a big heart."

"And a bigger voice. They make a strange couple, the Polish Baron and the Russian merchant."

"Even stranger if you knew more about them."

"Which I am hopin' you will tell me." Serov produced a package of Turkish cigarettes that he kept for such occasions.

The conductor took one, sniffed it, and lit it with a glowing wooden splinter he had stuck into the coals of the samovar.

"They make the trip to Kiev regularly, I'd say, once a month or so. But only recently, since the Baron was pardoned by our late beloved Tsar-Liberator, Alexander Nikolaevich. May he rest in peace."

"So, what was he, a rebel in '63?"

"That's what his coachman told me. It was last winter, when the engine broke down at this very station. He was waiting for the Baron in case the repairs couldn't be made. I invited him in from the cold. He would have frozen sitting out there on his troika. He told me a strange story. The Baron was living in Kiev when the rebellion broke out. He joined up right away. I think he had some military training. There was a lot of fighting in the city. He was captured in the winter of 1864. They could have shot him. But he was sentenced to exile for life. I don't know how long he served. But one day he showed up at his old estate. It had been confiscated, of course. But the man who purchased it was Lev Ivanovich. The old coachman said that the merchant had let the place go something awful. Now here's the strange thing."

The conductor stood up, peered down the corridor, and returned to his seat. He took off his cap, and placed it on the seat beside him. Then he drew heavily on the cigarette, filling his lungs before exhaling noisily. Serov nodded to encourage him. He could tell that the conductor was enjoying the moment, working up suspense for his audience. Vasiliev had told him how writers did it. What did he call it? A fancy name. A literary device. That was it. What would he use next? The samovar ploy?

"How about a glass, my friend? The rest of them can wait."

Serov turned his head away to smile. The tea ceremony took a few more minutes, the conductor humming all the time."

"Yes, the strange part. Well, when the Baron showed up, unexpected like, Lev Ivanovich took him in. And within a few weeks, the Baron was installed in his old house with as many of the old servants as could be found. The Baron hired a new overseer; they say he's a German or a Jew. And from then on the Baron has been running the estate and turning over the grain to Lev Ivanovich. They say he's selling it. But who believes it? And the two of them, thick as thieves, run off to Kiev regular-like. Now what d'you think of that?"

"Except for being thick as thieves, it sounds like the merchant has found a partner."

"What's that about thieves?"

"You see, thieves are never thick. They usually rat on one another. Maybe the merchant wants to marry his children into nobility; or the other way 'round. It's been known to happen." He noticed he had offended the conductor. What was so strange about the story? Perhaps there was more to it.

"The Baron has no children. No, Lev Ivanovich has nothing to gain from it. He doesn't even like Poles; he doesn't even seem to like the Baron. They're always quarreling. Lev Ivanovich teases him all the time. Now is that the way for partners, as you call them, to treat one another?"

"Another unsolved mystery," said Serov. "I'll work on it. But won't the others be itchin' for their tea?"

Chapter Six

At the Main Railroad Station in Kiev a young man dressed in a frock coast signaled to them as they stepped out of their carriage onto the platform. He announced he was from the Governor-General's office and would have the pleasure of conducting them to their rooms. "At least they had the good sense to send someone in civilian clothes," Vasiliev murmured to Serov as they passed through the main hall. "No need to be any more conspicuous than we are." They took little notice of the chaos that seemed to be the salient feature of all Russian railroad stations. Peasants surrounded by burlap bags were sprawled on the floor around the third class ticket office, stolidly waiting for the next train, however late it might be. He caught a whiff of sweat and rotting food as he passed them. Some of them had probably been there for days. A gypsy girl sat on the floor by the exit, cradling a baby in her arms. Vasiliev fished a ruble out of his pocket and dropped it in her lap. The young man looked at him in astonishment.

"She looks no older than twelve," Vasiliev muttered. They had to push their way through a crowd of peasant pilgrims, mainly old men, coming into the station. The coach was emblazoned with the arms of the Governor-General. "So much for anonymity," said Vasiliev.

Outside the station peasant women were selling bunches of pansies and lilies, reminding Vasiliev that they were now in the South, and many things would be different from Moscow, where there was still snow on the ground. As they stepped into the barouche, the air was shattered by the ringing of church bells. "Well, some things are the same everywhere," said Vasiliev. The young man smiled. "We have only half as many churches as Moscow, just three hundred. But still it's a good number, don't you think?" They sped through the streets as though the coachman was determined to show these Muscovites that there were spirited horses in the South as well. Vasiliev noticed that the poplars lining the big avenues like Roman sentinels along the Appian Way were already in full leaf, shimmering in the spring breeze.

"We're going down Bibikov Street now, named after one of our best governors. My grandfather served under him." The young man was pointing out the sights. "There was no disorder in those days. But even he couldn't tame the Poles. They dominated the University until the rebellion. Most of them were gone by the time I attended. But three years ago a group of them were expelled for political activity. Now we're turning onto Kreshchatik. You must have heard of it even in Moscow." The young man laughed. "It's the most famous street in Kiev. Some of you northerners call it the only real street in Kiev. That's not fair, but the best shops are located here. There is our new City Hall. You can see Archangel Michael, our patron saint, standing on the tower. You will be staying at the Hotel d'Europe."

Why do we have to keep reminding ourselves we are in Europe? Vasiliev kept the thought to himself. But then he decided the answer was right in front of his eyes. Until they made the turn onto Kreshchatik the city had a provincial look. No stone buildings, only wooden cabins and streets empty of traffic except for peasant carts. Kreshchatik was the only thoroughfare that bore any resemblance to Moscow, with its gaslights and four-or five-storied stone buildings interspersed among wooden shops and restaurants. Perhaps he was just being a snob from the North, he thought. His first reaction to Bucharest during the war had been much the same. Later, when he let himself absorb the atmosphere of the city, he found it charming. Could the same thing happen to him in Kiev, where pogroms had left their ugly mark? As the barouche descended a steep hill into a ravine, he noticed that most of the important public buildings seemed to be strung out along the boulevard: the banks and stock exchange, the city hall and the Club for Polish Noblemen. He wondered whether Baron Szymanski was a member.

"There you are!" he exclaimed." The Poles still have their exclusive club."

"Yes, but no one speaks Polish in public any more, or at least I haven't heard them."

"Do you happen to know a Baron Szymanski? We met him on the train."

"The mysterious Baron—or perhaps all Polish barons are mysterious to us Russians. All the same, he does live a charmed life."

The barouche suddenly swerved to the right, and a horse-drawn tram thundered by.

"Crazy damned things. I advise you never to use them. They can't manage the hills very well. We had two runaway trams just last week. Several people were badly injured."

"It sounds like a dangerous city," muttered Serov. Vasiliev nudged him sharply, but the young man paid no attention.

"So, you were saying—a charmed life…"

"He was in thick of the fighting around Kiev in the Polish uprising in '63, got arrested in '64, and then survived more than ten years in a Siberian exile. Few men sentenced to life in exile are lucky enough to return at all, let alone in one piece, *and* get back their estate. But here we are at the hotel. I have the honor to extend to you a formal invitation," he said, removing an envelope from his jacket, "to a dinner at the home of His Excellency, Governor-General Alexander Romanovich Drenteln, Friday evening."

Vasiliev proposed a stroll before supper. He was a firm believer in the adage that you learn more about a city in the first hour you are there than you do during the rest of your stay. He immediately felt enveloped by a more lively, open and youthful atmosphere than he had ever experienced in a Russian city. Provincial indeed! He reproached himself. The street was crowded with well-dressed strollers. To his surprise Vasiliev found out later that many of them were workers from the mills or peasant girls employed in the cigarette factories. The men were clean-shaven except for long moustaches. "No chance to wear a beard as disguise," Vasiliev chuckled. Serov was more interested in the large number of blondes. Whenever a soldier met them, he snapped to attention and stood rigidly until Vasiliev passed. Women were selling flowers on every corner. They saw no sign of damage from the pogroms. Everything appeared normal except for a heavy police presence. As they walked past the Club for Polish Noblemen, Vasiliev slowed his pace.

"Our friend the Baron has also extended an invitation, not so formal. He didn't want to meet here, where presumably he is well-known. As we left the compartment he whispered in my ear, 'We must meet. It is urgent. I will send you a message.' His exact words. He was almost furtive. I guess Siberia teaches you to be conspiratorial if rebellion does not. What did you think of him, Serov?"

Serov reported on his conversation with the conductor. "Siberia seems to have taken a lot out of him. But that's what Siberia does. The merchant, what was his name, Lev Ivanovich? He seems to own the Baron or part of him. But is this our business?"

"Let's have a bite, Serov, and I'll tell you about the other matter that really troubles me."

The dining room of the Hotel d'Europe was almost empty. It seemed appropriate to order cutlets *po kievsky*. Vasiliev told Serov about the visit of Ben-Zion. "I'm still not sure what to do. It's an added complication."

"Could be a provocation. There's plenty who might not want you mixin' in all this."

"You may be right, but somehow I believe Ben-Zion. Besides, I can't help thinking that no matter what happens we'll not get out of this easily."

Serov mopped up the hot melted butter from his plate with a crust of bread. "That's our fate, Vasili Vasilievich. Always has been. So, what now?"

"We'll follow the usual drill. You'll work the streets, get a sense of how people feel—the workers and especially the Christian shopkeepers and artisans. How should we disguise you? What about as a water carrier? There seemed to be plenty of them about, and they are mobile."

"Have pity, Vasili Vasilievich! Did you see those metal containers? Heavy enough to crush a man, they are. I have a better idea: a pilgrim. Plenty of them about too, and they wander all over the place. I could carry a staff to keep my legs workin'."

"A brilliant idea. A pilgrim can ask questions without drawing attention. You'll fit in easily. They pour into Kiev every year. Tens of thousands of them. This is the high season for them. They flock to the Pecherskaia Lavra—the Monastery of the Caves. A good place to begin."

The dining room was beginning to fill up, mostly men in uniform with a few civil servants mixed in. Vasiliev ordered coffee.

"I'll pay my respects to the Governor-General. I'd rather be in the streets with you. That's the place to find out what's really going on."

"We could change places." Serov's face betrayed no expression.

Vasiliev laughed silently. "You'd quickly get bored by all the beautiful women and rich food."

"A little boredom is not a bad thing," Serov said holding his coffee cup suspended in mid-air.

"*Touché*, Sergeant. But they'd take one look at your stripes and send you off to the kitchen to be fed."

Serov took a sip of coffee. "That's a good place if you want to find out what's really going on."

"Have you been reading Dostoevsky on the sly?"

Serov shook his head. He was beginning to wonder how long it would take for Vasiliev to put him down. The moment had come. A gentle but firm reminder of their class difference that no amount of chess victories could erase.

"Well, that's what Fedor Mikhailovich used to think, or something like it. The real people were more likely to be found in the kitchen, he said. But of course, he kept sitting in the salon while he said it."

Serov grunted. He was not eager to go down that path. Chess was one thing, literature was another. Still, he couldn't resist a parting shot.

"What'll you be lookin' for?—in the salon that is, not the kitchen."

"My goodness, Serov, two touches in a row. All right. Joking aside. Papa gave me a lead. I'm pretty sure that the Governor-General's wife was an old flame of his. She could be a help in opening doors. I'm out of my depth in Kievan society. That's what makes this assignment so damn frustrating."

Vasiliev paused, moving pieces of silverware around on the table.

"As for our Jewish friends, we'll have to wait until they make contact."

As it turned out, the wait was a short one. When Vasiliev opened the door to his room, he saw a blank white envelope lying on the carpet. The message inside was hand-printed in capital letters. "How is your conscience?" it read. "If strong, a cab is waiting for you at the corner of Institute Street. The lamp on the left side will be lit. The horse is jet black. If you are fearful, bring an associate. The cab will be there until 11:00 p.m. It will return tomorrow night at the same time and place." There was no signature.

Serov asked only one question. "Should we wear our uniforms?"

"That does not seem to concern them. Let's go."

Chapter Seven

The cab headed toward the river but then turned northwest on Alexandrov Street and crossed into the Podol District, a low-lying area housing a large Jewish population, where the fires of the pogroms were still smoldering. Rising high over the sprawling district was the great eighteenth century Rococo church of St. Andrei the First Called. The cab then turned again onto the high

St. Andrei the First Called Seen From Podol

ground in Lukianov District and followed Kirilov Street past the Kirilov Church, climbing higher into the hills. Vasiliev had studied a map of the city, and he remembered what his files had told him. They were approaching the caves where Professor Antonovich had recently excavated human remains going back to the Stone Age.

They passed the last of the streetlights. A few log cabins were nestled in the ravines, but they too soon disappeared from sight. The horse was straining now to pull them up the sharp inclines. Only a pale quarter moon lit the dirt road that led them deeper into the hills. Suddenly, a lantern shone in the middle of the track, as if its shutter had been thrown open. They came to a halt. The light went out. They could make out nothing against the dark contours of the hills. There was no sound except for the snorting of the carriage horse. They sat in silence for a few minutes.

"I guess they're waiting to see if we were followed," said Vasiliev. "Good. We're dealing with serious people."

"Inspector Vasiliev, would you please step down and join us?" It was a young man's voice speaking perfect Russian, yet Vasiliev heard the trace of something different in his intonation.

"Yes, right away. Listen, Sergeant Serov will stay with the cab. I'm leaving him my revolver, so I won't be armed. He has orders to come looking for me if I don't return within an hour. The cabby will also stay where he is. Agreed?"

"Of course. We appreciate your trust. We too are unarmed. Your Sergeant can observe you entering the cave behind me. There is only one entrance to these caves. Shall we move to the next stage of negotiations?"

Vasiliev detected a slight ironic tone in the voice.

As soon as Vasiliev and his guide disappeared into the mouth of the cave, Serov stepped down and stretched, holding Vasiliev's holster high above his head. He told the cabby he was going to relieve himself. He then settled down on an outcropping of rock on the side of the track that gave him a commanding view of the surrounding landscape. His playmates had nicknamed him *stolb*, the pillar. Once he had taken a position in their games or an argument, he could not be moved. If necessary he could remain hidden and silent for hours. Now he seemed to merge into the rock, keeping himself amused by picking out the different night sounds and watching how the ground shadows changed as the high clouds skimmed across the surface of the moon. From time to time, he slowly raised his arm, holding his watch up to the faint light in the night sky.

The guide lit the lantern again, and Vasiliev noticed the entrance to the cave had been recently been cleared of brambles. The height and width of the tunnel surprised him. So this is where the men of the Stone Age sought protection from their enemies! And now the Jews found it a refuge. But there was a difference. The enemies of the Jews were not wild animals but other human beings.

The tunnel opened up into a large cavern feebly lit with candles. His guide extinguished the lantern, plunging the cave into semi-darkness, but not before Vasiliev had counted six men in the shadows. A familiar figure advanced to greet him.

"Inspector Vasiliev, the man with a conscience."

"Ezra Ben-Zion, the man who has awakened it."

"My friends prefer to remain anonymous, I'm sorry to say. They are willing to use only a given name. Real or not is unimportant. They are all trustworthy, bound by solemn oaths. They do not all agree about many things. What brings us together is fear and courage. Fear for our families and friends; courage to oppose our enemies. Does that sound too rabbinic? Forgive me if it does. We need your help to solve this hideous crime. We all have information that may be of use. We will answer whatever questions you may have."

"Let me be frank. I have already made it clear that I cannot help you unless you agree to let me inform the authorities…"

"No! No!" Voices broke in from all sides.

"Wait! And listen. I can do this in a way that won't hurt you— no reprisals, no punishment. Here's my plan. I'll let the Governor-General know…"

Again he was interrupted with cries.

"Hear me out, or else our negotiation, as your guide calls it, will end here." This brought a snicker, and the voice he now recognized said loudly:

"Do we always have to behave like cackling geese at a bazaar? For God's sake let the man speak. Inspector, I was your guide. You can call me David. I don't trust you any more than the rest of us do.

But I am not afraid to listen."

"Good. So, for the last time. I will tell the Governor-General… Listen, I know his reputation as an anti-Semite. He deserves it. There's no question about that."

The murmurs were softer and sounded more like approval. Vasiliev was encouraged to press ahead.

"So, we agree on one thing. But please understand you can't expect me, a policeman, to violate my oaths, any more than I expect you to violate yours. How many other policemen would agree to meet in secret with a group of unknown men in a cave outside Kiev? Be reasonable." The murmurs had stopped and he was greeted by silence.

"I'll tell the Governor-General the truth, slightly amended. I'll tell him I've been informed by respectable members of the Jewish community that Rabbi Meier was murdered. His friends and family did not report it right away. They were afraid of touching off more killings. I will tell him that you realized your mistake and regret it, that you've notified the Crown Rabbi of Kiev. That's the law and you have obeyed it. You'll have to make this report tomorrow first thing. I will also say that there is no need to reveal the details of the crime to the press. We don't want to inflame the public. Only the top officials will know: the Crown Rabbi, the Chief of Police and the Governor-General."

"Don't be surprised if one of them leaks it. Why should they protect us?"

It was David's voice again, backed up by the familiar murmurs.

"Why shouldn't they? What have they to gain? Drenteln may be an anti-Semite, but he's no fool. Right now he hopes things will quiet down. The last thing he wants is a wave of murders in Kiev. This is his city, remember, and his reputation is at stake. Petersburg is already unhappy with the breakdown of public order. Think about it. The killing of Rabbi Meier was so horrible that if it became known in Russia and then Europe, the Governor-General would be finished. His career would be ruined. You understand me? It is in his interest to conceal what has happened."

"Who objects?" Ben-Zion asked.

"What are our guarantees?" Another voice rang out.

"Your guarantees are my word and your anonymity. I can only

betray Ben-Zion. He is the only one of you I know. If he agrees, then you have no cause to object."

"No objection," David's young voice rang out.

"I will consult with the others," said Ben-Zion. He moved into the shadows, where five figures crowded around him. Vasiliev could see arms waving in all directions, casting grotesque shadows on the wall. The sixth man, presumably the one calling himself David, stood apart from the rest, but his face was also concealed in the shadows.

"We agree to accept your conditions, but ask you to swear on your honor as an officer of His Imperial Majesty not to disclose any details of our meeting, least of all the location."

Vasiliev had never put much stock in oaths, and this investigation was already overcrowded with them, he reflected. But he duly swore. He asked each man to give his evidence as briefly as possible. It seemed to him that Ben-Zion had organized them with some inner logic in mind. But Vasiliev wondered whether anything would come out of this. Six unknown men babbling in the dark in a Stone Age cave about the killing of a rabbi about whom he knew nothing, in a place he had never seen. He began to worry about his sanity—not for the first time, he mused. His fellow detectives liked to tease him about it, his sympathies with the underdog. "You're a regular *intelligent*," they used to say. "Reading Dostoevsky's *Insulted and Injured* again, Vasiliev?" And then the laughter. It was all in good fun. At least, that is the way he chose to take it. But underneath there was a sharp edge, an unspoken thought; he's after all half a peasant, that one. He had a sudden impulse to walk out. Hell, why not leave the matter in the hands of the local police? Then David began to talk.

"Rabbi Meier was our first beloved teacher. He had studied at the rabbinical seminary in Vilna. He belonged to the second generation of *maskilim*. Do you know what that means, Inspector? It's a belief in the teachings of Moses Mendelssohn, infused with the Russian spirit. He taught us to think critically, not just in the old tradition of Talmudic studies but to be useful to society, to break out of the mental world of the ghetto."

"But you betrayed him!" A voice cried out. "You turned to socialism!"

48

"He never reproached us," David whirled to confront a shadow. "He remembered his own rebellious youth."

"This is not the place to quarrel," Ben-Zion said. "The Inspector is a wise and patient man. But he is not Solomon, and he cannot solve the unsolvable. We ask him only to solve a crime. You must restrain yourselves. David, please—just the testimony of what you saw and heard; and Natan you will have your turn. No polemics!"

David thrust his hands deep into the pockets of his worn linen jacket. He missed the reassuring feeling of the lead pipe. But they had agreed, no weapons.

"On the night of April 26 Aaron and I were watching outside the *Bet Hamidrash* in Podol. Rabbi Meier was inside alone. We feared for his safety. There were gangs looting and burning all around us. We followed him to his house. We were going to keep guard the whole night. He was walking up the path. Suddenly, he seized his head in his hands and rushed into the house. The door was wide open. We ran across the street and heard shots. Then..."

"Wait," Vasiliev interrupted. "Take it slower, David. I need to know everything. Lead me through it. I wasn't there. A detective who has never visited the scene of the crime... well, it's a terrible disadvantage. You have to help me, be my ears and eyes. Be precise. Give me a sense of time. The Rabbi taught you to be precise—isn't that so? Remember the Talmudic training. Now put it to use."

David bowed his head. "We did not consult our watches, Mr. Inspector."

"David!"

"Sorry, Reb Ben-Zion—yes, I will behave. It could not have been more than a few minutes after Rabbi Meier rushed into his house that the first shot rang out. Then there was a short pause, less than a minute probably. Remember, we were running and afraid. The others—five shots, I mean—came fast, maybe as fast as you can pull a trigger. The door was wide open—no, it was sagging on its hinges. The window to the front parlor was smashed. What else? I don't remember how we got down the corridor. It was pitch black. But we know the house. We were feeling our way along the walls into the dining room. We didn't see anyone, didn't hear anything. It was terribly quiet. And the smell of gunpowder. We recognized it. We must have been on the heels of the killer, but we didn't hear him, you understand. Maybe he went out the side entrance. We didn't think about it at the time. If we had, we might have caught him. There was no light. We knew there were candles in the bureau. But it took a few minutes, maybe just seconds, to fumble around for the candles and matches. We've been in the house many times; we knew our way around even in the dark. Did I say the window to the right of the front door had been smashed? The door itself was hanging loosely, as though it had been broken open. I'm repeating myself, but the words don't always say how I felt. No matter. I stumbled over the Rabbi's body in the dark. We lit the candles and saw his face; it had been shot away. There was so much blood. We only found out later about the pattern—the cross, I mean. We called out but nobody was home, thank God. Ruth and Rebecca, his daughters, you know, one of them is always home. Later we learned about the anonymous letter. Someone had warned them to get out of the house. It was on a list to be burned down."

"Did you save the letter, Reb Ben-Zion?"

"I have it," said Ben-Zion.

"Good, I'd like to see it. Go ahead, David."

"So someone wanted the place to be empty when the Rabbi came home. You see, the place was always crowded with people, friends, refugees, God knows who else. An open house and maybe the killer had been there before. How else would he…I don't know. I'm not a detective. The girls had left a note for their father, telling him where they'd gone. We covered his face and went to tell them."

"You're sure you heard no one leave the house?"

"Yes, sure."

"So, it is possible that the murderer was still there. You didn't take a look around?"

"No."

"Is Aaron here?"

"No, but he will confirm everything I have said."

Vasiliev was tempted to ask whether David was his brother's keeper, but decided against matching Biblical quotations with these people. "And what then?"

"We changed our mind on the way to tell Ruth and Rebecca. Instead, we went to Reb Ben-Zion. He called the doctor and told the girls."

"This is our next witness, Inspector. We shall call him Mordecai."

"Good evening, Inspector. I am a physician at St. Vladimir Hospital. One of three Jewish doctors on the staff. I was at home with
my family when Reb Ben-Zion came to the door. It was after midnight but I was still up, reading. I went with him to Rabbi Meier's
house. David and Aaron had already returned to the house. They
had lit four candles. The Rabbi's body was stretched out by the bureau, one arm flung out to his left side, the other twisted under him.
His face was covered with blood. If the first shot had been to his
forehead he would have died instantly. I assume that is what happened for the other wounds were regularly spaced. When I cleaned
the blood off his face, I saw the pattern. The shots were fired at very
close range. There were bullet holes in the floor under his head. The
Rabbi was already prone when the killer fired the last five shots.
Strange, that he could have done this in the dark. He must have
held the gun right up against the Rabbi's face. One of the bullets
was not deeply imbedded in the floor. It must have been deflected
by the hard bone of the cranium. I was able to dig it out. I saved it.
It's over there, wrapped in a handkerchief on the stone shelf to your
left. I am not a ballistics specialist. I don't know much about bullet wounds. But you don't need my help with that. The two young
men carried the body into the bedroom. We washed the Rabbi's
face and we covered it with a shawl. The four of us talked it over.
We decided not to inform the police. As you know, we were afraid
others might try to copy the crime. These are strange times. I think
you are right. We made a mistake. But I hope you understand our
fears. As for the Crown Rabbi—well, he is a government official.
His first duty, he thinks, is to the state. I understand your reasons
for questioning our decision, but at the time it seemed best. Then
all four of us went to tell the girls, Ruth and Rebecca. They are the
children. Their mother died many years ago. Rabbi Meier never
married again. We persuaded them not to see the body. It was not
easy. If you have any further questions I will try to answer them."

"Thank you, doctor, perhaps at some later time." Vasiliev had
unrolled the white handkerchief; held the misshapen bullet in the
palm of his hand.

"Natan is next."

"I am Natan. I am a trustee of Rabbi Meier's synagogue so I'm not hiding anything. But I've agreed to follow the rules of anonymity for tonight. On the High Holy Days it is I who blow the shofar and recite the Havdalah at the close of the Sabbath day. I am... was honored to be the Rabbi's closest friend, although it was well known that we argued constantly. We were both *maskilim*, but he was more advanced than I; this is his word, 'advanced', meaning he was permissive of those like David who had—I will tread softly here, or Reb Ben-Zion will reproach me again—who had gone even further along the path of Enlightenment. Is that satisfactory David?"

There was no answer.

"Fine. I am here because I do not believe my dear friend was murdered by some madman, nor at random. You will not like what I am going to say, Inspector. I believe the Rabbi was killed as part of a conspiracy involving the forces of law and order. He was a thorn in the side of the Governor-General. He was endlessly petitioning St. Petersburg about the expulsion of Jews from the city, the brutality of the police raids. Even our so-called legal merchants suffered from petty harassment and indignities. Rabbi Meier would not rest until he had addressed the Governor-General about these as well. It is my firm belief that a police official—I am not saying the Governor-General but some underling—had the bright idea of eliminating this Jewish gadfly during the pogroms. You would do well, Inspector, to turn your attention to such types. And while I am on the subject, you also might find that your main line of inquiry, so to speak, the causes of the pogrom, will lead in the same direction."

"Nonsense!"—a new voice came out of the shadows.

"I did not expect your agreement, Meier-Michael. But let me say before you spin your fantastic tale, that my theory, however speculative, is much more plausible than yours."

"I expect we are now to hear from Meir-Michael," Vasiliev prompted.

"Inspector, I am glad that you have come to Kiev to reinforce the forces of order. I was a great admirer of Rabbi Meier, but deplored his flirtation with nihilists."

Vasiliev was not surprised to hear snorts and growls of dissent. Would any one of these six agree with any one of the others? He admitted to himself that he was getting an education in probable causes without moving from one spot. That rarely happened.

"Let them scoff! But this is not my point. It's not my counter-point either. Let me explain. The real instigators of the pogroms are the revolutionaries. They are what's left of the People's Will that carried out the assassination of our beloved Tsar-Liberator, Alexander Nikolaevich. May his soul dwell in paradise. Let me tell you, Inspector, I am a Jew, a believer, a *maskil* like most here. But I am a professional man, a graduate of Warsaw University. Yet I do not resemble a Jew. And I took advantage of my goyish looks to mingle with the *pogromchiki*. Does that shock you? It was better than sitting and waiting for them to burn down my house. I wore a Russian blouse and visor cap, boots, the uniform of the rioters. And what did I see and hear in this clever disguise of mine? There were agitators in the mob who knew what they were doing. 'To Brodsky's!' they shouted, in other words to the richest Jew in all Kiev. And when they got to his house, or one of them, they threw the furniture out the window while others were looting his vodka factory. Once this was done, the same agitators shouted, 'Let's get all the blood-suckers! What difference does it make, Christians or Jews?' You see we were in the Libed district, very fancy homes, I wish I could afford one. Some Jews live there, but mainly Christians. And the agitators led the mob along the street, pointing out one 'bloodsucker' after another, all goys! I don't know how it would have ended. At that point the Cossacks showed up. We all wonder what they were doing up till then. No matter. It was obvious! The revolutionaries were trying to turn the crowd around. To go from beating the Jews to overthrowing the bourgeoisie. A neat trick, if they could have pulled it off."

"And you think the revolutionaries were guilty of murdering Rabbi Meier?"

"Of course! Think for a moment. Who else carries around a re-volver? Who else has the skill, excuse me, the brazenness to carry out such a crime? And what does this pattern of the cross mean? No one has ever seen such a thing. But it is meant to signify the mind of a fanatic. And to arouse a Jewish response, among our youth. I point no finger, but there are Jewish youth who are thinking about revenge, who are thinking about self-defense groups, who are arming themselves. If they strike back...I leave the rest to your imagination. Kiev and other cities could be plunged into disorder, riot—yes, revolution. Just what the People's Will want. And one more thing, Inspector, don't think for a moment that the People's Will is as anti-Semitic as it is painted. No, there are Jewish members. Remember Aron Zundelevich! I have heard—and I have friends in strange places—I have heard that Zundelevich was the evil genius who got the terrorists to replace knives and revolvers with homemade bombs. Zundelevich, a typical Jew for all that. Do you know where he was when they caught him? Reading books in the St. Petersburg Library on how to run a centralized conspiratorial organization! And that was only two years ago. Arrested in a reading room! Oh, my sons of *Erets Israel*!"

"A powerful indictment, Moise-Michael. I assume you are the lawyer in the group." This brought laughter from the shadows. "But I take your speech seriously for all its eloquence," Vasiliev said.

"It is left for me to speak in front of my fellow Jews," said Ben-Zion. "The rest of our delegation are here as observers. They prefer to keep their counsel for the time being. I have already let the Inspector know of my suspicions. But to be more precise, which seems the order of the day, let me add a few details. We know from friends that in this city of Kiev a month before the pogroms, in March, a secret organization was formed called the Holy Brotherhood. We also know that it counts a number of high officials among its members. Its purpose is to defend the Tsar. Why does the Tsar need to be defended by a secret organization? What is wrong with the Gendarmes? Perhaps Inspector Vasiliev can answer that question, perhaps not. Now put yourselves in the place of these loyal, true Russians. How best to defend against the revolution?—they ask themselves. One answer is to incite pogroms and then repress them, blaming the revolutionaries for starting them. What is gained here? You allow good Orthodox Christians to vent their frustrations against the Jews, not the most popular people in the empire. By blaming the revolutionaries you rally to the throne the propertied classes, who fear disorders of any sort. Now remember how the moderates in the government, like General Loris-Melikov, tried to win over the population with liberal reforms and promises of a consultative assembly. Yet, in the end the Tsar was isolated, cut off from his own people. To prevent this from happening again, the reaction goes in the opposite direction. They frighten society with the specter of revolution, aimed not just at the Tsar but all good God-fearing property owners. And *voila*! If I may be permitted a foreignism, you have a united Russia against both Jews and the revolution. And the murder of our late lamented Rabbi, may his children be comforted, was a terrible symbolic warning to us. A threat. We should suffer in silence."

Vasiliev looked at his watch. In five minutes Serov would come bursting in unless he brought the meeting to a close. What did he have? Who were the suspects? He counted them up: half the government, the local police, the People's Will and a crazed lone gunman. Quite a night's work, he thought. He thanked Ben-Zion and his friends, and made his way to the entrance of the cave.

Chapter Eight

"Come in, Stepan, come in. You are most welcome."
Stepan was surprised that the Esteemed Person had greeted him at the threshold to his Kiev mansion. He would have to tell Vera. How would he put it? "Verochka, none other than the Esteemed Person came to door, as if I too was a person of importance. Yes, none other." That is what he would say to her, and she would be impressed.

"Good evening, Your Excellency."

"Yes, Stepan, a good evening it is, thanks to you." He led Stepan down a long corridor lit by gas lamps in brackets that seemed to be made of gold. But that would be impossible, Stepan reflected. They must be highly polished bronze. Think of the time it takes to made them shine. Stepan felt his boots sink into a plush carpet the color of spilt wine. What luxury, he thought. Perhaps now he and Vera could buy a carpet—nothing like this, of course, but a little Turkish carpet from the bazaar. It would do nicely, lying next to the bed. Yes—a thick Turkish rug with some strange design, very Oriental, would be just the thing.

"My good fellow, sit down here by the grate and warm yourself. There's a chill in the air, despite the bonfires outside." He chuckled.

Stepan could hardly keep his eyes from jumping around the room, landing on one object after another, thinking how he must fix every detail in his mind. For Vera. Paintings on the wall; they looked old to him. They must have come from abroad. He did not recognize the clothing the people in them wore, something plain and colorless. Just black and white. But the frames were so beautiful. They must be worth a good deal of money. He stared at the crystal chandelier and tried to count the strings of glass beads but there wasn't time. What about this small wooden table next to his chair? Its spindly legs looked like a borzoi's. It was covered with a damask cloth of the finest quality; surely from Kostroma? Yes, he had seen such things in the bazaar there. He was afraid of knocking the table over, so kept his arms folded on his chest. There was silver everywhere, he would tell Vera, on the big buffet and the small table—dishes and plates filled with the most delicious morsels. He spotted the caviar right away. He would bet his life it was Beluga, although he had never tasted it, only seen it in the window of luxury shops of the Kreshchatik. Two decanters of cut glass embossed with silver, one containing a dark liquid and the other a light one. He guessed they would be cognac and vodka. Could he choose? Why not both?

The Esteemed Person was watching him beneath his lower eyelids. Stepan knew that trick of his. Well, he wouldn't be caught napping. He was well aware that the man was far above his station. But he was certain he had figured out the Esteemed Person. Stepan prided himself on knowing people. It had saved his life more than once. Another secret to staying alive was to keep alert. The problem here was too many distractions. He wanted to remember everything to tell Vera. And his eyes kept straying to the caviar. What had the Esteemed Person said to him? Then he remembered.

"Yes, Your Excellency, a good evening in Kiev."

"They are on the run, Stepan, down every street, across every square, on the run."

"Yes, Your Excellency, on the run." But when would he be offered a sip and a bite? The Esteemed Person seemed to read him as well.

"Help yourself, Stepan. A small celebration. Oh, allow me. Ah, you wish to start with a little vodka."

My God, thought Stepan, tossing back a glass. What is this? It flows like liquid fire down the throat. Stepan's eyes roamed over the dishes; a bite of cucumber would be perfect now, but how stupid; cucumber would not be served on the chinaware of the Esteemed Person. But why have they cut the bread slices so thin and narrow. I'll not manage more than a dollop of caviar, he thought. Careful not to let a single one of those grey pearls roll off. He brought the morsel to his lips without incident and swallowed it. Vera would be pleased at his manners. But the effort was making him sweat.

"Our lads are running right behind them. But you, Stepan, have made them run in an altogether different direction. Do you know this?"

Stepan was concentrating on preparing another canapé of caviar. All this running made him nervous. To his horror, several little gray pearls rolled off the absurdly thin slice of bread into his palm. He dared not lick them up. Vera had warned him: "No licking of the fingers, Stepanushka. No matter what happens, no licking." He slipped the canapé into his mouth and quickly made a fist, trapping the beads of caviar, and squeezing them. He felt them liquefy in his palm. He stared longingly at the white linen napkins but did not dare to touch them for fear of leaving a telltale stain. The Esteemed Person was speaking again. Stepan felt a flush of annoyance. Why can't he let me enjoy my snack in peace, he grumbled to himself. What was he saying?

"…so there are others who are now talking of running all the way to Palestine. Let them go, eh? They may call it their holy land, but we have our Holy Russia. Who needs this Palestine? Now the Latins have control over the holy places and defile them. No, Russia is the New Jerusalem."

Stepan felt confused by such talk. "Beat the Yids and save Russia." Now that made sense. But what was this talk about a New Jerusalem? Why would we want to build a New Jerusalem? If we did the Jews would think it was their place. They'd come flocking to Russia from all over; we'd never get rid of them.

Stepan kept silent and drained another glass. He had forgotten about the cognac.

"You have done your work well; you have earned your reward." The Esteemed Person stood up and went into the next room. He returned with a small purse and gave it to Stepan, who could only take it with his left hand. Was this a sign of bad luck? He silently cursed the little beads of caviar that lay squashed in his fist.

"Now don't go and count the money, Stepanushka. It would be bad manners. He would be offended." So Vera had admonished him. Damn it, there was no way he could count it, deprived as he was of the use of his right hand. He stuffed the purse into his jacket pocket and noticed with satisfaction that the Esteemed Person smiled approvingly.

"Now there is just one small matter; shall we call it a difficulty arising from unforeseen circumstances?" The Esteemed Person made a tent of his fingers, a gesture Stepan disliked. He associated it with the commandant of the transit prison, who put his fingers together in just this way when he ordered an inmate to be flogged. The sight of it still caused a slight trembling in his legs.

The Esteemed Person was startled by the angry expression that twisted Stepan's features into a mask of savagery. He was clearly frightened, and looked over his shoulder as if to summon assistance.

"Nothing serious," the Esteemed Person hastened to add. "But we are cautious people, my friends and I. It is a virtue to be cautious, don't you agree?"

Stepan sat silently gripping his empty glass. He had been cautious. No one had any reason to reproach him on that score. What did they want now? Suddenly, Stepan wanted to leave this house and go home to Vera.

"You see, Moscow is sending some meddler down—as if there weren't enough fools in charge here. So we have to suspend operations, to put it quite simply. We think it would be advisable for you to take a holiday. We have arranged a little trip to Yalta. Ever been there? No? Well, we have even bought your ticket. You will find it in the purse. We thought second class would be appropriate; not because we are stingy—no, never stingy when it comes to rewarding good men. But first class? You might draw attention to yourself. You understand? The train leaves tomorrow morning."

"You mean I'm to stop now?"

"They are on the run, Stepan; you've done your job well."

The Esteemed Person laughed. Stepan was not fooled. There was nothing to laugh about. He had only just started. There was much work still to be done, and it could not be done in Yalta.

"Your Excellency," he began but stopped short. "Never quarrel with them," had been the last thing Vera said to him before she kissed him on the brow and sent him on his way. He knew she was right. She understood these people, because she had been one of them. "They are too strong." She had said many times. But he was worried that he would not be able to master his anger. It came over him so fast. He tried to recall Vera's face, her stern look as she warned him: "They are too strong." But the Esteemed Person was not a strong man. He was soft and flabby. Only the eyes were dark and piercing. But Stepan did not believe in the evil eye. Looks could not kill. He felt like smashing the table with its spindly legs and sending the crystal and silver flying across the room. For a moment he forgot where he was. Then he became aware of the Esteemed Person staring at him, looking terrified again. Stepan had often seen this expression in the face of his enemies. He passed a hand over his eyes and looked down at the carpet. It no longer seemed the color of wine but of spilt blood.

How much time had passed? Stepan wondered. It was very quiet in the room. He abruptly raised his head and forced a smile to his lips. They felt dry and cracked. He stood up. The Esteemed Person shrank back in his chair.

"Your Excellency is right, of course. Have to be cautious. No need to worry about me. The meddler from Moscow will not find me in Kiev when he arrives. I must go now and prepare for the trip."

The Esteemed Person staggered as he rose to his feet. He seemed relieved but nervous as he led Stepan to the door. Stepan extended his hand. The Esteemed Person grasped it as a drowning man might, only to feel an oily substance smear his palm.

The Esteemed Person frowned as he examined his hand. What a barbarian, he sneered, and rang for the maid. After he had washed his hands and rubbed them with balsamic oil, he drew a key attached to a chain of fine gold links from inside his blouse and unlocked a drawer in his desk. He removed a large tooled leather book, placed it on his desk and opened it. He stared at the long row of double columns, taking pride in his modern methods of bookkeeping. He selected his favorite quill and carefully inscribed Stepan's initials. Opposite on the same line he wrote the date, a sum and the notation "For services rendered." He closed the book, passing his fingers over the smooth surface and returned it to the drawer, which he then locked.

Stepan pushed open the iron gate more violently than was necessary and crossed the street into the darkness of the city park. He stood in the deepest shadows, watching the entrance to the mansion of the Esteemed Person.

He tried to recall the moment when he had become aware of another person in the house. Perhaps he had sensed it when the Esteemed Person had met him at the door. At least he should have known right away that this was no gesture in his honor. What a stupid thought that had been. He could not afford to make such mistakes in the future. Boasting to Vera about the favor the Esteemed Person had shown him. Tphew! He spat into the night. There had been something else, too: a slight noise when the impulse to smash the table had come over him. What was it? Not the creaking of a door opening or a floorboard yielding to a heavy weight. More like a click, but faint, as if coming from behind a partition or a drape, possibly from the next room. Now he remembered the half open door at the end of the study, outside the circle of firelight. Another lapse on his part, not to have taken notice. Still, what could he have done? It was good that Vera's voice had been in his head. A rash move in the direction of the Esteemed Person and he might have been shot down like a stupid beast stuffing his belly at a trough.

There was little traffic on the boulevard at this time of night. No one would be wandering in the park even in this elegant quarter. People were afraid, Jews and Christians alike. He thought of what could be done with the money now that things had changed. There would be less to spend. Vera would be disappointed. But he would make it up to her.

He dug deeply into his pocket for his amulet but it was not there. He felt a moment of panic. He almost missed seeing a man leave the house and walk briskly down the boulevard. Still trembling, Stepan followed him, taking cover in the foliage at the edge of the park. He was thankful that a cab had not been summoned. How did he guess that someone would leave soon after he did? More evidence of his second sight, he thought. But this was no reason to celebrate. Something terrible had happened. What would he do without his amulet? Suddenly he remembered where he might have lost it, and he cursed under his breath. The man turned and went down Aleksandrov Street. Stepan had to drop far behind but still keeping him in sight. Another turn and…Good God! Stepan could not believe his eyes. The agent of the Esteemed Person was entering the District Police Station.

Chapter Nine

Stepan felt he badly needed a drink. The problem was that all the Jewish taverns had been sacked, and many of them burned to the ground. He recalled with pleasure how he had joined the mob looting Brodsky's vodka factory. What a great time that had been. He must have drunk off a liter and then stuffed more bottles into his pockets. They smashed what they couldn't drink or carry. A pity they couldn't cart it all off. The boys got drunk too fast, and after while they couldn't find the neck of a bottle. But where was vodka to be had now? They said there were still some taverns open across the river in Rovnoe, but that was too far to go. He had to get back to Vera. He needed a drink first. How would it taste after the superior stuff in the house of the most Esteemed Person? Hell, he didn't care. Maybe it was better to get some tea. He didn't want to show up at home tipsy. He was wandering aimlessly now. Should he have stayed and trailed that damned spy of the Esteemed Person? For what purpose? He felt he was in trouble, but where was the danger coming from?

He felt the rage come over him. If he ran into a Jew now…A crazy idea. He stumbled through the Park of the Great Garden, past the big dance hall and galleries that had been rebuilt after the fire of 1875, looking for a place to quench his thirst. He went into the first teahouse he came across and slumped into a corner bench. He ordered strong tea. He gave the waiter to understand that he meant strong enough to stand on. When it came, he gulped the bitter brew and felt his heart race.

Looting Brodsky's Vodka Factory

He wondered how he would tell Vera. He was sure of one thing. He would not use the railroad ticket. Anyway, the Esteemed Person had only given him one. Stepan had never told the Esteemed Person about Vera. None of his business. Besides, you didn't give away information. Not for free. He opened the purse and took out the ticket. In a burst of fury he tore it into small pieces, which he threw on the floor. They wouldn't trap him that way. Reserved seat! It was just like giving the police his address. It was smart of him never to let anyone know where he lived. Yes, he had learned a lot in prison and then in exile. Always meet your man in a tavern; a tavern run by a Jew where you met to get the Jews running. That was rich. He laughed out loud, drawing some strange looks from those near him. Let them look. He ordered another glass. It was scalding, but he didn't care. After life in prison he never wanted to drink lukewarm tea again.

He kept mulling over how to tell Vera. He did not want her to scold him. But she would know what to do. That had been another smart thing, to marry a little *burzhuika*. Well, and who else would have had her, with that scar? You couldn't see the scar in the dark, and Vera was a wonder in bed once he had taught her what to do. While they were at it, he would think of that little dancer, Dunia Rakovskaia. No one got hurt and Vera was happy.

Stepan folded his arms on the table and lowered his head. He felt his mind was working like one of those new, steam-driven threading machines he had once tried to operate. Up and down at a furious pace. He did not notice that the teahouse was filling up. Two men had followed him in and were watching him from across the room. They nodded to one another and moved over to sit on either side of him. Stepan jerked up his head.

"You look like man who'd like a real drink, eh?" said one of them, a tall thin man in a worn frock coat. His shirt, with a frayed collar, was open at the neck. "Hey, didn't we see you at Brodsky's downing a bottle at one go?" asked the other, who might have been a docker. His cheap calico blouse fit tightly over his thick muscular neck and long arms. He nudged Stepan with his elbow. Stepan grunted. He didn't like being crowded.

"Listen, brother, we've still got a bottle from Brodsky's." The docker opened his coat so that Stepan could see the label. "Still uncorked. We'd like to share, but we're sort of hard up. If you could give us a few rubles, we could have a little celebration. What do you say, five rubles for half the bottle?"

Stepan looked from side to side. He felt tension in the back of his neck. The offer was tempting. The vodka was a superior quality; it would be almost as good as the golden liquid he had swallowed in the house of the Esteemed Person. He hesitated.

"Come on, Pavel, this one's scared of his own shadow and probably broke too. The hell with him. Let's get out of here." The docker pulled down his peaked cap and heaved himself out of his seat. The tall thin man shrugged and leaned over to Stepan whispering in his ear, "Take it easy little brother. See you when we beat the Jews again." He laughed, showing a mouth full of rotten teeth. The two men made for the door.

Stepan threw down a few coins and went after them.

"Not so fast," he said as he caught up with them. He was thinking to himself, if there's any funny business I'll belt the docker first and then kick the shit out of the thin man. They don't know what a prison fighter is like. He already had the five rubles in his hand. He wasn't going to fumble in his purse so that they could get a look at what he had.

"Hey, listen brothers, you're right. A real drink is what I need. I'd almost forgotten what Brodsky's was like. Here's your fiver." He had stopped under a gas lamp; no dark alleys for him.

"Oorah!" They shouted in unison, and the thin man tossed the bottle to Stepan. As he caught it with both hands, the docker stepped up to him and plunged a long knife into Stepan's side. He twisted it as he held Stepan close to him. The bottle of vodka fell and shattered. The docker let the dead body slowly slide to the ground on top of the broken glass.

"He sure as hell can't take a drink!" the docker shouted to no one in particular. A group of workers coming out of the teahouse overheard him. They glanced over, smelled the vodka, and shook their heads. "Christ, what a waste," said one of them, as they walked off in the opposite direction.

Chapter Ten

Together they left the Hotel d'Europe early in the morning but went in different directions. Serov headed for the bazaar to pick out his "new spring outfit" as he called it: a pair of linen trousers that showed signs of have been repaired frequently, a well-worn Ukrainian blouse, a shabby cloak, a pair of bast shoes and leg wrappings. He also persuaded a seller of rags and sticks to part with his own wooden staff. The price was ridiculously high. He packed the clothes into a cloth bag, and marched along the street of Podol, staff in hand, toward the fringes of the district. He passed rows of burnt-out stores; the smell of scorched wood filled the air. Pieces of crockery and furniture had been swept into gutters. Here and there an artisan or shopkeeper sifted through the wreckage of a workshop or store. An old woman sat moaning and rocking back and forth on a pile of debris. People turned their faces away from him.

Serov was looking for a room to rent. It shouldn't be hard to find one, Vasiliev had told him. He had been wrong. Terror still gripped the Jewish quarter. Strangers were not welcome. Serov saw plenty of evidence of fear, but no rooms, until he had almost reached the river-front at the very edge of the quarter. A small, handwritten sign in a window with clean curtains gave him hope. The curtains parted when he knocked. An old woman opened the door. She must have been reassured by his uniform. Serov held the staff behind his back. Judging by her dress and accent she was Ukrainian though her Russian was good. He asked for a room with a window on the ground floor and paid her a month's advance. He impressed upon her the importance of keeping her mouth shut about her new lodger. There might be strange-looking people coming to see him. There was no need to gossip about them either.

As he laid out his purchases on the iron cot, Serov thought about revolutionaries and the police, how they learned from one another. He and Vasiliev had picked up a trick or two from the nihilists. The whole idea of having a safe house came from them, Irina and her friends. He wondered who would end up having learned the most. He slipped out of his uniform, folded his trousers neatly, and hung them on the back of a wooden chair, the only one in the room. He placed his boots under it and looked around for a place to conceal his holster and revolver. The mattress was too thin, the table had no drawer, and there were no loose floorboards. He shrugged and stuffed them in one of his boots. He brushed his hair straight back. He pulled on his newly-bought rags and examined himself in a small cracked mirror hanging on a nail near the window. He would pass, he supposed. Vasiliev had taught him the art of disguise, endlessly repeating the same words; there was no need for an "elaborate artifice," as he used to put it. The point was to imagine yourself in another man's body. That meant changing the way you walked, the way you swung you arms, held your head and parted your hair. Sometimes it was good to have something like his pilgrim's staff to serve as a distraction from what Vasiliev called the "permanent features". But the movements of your body, your mannerisms and of course your speech were the key elements. Whenever Serov took on a new part, he reviewed his lessons. Here Vasiliev was the true master, no joke. There was no question of beating him at this game. Vasiliev had told him many times of how he had been trained since childhood by the old serf, Foma, who had spent a lifetime perfecting the art.

Serov imagined his new landlady's surprise if she would have seen a poor pilgrim emerge from the room she had just rented to a police sergeant. It amused him to think so. He walked quickly along Boris and Gleb Street, past the Boris and Gleb Church to the river road. He knew he had a long trek to the Pecherskaia Lavra—the Monastery of the Caves—where he would mingle with hundreds of pilgrims from all over Russia. He was hoping he would blend in.

In the meantime, Vasiliev was strolling down Anenkov Street, where he stopped to admire the Lutheran Church before turning east on Levishev. To his left he caught a glimpse of the Governor-General's house, where he would be dining that evening. In his pocket he carried a note presumably from Maria Alexandrovna, the Governor-General's wife. Delivered to his room while he was at the caves, it read like an imperial command: "Palace Garden, by the fountain. 9:00 a.m. Friday." It was signed with the initial M. Apparently, the old Count had not trusted him to make a discreet approach. Somehow he had passed a message to her about his son's coming.

As soon as he entered the gardens he saw her. His first thought was that she could not have made herself more conspicuous. She was wearing a pure white muslin dress with a white confection perched on her head. The bonnet might have been French, or was it Italian? Vasiliev did not know what was in fashion these days, especially in Kiev. A light blue half cloak was draped around her shoulders with studied casualness. A liveried servant stood a few feet behind her. She waved. Incredible, he thought. Was this the discreet approach? He strode up to her quickly and she extended her hand. He bent and brushed it with his lips.

"My dear Vasili, how wonderful to see you in Kiev. It has been a long time, but I shall not embarrass you or myself by saying how long. Now let me take your arm. We are going to parade around the gardens in a flagrant display. You see I learned long ago from your father that the best concealment is full exposure. He sent Alexander Romanovich a telegram informing him of your exact arrival, time and hotel, and respectfully requested that he take you in hand. My dear husband's response was, 'Doesn't the old fool know that official orders have come from Petersburg?' Old fool indeed! And now when I return home I shall say how we met by chance, you on your way to the Offices of the Appenage Administration. It's right across the park. I will leave it to you to explain why you were going there. But any excuse will do—renewing an acquaintance, a small favor for your friend, the Iron Colonel. Now, with my Igor safely trailing behind, out of earshot, we can speak without a soul overhearing us. I do believe all Russia is caught up in some vast conspiracy to betray someone or something. I fear I've been guilty of doing the same thing."

Vasiliev gave a silent laugh, displaying his crooked teeth and shaking his head, as she took his arm and guided him down the sandy path bordered with lime trees.

"Do you remember me at all?"

"To be frank, Maria Alexandrovna, I have only one image of you, and yet I would have recognized you in the midst of the imperial ballroom."

"Oh my, at my age I do not expect such outrageous compliments."

"But I also recall stories about you, from my mother. She said you were the only titled woman who treated her as a fellow human being. Did you see her often?"

"No, not often. She was lovely and had more dignity than most aristocrats I have known. You were always there to protect her, even as a boy."

"Yes, well I got in a few scrapes defending her honor."

"So I heard. Quite the young champion. But before you learned to fence or shoot you were handy with your fists. Let me see your hands now." She ran her fingers over the enlarged knuckles. "Wherever did you learn this boxing business?"

"Serov started me off, a real street fighter he was. I learned the finer points from a gymnastic teacher at the Page Corps. The lessons were private. As you would say, held in conspiratorial secrecy."

"How is Serov?"

"Angry that I did not bring him along."

"What a pair you made. How did you manage to survive as children?"

Vasiliev made a fist and held it up. She laughed, and suddenly she was the young girl his father must have fallen in love with.

"I remember your father telling me how you thrashed young Mitya Mikhailovsky, a prince no less and, even more impressively, two years older."

"His teasing got out of hand."

"Yes, and the old Prince, his father, complimented you."

"But Papa gave me a beating, the only one I ever received from him, and he told me why: 'Never on your own land.' What ever happened to Mitya?"

"He was cashiered for some scandal and demoted to a line regiment in the Caucasus. So your lesson did not stay with him." She stopped, opened her parasol, and gazed at him for a moment.

"How I miss Moscow."

"And Moscow misses you."

"Save your compliments for younger women. But that was nice of you. Yes, and I miss your father. Does that shock you?"

"No, I will not banter about this."

She sighed. "So what do you want from me?"

"Whatever you can give me, about the pogroms. Who started them, why it took so long to get them under control."

"Now that is a real compliment! To ask a noblewoman serious political questions. First of all, you will learn a great deal tonight. The guests all have their pet theories. They will be happy for a new audience. And from Moscow too. Perhaps they won't even wait for the cigars and brandy. They will all be out to impress you. Or else to convince you. I include my dear husband, His Excellency the Governor-General."

"And what is your theory, Maria Alexandrovna?"

"I have none—or rather, I have several, each one accounts for part of the story."

"You sound like an historian."

"You forget I was in the first class of the Fundukleevsk Women's Gymnasium. My friends and I opened the school. What glorious days those were. And now we are old ladies exchanging gossip. No. That's not fair. I'll take it back. What are we really? Suppose I told you we were another conspiratorial organization. Would that surprise you?" Maria Alexandrovna giggled like a school girl.

"We meet on Wednesdays for lunch, every week at a different house and, can you believe it, we discuss politics. You are the first man to know our secret. We have our own little network of informants, our servants and their families, the poor in the charitable institutions we patronize, and the shop girls who are a fund of information if you can tease it out of them. Most of us are married to important men who think us empty-headed. They talk carelessly in front of us. They would be surprised how their confidences are bandied about in our Wednesday sessions. Of course, we are all sworn to secrecy; that's the delicious part. So you have the benefit of opinion from half of Kiev. Last Wednesday we had our 'pogrom day'. Does that sound too frivolous? It was a serious discussion."

"I'm not so surprised. It would surprise me though if you all shared the same opinion." If thoughtful Jews couldn't agree, why should Christians? He would not easily forget the Babel of voices in the cave.

"We didn't take a vote, if that is what you mean. But everyone came with a story, and we tried to fit the parts together. It ended up looking like one of those patterned quilts you can buy in the market."

Two ladies bowed to them from a distance. Maria Alexandrovna waved them over. She introduced him as Count Vorontsov's son; they would have a chance that evening to hear the very latest gossip from Moscow. The ladies tittered appropriately, chatted for a few moments and walked on, leaning toward one another in animated conversation. "Now I won't have to explain you to anyone. They will do it for me."

"You really are remarkable Maria Alexandrovna. But let's get back to your little conspiratorial group. I'm interested to hear what they have to say."

Maria Alexandrovna twirled her parasol, causing the light to flicker as it fell on her features. Did she know what an attractive effect this produced? Vasiliev thought she must.

"From what we could piece together, my co-conspirators and I, there was no grand conspiracy. Do you believe in the spontaneous, Vasili?" She did not wait for an answer. "Of course, people just don't start beating other people. But some of them do not need to be told to do so. They make up their own minds. Still, they don't act in a vacuum. The riots did not begin in Kiev, but my husband had been warned that they might break out here. The warning came from Petersburg and the local police. Alexander Romanovich is an anti-Semite, as everyone knows. But he is also an obedient and loyal servitor of His Imperial Majesty. He took precautions. He even told the Jews to close their shops on Sunday. That was April 26, as you may recall. He ordered police and troops distributed throughout the city, some to protect public buildings, like the Arsenal, others to surround the obvious targets like Brodsky's mansion on Theater Street."

"But not his vodka factory."

"Ah, you've already had your ear to the ground. No, not the

vodka factory. But Vasili, let me tell you a sad truth. The authorities did not have enough men for the job. And the army was not willing to get involved. I don't know why. Perhaps they thought the peasant recruits would not fire on their fellow Russians who were, after all, 'just beating the Jews.' Another sad fact. Alexander Romanovich climbed into his carriage that morning and toured the city, calling for order. Do you know what happened? He was stoned for his trouble. He came back in a state; his cheeks were wet from tears of rage. 'God commands not to do evil to anyone,' he said to me, 'and the Tsar does not permit plunder and pillage.' Some people are saying that the authorities were responsible for the rioting. That's simply ridiculous!"

"What else does you network report?"

"Rumors of all kind were circulating in the city. Our servants were in the street because we sent them there. They heard that Russian workers were arriving by the shipload at the river port and leading the riots, but no one we know saw them come. A shop girl who was trying to get back to her house said that some better-dressed men in 'fancy jackets', as she called them, were stirring up the mob on Spassk Street. That's in the southern part of the Podol district. The Austrian consul told me personally that mysterious strangers went around with written lists of Jewish homes to be burned. The stories are endless. What do they amount to? Not just a quilt, but a crazy quilt. No pattern."

While Maria Alexandrovna was talking Vasiliev was thinking of the dead Rabbi. Some one knew what he was doing. It was impossible to convict, let alone arrest a mob. But he could try to hunt down one killer. As if Maria Alexandrovna had read his thoughts, she said: "Over a thousand people have been arrested. But they do not know what to do with them. My husband says the law is not clear. He has ordered them tried by military tribunals. But he will not prosecute people who picked up Jewish goods on the street. That I think is wrong. But I do not know the law."

"You paint a vivid picture, Maria Alexandrovna. You seem better informed than the press. Thanks for being so frank. Everything you say sounds plausible—the rumors, the confused impressions. I'm troubled by the size of the riots, larger than anything before this. And so many different explanations. The problem is that I'm just a simple detective. I have been asked to do something far beyond my capacities. All my professional training cries out: how can I investigate the crimes of a thousand men? This is what I ask myself. I have no answer."

"They speak of military tribunals."

"But are these men guilty of one crime or a thousand? Listen to me! Two years ago there was a trial in St. Petersburg of 173 for terrorism. These numbers tell us something is wrong. Perhaps we are not longer talking about crime but about a sickness, a sickness of society."

"You frighten me, Vasili."

Vasiliev realized he was thinking of Irina again, the mystery of her becoming a revolutionary. He felt a sudden impulse to ask Maria Alexandrovna why a young woman from a family like hers, educated in a Russian gymnasium, filled with the joy of life, would suddenly become a nihilist. But he caught himself. I am babbling to my father's old mistress. This is absurd, he thought.

"I apologize, Maria Alexandrovna. I am still depressed by the assassination of the Tsar. You ask me how you can help me. I need to see your husband privately before the dinner tonight. Can you arrange it?"

They had almost made a full turn of the Palace Gardens. Vasiliev noticed the flowerbeds for the first time. More pansies, laid out in different colors to form geometric patterns.

"Of course. Usually, he takes a rest for two hours before a reception. But if you arrive early, say at 8:00, I'll make sure he'll agree to see you. I'm very discreet, Vasili. Why I won't even ask you what your delicate mission might be." She gave him her girlish smile.

Vasiliev smiled back, revealing his crooked teeth. "But you just have, dear friend. It has to do with a murder case; one I might even have a chance of solving."

Chapter Eleven

Vera knew something had gone wrong when Stepan was not home by midnight. After he had come back from exile she had made him promise never to leave her again at night. For ten years she had spent the nights alone, dreading the bad dreams, exhausted at dawn. She stood by the window, her forehead pressed against the pane. There were no gaslights in this quarter of town. She could see nothing in the blackness. She went to the table, lit a candle, and holding it in front of her, returned to the window. As soon as she saw her reflection she let out a cry and dropped the candle. She fell to her knees and smothered the flame with her hand before it could ignite the curtain that dragged on the floor. Pain seared her palm, and she ran to the cupboard, where she found a dab of rancid butter to smear on the burn. With her back to the wall she slid down to the floor, and wept. When the tears stopped she began to listen intently. A wind had sprung up, and she heard a branch of the tree by the side of the house scrape along the roof. She had asked Stepan many times to cut the branch. He had refused. He could not touch someone else's property or else they would send him back to prison. Tomorrow she would crawl onto the roof and break off the end of the branch. Or else she would go mad.

She started to think again about the early days with Stepan, how strong and loving he had been. Her family despised him for his crude manners and lower-class speech. But what had they ever given her but grief. Stepan had taken her away from their hypocrisy and arrogance. He was a simple man. His thoughts were not always healthy, but she was able to tame them. Until that moment when he made the one mistake. But it was not his fault. She never understood why he had been sent away for ten years of hell. Damn them to eternity! He had come back changed in many ways. He hardly touched her any more, except to stroke her hair and mumbled her name so that she could fall asleep. But he never beat her. And now he promised to take her away. There would be money, "honestly earned," he had said.

She wept again, slumped against the wall, her palm stinging as if a nail had been driven through it. Just like Our Lord, she thought. And would they then pierce her heart?

At dawn she struggled to her feet. Her back ached, but the pain in her hand had subsided. She found a crust of bread, but there was no water. She went into the street, carrying a clay pitcher with a broken handle, and walked a long time before she saw a water carrier. She paid him a few kopecks and he filled her pitcher. She gulped down a mouthful, standing there in the middle of the street. She felt ashamed. Covering her head with her scarf, she trudged back to the cabin, hoping to see Stepan standing on the porch wondering where she had gone. But there was no one waiting.

She did not know what to do. There was no one to help her. Stepan distrusted the neighbors and never returned their greetings. They had ceased to notice him or her. She opened the cupboard and took down the sugar bowl. There were still a few paper rubles left. She took them out, then wet her finger and ran it along the bottom of the bowl, picking up a few grains. She licked them and replaced the cover. She folded the rubles in the waist of her blouse. Perhaps if she bought something for him to eat, he would come back to her.

A knock on the door. She almost fainted, grasping hold of the edge of the table to support herself. She tried to cry out, "a moment," but her voice cracked and she uttered an incoherent sound. She moved toward the door. Every step felt as though she were walking through tar. She watched her trembling hand reach out to lift the rusty latch, as if it belonged to someone else. The door swung open. Standing in front of her, blotting out the morning sun, was a tall figure in uniform. She gasped and stepped back.

"Vera Evgrafnovna Tikhonova?"

She nodded, unable to speak.

"Your husband is Stepan Korneevich Tikhonov?"

She nodded again.

"I must ask you to accompany me to St. Vladimir Hospital to identify the body of your husband, Stepan Korneevich Tikhonov."

"Why do you repeat his name?" she asked and collapsed at his feet.

The policeman went into the house, found the pitcher of water on the table, and poured its contents over Vera's face. She sputtered and coughed.

"Please follow me," said the policeman stiffly, and without glancing behind him, strode off down the street. She mechanically put on her coat and followed him.

She did not remember much of what happened over the next few hours. Numbness had crept over her. Another policeman, an officer, had asked her many questions. Later she tried to remember how she had replied. There had been the money, a great deal of it. Had she known about the money? "No," she had answered. Had she any idea of how he had made it, this former criminal whose passport carried the stamp of a long term prisoner and exile? "No," she knew nothing. Many questions, but all about the same thing: the money. Stepan had often told her, "If they question you about me, any time, you must always reply that you know nothing. And Vera, that is why I tell you nothing, so that you do not have to lie. They always know when you are lying. They have heard the best lies in the world, and they know all about lying."

And so once again Stepan had been right.

"We are holding the money," the officer finally told her, "until we find out how it was obtained, you understand? If it was obtained honestly, then we shall give it to you. If not, then it will be returned to its rightful owner. If that is not possible, then to the state treasury. Please sign the stenographic report of this conversation that the police secretary has recorded. You may retrieve the body tomorrow morning."

She had already turned to leave when a thought suddenly struck her.

"How did he die?" Had they already told her? She didn't remember.

"He was stabbed by a long knife outside a teahouse near the summer theater in the City Park. No one claims to have seen what happened. The investigation is proceeding."

Mechanically, she was wandering the streets, apparently without purpose or direction, until she found herself opposite the teahouse in the City Park. She crossed the path, keeping her eye on the man who was scrubbing the pavement in front of the shop, scraping away Stepan's blood. She felt suddenly calm as she stood over him, watching the last stain disappear.

The man looked up at her, an old man with deep crevices in his cheeks.

"Mother of God," he swore. "Blood and vodka, that's what flows out of a Russian body."

"A Russian body," she repeated under her breath. Wasn't that it? Stepan had cursed the Jews, and now they had taken revenge. She felt her mind clear like the sky after a summer storm. She understood now. He was killed but not robbed. They left him his money. So who would kill just to kill? One who hated him for what he was, a true Russian. Everywhere the Jews had been beaten. And now they were striking back. But wait! Stepan had always called the Jews cowards. Where did they get the courage to strike at a powerful man like Stepan? Perhaps she had been too quick to draw a conclusion. She had to go home and think. Stepan would want her to think and not judge like a woman, impulsively. She owed him that.

Chapter Twelve

Vasiliev had dressed for the reception at the Governor-General's and was about to leave the hotel when Serov knocked on his door.

"You look exhausted."

"Hard work, bein' a pilgrim," he grumbled, slumping down on the sofa. "I kept feelin' a bit over-dressed, if you know my meanin'. I'd almost forgotten what they were like. I should've torn my clothes more. God spare me, I don't know how they walk in their worn out *lapti*, like bits and pieces covered in mud and blood. And me comin' from peasant stock, you'd think I'd know. Maybe it's better posin' as a water carrier. At least you don't go thirsty all day."

Vasiliev poured him a glass of mineral water and sat down across from him. "Nothing stronger here to revive you, sorry. You can order a good dinner in the hotel restaurant. Can you tell me quickly? I have to meet the Governor-General in half an hour. How was it, a harvest or a famine?"

"A harvest you couldn't live on, that's for sure. The pilgrims don't care much about pogroms. They've come to see the treasures and the relics, kiss the gold cross over St. Sergius' body. Aside from prayin' and beggin' they jabber on about the sins of the city and the rumors of typhus. Seems like they didn't expect to run into ladies of 'loose morals', as they call them. Some of the tarts are pretty bold, comin' right up to the poor believers with their coarse invitations. You know, Vasili Vasilievich, I was surprised myself at how they swarmed around the pilgrims. I got talkin' to one or two of the girls. They didn't care much about the pogroms either. Just 'bad for business' is what they said."

"Nothing at all then?"

"Oh, the usual, that is when anyone said anythin' at all about it. They blamed the Jews for squeezin' them; and that stuff about Christ killers. Never could figure that out. It all happened a thousand and more years ago. If we start beatin' up people for what was done a thousand and more years ago, well, there'd be no end in sight."

Serov yawned and rubbed his eyes. "Dust everywhere. It didn't help the thirst much. The Monastery pumps water from wells, but there's always long lines to drink. People drink from the Dniepr, but there's those who say that's where the typhus comes from. So you die of thirst or typhus, take your choice."

"What about the safe house, did you find one?"

Serov told him, "And I left my pilgrim's rags there along with some other pieces. Time for a change; the thirst got me, Vasili Vasilievich. Tomorrow I'll come out as a water carrier. And another thing. There was talk of boats comin' from the North with Russians

Monastery of the Caves

who started the riots. You know the stories. It's always strangers who cause the troubles. So I thought I'd spend the day down by the river but this time on the bluffs."

"Won't a water carrier be out of place along the river?"

"There's that to worry about. But, as I say, there's some who prefer the well water for fear of the typhus."

"Go to it, Serov. I'll be off to let Drenteln know about our murder case. Later I'll tell you about the network of society women we have working for us."

"Ah, Vasili Vasilievich, you're always stealin' a march on me. Now the ladies I've been talkin' to aren't exactly society, but they do seem to be in touch with the male part of society, if you catch my meanin', and I haven't given up on them as a source."

Vasiliev laughed and patted Serov on the shoulder.

"Use your discretion."

Vasili Vasilievich arrived on the doorstep of the Governor-General's mansion at precisely 8:00. It was still light, and he turned to watch the last rays of the sun catch the golden domes of the St. Sophia Cathedral, the oldest church in the empire. The mansion itself was a massive stone-built, two-story, ochre-colored pile where Nicholas I and his son Alexander II, had stayed when visiting Kiev. Once past the security guards, Vasiliev was showed to Drenteln's study by Maria Alexandrovna's lackey, Igor. Vasiliev had last seen Drenteln in 1877 when the Russian Army had advanced to the Danube in the early months of the Turkish War. Since then he seemed to have added five pounds a year and the decorations had multiplied as well. Vasiliev had heard the rumors and gossip about Drenteln's Circassian mistress; "Just like the Sultan" was the joke in the officers' compound. But what had always impressed him, much as he disliked the man, were Drenteln's efficiency and his personal courage. He sat there with his desk cleared, his hands folded as though he had nothing better to do than pass the time with a lowly police inspector.

"Vasili Vasilievich, welcome to Kiev. It's been a while since we smashed a few Turkish heads, you and I. My wife tells me she found you wandering in the Palace Park looking for the Appenage Administration. And I thought I'd have the honor of being the first official in Kiev to greet you. But business with the land holdings of the Imperial family! It really doesn't sound like you."

"Your Excellency, you are really very kind to receive me just before your guests arrive. I'm afraid I took advantage of your wife's good nature to plead my case. I have always remembered how kind she was to me when I was a boy."

Drenteln placed his hands down flat on his desk. The time for compliments was over.

"Your Excellency, I am here on a delicate mission."

"But this I know. For once the official correspondence has reached me before its subject arrives."

"I beg your pardon, but I am speaking of another matter. I beg your indulgence for a few minutes to tell you a strange story—a true story and one which you will appreciate when you hear it from beginning to end."

"A charming way of telling me not to interrupt you, my dear Inspector. Surely you know I can afford to listen, unlike many others in high position, who shall remain nameless."

"My apologies." Vasiliev was having trouble finding the right tone. "A leader of the Jewish community has informed me that Rabbi Meier of the city synagogue has been murdered. Unfortunately, the crime was not immediately reported to the police. The details are pretty gruesome. It seems that the Rabbi was shot in the face six times, forming a crude Latin cross. The family and friends were fearful that the killing might inspire some imitators. They didn't report it immediately as they should have. They thought it could lead to more violence, inflame an already tense situation. I warned them that they were violating the law and must submit a formal report to the Crown Rabbi. I am happy to say they have done so. I promised to inform you personally and ask for your understanding of their negligence…"

"Criminal negligence, Vasili Vasilievich, if you will excuse the interruption."

"These were my very words, Your Excellency. But knowing your deep concern over the disturbances and your heroic efforts to contain them, I had hopes that you would understand that they were trying in their own way to further the same cause."

"But I do not think I was breaking the law in so doing, Inspector Vasiliev."

"I had no intention of equating the two actions. But merely to explain their motives."

Drenteln stood up. "The Jews have been guilty of many sins. This adds to the list. If they had come to me at once, I would have advised them, even sympathized with them. After all, Rabbi Meier was a famous man, a thorn in my side, but as I say well known in the city. His murder is despicable. The trouble with the Jews is that they are so suspicious of us, their own government, that they conceal everything from us. They live and breathe conspiracy, whether it's their rabbis or their revolutionaries. But they seemed to have confided in you. Can you explain why that is?"

Vasiliev also got to his feet. He expected the question, but realized there was no good way to answer it. "It seems that they have misinterpreted my investigation of a case some years ago in Moscow, a matter of forged bank notes. A Jewish artisan was blamed. I found the real forger. Perhaps they thought I was sympathetic to their race."

"You say they misinterpreted your actions. Yet, they appear to have been right in finding in you a champion of sorts."

"Your Excellency, I do not wish to be misinterpreted twice." Vasiliev felt that much as he had prepared to betray his own feelings, he gagged on the words. He managed to clear his throat. "I considered my principal duty to set them on the correct path, to return them to the law, and to prove to them the power of Christian forgiveness." He felt as though he had spat out something disgusting.

Drenteln raised his eyebrows and stared hard at him for what seemed to Vasiliev an interminable time.

"They have reported this to the Crown Rabbi?"

"Yes."

"And what was the delay. Twenty-four hours? No longer?"

"No longer"

"A small matter, then. But still serious. As a favor to you, Vasili Vasilievich, in remembrance of our joint army service under the direct command of Grand Duke Nikolai Nikolaevich. You can tell your Yid friends that Drenteln is a merciful man."

"You are very generous, Your Excellency."

"A favor given is a favor owed. Just remember that, Inspector."

Vasiliev bowed. The interview was over. The dinner party was about to begin.

The guests were already gathering in the salon when Vasiliev entered. He was surprised to recognize several of them. He went up to Maria Alexandrovna, whose smile faded as he drew closer. He realized that the expression on his face must have betrayed his feelings. As he bent over her hand she said quietly, "You look unhappy." She signaled a servant, who glided across the room carrying a tray. "Dom Perignon," she whispered. "It's ice cold."

He was not sure this would settle him, but he was very thirsty. "Are you up to meeting the others, or shall we chat for a few minutes?"

"Chatting sounds irresistible, but your guests might draw the wrong conclusions."

"In what sense, wrong?"

"In the sense that they will be conclusions."

"What a phrase maker you have turned out to be. I suspect you make them up to hide your true feelings. But that won't work with me."

"Nor do I want it to."

"Come then, let us start at the top of the pecking order."

She led him to a broad shouldered man. "This is our financial wizard, Sergei Iulevich Witte, now manager of the Southwest Railroads, but I fear we shall lose him quite soon to St. Petersburg."

Witte bowed. "My dear Maria Alexandrovna, you know railroads are my passion. They will transform Russia. They will carry me to St. Petersburg if anything does. I understand, Inspector Vasiliev, that you are not a casual visitor to Kiev. Don't look surprised. Gossip travels just as fast in Kiev as in Moscow. If only we could harness the speed of rumor to the steam engine we would amaze the world."

After a few minutes Maria Alexandrovna was called away. Vasiliev was left to listen to Witte's plans. "Someday, we will follow the path of the Americans. Marvelous how they built their transcontinental railroad. It binds their country together. We too will build one across our continent to the Pacific. Yes, some day not too far distant. But first the country must settle down."

"Agreed. And the pogroms could easily scare off European capital from investing in Russia and its railroads."

"A shrewd observation, Inspector, and right on the mark. The pogroms are bad for business. They are also morally wrong, of course, even though the Jews tend to be insolent. Take for example my boss, Jan Bloch. He put together the largest railroad line in Russia, eighteen hundred miles long. Imagine! Yet it was not profitable. So he called me in to make it so. It's all a matter of freight rates. But I would bore you to go on. This would be the first thing people would say about me. And what would be the second thing? Not my interest in railroads. Of course, Maria Alexandrovna is the exception here, as she is to all vulgar generalizations. No, it is something else, something that will interest you, Inspector. Have you heard about the Holy Brotherhood? Yes? Well! I would wager you have heard wrongly. You see, I am one of the founding members. So are Count Shuvalov and Prince Demidov San Donato. The rumors would have you believe we are a conspiracy to beat the Jews. You can see how absurd that is! Ours is a conspiracy to protect the Tsar. Perhaps you would like to join us? You have a superb record for having tried to protect our late August Master, Alexander Nikolaevich. But you had to act alone. Oh, I know the story, heard it directly from Count Loris-Melikov. As for the pogroms, they are a blight upon us."

"I am happy to hear this, Sergei Iulevich. Perhaps it would reassure the Jewish population if you made this known."

"Why, this is just what we are going to do. Prince Demidov San Donato is writing a book on the Jews, defending them against these medieval accusations and arguing for emancipation. Think of the talent they could bring to building a strong Russia."

Witte was interrupted by the Governor-General. "My apologies, Sergei Iulevich, but we have just been informed of a problem on the Southwest Line, an accident I fear. You are wanted." Witte shook Vasiliev's hand vigorously. "Remember my offer!" he said as he left.

Drenteln accompanied Witte to the door. Vasiliev drifted from one small circle of conversation to another. He had lost sight of his old acquaintances, Lopatkin and Szymanski. An elderly gentleman, whose name he had already forgotten, invited him to join a game of cards. Vasiliev politely declined. "Ah! You, sir, do not know us yet. It is said that Warsaw dances, Krakow prays, L'vov falls in love,

Vilna goes hunting and old Kiev plays cards. Well, sir what do you think of that?"

"I think it admirable. But most of those talents lie above my abilities, except falling in love. Still, I prefer to hunt bear rather than boar."

"Capital!" exclaimed the old man, although later when he repeated the exchange at the card table, he found himself unable to explain what was capital about hunting bear."

"Perhaps," replied his partner, "it has some symbolic meaning. You know, the bear is the most Russian of animals, while the boar is generally found in our Polish provinces."

Indeed, Vasiliev had *Pan* Szymanski in mind when he made his little joke. He had spotted the Polish nobleman standing alone in a corner of the room, leaning with his back against the wall, his arms folded, following Vasiliev's every move. Vasiliev gave him a questioning look. Szymanski came across the room, moving with an ease of manner that Vasiliev knew he could only imitate; it had not come to him in his mother's milk.

"Inspector! Would you like to take a stroll in the garden? I have something to tell you that may prove of more than passing interest."

Chapter Thirteen

A string quartet began to play as they left the room, and the faint strains of an overture in the Italian style could still be heard as the French doors closed behind them. The evening was warm, and there was a slight breeze coming off the river, bringing with it a faint, unpleasant odor. The Baron clasped his hands behind his back and bent forward as he walked, his eyes fixed on the ground.

"Inspector Vasiliev, these are strange times." He paused and went on in a different tone. "My goodness, what a clumsy opening! We hardly know one another, you see, and yet I have something very personal to say to you. This is what I mean by strange times, times when strangers confide in one another. Or rather, when they serve as messengers of confidences." He paused again.

"Do you mind if I smoke, Baron, and will you join me? I acquired the habit of Turkish tobacco during the Balkan campaign."

"And I lost the habit in my Siberian exile."

"There was something in Szymanski's tone of voice that sent a chill through Vasiliev. He felt his heart suddenly beat faster.

They stopped as Vasiliev lighted his cigar. Szymanski took advantage of the pause to dig into the sandy path with the toe of his boot, quickly making a small excavation. Vasiliev began to think the Baron was at a loss for words, even embarrassed. There was no sense prompting him; it would all come out in good time. It always did.

"Inspector, you know that I was an exile in Siberia, arrested in '64 for participating in an armed rebellion. You know too that I was pardoned and was able to return to my estate. But I left behind comrades who were not so fortunate. They are still there. Some-times, if you will forgive me saying so, Russia's mercy is unpredict-able, even arbitrary. Like its punishments. Don't you agree?" This time Szymanski did not wait for an answer.

"My comrades and I keep in touch. I confess this to you. It is no longer illegal, but the authorities frown on a lively correspondence. I am careful; we are careful. I had not heard from one of my close friends for many months. By chance a letter from him arrived the day after I made your acquaintance on the train. It was written in code. Or, I should say, a few harmless words let me know that a message in code had been added at the end of the letter. You know the technique, I am sure. Lemon juice, invisible to the naked eye but legible after the application of heat."

Szymanski had not stopped digging; his excavation had be-come a crater.

Suddenly, he jerked up his head as the French doors opened behind them, and a couple stepped into the garden, linked arm in arm. Szymanski pushed the sand back into the hole, leveled it, and tapped it down with his heel. He took Vasiliev's arm and guided him farther along the path until the shrubbery completely hid them from the house. When a large cloud obscured the moon, only the tip of Vasiliev's cigar could be seen flaring and subsiding in the darkness. The heavy moisture dampened Szymanski's voice so that it sounded to Vasiliev as though they were conversing under water.

"Yes, the writing was invisible. But we still take precautions. We use a number code, nothing very sophisticated, but unbreak-able unless you have the key. My friend and I have identical copies of *Pan Thadeuz*—you know Mieckiewicz's poem don't you?"

"Of course, the Polish national epic."

"Yes, every Pole knows great parts of it by heart. The numbers of the code refer to pages, lines and words. But no need to tell you more. The message is intended for you."

Vasiliev flung down his cigar and ground it into the sand with the toe of his boot.

"This sounds more and more fanciful, Baron."

"I know, but let me explain. My comrade was given the mes-sage in a moment of desperation. Someone trusted him to pass it on to another trusted person. They're links in our underground postal service to the outside. It's not easy to find a mailbox in Siberia. The message was addressed to Vasili Vasilievich Vasiliev, Inspector of Police, Moscow. That was enough. Now, I admit it's a curious coincidence that we met on a train to Kiev. But I have never been afraid of coincidences. They happen all the time in Siberia. You meet a man you knew in school sharing your cell. What difference does it make? If I had not met you, I would have gone to Moscow to deliver the message. Not for your sake, but to honor the trust placed in my comrade. The message is very short, but terribly sad. I have it fixed in my memory. I shall probably never forget it. 'Please help me. I cannot survive a winter in this place.' It was signed Irina. There is no Irina in *Pan Thadeuz*. So instead of a number the name was written out."

Vasiliev felt grateful for the darkness. A feeling of queasiness overcame him. It took an effort to keep his voice steady.

"I have to ask you a few questions."

"Of course, just so long as you do not ask for the name of my comrade."

"Where did the message come from—I mean which prison?"

"The Tiumen Forwarding Prison."

"Irina is a common name. How can I be sure that I know this woman?"

"In the letter itself, my friend describes a young woman that he met and admired. In the coded part this woman is identified as Irina. He mentioned some personal features—short, auburn hair, deep brown eyes, an oval face, strong, well-defined features, not pretty in the conventional sense."

"Were those his words, 'in the conventional sense'?"

"Excuse me, I believe he wrote 'in the traditional sense.'"

"Do you have the letter with you?"

"No, I burned it immediately after deciphering it. We are sworn to do this for security. Surely you understand that."

"Do you have any idea how long the letter was in transit?"

"It was dated March 2. So about two months to make its way here. It took more time than usual because of the spring floods in Western Siberia. In winter the roads are frozen; things move faster, and in mid-summer as well, when the roads have dried out. But you surely know this."

"How can you be sure that your postal service makes regular runs?"

"I am not at liberty to tell you this."

"What can you tell me about conditions at the Tiumen Transit Prison?"

Vasiliev was unaware he had taken hold of Szymanski's wrist until the Baron winced.

"I'm terribly sorry. I meant no harm. It's just that I have to know." He relaxed his grip.

"Of course, I understand," said the Baron, rubbing his wrist. "I will try to remember. So many prisons to remember. I can only tell you about the men's prison. They say the women's prison is much easier; I mean the conditions are better. The men's prison is badly overcrowded. We were lodged in a log barracks. I think this was the one with the wooden sleeping bench in the middle of the room. It slept over a hundred, though they say it was built for a score of prisoners. There is nothing else in the room except for a bucket for performing your bodily functions. The unlucky ones in the next barracks had to sleep on the ground. It was muddy and filthy. But they weren't the worst off. There were others packed into cells, ten men occupying a small space, ten meters by ten meters. I got to know a Russian nobleman, a political. He had been confined in Tiumen for six months in one of those cells. He said it was the worst experience of his life. He almost died. Yes, I remember now! He said: 'There we were, ten of us, all nobles living in this filth and pollution. But when the warden came into the cell he took off his hat. We were after all still his social superiors!' Christ Almighty, what a place this Russia of yours is!"

There was a long pause.

"The food?"

"Vasili Vasilievich, why go on? You can imagine what the food was like, for God's sake. Listen, the women's quarters were better—cleaner, less overcrowding. I never saw them, but in the yard the women talked to us. I believed what they said. "

"How long do they keep prisoners there before sending them farther east?"

"For politicals sometimes after a few months, sometimes longer. There are no rules. Most of the politicals end up in Semipalatinsk. Some are sent farther on."

"If I wished, could I get a message back to her?"

"We could help. You will have to write it out for us. We'll transcribe it into another letter, in code written like this one in invisible ink. I can't tell you how long it will take to be delivered. Lots of things could happen along the way. Don't you have another way of sending her a letter—a trusted friend, someone on an official mission?"

"I have to think about it. I am very grateful to you, Baron. You've taken a risk already. I understand you were doing it for your comrade. But still, it was risky, and I thank you."

"Let us go back inside. We shouldn't arouse suspicion. People might think we're conspiring." Szymanski's laugh sounded hollow to Vasiliev. Perhaps, he thought, exiles survive on their dark humor.

Chapter Fourteen

As Vasiliev and Szymanski entered the salon, the musicians were laying down their instruments. There was a light patter of applause. The guests were beginning to move in the direction of a lavish spread laid out on long tables in the next room.

"Vasili Vasilievich, you must excuse me but I never miss the occasion to fatten up at the table of the Governor-General. I don't suppose you care to join me? No, I didn't think so. Perhaps you are making a mistake, given the alternative heading your way." Szymanski bowed and turned away.

The figure of merchant Lev Ivanovich Lopatkin suddenly filled the foreground.

"Don't let me chase you away, Baron!" he cried out. But the Baron affected not to have heard him, and lengthened his stride toward the buffet.

"My dear Inspector, what a pleasure to see you again. And so soon after our first meeting. Now where do you think the Baron is rushing off to? How is your mission proceeding?" The merchant did not wait for answers to these questions. Instead, he took Vasiliev by the hand, as one would a child, and led him over to a group of men. Vasiliev took one look at their gold braid, their medals, and concluded that these were the chief officials of the city. Lopatkin made the introductions. To Vasiliev's astonishment, Lopatkin launched into a long monologue on Jewish responsibility for the pogroms. Vasiliev scarcely paid attention, thinking only of his conversation with Szymanski. The conditions must be so much worse than Irina had anticipated. Nothing she could have experienced, even living as an illegal, could have prepared her for the Tiumen prison. He found himself rubbing his side. He noticed that the men were beginning to look at him strangely. He clasped his hands behind his back and made an effort to listen to Lopatkin. Was he saying something about the Governor-General?

"I heard him repeat it just as I entered the room. He was speaking to that fellow from St. Petersburg, what is his name? Inspector, you must know." Vasiliev shook his head. "It's not important. What is important is that His Excellency has come round to my way of thinking on the matter. You see, when the pogroms broke out, he was convinced it was the work of revolutionaries. Well, I tried to set him straight. And now he's come round. The riots have nothing to do with politics. The people are fed up with the Jews exploiting them. It is that simple. How else can you explain the outbreaks everywhere in the South—all over, Kherson, Ekaterinoslav, and Kiev? We all know that the People's Will has been broken up. It's impossible to blame them for the all these riots. Isn't that right, Captain?"

Captain Rudov had just joined the group and been introduced to Vasiliev as a gendarme from the outlying districts who had put down the pogroms by flogging the rioters in the villages under his command.

"You are probably right, Lev Ivanovich. But the situation is still unclear. Perhaps Inspector Vasiliev can be persuaded to visit my district. We are in firm control now. I guarantee people will talk freely to you."

"I don't think Inspector Vasiliev will have the time right now." Vasiliev turned to face the speaker who introduced himself as the chief of the Kiev city police; "Novitsky, Vasili Dementevich, at your service. I just heard from His Excellency that Inspector Vasiliev will be conducting two investigations in Kiev. Isn't that so?"

Vasiliev tried not to look startled. He felt that he had had enough surprises for one evening. He inclined his head, hoping it expressed his submission to fate. He waited to be enlightened.

"Tell us, my dear fellow, about these two missions," exclaimed Lev Ivanovich.

Novitsky stared at Vasiliev. "Well?"

"Please," Vasiliev extended his arms. "I am always interested in how my assignments look to the world." He realized it was a clumsy evasion. But what alternative did he have? He could hardly say he didn't know what in hell they were talking about.

"We are all well aware of the Inspector's official mission to investigate the causes of the pogroms. What other instructions he might have been given remain, shall we say, confidential. But there is another mystery to be solved. It seems that the Rabbi of the main synagogue has been murdered." There were gasps of surprise. The chief paused, pleased at the effect he had made. "And as I informed His Excellency that our police forces were stretched to the breaking point and cannot spare any detectives, he agreed to hand the case over to Inspector Vasiliev, whose reputation we all know and appreciate."

Vasiliev felt he had been blindsided. Drenteln had exacted his revenge. Once he had told the Governor-General about the murder, he expected the investigation would be pursued on the official level. He would be free to act on his own. Drenteln had turned the tables on him. He was now saddled with being the responsible official. That meant being subordinated to the chief of police; he would be forced to submit daily reports; his every move would be scrutinized. And Novitsky had made it clear that there would be no help coming from his office; the police were 'stretched to the breaking point.' And all this falling like snow on his head at the same time Irina was calling for help. He cursed the hour when Ben-Zion had shown up on his doorstep.

For the next half hour Vasiliev parried questions about the murder with the excuse that the investigation had just begun. When the guests tired of their questioning and moved off toward the buffet, Lev Ivanovich stayed behind. He had been drinking punch all evening, but it did not appear to have had any effect on him. He kept urging Vasiliev to have another glass so that they could toast his future success.

"Perhaps you are tired? All these strange people! You must wonder who to believe! Listen, Vasili Vasilievich, there is no reason you should trust me. But I can assure you that you can. Put me to any test! I'll prove myself. Come, let's get out of here. The party is going nowhere despite the best efforts of our dear hostess, Maria Alexandrovna. My coach is waiting. Recently equipped with rubber wheels. You won't feel a bump as we roll over the hills of Kiev! Come, I promise not to bore you with my theories."

Vasiliev was tempted; he felt his mind racing in several directions. He needed to calm down and think things out. If Lopatkin would keep his promise and stop jabbering—but how likely was that? His side was giving him trouble, and he rubbed it furtively. He had not eaten since breakfast, and felt the need for something. The idea suddenly came to him of putting Lopatkin to a simple test.

"First, a quick bite, Lev Ivanovich and then I'll accept your invitation on one condition. As you have already promised: no serious conversation." He watched the merchant break into a smile that transformed his entire face into an expression of pure joy. He thought the reaction was overstated, but wasn't that Lopatkin to a tee. Only later did he recall the incident in a different light.

Lopatkin maneuvered through the crowd, turning aside all attempts to buttonhole Vasiliev. At the buffet he stood guard as Vasiliev washed down marinated chunks of fresh sturgeon and pickled mushrooms with Polish pepper vodka. Lopatkin intercepted one guest after another, squeezing an arm, bowing and scraping, but refusing to allow anybody to get close to Vasiliev.

"Now let's say our farewells to Maria Alexandrovna and be off."

Vasiliev caught her look of alarm as he raised her hand to his lips.

"I shall never forgive you, Lev Ivanovich, for spiriting away our honored guest so early."

"Ah, my dear Maria Alexandrovna, you really should be grateful to me. I have Vasili Vasilievich's best interests at heart. I'm afraid he hasn't yet recovered from his noble injuries."

Vasiliev thought it was a tactless remark, but Lopatkin seemed to have a storehouse of these on which to draw. For an instant he regretted his decision to leave with him. He could not afford to offend Maria Alexandrovna. But she let him go with a smile that reassured him; no real damage had been done. He would have been even more reassured had he overheard her orders to her lackey, Igor. But he knew nothing of this until much later.

Once they were in the coach Lopatkin fell silent for several minutes. Then he said, with what sounded to Vasiliev like a wistful tone, "Maria Alexandrovna is much admired. It is not easy to be married to our Governor-General."

Vasiliev gave a non-committal cough. He was determined not to encourage gossip about the Governor-General's marital problems. He leaned back against the cushions and closed his eyes, lulled by the gentle motion of the coach. It was a short ride, and Lopatkin said nothing more until they parted. "Please remember, Vasili Vasilievich, you can count on my assistance. I do not boast, but my business interests require that I know everyone of importance in Kiev. I learn everything of importance as soon as it happens — even, I dare say, before the Governor-General." Vasiliev thanked him and, feeling badly shaken, entered the Hotel d' Europe.

Chapter Fifteen

The mornings were still cool in Kiev. The three students walking along the Dniepr bluffs wore Scottish plaid scarves under their jackets, the symbol of the St. Petersburg radical students. They stopped on the high bluff overlooking the Tsar's Garden, called the Cuckoo's Dacha, and gazed up river.

The Dniepr Bluffs: the Cuckoo's Dacha

"What do you think, more of the barefoot brigands arriving to have their fun with us?" Aaron exclaimed, pointing to the Dniepr.

"I don't know, Aaron, those might be ordinary freight barges."

"Nothing's ordinary these days," said Aaron. He selected one of the large pebbles in the palm of his hand and hurled it in a high arc toward the river. It fell short.

"Why do you do that? It only draws attention to us," said the girl, tossing her head.

"A nervous habit, Rebecca, like you when you shake your curls."

"It's not the same thing."

"Listen, comrades, we have something better than pebbles and curls to talk about."

"Always the taskmaster. Eh, David?" said Aaron.

David snorted. "We have to decide what to do about Vasiliev."

"I can't understand why you didn't tell him what you found, David," said Rebecca. "It's crazy to think that we can play detectives ourselves. We're practically illegal in any case. Snooping around will just draw attention to us."

"Like my pebbles, Rebecca?"

"Oh do be serious, Aaron! Sometimes I wonder that we belong to the same family."

"Brothers and sisters can go along different roads; as for cousins like us…" Aaron tossed another pebble in the direction of the Dniepr. "Tell her, David. She has a right to know." Rebecca noted with satisfaction that Aaron had changed his tone. They would get down to serious matters now. The teasing was over.

"Listen, Rebecca, we all admired your papa and we want to get the killer. But how can we trust the police—even a man like Vasiliev, who has this big reputation? But it's only a reputation. What do we really know about him? Reb Ben-Zion vouches for him. But Reb Ben-Zion isn't one of us."

"What do you mean, David? Reb Ben-Zion is like family."

"Of course, Rebecca, But we've gone beyond him—I mean he's still a believer, and not just in Judaism, but in law and order. You've told me yourself that he has no idea what you are up to."

"I know where I stand, David. We may be revolutionaries now but we are still Jews."

"Hey, let's not get into that discussion right now. We're trying to decide on a practical action." Aaron stuffed the pebbles into his pocket and brushed off his hands. He reached back into his waistband for the reassuring feel of his revolver. How could he have forgotten that he had left it hidden in his room? He had taken pains to slit the mattress along a seam and slide the revolver into the cotton wadding, so that it couldn't be detected even if someone lay on top of it. Now he regretted having promised the others not to carry it around for fear of being stopped by the police, and searched. He was beginning to understand how those American cowboys felt when they had to leave their guns outside the saloons—or so the novels of Karl May had led him to believe. The only weapon they had was David's pipe. That was the compromise between the 'hards' like himself and the 'softs' like Rebecca; recalling it made him smile. He was beginning to wonder, though, whether Rebecca was really a 'soft.'

They were walking high on the bluffs toward the Monastery of the Caves, its golden cupolas bright in the morning sun. They stopped to watch two men wade into the Dniepr and then dive, though it was too early in the season for most swimmers. A few other onlookers gathered by the retaining fence. They were pointing back to where the barges were tying up and unloading. In the far distance, on the other side of the river, the flag of the Yacht Club was snapping in the breeze. A water carrier was not having much luck selling to the strollers, but he was chatting with them.

"Do you have it with you?" Rebecca asked.

David reached into his jacket and pulled out a small object that he placed in the palm of her hand. She turned it over and held it up to the light.

"It looks like some votive figure, carved from ivory."

"Or bone. And the thong that must have attached it around the neck—smell it!"

"Strange. It isn't leather. Or else it has been treated with some substance. Listen, David, if you don't want to show it to Vasiliev yet, then you can at least get an expert opinion. It must belong to the killer. The thong looks worn where it broke when...when..." The tears started in Rebecca's eyes. David silently handed her his handkerchief. She gave him the votive figure and dabbed her eyes. "Sorry, it just came over me, you know...when...the moment that this thong broke."

The group of onlookers had turned to walk in the direction of Askold's Tomb, apparently bored watching the swimmers. The water carrier tagged along behind them. Five men had left one of the barges and were climbing the slope behind the students. The church bells suddenly began to ring, sending clouds of river birds into the sky—ducks, sandpipers, loons and snipes. The cacophony of cries drowned out the harmony of the bells.

"What do you suggest?" David asked.

"Take it to Professor Antonovich. Ask him to recommend someone in the Ethnography Department. They'll know what it is. If that leads somewhere, then we can follow. If not, then we go to Vasiliev, agreed?"

The men had disappeared in the trees. They emerged at the crest of the path and began to run towards them.

"Look out! They've got sticks. They're after us. Rebecca, here take the figure and run like hell!" Rebecca hesitated a fraction of a moment, then kicked off her sandals and, with surprising speed, raced down the causeway, screaming for help. The group of onlookers scattered. The water carrier seemed rooted to the spot. She ran right at him, waving her arms. He pulled the straps off his shoulders and let the metal water container fall to the ground. It rolled down the hill toward the Dniepr. He raced past her, shouting, "Get the police! Run as fast as you can!" He was still a few meters away when the five men caught up with David and Aaron. David sank to his knees, whipped out the pipe from his jacket and swung it in a wide arc. It landed with a sickening crunch, followed by a piercing scream. The stricken man collapsed. David raised the pipe again. Aaron had pulled out a handful of stones from his pocket and hurled them at the man closest to him, striking him full in the face. He fell to his knees, blood streaming down his cheeks. With a savage cry the other three men hurled themselves on the two boys.

Chapter Sixteen

Vera woke up early and immediately got out of bed. She had slept soundly, and was surprised at how energetic she felt. Then she remembered her dream. She had been sitting in the classroom of her old school. The teacher had been questioning the students, and she was afraid her turn would be next. When the teacher finally called on her, she answered without hesitation. She was no longer afraid. She outlined her plan, and the teacher smiled at her benevolently. "Vera has got it," she said.

Vera washed hurriedly and ate a crust of bread soaked in water. She was hungry, but her plan would solve that problem too. She brushed her skirt with her hands and shook it vigorously. She put her amulet around her neck. She held it in her palm, wondering where its twin had gone, the one Stepan always wore. Had his killers torn it from his neck? She held it for a moment longer, squeezing it with all her strength. Then she opened the door and peered outside. She watched the sweepers come back from their nocturnal work, gray as the dust they had been collecting. The sun was just clearing the tops of the low wooden cabins across the street. It would be a cool clear day.

She made her way along the muddy street, stepping on the wooden planks that were scattered in front of the cabins. Her shoes would be ruined by the time she reached the teahouse where Stepan had been killed. It took her an hour to get there, but she realized she was still too early when she saw the windows shuttered. She walked aimlessly around the neighborhood, keeping her eyes fixed on the ground so that nothing would distract her. The dance hall was closed and the galleries were still half-empty. She thought about Stepan, how he promised to take her away. The last night they were together he seemed to be happier than she had ever seen him. He had listened to her advice as he always did, with that intensity of his that sometimes frightened her a little. But she had been reassured. He would obey her instructions. He respected her. Yet, she reflected, she was not a woman of the world. All she knew about people had come from living with her family and from books. Her mother was a stupid woman, completely enslaved to her father, a lawyer who went to bed drunk most nights and then repented on Sundays, when he forced the entire family to fast with him. Her two brothers were wastrels. But her grandmother had taken a liking to her and she had a little money, enough to pay for Vera's schoolbooks and uniform. Vera had turned out to be a good student, bright and obedient. Granny liked that. She would give Vera a few coins on her birthday, admonishing her not to tell her parents or brothers. Vera would buy books. Vera could still recall every book she had read out loud to Granny. The day Granny died, Vera felt part of herself had also perished. She had to leave school and become a seamstress. Her life would have been unending drudgery, she thought, if it had not been for Stepan.

He too had been lonely, though he never told her much about his past. They used to sit on the bluffs overlooking the Dniepr and talk. She would tell him about her family, the people from books, mixing the two together, making believe they were all real. He thought she had "a way with knowing" as he put it.

Her meandering walk had brought her back to the teahouse. She stood to one side, watching a man taking down the shutters. She was staring so hard that she did not see the beggar sidled up to her. "Give us a kopek in Christ's name." He startled her. She only had a few coins left. Why share them? Then an idea struck her.

"Listen old man, you have to earn your coin."

"Eh. What's this?" He stepped back. She smelled him now; his shaggy unwashed body offended her. But he might be useful.

"Tell me, old man, is this your station?"

The man giggled and screwed up his eyes. He raised his hands in supplication. "I stand on God's little patch of land."

"Good, then you will have knowledge. Tell me about the man

who was killed over there. You saw it, didn't you? Now, don't be fearful. I was his wife. I want to avenge him. Here's a coin for you if you help me."

He glanced at the coin in her hand.

"That's little enough."

"I don't want much!"

The beggar looked around, and she watched the expression on his face change. He had dropped his pose as a holy fool.

"What did they look like, the ones who attacked him?" Vera was sure there had to be more than one man. Stepan was too strong. "There was more than one, isn't that right?"

He nodded.

"And did they look like Jews?"

The man laughed, "Jews? No, my little soul, they were as Russian as you and me. Jews? Your man was too big for Jews, even an army of them."

"And did they say anything to him?"

"Not a word." His eyes fixed on her. He stepped closer. His breath was terrible. "They came up to him, friendly like, tossed him a bottle, and when he caught it they slipped a knife into him. You see, he had to catch it with both hands. That way he couldn't defend himself. He went down like a tree, and the bottle smashed. The two walked away. A crowd gathered. I knew the police would be next. I left."

Vera felt the prick of tears in her eyes. She extended her arm as far as possible and dropped the coin into the beggar's upturned palm. Then she crossed the pavement and entered the teahouse.

There was only one man inside, seated at a table near the entrance to the kitchen. He was pouring tea from a cup into a saucer and blowing on it. She recognized the china was good quality, something that would not be served to an ordinary customer. He placed a large lump of sugar between his front teeth and sipped the steaming tea. She sized him up as the manager. She sat down at a neighboring table and ordered tea. She felt in her pocket for her last coin.

"Good morning," she said after she had been served her tea. "I'm a poor widow who needs your help. No money, I'm not begging. I need to know."

She watched him turn toward her, a fat man with long greasy hair and a cunning look on his face. This will not be easy, she thought.

"A need to know, do you hear, Egor?" He called over to the waiter who had slouched down in a chair against the wall. "Knowledge of what, my dear? Why people beat the Jews? Whether the world is flat or round? Whether the Holy Spirit emanates from the Father, or as the heretics have it, also from the Son? To know is a lifelong task. And who lives long enough anyway?"

"My name is Vera Evgrafovna. My husband Stepan was killed on the street outside. I want to know only about his last minutes of life."

The manager leaned forward, pushing aside his teacup. "There are police in this city who occupy themselves with such questions — that is when they're around, eh, Egor?" Egor made a strangled noise in his throat. Vera could not tell whether he was laughing or choking to death.

"The police, when they are interested as you say, are after murderers. God be with them. I want only to know how he was, my Stepan — sad or happy sitting here in your teahouse. You see, I was home waiting for good news. Was I right to wait?"

"Sad or happy? She wants to know, Egor, about a state of being. Madam, I am a teahouse manager, not a physician of the soul. Well, what do you say, Egor? You were the last person to see this Stepan alive, except for the murderer. You are not a suspect, Egor. Don't worry. I can vouch for you." The manager smiled, showing rotten teeth. Too much sugar, my man, thought Vera.

Egor looked around the room, hoping for a customer to rescue him.

The manager sipped some more tea. Vera listened to the carts rumble by on the street outside. She folded her hands in her lap and stared at Egor.

Suddenly, the manager pounded on the table, rattling the saucer and sloshing tea out of the cup. Egor jumped, as if he had been struck.

"Damn it, Egor! Tell Madam what you saw and heard. She is suffering, and you cringe over there like some beaten cur. Speak up!"

Egor tottered to his feet and bowed to Vera.

"Sad or happy, I cannot tell. But he was angry. He drank his tea like an angry man."

Oh my God, another teahouse philosopher, thought Vera.

"Yes, you can tell these things after a while. An angry man who showed his anger in a strange way. He sits over there at that bench under the picture. He orders tea twice. The second time he could hardly wait for it to cool down. Then he pulls out a small bit of paper from his pocket. God knows what it is—well, maybe tickets. Yes, yellow, like, say, a railroad ticket. And he sits glaring at it. Then he tears it up and throws it on the floor. He swallows the rest of his tea. Must have burned his throat. He gets up and leaves. I saw him no more."

Egor bowed again and rushed off to serve a postman who had just entered the shop.

"So there you have knowledge, my dear. From Egor, the observer. What else has he in life but to observe?"

"Do you sweep the floor every evening?"

"I do not sweep the floor," the manager grinned again. "But yes, unfortunately for you we have a *baba* who sweeps up. Unfortunately, I say, because if Egor swept up, you can be sure he would have looked at these tiny bits of paper and figured out just what they were.

"And this *baba*, do you know where she lives, or do I have to wait until she comes here again to find her?"

"My, my! You have the instincts of a detective. No address for the *baba*. She will come again tonight, at midnight. You are welcome to continue your investigation, Madam Inspector. But in return, no running to the police. The crime was not committed on the premises, as my legal consultant assured me. So we are not involved. A favor for a favor, my dear. Do you agree?"

"Of course. In any case you could always tell them I was mistaken. You never told me anything, neither you nor Egor."

"This is a smart lady," the manager called out to Egor as the waiter passed on his way to the kitchen.

Vera put down her last coin and left the teahouse. She fingered her amulet. Her mind was in a whirl. Her heart was pumping hard from the strong tea and the lack of food. If she only had more time!

But as the next step in her plan she had resolved to get a job. Without money she could not feed herself. She had considered the possibilities while she had wandered around the neighborhood. The best would be to find work as a seamstress again. But she knew that would take time. She needed something to tide her over, a job that provided food. What could it be?

"So Egor, very good!" said the manager after Vera had left.

"Just enough knowledge. No need to say whose men took such an interest in that miserable wretch—what was his name? Stepan."

Chapter Seventeen

Late that same night, Vasiliev, still in uniform, was stretched out full length, his boots extending over the edge of the hotel bed. He was staring into the darkness, holding Serov's message between his fingers, folding and unfolding it He needed to talk to Serov. There was no one else he could trust, not about Irina. God only knew what had happened to him. Was it a mistake to have sent him off on his own? Vasiliev cursed out loud and was startled by the sound of his voice. Kiev was still an unknown quantity for both of them. Better to have stayed together. Perhaps he had gone back to the safe house. That would make sense. If he was going to be a water carrier, he had to be careful. He couldn't be seen running back and forth from a hovel to the most luxurious hotel in Kiev. If anyone were watching, that is. And it always paid to assume that someone was always watching. Vasiliev felt he had very little time. He had to make up his mind quickly. What were his choices? He tried to review the alternatives, but found it difficult to focus his thoughts.

Suppose Serov were here, what would I say to him? He turned toward the window. His eyes were getting used to the darkness, and he could make out the faint outlines of a chair. He imagined Serov sitting there, and he began quietly to talk to him.

"Irina is calling for help. My dear fellow, what can I do? The last time I saw her she warned me against any romantic escapades. But that was before she was transported, before she had to face the prison conditions in Tiumen. Let me tell you what the Baron said." Vasiliev repeated word for word his conversation with Szymanski.

"So you see, my friend" —his voice falling to a whisper— "Tiumen's a real hell-hole. She knows her own strength and fears that she won't be able to hold out. I've already written to Ivan in St. Petersburg. He'll take my petition to Loris-Melikov. But there's a problem here. Loris-Melikov is no longer Minister of Interior. I don't know how much influence he still has. He'll remember me well enough. After all, he was the one who assigned me to the Ushakova murder case. He knows we went on to uncover the conspiracy to kill the Tsar. He can't forget that you and I, with Irina's help, damn near saved His Majesty's life. Doesn't he owe me something? Or does he think that the Stanislas squared things between us? Without Loris-Melikov, the chances for a pardon are practically nil. The trouble is our new Tsar no longer has confidence in him. You don't know the new Minister of Interior, Ignatiev. Appointed less than a month ago. Just our luck! He's a scoundrel, a liar, and an anti-Semite—I knew him in Constantinople. No, there's no hope in that direction."

Vasiliev groaned and turned on his side. He swung his legs over the edge of the bed and sat up, covering his face with his hands. He looked toward the chair again. There seemed to be a kind of shape there. Had Serov come in silently? He shook his head. This is the way to madness he thought. But he went on. "What about the Tsar himself, Alexander, the third of that name to occupy the throne? He saw me holding his dying father, the royal blood spattered all over me. But does he even remember? He was shattered himself, down on his knees begging his father's forgiveness. And me sitting there, covered with royal blood, cradling the Tsar's head. Maybe Ivan can get to him. An outside chance! What else, Serov? Resign, head off for Siberia, and execute a daring rescue. I couldn't ask your help in this, my dear friend. So I would have to do it alone. And then what? Flee to China? America? Drag Irina across a thousand miles of trackless wilderness? Resign, disgrace my father, end my life in Russia, and leave you to suffer the consequences? The assistant of a rebel and a traitor? Mother of God, spare me from that!

"Suppose I could get her sentence reduced, allowing her to live as a free exile. I could send her money so she'd be able to live decently. Then, after we've cleaned up this mess, I could resign with honor. You too. We've got good record! Take up the management of *Nettles*. Work for her full pardon—or even better, join her. I have enough saved to buy a small property. We could raise Merino sheep."

Vasiliev slapped his head.

"Dreams, fantasies. I'm jumping too far ahead. Right now—get her a message! Ask her to wait. Can I ask this of her? How long do you wait in hell before you begin to rot? Not too long! We need to work fast, Serov. I have to finish things up here. The report on the pogroms is taking shape. I've some ideas. Keep bringing me what you hear. What about the Rabbi? Listen, my first idea is that this was not a random killing. What then? I have the feeling there was something special about him. We can eliminate the Jews. Except for a renegade, no Jew would do this. Unless... No, too fantastic. He was singled out because he stood for something. Or else...No, too many possibilities. We've got to narrow them down. Thank you for listening, Sergeant!" Vasiliev smiled at the chair. It was empty again. He chuckled softly. "You were always a good listener."

The next morning Vasiliev checked out of the hotel. He left no forwarding address, but instructed the porter to hold all messages for him. He sent his portmanteau to the baggage room of the railroad station. It was a move, however feeble, in the right direction. Then he made his way to the safe house. The landlady informed him that Serov had not spent the night there. He gave her a coin and she let him into the room. Serov's uniform hung on a nail in the wall. There was no sign of a message. Vasiliev felt uneasy. Now he was sure. It had been a mistake to separate so early in the game. He took out his notebook, scratched a few lines, tore out a page, and slipped it under the candlestick on the table. He walked down to the embankment and hailed a cab. He gave an address in the Podol. The cabby shook his head. "I dare not go there, officer. There's bound to be more trouble. You can fine me if you like."

Vasiliev jumped out of the cab and slammed the door. He walked on farther and hailed another cab. "I'll need to double the fare," said the cabby. They rolled past the burned-out shops and turned down a leafy avenue. Vasiliev was no sooner out of the cab than the cabby whipped his horse into a gallop and disappeared around the corner. Walking up the path, he noticed the boarded up window on the ground floor. The door looked as though it had been recently repaired. It opened a crack. An old man wearing a yarmulka and phylacteries peered at him. The door closed again. Vasiliev heard scurrying feet. Then the door swung open, and a young woman wearing a black dress stood in front of him. She was very pale. Vasiliev was struck by how beautiful she was. Masses of glossy black hair swept back on one side and held in place by a set of combs framed an oval face. Her eyes were dark, with glints of silver, and moist, as if she had recently been crying. But Vasiliev later discovered they always looked this way, giving her the appearance of someone in need, vulnerable to the slightest hurt. Her lips were full, naturally rosy—she wore no cosmetics—and trembling, not with fear or nervousness, as he also discovered later, but with suppressed emotion. As a student of physical types, he found her unique in his experience. He felt a strange sensation come over him, and he had to make an effort to compose himself.

"Please forgive me for interrupting your period of mourning. I am Inspector Vasiliev and…" But he did not get the chance to finish. The young woman closed her eyes, and her body swayed, as if she were going to faint. Vasiliev reached out to steady her, but then let his arms drop. She placed one hand on her heart, and the other gripped the doorframe. He saw real pain, but her gesture seemed somehow contrived, almost operatic, as if she were about to burst into an aria.

"You are Serov's friend!" she gasped. It was not the greeting he expected, and he felt a pang of fear. "You must come in! Please wait." She turned and hurried off down the corridor, crying out "Rebecca, Rebecca! He has come!"

Vasiliev stood rooted on the threshold. A moment latter another young woman appeared, also dressed in black, also beautiful, but younger. She bore a strange resemblance to her sister, as if Nature had decided in its whimsical fashion to produce an exact replica but had then miniaturized. The same luxurious black hair, though falling freely to her shoulders, the dark eyes, but dry and steady, the features smaller, more sharply drawn. She gave a different impression—serious and more subdued. She extended her hand. As he expected, her grip was firm

"Inspector, I am Rebecca, Rabbi Meier's daughter. You just met my sister, Ruth. I am a friend of David's. He has been searching for you, but you disappeared from your hotel. Please come in. You are most welcome here."

Vasiliev followed her past an ornately carved bureau and a large polished mahogany table. He realized this must have been the scene of the murder. She led him into another room where a sofa and two large armchairs had been pushed against the wall. He noticed the marks they had left on the thick Oriental rug, representing the tree of life that covered most of the floor. The slight odor of furniture polish hung in the air. She motioned him to a chair, and sat across from him.

"Inspector, your Sergeant Serov saved our lives."

"And what about his own life?"

"What do you mean?"

"My God, girl, is he alive?"

"I'm sorry—of course you didn't know. Yes, he's alive. They broke his arm and he's badly bruised. But David said he was magnificent."

"Now that you've told me the important thing, please begin at the beginning." Vasiliev suddenly recollected his first meeting with Ben-Zion. Hadn't he used the same words?

Vasiliev studied her as she collected her thoughts. She tossed her head, her long black curls brushing her shoulders. The gesture reminded him of Irina. He seemed to recall that if Rebecca were to marry into a strict Orthodox family, she would have to be shorn, just like Irina when she entered the prison. He shuddered involuntarily.

Earlier, Rebecca had persuaded David that they had to tell Vasiliev everything that had happened to them on the bluffs. "We'll leave out politics!" David had insisted on that point. "He already knows too much about me from the caves. No reason to test the limits of his tolerance," he had said. Poor Aaron, she thought. He was in no condition to disagree.

Chapter Eighteen

Rebecca seemed preternaturally calm as she told her story, how the five men had disembarked from a barge and rushed them on the bluffs, wielding heavy sticks; how she had run, calling for help; and how the water carrier had dumped his container and tore past her, shouting at her to get the police. She had turned to watch him, and saw David go down on his knees, striking one man with his pipe, while Aaron had thrown his stone missiles into the second man's face, stunning him. She described how she had caught up with several strollers, and breathlessly begged for help. One of the young men in the group had dashed off and waved down a Cossack patrol just rounding a bend on the river road. They came up at a gallop. From a distance she had seen Serov, as she now called the water carrier, plunge into the pile of struggling figures. He pulled out one man and struck him full in the face. "A terrific blow, it was. The man was much bigger than Serov, but he went down like a fallen oak." Another man had wrenched the pipe from David and was beating Aaron. Serov had kicked him aside and then seized the man who was astride David by the collar and the seat of his trousers, lifted him in the air as if he were a sack of potatoes, and threw him over the edge of the bluff. The man disappeared from sight. "He may have fallen all the way to the river," she said. But the third man hit Serov from behind as he was turning. He fell on top of David. By this time the Cossacks were bearing down on them. The man dropped his stick, jumped down the hill on the opposite side of the river road The Cossacks dismounted and pulled the man Serov had knocked down to his feet. They spoke a few words to him and let him go.

Rebecca paused and put a hand to her throat. Her voice had grown hoarse. She rose from her chair and went to a table in the corner, where she poured two glasses of water, handing one to Vasiliev. She tossed her head before speaking again.

"I ran back shouting something, I don't remember what. The Cossacks stood over David and Aaron and Sergeant Serov as if they were trying to decide what to do with them. As I got nearer I could see the blood on their faces. I mean David's and Aaron's. The Sergeant looked like he was in great pain. But he pulled something out of his blouse and showed it to the Cossacks. They glanced at one another and helped him to his feet. I ran up and cried out, 'Take them to St. Vladimir!' They looked at me as if I had dropped from the sky. 'Dr. Margulies will take care of them,' I said. One of the Cossacks said 'the Jew doctor' and the others nodded. The Sergeant spoke to them quietly. One of the Cossacks mounted and rode off. In a few minutes a cab appeared. They lifted Aaron inside. David was on his feet, smiling at me as he walked to the cab. He was holding his side. The Sergeant got in, and I squeezed in next to them. When we got to the hospital I asked for Dr. Margulies. You met him, I think, in the cave. He came right away. He gave a lot of orders and told me to wait. In an hour he came back and told me that Aaron was badly hurt and he was going to consult a specialist, perhaps operate immediately. David had suffered a concussion, a bruised rib, and some other injuries. The doctor had set the Sergeant's broken arm and insisted he and David stay in the hospital overnight. We still didn't know who our savior was.

"When I returned the next morning, Dr. Margulies told me that Aaron was going to live but would always have a limp and might lose his sight in one eye." Rebecca's voice broke. "He is my cousin you see and we grew up together. It is very hard, after papa, now Aaron." She sipped some water. Vasiliev felt bound to say something.

"My heart goes out to you. This is a terrible thing. I am ashamed for my country."

She lowered her head and then looked him straight in the eye. "We will change it some day!" she said, with a fierceness that surprised him. Again she reminded him of Irina. My God, he thought, will we lose all our young people because of this insanity?

"And Serov?" he prompted.

"Yes, I'm sorry; you want to know about him. And there is more too about the murder of my father." She looked toward the door. Vasiliev turned and saw the old man, who had removed his phylacteries. He shuffled from one foot to another. "You must eat, Rebecca," he said. Rebecca smiled at him and said softly, "Thank you Reb Moishe, not now."

"The Torah says 'You shall guard your souls,'" he said, and vanished.

"The next morning I visited the Sergeant." Rebecca went on. "He had tried to leave the hospital, but it turned out that his ankle was so swollen that he couldn't get his boot on. He seemed very distressed. He asked me who I was, and when I told him he brightened up for an instant. Then his face became sad. He told me how sorry he was for my loss. I couldn't understand who this man could be. He was not a Jew, but so sympathetic. I said it was only fair that he tell me who he was. He laughed and swore me to secrecy. He said that he must get a message to you. Then David came in, hobbling, his head bandaged. He thanked the Sergeant. That's when he said to him, 'You were magnificent.' The Sergeant looked pleased. But then he looked strangely at David. 'Didn't I last see you by the light of the moon, coming out of a cave?' David was startled. Then the Sergeant told him who he was. He was joking. He said we now formed a 'secret society'. We promised to find you, but you found us first."

Vasiliev thanked her. A smart girl, he thought. "But what is this about your father's murder? Wait a moment. I have to tell you first—Kiev has put me in charge of the investigation."

Rebecca drew a small object out of her dress pocket and handed it to him. It looked like nothing he had ever seen before.

"David and Aaron found this near the body of my father. They hesitated to show it to you. They had their reasons, but that isn't important now. Yesterday, after I visited the hospital, I took it to Professor Antonovich—you know the archaeologist who first explored the caves where you met David. He thought it came from the North. He took me to see his colleague in the Ethnography Department of the University. The professor examined it under a magnifying glass. Then he compared it to some sketches one of his students had made on an expedition to Western Siberia. He said it was an amulet of the Ostiak tribe."

"The Ostiaks? That makes no sense. They are a semi-nomadic tribe, a reindeer people. They roam over the tundra."

"That's what Professor said."

Vasiliev held the amulet up to the light. "The thong must have broken…" He checked himself when he saw the expression on Rebecca's face.

"But Ostiaks? Why would they come to Kiev? Unless of course…" He paused again and then muttered, as if to himself. "Yes, that must be it."

He turned the amulet over in his hands. It was smooth, as if the edges had been worn by constant rubbing.

"I don't understand," said Rebecca.

"The Ostiaks live in a Siberian wilderness, a region where many exiles are sent. Let's assume that the man who dropped this is not a tribesman, but an exile, a former criminal—not a political—who was hired to kill your father. That would explain some things, but raises other questions. Let's make a second assumption, or a guess. I'm a great believer in guesses. Let's say the killing was not connected to the pogroms. At least, not directly. Perhaps your father was not murdered because he was a Jew. Or not *just* because he was a Jew. It's complicated. The symbolism of the cross—horrible, but it might have been intended to mislead the police, to disguise the real motive. You see what I'm getting at? So I have to ask you. Did your father have any personal enemies, or was he somehow involved in something, I don't know what? Politics perhaps? I'm just grasping at straws right now. Trying to get you to think of any reason someone might do this and then try to hide the real reason."

Rebecca sat motionless for a long moment, knitting her brows. Then she shook her head so that it seemed her curls were dancing on her shoulders. Vasiliev wondered what her relations were with David. The boy would have to be made of stone not to fall in love with her.

"Nothing comes to mind, Inspector. Father was beloved by everybody. It's not a matter of filial piety here. You can ask anybody. Even on religious matters, the conservatives respected his great learning, even though he was a *maskil*. Do you know the term? It means an enlightened one in Hebrew. He believed…well, that's not important right now. The devout Orthodox opposed him on theological grounds, but they had to acknowledge him as a great scholar. And the radicals who had left the faith had been inspired by him when they were younger. Still, they respected him as a wise man, even though they disagreed with him."

"I wasn't thinking necessarily of the Jewish community or even Jewish revolutionaries, but of someone who had a grudge against him or who saw your father as a threat for some reason or other."

"I can't think of anyone like that. I'm not home so much any more. I've been attending the women's higher courses at the University. You know about them? They've only opened recently. Yes, well—father and Reb Ben-Zion taught me so well that I was admitted, one of the few Jewish girls. Perhaps my sister Ruth would know. She was here most of the time, running the household. She would know more, I think. I'll call her."

In a few minutes Ruth appeared or rather, as Vasiliev later put it to Serov: "She made her second stage entrance. I was able to compare the two sisters. Ruth was a classic beauty, and even in her deep mourning there was something very feminine, even flirtatious, in her manner. Rebecca, though younger, seemed more mature—thoughtful, even though she too was stunning." Serov immediately regretted having missed the interview.

Vasiliev questioned Ruth, but she seemed to know very little of what happened outside the household.

"Did your father have any relations with the secular authorities, or perhaps with people in the Christian community?"

"Oh, Inspector, I am not much help. My father never talked to me about such things. He was very loving, but he didn't think I had much of a head for practical affairs, and Rebecca was so seldom here."

"Did your father leave any papers aside from his scholarly work?"

"Why, I suppose so. They would be in a cabinet in his private study. It was always locked, and he carried the key with him."

Rebecca suddenly looked up. It seemed to Vasiliev that she had lost a bit of color. "Ruth, did Reb Moishe find a key on papa when he prepared him for burial?"

"I never asked. But he would have told me, if he had, wouldn't he?"

"We can ask him now."

"He's gone home."

"May I see the cabinet?" Vasiliev asked.

"Of course. It is in the back of the house. The study faces the hill." They went into the corridor where several men brushed by them, muttering in Yiddish to the two young women. There were people in every room they passed. The house seemed like a hotel to Vasiliev. Rebecca led the way to the study. Bookshelves lined the four walls. Vasiliev glanced at the titles in Hebrew, Russian and German. A few prints of the old ghetto in Vilna stood on the shelves; a large mahogany desk and a long table made of lime wood occupied the center of the room. Piles of neatly stacked books covered most of the flat surfaces. Ruth turned to Vasiliev as they entered the study. "You must wonder about our lively household," she said smiling. "Father's relatives are here, our friends, and people who are seeking refuge. Some have lost their homes. My goodness, sometimes we have twenty for supper."

"But the night of the pogrom the house was empty."

"Yes, we had been warned to leave."

"Did you ever find out who sent you the warning?"

"No."

"You're a very practical woman, Ruth, or else you couldn't manage such a big household," Vasiliev said. Ruth blushed. She dismissed the compliment with a wave of her hand. Vasiliev found her charming, if a bit theatrical. He wondered where she had learned all these gestures.

"Does anything look out of place?" Vasiliev asked her as he glanced around the walls of the study. Rebecca was standing in front of a bookshelf, running her fingers over the old leather bindings. She seemed lost in thought.

"Why, no! Father was very tidy. Even when he was working with manuscripts, they were carefully arranged. Here on this table. When he'd finished with a book he returned it to its proper place on the shelf—not like most rabbinic scholars I have known."

"And this is the cabinet?"

Vasiliev sat on his haunches and examined the double doors

fitted with two polished brass handles. There was no indication that the lock had been forced, no scratches around the keyhole. He stood up and started to leave the room, then stopped short. A thought had occurred to him. Rebecca looked at him curiously. He went back to the cabinet, crouched down again, and ran his fingers along the edges of the double doors. He felt something move. He took hold of the two handles and pulled. The doors swung open. They had been left unlocked.

Ruth gasped. Rebecca knelt down beside him. "This cannot be," she said.

The three shelves of the cabinet were empty.

Chapter Nineteen

Vasiliev spent the morning in the library of St. Vladimir University reading ethnographic reports on the crafts of the Ostiaks and other Siberian tribes. He arrived at St. Vladimir Hospital at noon. He brought some of Serov's favorite *kolbasa* and cheese. The corridors were packed with makeshift beds. There was a smell of carbolic acid and human excrement. It took Vasiliev some time to locate Serov's ward. It was cleaner and lighter than others he had seen. There were ten patients, all of who seemed to have casts on their arms or legs. When he entered the room, Dr. Margulies was standing at the foot of Serov's bed. Vasiliev recognized him as Mordecai from the Caves.

"Inspector! How nice to see you in daylight. My real name is Mikhail Borisovich Margulies." He said extending his hand. "And here is the hero of the moment." Vasiliev touched Serov lightly on the shoulder. "Yes", said Margulies, "he has done more for the status of water carriers than a three month drought."

"The doctor comes in to entertain me, you see, Vasili Vasilievich."

"He also seems to have done a good job with your arm."

"It was a really just a hair-line fracture. Your Sergeant has powerful muscles in his forearm. A hard blow with a thick wooden stick would have shattered the bones of a lesser man."

"And the ankle?"

"Badly sprained, but it too should heal quickly if we can tie him down long enough." Margulies laughed, and gave Serov a mock salute as he left the room.

"I must tell you, Vasili Vasilievich. I like these Jews."

"You may be one of the few philo-Semites in the city, Serov. And what is this?" Vasiliev pointed to a bouquet of spring flowers in a water-filled bottle by the side of the bed. "More tributes from your admirers?"

"There was no note, but I suspect the girl, Rebecca."

"I've heard her version and now I want yours."

Serov lowered his voice. His account added little to what Rebecca had said. "What really surprised me, Vasili Vasilievich, was the way the Cossacks treated us. They behaved badly. They saw what happened, far away as they were. But they let the swine get away with it. They just let 'em go. And they didn't much care for me, even after I showed 'em my police card. There's somethin' rotten in this city."

"Rotten perhaps, confused certainly. One night with the higher ups convinced me that no one from the Governor-General on down has a good idea of why the pogroms broke out, or how to control the mob. They don't agree on who was responsible. I get a sense that police, army and Cossacks are acting—or not acting at cross-purposes. What do you think?"

"Well, Vasili Vasilievich, the street is alive with rumors. Some see the revolutionaries behind it all; others blame Jewish greed. I've heard said that Russian hooligans started it all. I don't know. It's too hard to sort out. Everybody agreed on one thing. Not enough police on the streets. Could be, there just aren't enough police in the city. I mean to handle a pogrom. And then there's the army. People ask where were the soldiers?"

"Our Jewish friends don't agree either. I'd like to see the orders issued to the police and army units. Something's not right. But I can't put my finger on it. Not yet."

"And what about the killin' of the Rabbi?"

Vasiliev had no chance to answer.

An orderly came into the ward and looked around. When he saw Vasiliev, in uniform, he hurried over. He was carrying a large basket. "Is the patient, ah…" He groped in his jacket which, Vasiliev noticed, was not too clean.

"…ah, the patient Serov here; are you the patient Serov?" He held out the basket. Vasiliev took it and set it down beside the bed.

A note was attached.

"For gallantry in action," it read. It was signed 'Lev Ivanovich Lopatkin.' The basket contained fresh fruit and small, freshly baked cakes.

"What a strange fellow," Serov said. "Why should he care about me?"

Several other patients were straining to see what the basket contained.

"Brothers, don't let this go to waste. Help yourselves!" Serov called out to them. Vasiliev handed the basket around and each patient took a piece of fruit and a cake. They mumbled their thanks between bites. "The legend of Serov grows," whispered Vasiliev. Serov laughed.

Vasiliev told him about the missing papers. "Too bad the Rabbi was so secretive. The girls don't know anything about the papers. There were always people coming to visit him. Ruth remembers them by sight. She said some were carrying briefcases or folders. But the Rabbi always received them in the study and made sure the door was shut. No one dared interrupt him then. Even Ben-Zion hasn't a clue about the content of the papers. Someone, probably the killer, got hold of the key. But there's a problem. Would he dare to go back to the house later for the papers? He wouldn't have had time after he shot the Rabbi. David and Aaron were in there too quickly. The Rabbi carried the key with him at all times. We have to know who had access to the body. It seems a Reb Moishe prepared the Rabbi for burial. He might have seen something. The girls are eager to help. But I don't want them to get too involved. They gave me Reb Moishe's address. I'm hoping he might be able to tell us about the key to the cabinet. But we've got something else. A curious thing."

Vasiliev drew his chair closer to the head of the bed. He took out the amulet and showed it to Serov, screening it from the other patients. "Thanks to your 'gallantry in action', as Lopatkin puts it, our young Jewish friends trust us. It's probably Ostiak..." Vasiliev stopped in mid-sentence. Serov was staring wildly at the amulet. He grabbed hold of Vasiliev's hand, bent over, and brought the amulet close to his eyes. The abrupt movement caused him to grunt with pain.

"Easy does it, Sergeant! What's wrong?"

"Vasili Vasilievich, I've just seen its twin, I mean another just like it."

Vasiliev looked startled. "What d'you mean?"

"Early this mornin', the woman who empties the slops, she was wearin' one just like it. It was hangin' around her neck. When she bent over to get the pan, it swung out, just inches from my nose. I saw it as clear as this one."

Vasiliev closed his fist on the amulet and stood up. "What did she look like? I've got to find her, now!" In a moment he was out into the corridor, stopping everyone in a white uniform. No one seemed able to help him. He found his way to the administrator's office. The secretary or assistant was arguing heatedly with a woman in a gray dress wielding an umbrella. He tried to interrupt, but the woman turned on him in a fury. She ranted for several minutes before stalking out of the room. The secretary slumped in a chair. "I can't cope any longer!" she sobbed. Vasiliev spoke to her softly, trying to calm her down.

"Listen, my dear, I need your help. It's about one of your staff. She empties bed pans." He described her in Serov's words. "She is small, thin, fair hair streaked with gray. Her eyes are light blue and prominent, as if she were suffering from some disease. She has a long scar on her forehead. She worked in ward No. 19 this morning. Where is her employment form? It's a police matter."

The secretary looked dazed. "What could be wrong?" She seemed unable to focus on what Vasiliev was saying.

"Where's the administrator?" he demanded.

"She's out sick."

"Who's in charge of hiring here?"

"She is."

"Where do you keep the records?"

"In her office. But it's locked, and we don't have the key."

"That's impossible. How can you lock up the records?"

"Nadia Pavlovna doesn't want anybody snooping."

"Is there no section manager, no one in charge on the floor?"

"Please don't shout! There is the day attendant, if you can find her. They are all irresponsible. We can't cope!" The secretary began to weep again.

Vasiliev left the office and went back into the corridor. Several new patients had just arrived on dollies. They were surrounded by orderlies, doctors, and people from the street. Everyone seemed to be shouting at once. Vasiliev felt himself getting angrier as he watched the confusion grow. Ambulatory patients began to stream out of the wards to find out what was going on. Vasiliev spotted Dr. Margulies, who was trying to get things under control. But someone in the crowd shouted, "We don't need the help of a Yid." Dr. Margulies fell back and retreated to the end of the corridor. Vasiliev caught up with him.

"Damn those swine," he said.

Dr. Margulies smiled grimly. "I should be used to it. But when it happens here, in the hospital, it's hard to take. What is it, Inspector? Can I help you? Is there something wrong with the Sergeant?"

Vasiliev described the woman with the amulet.

"I wish I could help. But ever since the riots, orderlies have been leaving without notice. The replacements are temporaries. They're hired every day. I don't know most of them any more. But the administrator, Nadia Pavlovna…"

"She is out sick."

"Again! The place is coming apart, my dear Inspector."

An orderly ran up, begging Dr. Margulies to attend to a patient in ward 21. He left Vasiliev, shaking his head.

Vasiliev stood in the corridor, people swarming around him. He rubbed his side as he walked back to Serov's ward.

Serov read Vasiliev's face. "She'll come back around ten o'clock. The night shift, I'm pretty sure. Why didn't I think of that before?"

Vasiliev sat down on the chair. The time had come to tell Serov about Irina. The other patients were gathered around a man still nibbling on his piece of cake. He was telling them what had happened in the corridor.

Vasiliev smiled to himself as he told Serov for the second time about his meeting with Szymanski. "You see the problem, Serov. I can't leave her out there. But I don't see how I can break her out if we've got no place to run. Here's what I thought I should do." Vasiliev outlined his plan. Serov responded as Vasiliev had expected. He grunted and whistled softly from time to time. It was Serov at his most eloquent.

"Listen my friend, the main thing is to finish up in Kiev as fast as possible. We'll be free then to help Irina. First, I'll retire. How about joining me? We'll run *Nettles* together, make it our base. Then we'll take off for Siberia. I'm sure we can get Irina released from prison. Local officials are always ready to make some extra money. She may have to live in exile, but we can find her a decent place to live. Meanwhile, Ivan will be working to get her a full pardon. A new life for all of us."

Serov closed his eyes for a moment. He knew what he had to say.

"It's a good plan, Vasili Vasilievich, a good plan. But as you say, there's no time to lose. And here I am half-crippled and of no use to you. Who else can you count on?"

"We're not going to get much from the police. They're moaning about being overstretched. I don't know about the army. They're next on my list. Our young Jewish friends are eager, but inexperienced. Besides, David sounds like a radical. That's all we need, to team up with radicals again. The merchant Lev Ivanovich offers his services, but I can't see what use he might be. Maria Alexandrovna is a great source of information. Szymanski? As a messenger, perhaps, but nothing else. Here we are again, Sergeant, just like the Ushakova case. We're thin on the ground."

Vasiliev was thinking back to when they had failed to save the Tsar's life. Russia had always paid a high price for the lack of good men.

"Never mind. We'll follow the leads we have. Tonight the woman with the amulet will be back. You might have to tackle her alone. It all depends on whether I can get hold of Reb Moishe."

Vasiliev left the hospital and hailed a cab. He gave an address in the Podol district. The cabby looked at him skeptically. "I'll take you to the boundary line of the district. But no cab will go beyond that any more."

"That's nonsense. One took me yesterday."

"That was yesterday," said the cabby. "Are you going or not?"

For an instant Vasiliev thought of commandeering a police cab. But he decided against it. He did not want any favors from the chief of police. On the spur of the moment he changed his mind and ordered the cabby to take him to the Bessarab bazaar. He passed several stalls until he found one that sold respectable looking second-hand clothes. He picked out twill trousers and a dark jacket to match, a broad brimmed hat, and a pair of worn but serviceable black leather boots. Next he went to an apothecary shop and bought some cosmetics. No time to make his own, as Foma would have insisted. He rejected the idea of a wig.

As he walked to the safe house he thought about his old tutor in the art of disguise. He often wondered why Foma had stayed on the old Count's estate after the emancipation of the serfs in 1861. Long before then the Count had given him a passport so that he could work anywhere and send back a few rubles as *obrok*, payment in cash. He had traveled all over Russia, picking up odd jobs, keeping his eyes and ears open, storing away vast amounts of local lore, mastering regional accents. He could have disappeared any time into the nether world of the *brodiaga*, the floating vagrant population that from time immemorial had tramped the byways of Russia. But he had always come back. As Vasiliev grew up, Foma traveled less. Vasiliev thought about it. Was it because he wanted to spend more time with his young pupil? Teaching him everything he knew? Well, not quite everything. That would have been impossible. But teaching him how to imitate the regional accents, dress, and habits of people from every social class and how to master all the arts of disguise. Vasiliev found out later that even apprenticeships of the Imperial Theater provided no better training for actors.

On his way to the safe house Vasiliev took every precaution to avoid being followed. He knew he was conspicuous in his uniform and couldn't easily lose himself among the strollers. He passed the house and doubled back. Nothing suspicious caught his attention. What a strange business! An inspector of his Majesty's Imperial Police slinking about in his own country, forced to act like a criminal. This is not what he expected when he joined the force.

Once inside the safe house he spent the following hours transforming himself into a merchant. He examined several passports he had stowed in his bag, and finally selected one that identified him as a merchant of the second guild. Not too ostentatious and not too plain. A man content with his standing in the middle rank. He had debated with himself about taking on the identity of a Jewish merchant, but concluded the risk was too great. He watched at the window until he saw the landlady cross the street, a wicker basket over her arm. Then he left the house and walked down a broad avenue that led into the Jewish quarter. He had memorized the street plan and soon found the address that Ruth had given him. He took in everything at a glance and felt his heart sink. The house of Reb Moishe was a burned out shell.

Chapter Twenty

Maria Alexandrovna was reclining on a Louis XV *chaise longue* in her boudoir, absentmindedly trailing her fingers over the silk upholstery. She regretted that she had not been kind to her milliner. It was not the poor woman's fault. The latest hats from Italy had been attractive enough, but her mind was on other things. She had always prided herself on understanding Drenteln. She had no illusions about loving him and did not know whether he loved her, not in the conventional sense. Or was true love always unconventional? It certainly had been with Count Vorontsov. Why had they not married? She felt the shadow of Vasili's mother had stood between them. Outclassed by a serf girl! And yet he would not marry her either. A strange man! And Vasili had never married either. Who was he saving himself for? She wrenched her thoughts back to what was disturbing her now. Whether Drenteln loved her or not, he had always confided in her. He respected her opinion, though he did not always take it. But now, what was she to think of the mysterious goings-on in her own household?

She stood up and went to the window. The rain that started it all was still falling in heavy drops. But she recalled that the first indications had come earlier, before the storm. It began with the invitation. As usual, she had made out the guest list and shown it to him. As usual, he had approved. Then, later the same day, after lunch, he had casually suggested adding two more names, the merchant Lopatkin and the Polish Baron, Szymanski. At first she had thought nothing of it, probably because she was getting ready to go out. In the coach it had occurred to her how curious the request had been. The Governor-General did not consort with merchants, and he could hardly have any sympathy with Poles. It had been a Polish revolutionary, Leon Mirsky, who took a shot at him just two years before.

She watched the rivulets trickle down the long panes of glass. Why did raindrops on the window always remind her of tears? Too many sentimental French novels! She cast a disdainful look at the book with yellow covers lying on her bedside table.

"Concentrate, Maria, for heaven's sake," she murmured to herself. She recalled all the inquiries she had made. Her friends at the charitable circle, just yesterday. They told her about Lopatkin. Rich, a railroad baron, well connected at court. "They say he was one of Princes Yurovskaia's advisors—unofficial of course, my dear—in railroad speculation," one of her friends had confided. Then she remembered that Drenteln had scornfully mentioned the same thing when Ekaterina Dolgorukaia, now Princess Yurovskaia, had married the late Tsar Alexander II. "What's really shocking," he had said, "is not that he takes a new wife before the empress is cold in her grave, but that she dabbles in railroad concessions. Sordid business!" If it was such a sordid business, and Lopatkin had been her adviser, then why on earth would the Governor-General invite him to his house? When she found out more about Szymanski, she was even more puzzled by Drenteln's interest in him.

The dowager of a general in her circle had told her that the Baron had been a young blood in the years before the Polish revolt of 1863. He had thrown himself into the fighting around Kiev, got himself captured, and was sentenced to exile for life in Siberia. But he was pardoned recently and restored to his estate. This had happened before Drenteln was appointed Governor-General. What was the reason for inviting him? She searched her mind. He ran a big estate and was a member of the Polish Club. What else? He was considered something of a mystery man, although no one could tell why this was so. None of this told her the reason for inviting him. Was it because he and Lopatkin were successful business men? Of course, the local economy was important. That was why Witte had been invited. But he was at least a state official. If that was all there was to it, she wondered, then why hadn't her husband consulted her. He didn't even ask her to pay them particular attention. That's what he had done so often in the past with important guests. So this time she had practically ignored them. Was this what he wanted?

She listened to the thunder roll over the hills of Kiev. The storms had begun yesterday, driving her home early, unexpectedly. She recalled how Igor had met her at the door with that warning look she knew so well. Her thoughts strayed for a moment. How much like his father Igor had become! Probably just like his grandfather too, though she could scarcely remember him from her childhood. She had brought Igor and his father to Kiev. The old man had died shortly after. Igor was her last link to Moscow. She had come to rely on him for delicate missions. Nothing intimate or scandalous—just delicate. He had already reported how he had followed Lopatkin's coach the night of the party. Why had she been so concerned about Vasiliev leaving in the company of the merchant? She could not explain it, even to herself. Perhaps because she did not know this man, Lopatkin. Perhaps she felt overly protective of Count Vorontsov's son. Couldn't a senior police officer like Vasiliev take care of himself? She argued with herself. Perhaps Kiev had become a dangerous place not only for Jews but also for strangers from Moscow.

Igor had taken her umbrella and signaled with a motion of his head. She glanced at the coats hanging in the corridor, one of an officer of the Gendarmes, another an old-fashioned cloak with a worn velvet collar of distinctive Polish cut. Igor had led the way past the door of the Governor-General's study. He had paused, bowed to her and turned away, heading for the pantry. She had heard the murmur of male voices, knocked, and quickly opened the door.

It had surprised her that Drenteln was not seated behind his desk. Instead, he was standing next to the deal table, in conversation with two men. She was even more surprised, despite Igor's unmistakable signal, to recognize Captain Rudov and Baron Szymanski.

"Oh, Sasha, I'm sorry, I didn't know you had company. There's a storm coming up and I came home early. Captain, Baron, excuse my interruption." The three men had bowed. She had closed the door and went to her room.

"Now what does that all mean?" she kept thinking.

Vasiliev questioned several people in Reb Moishe's neighborhood in the Podol. He soon realized that the Jews had become suspicious of strangers looking for one of their own. He retraced his steps to the safe house, changed back into his uniform and took a cab to Rabbi Meier's house. Surprisingly, Rebecca answered the bell. He explained the problem. She volunteered to find Reb Moishe with the help of David, who had been released from the hospital. Vasiliev returned to Serov's bedside to wait for the woman with the amulet.

Rebecca and David spent several hours searching for Reb Moishe before they found his sister-in-law. She told them in a trembling voice that Reb Moishe had left Kiev for the small town of Shuliavshina. "He was a frightened man."

"It's the first stop on the rail line," said David. "Do you want to get back to Vasiliev?"

"No, let's find Reb Moishe. Vasiliev would be even more conspicuous in Shuliavshina than in Podol. Besides, if Reb Moishe is frightened now, he'd be terrified if a police inspector showed up. I'm sure that he knows something about father's murder. He'll tell me if I ask him point blank. Strange—he didn't seem frightened yesterday."

"We'd best split up. I'll go to the local synagogue, and you look for a restaurant where they supervise the *kashruth*. He's bound to be in one place or the other," Rebecca said as they boarded the train.

"I'm glad you volunteered for the synagogue. I don't think I could go in one any more."

"It doesn't appeal to me either, but we haven't got a choice."

The third class carriages of the train to Shuliavshina were crowded with Jews fleeing Kiev for the shtetls in Podolia, to villages where their ancestors had lived long ago. Rebecca and David were forced to stand, crushed together and jostled uncomfortably throughout the slow journey. They emerged from the train shaken by the sight of weeping women and crying children clutching overstuffed suitcases, canvas bags, and boxes tied with string. Lacking the fare to continue on the train, people were trudging on foot into the countryside. One couple caught their attention. How dignified in defeat! thought David. They were grim-faced when they entered the town.

Jewish Couple Fleeing Kiev

David found his way to the one restaurant in Shuliavshina "where the pious eat," as a Jewish tradesman told him. He ordered a slice of cherry cake with powdered sugar and tea. The waiter seemed miffed that he was occupying a table without ordering a full meal. David realized he had made a mistake, but he couldn't afford to pay for anything else. Now they would tell him nothing. The owner shook his head at every question. David looked around angrily. These foolish old men, sitting here waiting to be beaten, he thought. Then he felt badly and left the restaurant, slamming the door.

Rebecca pulled a shawl over her head, entered the small wooden synagogue, and climbed to the balcony. She had brought with her a *siddur* printed in Jerusalem and bound in wooden covers, from her father's library. It had been years since she had said her prayers. As she murmured them she suddenly felt a strange sensation of almost physical revulsion creep over her. She was afraid she might faint. She grasped hold of the wooden rail and glanced around at the women sitting near her. They appeared to be poor, and prayed from a large *siddur* bound in a dark cloth cover, with the Hebrew text on the top of the page and a Yiddish translation on the bottom.

She was overcome by feelings of pity and anger. She couldn't even remember when she had become truly rebellious. No doubt a gradual process, she thought. There were times when she struggled and failed to understand papa. He treated her and Ruth too as creatures with brains worth cultivating. But then, he was tied to so many of the old beliefs, the separation of women in the synagogue, the shaving of their heads when they got married. Sometimes she could barely contain herself. She felt this was one of those moments.

She struggled to get control of herself. She stood up and peered through the curtains screening the women's section. She caught a glimpse of Reb Moishe. The sermon seemed to go on forever. She felt the words washing over her, but leaving her dry. When the voice stopped she automatically kissed her prayer book, then with her fingers rubbed her lips in surprise, and hurried down the stairs. Reb Moishe had rushed out. He was walking alone down a muddy street lined with lime trees, his head bowed. She followed him until they were out of sight of the synagogue. She thought carefully about her next move. She wanted to avoid startling him. Braving the mud, she crossed the street, and, lengthening her stride, she rapidly got well ahead of him. Then she crossed back to his side and stood waiting for him to recognize her. When he saw her he stopped in his tracks. His whole body swayed for a moment, before he reached out to support himself against the trunk of an enormous lime tree. She smiled and waved at him. She had never seen a man's face so distorted with fear.

She held out her hands to him. "Reb Moishe, I have been searching everywhere for you! I need your help, please!"

"No, No," he stammered, "I cannot help you. May God forgive me! Do not ask, my dear Rebecca. I am not to blame."

"Reb Moishe, you loved the Rabbi and he loved you. He has been violently taken from us. I seek vengeance. You must help me. When you prepared the Rabbi for burial you found a key in his pockets. What did you do with it? This key will unlock the mystery."

Rebecca was afraid that Reb Moishe would collapse. She took his arm.

"Come, where do you live? You can rest there and tell me."

"No, I cannot!" He looked around wildly. "I cannot involve them! They have given me shelter."

"Where then?"

"Further on, down this street, then off to this side, a small park by the stream."

They walked together silently. Rebecca, holding his arm, felt his whole body trembling. The park was nothing more than a bare open space with a few stunted lime trees and forlorn bushes. Reb Moishe collapsed on a wooden bench. Rebecca noticed one of the slats was missing. She stood over him. "I do not blame you. I only want the truth." She spoke now in Yiddish.

He looked up at her. "Rebecca, my child, I'm not afraid for my life. I have long been ready to meet God. They know this. The danger hangs over my family, my innocent niece, Bathsheva. If my lips are unsealed, she will suffer great injury or worse."

"No one shall know what you tell me. I will not share this knowledge with the police. I will look into my own heart and then decide what to do." She was aware of having adopted the stilted cadences of his speech.

"You must swear this to me!"

"I so swear on the memory of my father, may he rest in peace."

Reb Moishe drew a deep breath. For a moment she was not sure he was capable of uttering a sound. Then he began in a quiet voice. "I found the key in the Rabbi's pocket and set it aside. As I was washing the body, a man came into the room. I can see him now, very tall, lean, with the face of an ascetic. He said he was from the rabbinic court. I remember having seen him in the house several times, though never when Rabbi Meier was there. He asked if I had found a key to a cabinet. He said he needed it to gain access to some legal documents. I should have asked you first, but no one was around, and I was distraught. I gave him the key. I didn't notice whether he came back or not. I forgot all about the key until yesterday. A man who claimed to be a detective came up to me on the street outside your house. He demanded to know where the key was. I told him about what happened. He said the key had disappeared and the responsibility sat on my head. He said that if I did not recover it I would bring down the wrath of the Christian community on me and my family. I couldn't understand this! He said the cabinet contained documents of importance to the future of Kiev. I had to swear—I shall never forget the cruelty in his face— never to say anything to anyone about the key. I was terrified. I promised him to look for the key. I returned to your house and searched the room where I had last seen it. But there was no trace of it. I knew the threat from the detective was a real one. I rushed to my brother and urged him to flee Kiev with his wife and daughter. I cannot tell you where they went. But now I am cursed!"

Reb Moishe began to weep. Rebecca sat next to him and cradled his head on her shoulder.

Chapter Twenty-One

Ward No 19 had grown silent. The candles had been extinguished. Vasiliev sat in the dark beside Serov's bed. At midnight the door to the ward opened and a woman holding a candle entered. She was dragging a large metal container into which she emptied the slops from the bed pans. When she came to Serov's bed, Vasiliev lit a candle and held it up.

"It's not her," said Serov.

"Where is the regular orderly?" Vasiliev asked.

"There ain't none," the woman answered in a rasping voice. "You gits what shows up." She seized the pan and emptied it.

"Damn it! People keep disappearing in this case." Vasiliev got up and went to the office of the administrator. It was locked. He went down the corridor to the night attendant. What did she know about the schedule of orderlies? He wanted to know. She could not tell him anything. As Vasiliev turned way a nurse appeared, and the attendant mumbled a question that he did not hear. The attendant turned to him.

"Listen, Inspector. The woman you want quit after a day's work. She complained to Nina here that the work was filthy and she couldn't stand it. She stuffed herself full at the buffet though. That's clear."

"No address, I suppose."

"No, we just hire them off the street. It's hard to get people. The work is wretched. They'd rather get a job sweeping."

Vasiliev returned to Serov. "How do you feel about getting out of here tomorrow?"

"The leg's mendin' well. Of course, I'll have the cast on the arm. So I can't be wanderin' around like a water carrier. Perhaps bein' a beggar is the only chance."

"Good! Here's what we'll do. You'll spend the day begging at the bazaar and questioning the tradesmen. I'll go to police head-quarters. They should have records of criminals sentenced to exile who have come back to Kiev. We might be able to trace our man that way. I hope Rebecca and David have found Reb Moishe. I'll write Irina and explain how we plan to get her out of there."

The following morning Vasiliev was having his breakfast in the hotel dining room when Maria Alexandrovna's Igor came in, bowed, and handed him a note. She asked to meet him at 11:00 o'clock at the church of the Yakol monastery overlooking Askold's Tomb. A strange choice, thought Vasiliev. No more exposure to the public gaze. He scribbled a reply and gave it to Igor, who left with-out having spoken a word.

He spent the rest of the morning composing a letter to Irina for Szymanskii to send by his secret courier. He kept searching for the right words. He tried to imagine what her daily life would be like. He kept tearing up what he had written. He thought it was the hard-est message he had ever composed. A vague uneasiness was nag-ging him. He couldn't pin it down. He read over the final version of the letter. It sounded stilted. Well, it wasn't supposed to be a love letter. He stuffed the torn pieces of the early drafts in his pocket. As he was leaving the hotel, he glanced at the clock. It was 10:45. The desk clerk called him over and handed him another note, written on a scrap of cheap foolscap. He recognized Serov's hand. "Come quick to the bazaar. Mordvinov's Shop selling kitchen pots, third row. Urgent information on Irina. No uniform." Vasiliev asked the clerk for a sheet of stationary and scribbled an apology to Maria Alexandrovna. He gave instructions to the hotel messenger boy and called a cab. He went first to the safe house where he turned himself back into a merchant. Another cab took him to the Gostiny dvor in Podol and dropped him by the Fountain of Samson, popu-larly called the Lion. Pilgrims were washing their feet in a stream of water gushing from the sculptured mouth of a lion's head. In a large circle around the fountain scores of petty traders catering to the pilgrim trade were selling small icons, crosses, ribbons. A blind *bandurist* was singing a mournful tune, strumming his lyre. The old Ukraine of Gogol was still alive, it seemed.

Vasiliev pushed his way through the crowds, being jostled, asking directions. Mordvinov's turned out to be situated among the wooden shops on the third row off the square. When he got there Serov was sitting on the ground outside, holding a rusty can that held a few coppers. Vasiliev dropped a coin into the can and strolled on. Serov struggled to his feet in a good imitation of a man in great pain. He hobbled behind Vasiliev, who stopped to examine several pairs of gloves displayed on a coarse cloth. An old man jabbered at him. Serov brushed past and wandered down the trade rows, coming to a stop at a stand where a young woman was selling cheap trinkets. He winked at her. She tossed her head. Serov nodded in the direction of Vasiliev, who sauntered over and began to look over the objects on display. His eye was immediately caught by several small carvings made from bone or ivory.

"Well, these are pretty pieces." They began to bargain. Vasiliev held them up to the light one by one. Behind the stand there was a tarpaulin held up by poles to provide a rough lean-to. Bundles were stacked against the poles to give them support. An old woman, or a woman who looked old, was crouched down on one of the bundles watching the trading. Serov had slipped away.

"They tell me you are something of a collector, Your Honor," said the young woman. Vasiliev giggled, having learned from Foma's training and his own experience that giggling was an excellent way to dissemble.

"Yes, but I always have to know where my pieces come from, a bit about their history, you know. There are so many fakes around."

"Oh, these are genuine pieces from the North."

"How can I be sure?"

"Well, Anna Andreevna, back there can tell you about them."

The woman came out of the shadows. Vasiliev saw that she was not, in fact, old. Her features were worn and lined, but her body was straight and muscular under the thin rags she wore.

"So, Anna Andreevna, tell me about your pieces."

"I've brought them from the North." Vasiliev was surprised to hear the accents of a cultivated voice.

"Yes, well—the North is a big place. Where exactly?"

She stared at him for a long time. "Does it make a great difference to you?"

"Of course." Vasiliev spoke about different styles of carving, trying to remember all he had read in the library. "So, I'd like to know where you picked these up."

"That beggar friend of yours asked the same question."

Vasiliev laughed. "Yes, he is my advance agent. He can smell out a bargain like a hound dog."

"This one is from the Tiumen Region." She picked up a carving with a bear motif.

Vasiliev held the piece for a long time as if he expected it to yield its secret. "Well, of course, but…" He bargained with her just long enough to avoid appearing too eager. In the end he seemed to hesitate, and then to give in reluctantly. "All right I'll buy it. Here's your price." The woman's callused palm was hard as wood when he touched it "Well, how about celebrating? I'm treating to tea. There's a seller with a samovar right over there."

They stood for a while silently sipping their tea and watching the trading. "So, you must have known Irina Davidova," he said, trying to keep his voice under control. She did not look at him, but kept her gaze fixed on the passers-by. "I see that your beggar friend is more than a buyer's agent."

"Listen to me, Anna Andreevna. I have no reason to ruin your life. That's already been done, I think." Vasiliev had dropped his merchant's patter and shifted to his normal voice. "You've been an exile or a prisoner, hard labor if I can judge by your hands. The chances that a lifer would have been pardoned are slim. That just doesn't happen. Let's say a miracle occurred and they released you. You would never be allowed to live in a major city like Kiev. So you left your place of exile, illegally. And you are trying to eke out a living, selling objects you picked up in Siberia. An Ostiak carving? That could mean the Tiumen region. If your place of confinement was there, then you might have been a while in the Forwarding Prison. That's what the beggar thought. He knows about such things. Chances are you ran into Irina Davydova. That would be my guess. I can tell you come from an educated, noble family like she does. Am I right?"

Vasiliev studied her face. It showed no signs of emotion except for a slight tightening of the jaw muscles.

"I have a special interest in her, an honorable one. You'll have to trust me on this. You haven't much choice. If you tell me what you know, I'll forget about our meeting."

"Would you like to buy another trinket?" she asked.

Vasiliev flinched. He thought of how humiliating it would be for Irina if she were reduced some day to haggling at a bazaar. But perhaps he was being unfair to this woman. For an exile pride was an expensive commodity. This woman must have survived by her wits for a long time.

"Of course. What do you recommend?"

They returned to the stand.

"Come back here, and I'll break open this bundle." She produced a fine walrus tusk carving. Vasiliev did not bargain this time.

"Your Irina Davydova is a strong one. I recognized the type. I was like that myself once, ten years ago. She adapts quickly. No complaining, tries to help others. Retains her dignity in the face of coarse treatment. You can imagine what the wardens and guards are like. They respect her. How long that will last I don't know. The new warden of the Forwarding Prison is a decent man compared to his predecessor. Of course, the place is hideous. But the women have it better than the men, especially the politicals. She and I only exchanged a few words before I..." she hesitated for the first time "...before I made my way west. That is all I can tell you."

"When did you last see her?"

"Two or three months ago."

"Thank you, Anna Andreevna. I'll keep your secret." Vasiliev felt he should say something more. But he could no longer be sure of how to react. Here he was, a policeman unwilling to arrest an escaped convict. He assumed she was a political, but he couldn't be sure. Even so, under Russian law she was a criminal. So what about his lecture to Reb Ben-Zion about the sanctity of the law? Was it just Irina standing in his way? He thought of what he had once said to Serov when they made contact with her nihilist friends: "There but for the luck of the draw go I." Was this really true?

She had been wrapping the carvings in newspaper, tying the bundle with string. Vasiliev noticed how she had trouble with the knots. Her fingers were stiff. Arthritis from exposure to the cold, he thought. How long does it take for that to happen?

"Farewell and good luck!" was all he said. He tucked the package under his arm and left the bazaar.

Chapter
Twenty-Two

Vera had slept badly again. She dreamed of Stepan lying in the hospital, his legs amputated. She woke up in a cold sweat. She vowed she would never return to St. Vladimir Hospital. She counted the few rubles she had earned and tried to recall the flavors of the hot meal she had eaten in the buffet. She breakfasted on the bread smeared with mustard that she had taken from the buffet and stuffed in her pocket. But this made her thirsty. She went outside and found a water carrier. She did not know what to do next.

A disturbing thought nagged at her. It had something to do with their early days in the cabin. A vague memory of the dream came back to her. This time Stepan was down on his knees in the icon corner. Yes, that was it. She had really seen him there once before. She remembered clearly having come back unexpectedly from shopping. The stores had run out of fresh milk. When she came through the door, he had jumped to his feet. There was a strange look on his face. At the time, she thought he might have been praying. Perhaps he had become a believer during his life in exile. It happened all the time. But that wasn't it. Then she had forgotten about the incident. Now she wondered: had he been hiding something, perhaps something worth selling, something he had put away in case they were really hard up? It would be like him. He would surprise her by pulling out a wad of rubles when she was in despair. With a sheepish smile he would confess that he had saved it for bad times.

She knelt down on the floor and murmured a prayer, then ran her hands over the boards until she found a loose one. She pried it up. There was a small space underneath. She reached in, and immediately pulled back as if she had been burned. She rocked on her heels, pressing her hand to her mouth. She might have been mistaken. Her hand was trembling as she groped again in the small space. The object was cold, not hot, metallic—a revolver. Her fingers trailed over the surface; then she rubbed her hand against her dress as if to cleanse it. She put the board back in place. How could she sell that? They would ask questions, perhaps even call the police, arrest her. She shuddered to think what purpose it might have served. She stretched out on the floor and wept for a long time.

She felt cold and stood up, wringing her hands. There was only one chance left, she thought. She hesitated to take it. Stepan had told her all about the Esteemed Person. But they had decided not to tell the Esteemed Person about her. She had advised Stepan to go by himself. If he was alone the Esteemed Person would trust him. She knew where he lived. Stepan had shown her the house one day when they were out strolling. She remembered how impressed she had been by its size and the gardens surrounding it. "Right across from the park too!" she had said to Stepan. Would the Esteemed Person help her if she appealed to him? The worst he could do was refuse or turn her out of his house. But she could not go back to the hospital, and there was no time to find another job. She already owed the landlady for more than a month. The old witch was perfectly capable of throwing her into the street if she did not pay.

The storm had cleared the air. She thought that was a good sign. She examined her clothes. The dark brown dress would be best, but she noticed that the hem needed stitching. She sat by the window, her head bent over her work. She knew she was a good seamstress. Perhaps the Esteemed Person himself would hire her. She took out her old brown shoes. They were caked with mud from the road. It hardly made any sense to clean them, but out of habit she scraped them with a dull knife. The soles were almost worn through. She wondered whether they would last out the day. She shuddered to think of the mud seeping through them.

She walked all the way to save the fare. At the last minute her courage almost failed her. The house looked even more imposing than she remembered. She stood facing an iron gate. Suppose it was locked. What would she do? There was no bell. She pushed the gate and it swung open. She mounted the stone steps. Her heart seemed to be beating faster with every step. She rang the bell and heard chimes. A tall man with a thin face opened the door.

"My name is Vera. I was Stepan's wife. I would like to speak to the Esteemed Person." She suddenly realized she did not know his name. Would the nickname she and Stepan had used seem foolish? The man frowned and opened the door wider. "Please wait," he said. It seemed to Vera that his voice belonged to someone else. It was too deep and resonant to come from such a thin frame.

She stepped inside. It was cool in the foyer, and she inhaled a pleasant odor.

A chair of wrought metal stood by the door, but she did not dare sit down.

In a few minutes the thin man came back. He motioned to a pair of slippers by the door. She flushed as she bent over to remove her muddy shoes. "Please follow me." He led her down a long corridor. She felt her feet sink into the deep pile of the carpet. It reminded her of the color of burgundy wine. Elegant brass fittings held gas lamps strung along the walls of the corridor. She tried to imagine how this all must have looked to Stepan. The thin man knocked on a polished wooden door and opened it for her. She entered a large study with many books. As the door closed behind her she felt a slight draft; it stirred the crystals of an immense chandelier overhead, emitting a sound like the tinkling of distant church bells. The Esteemed Person was sitting behind a desk. Vera admired its elaborately carved legs, shaped like the paws of a wild beast. The paintings that hung all along the right hand wall reminded her of those in the Tretiakov Gallery in Moscow, where her father had once taken her as a young girl. It had been a private gallery like this one. There had been some business dealings with Tretiakov. Otherwise, they would not have been admitted. She had felt important then, but now she felt somehow diminished.

"My dear Vera—may I call you that? I was terribly upset to hear about your husband's death." He did not invite her to sit down, so she stood in front of the desk. She felt like a pupil in the fourth form facing the terrible Mr. Ivaniushkin.

"Stepan was a man of rare qualities. He had firm ideas and was reliable. But he never told me he was married. How curious."

"We were afraid you might not entrust him with important work if you knew he was married."

"Really? And what important work would that be?"

"He did not tell me, except to say that you were a generous patron and we would soon be able to live like decent people."

"I can tell from your voice and bearing, Vera, that you come from a family that was used to living decently. How can I help you to live decently again?"

Vera felt a glow of excitement and gratitude toward the Esteemed Person. He understood her perfectly. She hadn't even had to ask, let alone beg him.

"You see, the police confiscated the money you paid him. So I have nothing. You are kind to offer help. I only ask to find honest work. To earn my living. I am a good seamstress. But I have no references because I come from Moscow. I have never worked here."

"A seamstress you say. Capital! I have just the place for you. A milliner's shop. The proprietress is a distant relative. She has just lost one of her girls. The wages are fair. Why you could begin today! Are you ready to go there now?"

It was arranged that the tall thin man, bearing a letter from the Esteemed Person, would accompany her. Vera thanked the Esteemed Person, but not too profusely; that would not do, she reminded herself. After all she came from a decent family and did not have to toady to anyone.

She was exhilarated walking to the cabstand. She hardly noticed that the tall thin man did not speak to her. There was only one cab waiting. Just as they reached it a young man rushed across the street and jumped into the carriage, shouting an address. The tall thin man did not appear to be upset. Vera thought this was curious. Stepan would have been very angry. They waited five minutes until another cab drew up. Vera thought the horse was a poor specimen, and the body of the coach looked battered. She gave the tall thin man a quizzical look. But he seemed to take no notice, and handed her into the cab. Then, instead of joining her, he leaped onto the box with the cabby, and they drove off.

They headed toward the Dniepr, and Vera soon lost her bearings. She could not see where they were going. The curtains had been drawn tightly and she was unable to pull them open. She began to feel uneasy. She heard the two men talking. But she couldn't make out what they were saying. The horse slowed to a walk, almost coming to a halt. Vera felt a jolt, as if the cab had become lighter. Then it started to go downhill, rapidly gaining speed. Vera was suddenly frightened. She tried with all her strength to pull the curtains open. But they seemed to be sewn together and were too thick to rip apart. She pressed down hard on the door handle, but it would not budge. In terror she realized that she was in a runaway cab. The cabby and the tall thin man had jumped off at the crest of the hill. She heard the bells of St. Andrei the First Called and she knew she was hurtling down the Andrei Descent, the tallest hill in Kiev. Had they left her to die? She began to scream, but the thick curtains muffled her cries. She could feel the pounding of the horse's hooves through the thin boards. Strollers stopped to watch in horror, pointing to the cab. As it careened around the first sharp turn, the wheels struck the curb violently, cracking an axle, and hurling Vera to the floor. The other wheel broke off and bounced down the hill. The horse lost its footing, stumbled, and crashed to the ground. The cab overturned, collided with a stone wall, and broke up. People were running from all directions. They gathered silently around the shattered body of the cab and the dead body of the horse tangled in the traces.

The Andrei Descent and the church of St. Andrei

Chapter
Twenty-Three

Vasiliev went straight to the safe house. He sat for a long time on the wooden chair, examining the two pieces he had bought from the escaped exile. What to believe, he asked himself. This woman claimed to have seen Irina, active and strong. At the same time she was supposed to have dictated the despairing message to the Pole. Of course, there was no way of telling the exact sequence of events. It may have been that shortly after the woman made her escape something terrible had happened to Irina. He could not think of any other answer. He tried to imagine what might have changed. After a while he stood up abruptly, and put on his uniform. The possibilities were too many and too terrible to contemplate. He left the bone carvings on the table and made his way back to the Hotel d'Europe. It was early in the afternoon.

Igor was waiting for him in the lobby. He handed Vasiliev another note from Maria Alexandrovna. "Please go with Igor. He will know where to find me."

Igor pulled out a pocket watch from his waistcoat. "Maria Alexandrovna will still be at the Nikol Monastery. If we hurry we'll catch her. Otherwise, she'll go to the Botanical Gardens where the director is giving a party. It will be less convenient to talk there."

There was little traffic, and the cab lost no time in crossing the city. When they entered the monastery grounds, Igor pointed to the figure of Maria Alexandrovna seated on a bench under a chestnut tree in full bloom, talking to a monk. Then Igor disappeared. The man seems like a phantom, thought Vasiliev. Maria Alexandrovna greeted Vasiliev with feigned surprise. The monk rose, murmured some words of thanks, blessed her with the sign of the cross, and left them.

Vasiliev began to apologize and explain, but Maria Alexandrovna cut him short.

"Never mind! The monks gave me a nice lunch, and now I only have a few minutes to tell you what you should know. When I came home early and unexpectedly from my charitable circle, I found the Governor-General had visitors. I could say he was in intimate conversation with Captain Rudov and Baron Szymanskii. They make an odd company, Vasili. This is the second time within a few days the Baron has been a visitor. But my husband has no love for the Poles, to say nothing of former rebels! The Baron may have been pardoned, but that does not remove the stigma. I cannot imagine what business he has with the Governor-General. As for Captain Rudov, he's a Gendarme officer. But he is not under the Governor-General's command. I noticed that both the Baron and the Captain took an interest in you at the party. Am I right in thinking that *Pan* Szymanski and you had a long discussion in the garden? I asked Igor, you see. He remembered seeing you go out together through the French windows. Then Captain Rudov asked me whether I might persuade you to visit his district. He had already invited you, he said. At the time I thought nothing of it. But now, I don't know what to think. I'm not spying on you, Vasili; please don't think that. But since you arrived people have been behaving strangely." She glanced at her watch. "My goodness, it is late! Just one more thing. I was worried too about your leaving with that merchant, Lopatkin. He was another unusual guest in our house. Why did you leave with him?"

"I'd met him on the train coming in. He offered to drive me home. I probably looked pretty upset. Your party was a lovely affair, Maria Alexandrovna. But I heard some bad news there, that's all." He raised his hand. "I'll explain later. Lopatkin offered me a way to leave as politely as I could. Please don't misunderstand. It had nothing to do with you."

"I see. Then my feminine intuition was wrong. My turn to apologize. I was worried enough to have Igor follow you. Does that shock you? It sounds foolish now when I think about it. He returned and told me that Lopatkin had brought you back to your hotel. But Igor may be even more suspicious by nature than I am." She laughed as she rose and took his arm. They walked toward the gate. "What I mean is that he kept following Lopatkin. Now this is the strange part. Lopatkin's coach returned to our house and stood in the drive. After a few minutes a man emerged from the shadows. He climbed in with Lopatkin and they drove off together. Igor was sure that the man was Baron Szymanski. Does this close some kind of circle? My dear Vasili, do be careful. Au revoir!" Her coach was waiting outside the monastery walls. Igor was nowhere to be seen. Probably following somebody, thought Vasiliev.

Vasiliev was of half a mind to turn back to the garden of the monastery, sit under the shade of the ancient trees, and try to sort out the information Maria Alexandrovna had given him. Did anything she said have meaning for him? He touched the pocket of his jacket and felt the folded sheet of paper. His message to Irina. Could he afford to wait another day before handing it to Szymanski? Now he held two pictures of Irina in his mind. Was she cowering in the corner of a filthy, stinking cell, having lost all hope? Or was she moving from bunk to bunk of the women's barracks, speaking a word of encouragement, sharing her rations with the weak, ministering to the sick? God, he had never felt so indecisive in his life. He asked himself what he would do if he were not in love with Irina, if she were just an innocent victim of the system, unfairly sentenced to exile. It came as something of a shock when he realized he would act more cautiously. If he only knew the warden at Tiumen. Could Ivan help him?

What made him hesitate? He imagined Ivan's voice, tinged with irony: So Vasya, consorting with revolutionaries now! Ivan would be only half joking. He had never told Ivan about Irina, how she had risked everything to help him try to save the Tsar's life. And for that she had earned exile. But Vasiliev knew that his relations with her could compromise Ivan as well. He would have to be careful in wording his appeal. But there was no other way. He hailed a cab. "The Central Telegraph Office," he said.

Rebecca and David returned from Shuliavshina the same day. They huddled together on a wooden bench in a third class compartment. The car was almost empty; no one was coming into Kiev. But they still spoke in whispers. Rebecca chewed on an apple as she related her meeting with Reb Moishe. "Something happened to me back there," she said. "I think I'll always remember Shuliavshina as more than a wretched Ukrainian town."

"Tell me," said David. "And give me a bite of that apple. I still have the taste of that tart in my mouth. It was too sweet."

"Here. But we're going to have a serious talk now, aren't we?"

"Agreed. Go ahead."

"Maybe seeing Reb Moishe was just the final straw. Being in the synagogue got me going. You know how we've always wondered whether we could be Jews and not believe in Judaism? Well, I think I've crossed the line. It's terrible to say it! I think of papa all the time. But I can't help it! I must have lost my faith long ago, but standing there with all those women, shut off from the men, listening to the sermon on the giving of the Torah. 'Everyone that thirsteth, come ye to the waters.' I could hardly stand it. I wanted to shout out loud, 'The waters do not quench our thirst for justice. They just go on beating us!' Look how they threaten us, like poor Reb Moishe."

"I've told you that, Rebecca. That's why Aaron and I appointed ourselves your father's bodyguards. Rotten job we did, I admit. But we have to defend ourselves. They would have killed us on the bluffs..."

"And almost did, except for the Sergeant. That was just luck. What I've been thinking, David, is that we Jews are not strong enough to defend ourselves without help. And we can't expect it from the police or the army or even enlightened Christians like Serov and Vasiliev. They won't always be at our beck and call."

"But we can form a militia, like they did in Berdichev. They stopped the Russian workers from getting off the train, didn't they?"

"Yes, but they had to bribe the police chief to let them organize. That's the problem, David. There is no purely Jewish solution. We have to join forces with others, with the People's Will."

"God almighty, Rebecca, you're going too fast for me! Something did happen to you in Shuliavshina. You lost your reason. The People's Will! They're terrorists and what's even worse, anti-Semites."

"You're wrong, David. Since papa was killed, I've been talking to students at the University, some of the members. They're eager to have us join."

"What do you mean? Listen, I've talked to some of them too. I even saw a draft of a proclamation by some idiot named Romanovsky…"

"You mean Romanenko, I've seen it too."

"Well, isn't that enough for you? It is the worst kind of Jew-baiting. Just imagine the effect if it gets published. He's a member of the Exec-Com of the People's Will."

"Listen, David, this man is not representative."

"How do you know?"

"The students are appalled by this kind of talk. They're already drafting their response. They will send it to Tikhomirov and others. They'll set the record straight. The point is that a real struggle is going on in the People's Will. If we join them, we can make a difference. But if we get on our Jewish high horse…"

"This is madness, Rebecca! In Kiev they're already blaming the pogroms on Jewish revolutionaries. You know it! The pogroms are supposed to be a training ground for mass revolt. It's crazy, but if people believe in blood libel they'll believe anything about us."

"If they believe it already and we gain nothing from it, then why not make it true and gain something by it."

"Oh, that sounds very profound, Rebecca, but I don't see what we gain."

"Don't patronize me, David! We are having a comradely discussion, a discussion between equals. You can't banish me back to the balcony."

David closed his eyes and leaned his head back on the wall of the compartment. "All right, I'm sorry. Just tell me what we gain."

"We gain an organization that will protect us—not as Jews, but as revolutionaries who happen to be Jewish. The aim is to overthrow the entire system. It's the only way to emancipate us as Jews—to abolish the Pale and all the restrictions on us, and not only us. That's the point. The revolution will abolish all religious discrimination against Catholics and Old Believers, and even the sectarians. So, let the *skoptsy* castrate themselves! Who cares? It's all of us or none of us."

David looked out the window at the fields stretching without a break to the straight line of the horizon. Long rows of peasants were moving slowly across the land. Scythes flashed in the sunlight. They were bringing in the winter wheat, the golden durum of the South. In the meadows women and children were tending herds of cattle. "And what about them?" He jabbed his thumb against the pane. "The peasants hate us. And the People's Will is a peasant party. When push comes to shove and the choice is between organizing the peasants or organizing the Jews, you know who is going to get pushed and shoved."

"Oh that sounds very profound, David."

David jerked his head around and saw Rebecca silently laughing.

He knew he could not resist her. But he felt he had to try.

"David, we're getting close to Kiev. But I have to say this. It may sound too theoretical. The peasants hate us because they only see Jews as tavern owners and moneylenders. Who likes tavern owners and moneylenders anyway? If they see us fighting for their interests, it will be a different story."

"All right. To be continued. But—one last question."

"I'll bet it *isn't* your last question."

"You are relentless, Rebecca. The last question on this trip, then. What about terror?"

"I've thought about it. You'll have to wait for my learned disquisition on terror. We are in Kiev."

Chapter
Twenty-Four

Vasiliev had drafted the telegram to Ivan several times before he was satisfied with the result. Why was he having such trouble writing messages these days? The point was to get the wording as simple as possible, but still be clear. He had to admit this wasn't the main reason why it was so difficult to strike the right tone. "Urgently need details on living conditions of exiled political Davydova, Irina Nikolaevna, Tiumen Forwarding Prison. Outcome will determine success of this mission." It wasn't often, he reflected, that he felt obliged to deceive Ivan. But the more he thought about it, the more he realized there was no deception here.

He sent off the telegram and walked on to the Central Police Station. On the way, he dropped in on Oglobin's bookstore. It was a huge place. He spent a few minutes looking in the poetry section. He quickly found what he wanted. Not an indulgence, he told himself, but a spiritual necessity. The bookseller kept staring at him. How many police officers came into his store? How many read poetry? How many read poems by Nekrasov? He turned to the poem about the wives of the Decembrists.

The police station looked like a dilapidated fortress. Bricks were missing from the façade; the stone steps were cracked and worn down. Inside, the walls were spotted with watermarks. The paint was peeling on the staircases. On the landing two plainclothesmen were having a smoke. They ignored him. Vasiliev passed suspects in manacles crowded together on wooden benches. They looked as though they had just been dragged out of the Dniepr. Were they *pogromshchiki*? An armed guard stood over them, his eyes half-closed

156

in boredom. Vasiliev pushed open a door marked *Detectives*. Desks were scattered around the office in no particular order, as if they had been just dumped there by the movers. Only one was occupied. The man did not look up when Vasiliev entered. He walked passed him, knocked on the door marked *Chief*, and entered. A secretary waved him into the inner office. It did not seem any more cheerful to Vasiliev than the rest of the place. Stretched too tight, they had said. More like broken beyond repair.

Above the chief's desk hung the obligatory portrait of the new Tsar, Alexander III. Vasiliev had only seen him once, the day his father, Alexander II, had been assassinated. The portrait did not make him appear any more regal. Vasiliev couldn't help thinking that if you took off the medals and the uniform, the Tsar would look just like a butcher on Hunter's Row.

The chief was Novitsky, a man with the reputation of tough honesty. He greeted Vasiliev in a friendly fashion, rang a bell, and called for tea. The secretary wheeled in a samovar and poured. She handed Vasiliev a small dish of plum jam. Novitsky grinned. "We're trying to civilize you, starting with Ukrainian fruit preserve. You have nothing like it in Moscow, believe me!" He got up from his desk and came around to sit with Vasiliev on the sofa. More surprises, Vasiliev thought. His own chief wouldn't have budged for a visitor.

"So, how long have you been at it here—two weeks? Time enough for you to report in, isn't that so? Let me be frank, Vasili Vasilievich. None of us here in Kiev like being investigated from the North. Moscow and Petersburg have had their problems with the People's Will. But we face a very different situation. Terrorists are one thing. But here, public order has broken down. We did not expect this. Twenty years ago I witnessed the Polish rising. That was bad. This may be worse. Back then we knew who the enemy was. But now? Then, we Russians were united. Now, we are blaming one another. The police have taken the heaviest fire. But I swear to you, we were out on the street in full force. Three days before the big riots I sent my men into the Podol and Lybid districts to warn the Jews to stay indoors. Shut their shops. They didn't like it. What else could I do? When the riots broke out we were overwhelmed. I appealed to the Governor-General for help from the army. No response for several days. Absolutely nothing. Then orders came down. 'Repress the disorders!' Where from? I don't know. The troops began firing on the rioters. You understand, Inspector? On our people! Well, maybe it was necessary by then. But it could have been prevented. I mean the shooting. A show of force the first day. Call out every available man. You know what I mean. It wasn't done. As soon as the word spread about the shootings, the riots stopped. The Governor-General told me that he regretted not ordering the troops into the street earlier. Excellent! But the papers all blame the police. I'm telling you this so that you can tell them in Piter. God knows what Drenteln will report! I count on you to clear the record."

Vasiliev had taken out a small notebook and was making notes. He took a sip of tea and tasted the jam. It was good, as good as the apple jelly that Serov's mother made. He did not tell Novitsky that. He made the appropriate noises of appreciation.

"These things shouldn't be allowed to get out of control. Thanks for your frankness, Vasili Dementevich. I'll pass on your comments to Petersburg. They're worried sick, you know. Europe has given us a beating on this. If we can show we're doing our best…well, you know how it is."

Novitsky leaned back and smiled. "They said you were a reasonable man, Vasili Vasilievich. Now, how about your case? Any progress? By the way, it wasn't my idea to saddle you with the Meier murder. Perhaps it looked different at Drenteln's. But I too have to take orders."

Vasiliev nodded. He sipped more tea. "Here's what I have now. Not much. But something." Vasiliev told him about the amulet and the missing documents. "So I'm following up both lines. They've got to be connected. The amulet leads one way. I'm guessing the killer was an ex-convict, a hired gunman. Finished out his term and was looking for a job. The documents take me in a different direction." Vasiliev wondered whether he should expose Novitsky to his theory of scientific guessing. He decided against it.

"The bloody cross wasn't a symbol of anything. It was done to mislead, to muddle things. The real motive was to get hold of the papers. But the killer didn't have time to steal them. Maybe that wasn't part of his assignment. In any case they were picked up later."

Novitsky raised his hand. "What do you mean, didn't have time?"

"It seems he was interrupted by members of the household." Vasiliev didn't feel ready to involve David and Aaron. He hurried on. "I'd like to take a look at your files for the past ten years. If the killer had been arrested and sentenced here in Kiev, then we should be able to trace him. You said that there hasn't been much crime in Kiev since the Polish revolt. The list of suspects shouldn't be long."

"Of course, of course. Only I must warn you, my predecessor was not a well-organized man. I'm not responsible for what passes here for a filing system. And suppose this hypothetical killer was not a *kievlianin*? You may not know it, but the criminal element in Kiev is largely made up of Russians from the North. There were plenty of them involved in the pogroms, I can tell you! So what then?"

"Then I may have to advertise for him in the local paper."

The Chief looked at him in astonishment for an instant before breaking into a series of guffaws. Just like six rapid shots, thought Vasiliev. "They say you are one of a kind, Vasili Vasilievich, one of a kind." The Chief picked up a small silver bell from his desk and rang it energetically. The door flew open and a young constable saluted and clicked his heels.

"This is Kablukov. We call him 'our Prussian' for reasons that should be obvious. You see, we too have a sense of humor." The Chief winked at Vasiliev. "He'll show you the files, such as they are. When you're finished, come back, and we'll have a drop of something more bracing than tea."

Vasiliev followed Kablukov into the basement of headquarters. The windows were heavily barred, and so covered with dirt that candles were needed to light the way. Vasiliev told the constable what he was looking for. Kablukov laid a forefinger against the side of his nose, as if to show how seriously he took the request. Then he lifted a candle above his head and ran the same forefinger along the edges of unmarked files, packed between cardboard covers and tightly bound. He reached the end of the row. He continued along the second and third rows in the same manner. Abruptly, the finger stopped. Vasiliev could see no difference between the file Kablukov pulled out and any of the others. The constable set the file down on the rough surface of a wooden trestle table and placed his candle next to it. He bowed, and retreated into a dark corner. A disembodied voice came out of the gloom. "When Your Honor has finished, you have only to knock on the table." Vasiliev could no longer see him. He heard a scraping noise, as if a stool or chair had been dragged across the stone floor. He sat down on the wooden bench by the table and began to untie the thin cloth strips that held the cardboard covers together. A strong odor of mold assailed his nostrils. The left margin of each page had been sewn into a rough sort of binding. The pages were numbered consecutively.

The file consisted of judgments of the Kiev Circuit Court. The first document was dated January 13, 1871, the day after the New Year in the Old Style Calendar. Vasiliev turned the pages carefully to avoid raising dust He read through January, then February, and into March. He noticed immediately that after the judgment of March 8 a gap appeared in the pagination. He examined the binding. There was no trace of any pages having been removed. It had been done very skillfully. But there had been no way to alter the pagination. He continued to read into March and April. His eyes were beginning to tire, but he kept reading to the end of the year. No additional pages had been excised.

Vasiliev closed the file and tied the strings, using the same knot that had been used to bind it together. He then rapped on the trestle. Kablukov emerged from the darkness. He took the file from Vasiliev and examined it. Then he set it back on the table, loosened the strings and retied them with a different knot.

"You are a very precise fellow. I understand why they call you 'our Prussian'. Let me test your memory. Who has asked for this file within the past month?"

"No one, Your Honor."

"You are quite sure."

"Yes."

"Has anybody asked to see other files from about the same period?"

"Yes, Your Honor."

"From the same shelf?"

"The one below it."

"From where you are seated back there in the darkness, is it possible for you to see me as I sit here."

"No, Your Honor. There is a partition that screens me from the reader, giving him a sense of privacy."

"So, if I consulted another file without asking you, you would not know about it."

Even by the light of the candle, Vasiliev could see a puzzled look come over Kablukov's face.

"Why no, I wouldn't. But who would wish to do that?"

Vasiliev smiled at him. "Just a theoretical question. Thank you. You've been more help than you know."

Kablukov replaced the file and led Vasiliev back to the chief's office.

"So, Inspector, any luck?"

"Your Prussian is a very observant young man. I think he'll make a good detective some day."

"Really? I'm glad to hear you say that. Some of the men think he's too pedantic."

"I don't want to sound like an oracle, but I think there's a difference between pedantic and thorough."

"Bravo, Inspector! I shall quote you as an authority from Moscow. That should silence the quibblers." The Chief took a bottle out of his desk drawer.

"As for luck, I'd say—without wishing to sound like an oracle again—that we all rely on a bit of luck. Recently, mine has to do with knots."

The Chief didn't miss a beat as he poured a dark liquid into two brandy glasses. "Well, here's to Lady Luck, Inspector! May she always be with us and not against us."

They drank in silence.

"Tell me, Vasili Dementevich, d'you keep a record of visitors to your files?"

"That's hardly necessary, Inspector. If somebody shows up once in a month we call it heavy traffic."

"So you remember your visitors well."

"Try me."

"Over the past month, say—or, since they're so rare, let's make it two months."

"Easy. Since the riots broke out, not a single soul. Before that, the last visitor was our colleague, Captain Rudov. If I remember right it was early in April. He was interested in an old file. I don't think he found what he wanted." Novitsky put his glass down. "A wee bit more?"

"No, thank you. I promised to visit a patient in the hospital."

"Nothing serious, I hope."

Vasiliev found Kablukov in the corridor reading the announcements posted on the wall.

"Than you again, constable. Captain Rudov told me you would be a great help. He and I must have been looking at the same files."

"No, Inspector. He consulted the files for 1861, on the shelf just below yours."

"Of course, now I remember. Something to do with the peasant disturbances after the announcement of the emancipation."

"That is what he said, Your Honor."

Vasiliev left the building, thinking about the small mistakes people make when they are doing something wrong. Rudov should take a lesson in tying knots from our Prussian, he mused.

Chapter
Twenty-Five

David arrived at the University early the day after the visit to Shu-liavshina. He went immediately to the student buffet, where he sat at his usual table. Within a few minutes three other students joined him, bringing glasses of tea and a plate of fresh rolls.

"Where is Natan?"

"David, listen to the bad news. Natan is leaving Kiev. He's packing right now."

"Where is he going, home to Berdichev? It's worse there!"

"No, David. Palestine."

"What? Impossible! He wouldn't desert us."

"Right! Just what we said to him." The others nodded. "But he doesn't think of it that way. He told us he couldn't find justice in a Christian country, especially Russia. There's a real exodus, David. The Jews are leaving Kiev in great numbers."

"I know that, but not to go to Palestine. What's there but Arab shepherds and old bad memories? Listen, the hell with Natan. I'm staying. What we need now is to build a self-defense force. I've been talking to some Jewish veterans of the Turkish war. They can help train us."

"David, be realistic. The Kievan Jews are not up to it. We should go to Odessa or maybe north. They say that the People's Will is re-viving in Vilna."

"Good for them. And how do you expect to feed yourself in Vil-na? Here the University is the perfect base. So, the Jews are leaving Kiev. They'll come back when things settle down. In the meantime, we can build the scaffolding for a strong movement, and when they come back we'll pull them in."

"You're still thinking of going it alone?"

"Not alone. I thought I could count on you three to start with."

A student monitor walked past them. They fell silent. David reached for a roll, broke it in half, and chewed it furiously.

"Look David, the People's Will already has the scaffolding. If you want to call it that. Aren't you forgetting that we Jews were in on it from the beginning? Do we have to read the honor roll for you? Zundelevich, Tsukerman, Iokhelson, Aronchik—on and on. We helped them plan the attacks on the Tsar. What would they have done without us? And don't forget the women—Lichkus and Hesia Helfman. Did you know that Helfman is pregnant? Rotting away in Peter and Paul Fortress! These are our martyrs."

David felt the ground slipping away from under him. First Rebecca, and now his best friends, sounding the same note. He wished Aaron were there with him. He took another bite of roll. He felt hemmed in. He glanced at his watch.

"Law lecture in five minutes." His friends looked at one another and shrugged. They got to their feet as a body. One of them punched his shoulder.

"Come on David, don't let us lose you."

"It's not a damn child's game!" he blurted out.

Rebecca was waiting for him by the door to the auditorium.

"We have to speak," he said. She put her hand on his arm. "What's the matter? All right, let's skip the lecture. It's not going to tell us anything we don't know already."

They went around to the rear of the University and pushed open the gate to the Botanical Garden. It was still too early for the flower displays and the big crowds; anyway, they would flock to the North Garden. They walked down the steep path under a canopy of chestnut trees and found an empty bench on one of the smaller paths. David felt his life was at a turning point.

"When do we see Vasiliev?" he asked.

"Tonight. If he picks up his messages at the hotel. I've been thinking a lot about it all. I get up in the middle of the night and sit at the window. I imagine papa returning from services, coming up the path to the house, still deep in thought. You remember how even as kids we were inspired by his sermons? Then we drifted away. How did it happen? We still loved him."

Botanical Garden

David felt hypnotized by the sight of her curls swinging around on her shoulders. He had the sudden urge to stroke her hair. But he held back.

"*Fathers and Children*," he quoted.

"I suppose so. But even Turgenev could not describe the pain." She turned to face him. "David, all I want now is revenge."

"Not a healthy emotion," he said.

"I have a question I've wanted to ask you. If you had run into the killer that night in the house, would you have shot him?"

"Aaron had the revolver."

"Don't quibble. If you had had the revolver, then?"

"Probably."

"So, what's the difference? I mean between executing the killer then and doing it now."

"You know the law. Self-defense as against premeditation."

"But the law pertains only to innocent victims."

"That's debatable. But all right, then. The state has a monopoly of coercion. It's a protection against private vengeance."

"But we agree that this state, this Russian autocracy, is illegitimate; we agree that there is no justice for Jews; we agree that you and Aaron violated the law by carrying around concealed weapons. For God's sake, David! Can you honestly be a revolutionary and quote the Code of Laws at me?"

"Easy, Rebecca! You're talking about personal revenge; I'm talking about justifying political violence."

"Just because he was my father? This was not a casual murder. This was a political assassination."

"We don't know that. There is the problem of the missing documents. They might give us a different motive."

"The six shots in the form of a cross, David. You are forgetting that!" Her eyes were blazing.

"Why are we fighting? Is this your disquisition on terror? What do you want to do, for us to do?"

"If you are with me, we're going to hunt him down. We already promised Reb Moishe we wouldn't tell Vasiliev about the key. About who took it. I think I remember the man he described. Ruth would surely know who it was. We'll track him down. He's the killer, or he'll lead us to him."

"And if and when we find him?"

"We will execute him in the name of revolutionary justice."

David was about to ask, and would your father approve? But once again he held back. That would be a monstrous thing to say.

"So what do we tell Vasiliev?"

Rebecca reached out and seized David's hand. Tears glistened in her eyes. "You and Aaron are the only ones I can count on. Thank you David."

David did not remember promising anything. But he remained silent.

"We tell Vasiliev that we found Reb Moishe, but he knew nothing about a key. He fled Kiev because he was afraid for his life, like so many Jews. He was part of the exodus. We tell him that Moishe swore us to secrecy about his whereabouts. That's all."

"And you think Vasiliev will be satisfied?"

"I don't give a damn. He'll have to find his own way. That's what great detectives are supposed to do. Not employ Jewish student revolutionaries to do their work. We have two clues—the key and the amulet. Didn't it seem strange to you that the amulet came from Siberia? Ask yourself who comes from Siberia. Merchants, retired soldiers and exiles who have served out their terms. Or else escaped. My choice is the ex-convict. A hired killer. Somebody wants to sow panic among the Jews. Riots are one thing; they may or may not be the work of a conspiracy. But an assassination like this? It's hard to explain it *except* as a conspiracy. It terrifies the leaders of the community. We've seen it happen. The troops protected Brodsky against the mob. But they couldn't protect the Rabbi against a gunman. You see? Maybe stealing the papers was just laying a false trail. You know, to confuse the police. So, how do we find this ex-convict? We go where they know about such things. The Jewish underworld. It's not a big place. No killers for sure. But I'll bet they'll know about the ex-convicts coming back from Siberia. We'll start with Reb Alter Kaniever's Inn."

"That dump."

"You don't expect to find crooks dining at the Hotel d'Europe, do you?"

"You can't go there, Rebecca. The only women in Kaniever's are prostitutes."

"Then, you'll go alone." Rebecca looked at him intensely. Then her face broke into a smile for the first time that morning." Oh David, if you only looked more like a bandit."

Chapter Twenty-Six

Serov felt tired but still alert. The thin strip of light under the door caught his eye. It might be a safe house, he thought. But never take chances. He stood stock-still. He was the *stolb* again, the pillar of his boyhood games. How many minutes passed? He was listening intently. The silence was broken by the rustle of paper. It sounded like the page of a newspaper being turned. He had to smile. How many assassins would be reading the news while waiting in ambush? Nevertheless, he inserted his key quietly and flung the door open, moving to one side as he did. Vasiliev looked up from a pile of papers that were scattered over the table.

"Still master of the silent approach, eh Sergeant?"

Serov showed immediate interest in the plate of sausage, cheese and bread. A bottle of red wine, uncorked, stood in the middle of the table. It would be just breathing. As Vasiliev had taught him. He really couldn't tell the difference between a wine that was breathing and one that was not. But he chalked that up to his plain tastes. "Are we to be celebratin' an event?"

"Only the end of another frustrating day. As soon as I turn around something else disappears—keys, documents, people."

"As it should be in any good mystery."

"After you've washed up, give me some good news." Serov dipped his hands in a basin of water, shook them vigorously, and seated himself at the table. Vasiliev swept off the papers. Serov took out a knife from his boot and applied himself to his supper. Vasiliev filled two tumblers with wine. They toasted Irina. Serov brushed the last few crumbs from the table. He adjusted the sling on his arm

170

and gave his report. The bazaar was still "skittish as a young mare," he said. There were the usual rumors and stories of strange men popping up to lead the rioters. But no eyewitnesses.

"Most people agreed on one thing. If the soldiers had come out early and in force, it would have ended as soon as it began." Serov wiped his knife on his kerchief and slipped it back into his boot. He explained how the troops had been dispersed in small units. Some were placed on the walls of the Arsenal, where the Jews had fled for protection. Others surrounded City Hall. "Some people told me the soldiers just stood by. Watched the rioters burn down shops. In other places, it seems, they tried to control the rioters. But no one paid 'em attention. I tell you, Vasili Vasilievich, the more I'm out there, the more confused I get."

Jewish Refugees in the Arsenal

"It's the same with the papers. They're not much help. The journalists have different theories. Just like our Jewish friends. What to think? I change my mind every hour. It seems that way, at least. You can put some bits and pieces together and it looks like a conspiracy. Police, army, local officials all involved. Then you think— that's too fanciful. Who'd be coordinating it all? But the alternative doesn't make any more sense. A random and unconnected set of events? But they were so widespread. Not only Kiev but all over the southwest. Could this be just accidental? I'm beginning to think the pogroms were something else."

"What's left?"

"I'm not ready to say. Not just yet. Give me some time. I don't think we're going to find the answer in the streets. I'm not saying your work was useless. What you've told me helps. You see if we eliminate the two extremes—conspiracy and chance—what's left is something in between. Lots of space there. The trouble is I can't stay with the one problem. Don't forget we're on the Rabbi's case too. We can rule out chance there. But I still don't have a motive. And I keep feeling the pressure to finish it all fast."

Vasiliev poured the last of the wine. He half closed his eyes and began to tell Serov about the meeting of Drenteln, Szymanski and Rudov. He explained how Rudov was probably responsible for destroying the court records of a case in April 1871.

"Our boys in blue again," said Serov.

"Right! But it's not clear what they're up to. Or even whether Rudov is acting alone. Why would he try to cover up a crime like the murder of the Rabbi? Both he and Drenteln may be anti-Semites, but they both came down hard on the rioters. Why crush the *pogromshchiki* with one hand and murder a leading figure in the Jewish community with the other?"

"And what is Szymanski's game?"

"I'm hoping to find out. If only Ivan can tell us more about Tiumen." Vasiliev rubbed his side.

"I can't help thinking that the missing documents are the real key. But no one has any idea of what they contained. Did the Rabbi have a secret life? You know, Serov, I haven't much of an idea about him. They call him a *maskil*, an enlightened Jew. A serious scholar. But tolerant of youth, especially his own daughter, Rebecca. Was he a man made for causes? Whatever the case, the ritual murder was a blind.

"Reb Moishe might be able to tell us about the key. Our young Jewish friends have the best chance to find him now. Novitsky told me something important today about the pogroms. You see how I keep jumping from one problem to another. Well, it can't be helped. He was trying to persuade me that the police couldn't cope. Things got out of control. The army did nothing or nothing right. We need to find out who issued the orders to hold them back. Strange that they broke up into small units. It made them less effective. Was that deliberate? Sounds far-fetched. Or else it was plain stupidity. Either way, Drenteln looks bad. He has a lot to answer for. First let the rioters cut loose, then shoot at them. Put it that way and his career is over."

Vasiliev was pacing the room now. "We'll go at this in the same way as before. I'll try to make contact with someone in the Kiev Military District command. Bypass Drenteln's office. If he finds out what I'm doing he could throw us out of Kiev. You'll make the rounds of the soldiers' hangouts. In uniform, of course. Barracks gossip usually gets things right. We'll see if our sources tally."

Serov had been tapping his cast. "Damn thing itches and I can't scratch it. Oh, I'm listenin'. Here I was just gettin' used to beggin' for a living. You know, Vasili Vasilievich, I met some down and outers makin' a better livin' than me. A Sergeant in his Imperial Majesty's Police Force! If I just had an ugly mug. Why who knows? I could retire early."

At the Jewish Hospital they told David that Aaron had been transferred to the Military Hospital. Dr. Margulies had ordered the move. According to the nurse in Aaron's ward, a specialist there would operate on Aaron's eyes. "A colleague of Dr. Margulies in the Army Medical Services during the war. It's really a special favor, considering," she said. David understood that 'considering' meant an exception was being made for a Jew. He felt very angry. Aaron was in a room with only four other patients. David's first thought was, why do people always look diminished in a hospital bed? He did not notice at first that Aaron was highly excited.

"Sit here, on the bed, David. They won't mind. Listen I have something really important to tell you!" Aaron fumbled for David's hand. He squeezed it hard.

"I know, Aaron. They told me that a specialist—"

"No, no! It's not that. Something really important." David had to smile.

"When they brought me over here there was an emergency, and they had to leave me on a stretcher in the receiving room by the entrance. They carried in this woman, a terrible accident, a runaway cab. She got all smashed up. They put her behind a curtain, but I heard everything they said. Mostly doctor's talk. I couldn't understand much. But then one of the nurses said, 'What about this thing around her neck?' And a doctor, I guess it was—anyway, a male voice said, 'Cut it off!' And then, David, it was like a revelation. I saw the curtain move. A hand reached out and dropped this object into a tray. Right on the table between our two stretchers. David, it was the amulet!"

"Can you be sure?"

"How many times did we handle it, you and I? And there it was, right under my nose! I could have reached out and touched it. The injured woman behind the screen, she must have been the orderly in the Jewish Hospital. In fact I'm sure of it. Remember, she bent over right next to my bed. The amulet was that close. No mistake."

"Is she alive? What did they do with her?"

"I don't know. They lifted me out of there just after that. But listen! Be careful in poking around. A Jewish boy asking about... well you know how it is."

"How about Dr. Margulies?"

"He isn't a resident here, just has this friend, the eye specialist, 'ophthalmologist' they call him. They were comrades in the war. But I don't want to ask him either. I'd have to invent some far-fetched excuse. What about Rebecca? A woman is less likely to raise suspicions."

"Rebecca is getting herself involved in some pretty wild stuff. We have to talk about that some time. I'm worried she'll pick up a police tail. Since we agreed to keep Vasiliev out of it...Well, we'll have to find someone else. Not involved in politics."

"How about Ruth?"

"Ruth! She's the last person I would think of."

"Exactly, just what I mean. She would be above suspicion."

"What do we tell her?"

"I'll think of something while they're working on my eye. It'll keep me distracted." Aaron grinned.

David spent the afternoon at the University. Later on he could not recall a word of the two lectures he had attended. He kept wondering how to prepare himself for a night at Kaniever's Tavern. He went over in his mind what he knew about the place. It was all second hand, but from friends who had been there. Years ago Reb Alter had turned it into a refuge for Jews who sneaked into Kiev for a short time. Most of them were dealers of one sort or another, without the proper papers to live in the city. They lived in constant fear of the police, and often survived by distributing bribes to the local constable or even the district police chief. They also paid off the yardmen in the neighboring buildings who served as the informal eyes and ears of the authorities. Periodically, the police and gendarmes would get orders to organize a sweep of all the Jewish inns, usually in the middle of the night. If you got caught without the proper documents, the police put you in the slammer with common criminals. The next day they escorted you back to your hometown along with the thieves.

Kaniever earned a reputation as the smugglers' shield. He made sure that no contraband was stored in his establishment. He distributed generous bribes to the police. They let him know when the sweeps were coming. Once he got the word, he ordered all the contraband goods the smugglers had with them to be hidden in various secret storerooms, trunks, and closets. The police would normally give his place a superficial search. As soon as they left, he would stride through the corridors, a patriarchal figure with masses of white hair and a white beard, calling out to those hidden in the attic, "Jews, don't be fearful! Come on down. The demons have disappeared. The inspection is done. Come on let's have fun!" There were stories about the fabulous celebrations that followed. Girls would suddenly appear, the samovar would bubble madly, whiskey would flow, platters of dried bagels and smoked fish would be laid out, and there would be talk of miracles—until Kaniever made the rounds of the tables collecting from each customer a ruble and a half for the cost of the raid. David hoped there would be no raid the night he dropped in on Kaniever's.

He waited until 11:00 before went into the inn. The place seemed quiet. Was it too quiet? He wondered. Then he put it down to nerves. He ordered a whiskey, a drink he hated, but he worried that he would seem out of place drinking anything else. Suddenly, he felt very foolish. What was he doing there? How was he going to strike up a conversation with any of these men? He looked around. The entire far wall of the room was taken up by a wooden counter loaded down with kegs of whiskey, beer barrels, copper measuring cups, and mugs lined up on a long copper tray. Above him a heavy square beam supported the ceiling, its surface carved with names and dates that meant nothing to him. Behind the counter was a fat woman with a long braid hanging down her back. She was picking her nose. In one corner three old men were bent over their soup bowls. A few younger men were sitting in the other corner. Two of them had girls on their laps. A haze of cigarette smoke hovered above them. The whole place reeked of roast meat.

He nursed his drink. A waiter in a dirty white apron came by several times and gave him an expectant look. After a while he just sneered when David shook his head. He felt he was not blending in very well.

Just before midnight the door crashed open. A boisterous gang of young men burst into the room. "Hey, Rachel! Ten glasses of lager!" The girl at the bar suddenly moved quickly. They pulled together two tables, scraping chairs along the floor of wooden planks. One of them got up and went to the counter. "Watch out, don't give us half a glass, Rachel!" The rest laughed raucously. A white head peered around the corner of the kitchen. "Don't be cruel boys, don't be cruel." The head disappeared. The young man standing at the counter shrugged his shoulders. Then he made a signal to the others, and turned to go to the back door. As he passed David's table he glanced down and stopped short.

"My God, it's David Pressman! What the hell are you doing here?" David lurched to his feet, but the young man pushed him down. He swore loudly, but good-naturedly, grabbed a chair, and sat down. "Davy the giant killer! Have you fallen so low?" Some of his friends began to glance over. David felt the heat in his face.

He was grateful that it was too dim in the inn to see his flushed features.

"Greetings, Mendel."

"David, this is not a good sign. Drinking alone in a smuggler's tavern—you the brilliant scholar, university student."

"All right, Mendel, cut it out!"

"Cut it out, the man says." Mendel swiveled in his chair to address his buddies. "Boys, this is a real treat. Let me introduce to you the star of my youth, David Pressman, Davy the Giant Killer." Several glasses were raised in their direction. The three old Jews kept eating, bending even lower over their soup. One of the men in the corner with a girl on his lap cried out, "Order, order! What d'you think this is, a bordello?" Everyone except David laughed. "No, this is a public lecture hall, and I'm giving the lecture," Mendel said. Suddenly his voice changed. He began to speak in the accents of an educated man as if it were the most natural thing in the world.

"Now, how you will ask did the vagaries of life first bring together Mendel Bornstein, the future smuggler and David Pressman, the future university student? David gripped his glass tightly. If I wanted to be integrated, I've got my wish, he thought.

"I, Mendel the Smuggler, do hereby testify that everything I say is the truth the whole truth and nothing but the truth. I speak as an expert, for I was an eye-witness to the extraordinary exploits of David Pressman—Davy the Giant Killer as he was fondly known to old and young alike. In the gymnasium where we toiled together, David was always first in the class."

David lifted his head and slammed his glass on the table. Mendel jumped and stared at him. "Yes, brothers!" David shouted, surprised to hear the strength in his voice, "And one Mendel Bornstein was always number two, but very close behind."

Mendel bowed to the room. Everyone was listening including the three old men who had put down their spoons. Rachel the barmaid was leaning on her elbows. The waiter was lounging against the door to the kitchen. Even old Kaniever had stuck his head back into the room.

"But there is more! So prick up your ears and set aside your raucous celebration for a moment. One fine day in the bazaar, the old cart of Sholom the Hunchback overturns. Sholom always loads it with junk, without concerning himself with the rational and orderly disposition of his goods. Isn't that true, David? Yes! Now when this pile of shit turns over, old Sholom disappears underneath. Those of us in shouting distance hear his piteous cries. His horse is thrashing around something awful. Buried under his cart lies Sholom, a victim of his own greed and stupidity. But his misfortune does not deter our hero. David—still a schoolboy, you understand—crawls under the cart. He has a knife, though where he obtained this deadly weapon is to this day unknown. And he cuts the horse loose. The beast staggers to its feet, and without even a gracious nod in the direction of its savior, it takes off down the street, scattering pie-sellers and rag pickers in its wake, and is no more seen by man or woman. There are those who swear it ran right off the embankment into the Dniepr, or launched into space. But who believes these superstitious Jews? Their accounts must be dismissed as fantasy. Meanwhile, we are witnessing a miracle. The cart begins to move, up and up, tips and teeters to one side, as if to right itself! Well, not quite correct. It does not perform this act by its own volition. No, no! Wait! There in front of our unbelieving eyes lies Sholom the Hunchback, still crying piteously but in fact free. Someone—was it me? I forget—hauls him out. And then we all watch David peer out from the wreckage. The lad had seized a length of iron pipe that Sholom had wrested from the wreck of a river barge and stuffed in his cart. Davy has used it as a lever to raise the cart. Of course, this requires both brains and brawn. David crawls out, to cheers of the assemblage. A moment passes. Suddenly, the iron bar slips. The cart collapses and disintegrates before our very eyes. No matter everyone is safe! And do you know what David says when we praise his exploit? He is panting and covered with all kinds of shit, but he manages to blurt out two words, 'Archimedes' lever.' Now friends there you have a picture of the scholar-hero in action!"

Mendel paused. His buddies have broken into applause. Mendel bowed, sweeping the floor with an outstretched arm. David shook his head. But Mendel had caught a glimpse of the faint smile so familiar to him from those early days. He clapped David on the back.

"So how does this explain the nickname of giant killer, Mendel?" shouted Rachel.

178

"Ah," Mendel said, "That is another story!" More raucous laughter broke out all over the room.

Mendel sat down next to David, and lowered his voice to a harsh whisper. "All right, brother. What errant wind has blown you this far off course?"

"I wanted to meet someone like you."

"David, this flattery does not become you."

"All right Mendel, listen and believe."

Chapter Twenty-Seven

The Sapper Barracks were located in the southern part of the city across the railroad tracks from the suburb bearing its name. Vasiliev had no trouble finding the office of Major Sevin, an acquaintance from the Danube campaign. He had picked his name out of the officers' roster in the headquarters of the Kiev Military District, and had sent his name ahead. Sevin was delighted to see an old comrade-in-arms. He immediately invited Vasiliev to dinner at the officers' mess. Vasiliev persuaded him to dine instead at a small restaurant in the Sapper Suburb, hinting that he preferred that their meeting be discreet.

"So, Vasili, you are going to have to pay for this discretion with an inferior meal. But the wine cellar is more than adequate. So fire away with your questions before I lose the ability to give straight answers."

"No chance of that. My questions are hardly profound. But let's have a toast to the old days on the Danube."

"What? Not to the new emperor?"

"That comes next, of course."

They studied the menu. Sevin suggested they leave it all up to the owner, who knew something about country cooking. "It's safer here."

Vasiliev told Sevin about his assignment, and made him swear not to gossip about their meeting. "Just tell your comrades that I wanted to reminisce. You know—old friends going over the battlefields and that sort of thing. I just don't want to stir up a lot of trouble with the Governor-General. We're on good terms and I want to keep it that way. But I also have to write a report, you understand."

Sevin nodded, raised his right hand in a mock oath and added in a serious voice. "I'm glad you looked me up, Vasili. Trust me to keep my mouth shut. So you want to know about the army and the pogroms. All right."

Sevin signaled to the waiter for another bottle of burgundy and settled back in his chair.

"You have to understand something if you don't know it already. It's about the new Minister of War, Vannovsky. True, he's only acting minister, but he'll be the next one to be sure. He's Drenteln's boy. The Governor-General got him assigned to the Kiev Military District before the war and pushed him up the ladder. So Drenteln is protected at the highest level. This is one reason I can be frank. Nothing I say or anybody else in the district says can hurt Drenteln. You get the picture? He's virtually impregnable. Easier to storm Plevna—and you remember how tough that was. So, whatever you write about him that puts him in a bad light will be discounted or suppressed. Make you feel better or worse?"

Vasiliev shrugged. "I can't imagine toppling the Governor-General, believe me. Just want to get the full picture. It might come in handy some day when things at the top look differently."

"Spoken like a true son of the Iron Colonel. Oh, I know about your old friend, Ivan. The man who knows where all the bodies are buried."

"This soup isn't half bad," said Vasiliev dipping his spoon into a rich Ukrainian borshch.

Sevin laughed. "I told you. The local product is safe. All right, I'm not going to pry into your affairs. Another thing, though. Let me be clear. The Sappers weren't involved. Confined to barracks during the riots. We're not always trusted to do the right thing. It's our training. We have a certain reputation for being brainy. And that can be a problem sometimes. You remember the conspiracies at the Petersburg Military Academy? All engineers. So what I have to say comes from my friends in the infantry units. I'm not saying they're not bright, but—well, you know what I mean."

Vasiliev nodded and kept working at his soup. "Don't let it get cold," he said.

"God, you won't be drawn will you. All right, these are tough times."

Sevin ate silently for a few minutes, dabbed his mouth with his napkin and drank off another glass.

"They're a little slow here. It'll take a while to prepare the *zakuski*. So, here's what I know. The orders came down straight from the Governor-General. Very detailed—unusually so, I am told. Units no bigger than squads were assigned to protect specific buildings. Mostly government offices, but also some big commercial establishments and the homes of wealthy Jews like Brodsky. The orders— that is the first set—were to show fixed bayonets but not to fire on the rioters, even though live ammunition was handed out. No fraternizing with the crowds allowed. Officers given the discretionary authority to negotiate with the rioters."

"Negotiate? Was the word actually used in the orders?"

"So I am told. The word spread by mouth. 'Warn the rioters! Any attempt to break through the cordon of soldiers will be answered by force.' But there were no instructions for our boys to disperse the crowds. 'Just keep them moving.' That meant moving away from the protected places."

"Is that all?"

"Officially, yes. But there were rumors. I don't know where they started. We were supposed to be short handed. So any attempt to break up the crowds could be disastrous."

"For whom"

"Unstated."

"Here come the *zakuski*. Let's take another break. Best concentrate on the mushrooms. I wouldn't trust the fish."

"And what changed, then, after day one?"

"The new orders simply read, 'Repress the disorders.' Then the firing broke out. The officers were angry, the men were tired. They'd been on duty for twenty-four hours. No hot meals. Hard to take the baiting from the crowds, calling out insults; you know how it is. The new orders came as a relief. Hell, they just leveled their rifles and fired. No aiming over the head. Right into the mass. How about that?" Sevin was waving his fork dangerously.

"Lucky they rationed the ammunition. Six cartridges apiece. The first volley was enough to disperse the crowd without killing hundreds. Some say the change came after Drenteln was stoned on his peace ride through the city. That's what it was called. But you know how these things are. Who fired first and why? You'll never figure that out."

"What do you make of it all? What did the men say? I mean the ones who were out there."

"Well, I only spoke to the officers. Even they had some wild stories. You can imagine how it was in the ranks. One thing came up again and again. I checked with my fellow Sappers, the ones who had comrades in the infantry. They heard much the same thing. Drenteln had been agitating for more troops for the district. He had prior intelligence about the pogroms, you see. He had gotten annoyed at the answers he was getting. He thought he was being set up. I can't imagine who would try that trick. But you never know! Anyway, he got the bright idea, it is said, of letting the rioters have their way for a few hours and then cracking down. But things got out of hand quickly. His peace ride boomeranged. He panicked and ordered the shooting. Then to cover himself he complained that he hadn't enough men. Apparently, he also blamed the police for not doing their duty. Oh, yes, and he switched stories about the pogroms. First he said it was the fault of revolutionaries. But someone must have warned him how that would look. You can just imagine—Petersburg would ask embarrassing questions. How could he have allowed the People's Will get so strong in Kiev? And so on. After all, they were supposed to be finished as a movement. But you know this better than I do."

"Not a pretty picture. It fits with what I've found out. Makes sense in a crazy way. But what in God's name can be done about it?'

"That, my friend, is no business of mine. But let the wine flow now. I'm out of answers. Tell me about your life in Moscow."

Chapter
Twenty-Eight

Later the same night, back at the safe house, Serov had little to add to what Vasiliev had learned. He had made the rounds of the few taverns still open, 'Christian watering holes' the soldiers called them. After a few beers the rankers had been willing to talk. They complained things shouldn't have gotten to the point of firing on the crowds. They blamed the Jews for starting the riots. The usual grumbling about money lending and smuggling. But there was another twist. The same men accused 'them', giving a thumbs up gesture, for managing things badly. "You know what they means, Vasili Vasilievich," said Serov. "'Them' is the people at the top." Still, the soldiers had praised Drenteln for showing a lot of guts on his peace ride through the city.

Vasiliev wondered how his report was going to read in Petersburg. "Any way you look at it," he said, "there's plenty of blame to go around. But it will be hard to pin it on Drenteln. The final responsibility was his. But it also seems that he is invulnerable. I wonder whether there isn't a chink in his armor?"

It was another time when Serov missed his right to 'beg pardon.' But he felt a need to reply. "Nothin' new in Russia."

The next morning the temperature shot up, as if to reproach Vasiliev for having left his summer uniform in Moscow. He remembered his father's cranky complaint that Peter the Great had made only one mistake, but a big one. "He should have moved the capital to Kiev," the old Count said more than once, "and not plunged us in an icy swamp in the north. To say nothing of the fogs. We could just as well have reached Europe through the Straits and the

Mediterranean as the Gulf of Finland and the Baltic." Well, thought Vasiliev as he breathed in the fresh air, maybe not so cranky after all. He stopped at a café on his way to the Meier house where he treated himself to a hearty breakfast of *blini*, sour cream, and strong tea.

He kept reflecting on the way he had slipped into an easy relationship with the young Jews. He was beginning to worry about his feelings for Russia's radical youth. It had been the same with Irina and her nihilist friends. True, not all of them. But Letchik, the healer, was a good man and he was with her now. A strange position for a police inspector. More than strange—perverse. In the eyes of the law, subversive. What was really behind it? He began to wonder where his sympathies lay. Not with revolution. Certainly not! But not with 'them' either.

He asked for the bill, paid, and decided to walk. The wind had shifted to the north, dispersing the unpleasant smell from the Dniepr. The clouds were piling up into impossibly lofty towers, then breaking up into grotesque shapes and scurrying off. The street was filled with perfumed air. It seemed that there were flower sellers at every corner. He was tempted to buy a bunch. How silly it would be to show up for an interrogation with flowers. He thought about seeing Ruth again. He couldn't deny that he was strongly attracted to her. Young radicals and beautiful women! What was happening to him? Was all this southern air and light affecting his brain? He glanced at the street signs and made a sudden turn heading for the Hotel d'Europe. There might be a message waiting from Ivan. His thoughts turned elsewhere. How long every day must be in the Tiumen Prison!

As he approached the hotel desk the concierge reached back, pulled a thin yellow envelope out of a mail slot, and handed it to him. Vasiliev carried the telegram to the far end of the lobby. He sat down on a couch, turning it over in his hands. Then he ripped open the envelope and read the short message. He read it a second time, as if he couldn't believe his eyes, then folded it into the pocket of his blouse, and glanced around the room. Two ladies in long white dresses were seated by the tall, glass window, deep in conversation. An older man, wearing an elegant linen suit and sporting a monocle, was reading the daily *Kievlianin*. No one was paying him any attention.

He stood up and went to the writing table. He pulled out a sheet of paper from the drawer, dated it and addressed it to Baron Szymanski. He wrote swiftly as though he had long prepared the letter in his head. Then he wrote another much shorter message, which he inserted into an envelope embossed with the crest of the hotel. He handed it to the concierge and asked to have it delivered by hand within the hour. Then he reserved a private room in the hotel for five o'clock that afternoon.

The sun was at its zenith when he rang at the Meier House. Ben-Zion answered his knock at the side door, a startled look on his face. "Ah, Inspector! Good. One never knows these days who comes to the door of a Jewish household." He led him through the familiar rooms, where people were seated in small groups or lounging in sofas reading. "Who are they all?" Vasiliev whispered to Ben-Zion. "A few relatives, mostly Jews who have lost their homes and seek shelter here until they can get their bearings. Rabbi Meier always kept an open house. Now the girls continue the tradition, but it's become a burden. So many mouths to feed. Ruth performs miracles."

They found Ruth in her father's study. She was arranging books on the shelves, although they looked to Vasiliev as if they were in perfect order.

She smiled at him. "Rebecca is at the University. She'll be back late. I'm sorry."

"I came to see you, Ruth." Vasiliev found himself dissimulating. He smiled at her, suddenly aware of the contrast between her dazzling white, perfect set of teeth and his own crooked set. He hadn't thought of his teeth in a long time. He rubbed his side. He would have been surprised to learn that Ruth regarded Vasiliev's smile as part of his charm. From the very first time she met him she regretted he was not Jewish. Of course, there were cases of mixed marriages, but not involving a girl who was so deeply religious. Still, she wondered idly, what it might be like to be the wife of a police inspector. What a scandal that would cause! She invited him to be seated and ordered a samovar.

"Serious gentlemen normally call on Rebecca," she said.

"This is hardly a social call, Ruth."

"Of course not. What I meant was that men with a serious object in mind, scholars and students, find Rebecca to be more thoughtful."

"Possibly that is so. But for the moment I'm interested in what you have to say. Let's go back to the question of the missing documents. Who might have taken them? Do you have any suspicions? It seems that every time I come here a different person answers the door. It's possible, then, that a stranger might simply walk in with some story or other. You see what I mean?"

They were interrupted by a servant who brought in a samovar and an assortment of jams. Ruth made tea, nodding her head as if she were running through her mind the visitors who crowded the rooms of her house.

"I'm sure of one thing, Inspector. No one could be in the house for more than a few minutes without my knowing about it. You see I have a system. I've never told anyone about it before." She looked up at him. He noticed for the first time her extraordinarily long eyelashes. She handed him a cup and saucer. He remarked on the beauty of the tea service. "So you notice these things too. Not many men would."

"I have a close friend in Petersburg who is a real connoisseur. He has taught me a lot over the years."

"But you yourself are not a collector?"

"No—like your father, I collect books." At the mention of her father Ruth lowered her gaze. "But not the same ones," he went on. "Poetry, books about poets." Her features went through another rapid change. "A poetic policeman," she gasped. "How extraordinary." Her eyes were dancing merrily. He felt thrown off his stride.

"A topic for another day," he said gently. "How about telling me about your system."

She settled back in her chair and peered at him over the top of her cup. "You might have wondered about all the people in our house—strange-looking to you, perhaps. Papa thought it was his moral obligation to keep the Rabbi's home as a refuge. One of his many unorthodox ideas. Don't worry. I keep tabs on them. I choose someone different to answer the door every day. They think of it as a kind of favor. In return they have to report to me. I make it my business to introduce myself to each visitor. I ask for names and addresses and recommendations. My father never knew about this system. He would have disapproved. Rebecca did not much care for it. It didn't look like a system because there were so many different people acting as my greeters. That's what I used to call them. Never to their faces. Only to myself. I don't believe in having servants greet my guests. They do other kinds of work."

"Very clever," murmured Vasiliev. He felt her smile was also a kind of favor. He wondered why its effect on him was so strong. He could imagine men and perhaps women too, making a special effort to bring it to her lips.

"And I think I can tell what your next question will be. Has anyone who came to the house in the past few weeks seemed suspicious or out of place?"

"You make it easy for me", he said hoping he would be rewarded again by another smile.

"Three come to mind. A young man who called himself Pinye Lisak, a fiery redhead with a bandage over one eye. Dressed in cast-off clothes that did not fit. Not that his appearance was important— just giving you a description. Reb Moishe found him rummaging around in the bureau drawers, probably looking for silver. We keep it locked up. He said he was looking for a blanket. So I gave him one and told him to leave. He was only here a few hours. He didn't seem like the type to steal documents. My goodness! Listen to me! As if I would know! What I mean is he didn't seem to be anything more than a petty thief. The second person was a woman. She had already gone gray, but she must have been pretty when she was young. She looked battered. She wandered around from room to room, quietly weeping. When we tried to help her she flew into a rage and cursed us. She stayed for several days, but was always getting into fights with people. She said she was the wife of a rabbi from Vitebsk. But she didn't know her prayers. I don't know whether she was crazy or not. But sometimes a crafty look would come into her eyes. Then one night just after father was killed she disappeared."

Ruth paused and rested her hands on her knees. "Finally, a man who came to the front door like you, Inspector. Oh! I'm sorry. I'm not criticizing you. You couldn't know. For us Jews that's not polite. A Jew would never do this. He would come to the side door. He came the day after Papa was killed. It was a terrible time for us. I was so distraught. I was not paying close attention to who came and went. Reb Moishe was very good. He made a list for me. This man said he came from the rabbinic court at Berdichev and had witnessed the pogroms. He told us about the Jewish militia, who armed themselves with clubs to turn back the Russian workers coming from the North on trains. He said he'd been sent to do the same thing here. But the pogroms were over. He was very vehement, but he only stayed one day and left without saying goodbye. Again this was a violation of good manners. But I don't think he was a Jew."

"You say Reb Moishe made a list. Is this man's name on it?"

"Yes, I remember it. His name was Pavel Tsukerman. But I doubt he gave his real name. Don't you think it's unlikely?"

Of course, but people make mistakes in choosing false names. They unconsciously betray themselves."

"That makes sense. You know he took a lot of sugar in his tea. I joked with Rebecca about it. 'A man becomes his name', she said. Rebecca was always the clever one." Vasiliev resisted the temptation of contradicting her.

"Now, can you give me a description?"

"He was very tall, taller than you. He was thin, I would even say skinny. He had lank dark hair combed back from his forehead without a part. He moved strangely, I would say stealthily. But, you see, I didn't like him, so I use all the negative words." She gave a short laugh; that too he found charming. "His face was narrow. Everything about it was narrow—his nose, his jaw. He did have a good Jewish nose." She laughed again. "He carried a prayer book, but it was easy enough to get hold of one then. Sad to say you could pick them up on the streets of Podol after the riots."

She clasped her hands on her knees, pressing her skirt tightly around her legs. Her gesture appeared perfectly natural, yet it had a disturbing effect on him. Vasiliev felt himself admiring the outline of her legs. She seemed to be innocent and seductive at the same time. How different she was from Irina, in every way. The thought was like a douche of cold water. He stood up abruptly.

"You are marvelously observant, Ruth. I think I could pick this man out of a crowd. You've been very helpful. The police might recognize him from your description. If you think of anything else, please send me message at the Hotel d'Europe." He registered the look of disappointment on her face. Did she expect him to say more?

"Should I leave by the side door?" he asked, realizing how feeble was his attempt at a joke.

"No, Inspector, you may always come in the front door."

Chapter
Twenty-Nine

Vasiliev's visit made him feel uneasy. Ruth's sensuous beauty was beginning to arouse him. She turned out to be less feather-brained than he had thought. Hell! Damning her with faint praise wasn't going to help. Whatever her formal education, she was clever. He kept going over their conversation. There was nothing remarkable about it. Except for one thing. For a moment he had almost forgotten about the meeting with Szymanski. What did that mean? It was insane to think that anybody could replace Irina. But she was a thousand miles away, and Ruth was here. How could he even compare them? He hardly knew this girl. He kept reproaching himself. At the same time he recalled how she had pressed her hands around her knees outlining the shape of her legs. And what did her parting phrase mean? A *double entendre* or an innocent remark? He tried to recall the intonation in her voice. Damn it! There was nothing to it. He was day dreaming like an adolescent. He jammed his hands into his tunic pockets and looked around. He hadn't even noticed where he was going. It was then that he caught sight of a man about fifty meters behind him, who suddenly pivoted on his heel in the middle of the block and hurried down a side street.

Vasiliev quickly retraced his steps and also turned the corner, where the road curved sharply down a steep hill. There was no one in sight. Below him he saw the statue of Saint Vladimir, the Kievan Prince who, a thousand years before, had ordered the mass baptism of his people in the Dniepr. For some reason he recalled the legendary story in the Primary Chronicle: how Vladimir had decided to abolish paganism, and had sent out missions to report back on the attractions of the Orthodox Christian, Muslim and Jewish faiths. The prince then ruled out Islam because the Koran prohibited drinking alcohol and Judaism because God had cast out the Jews and scattered them on account of their sins. But the mission to Constantinople reported back that when they had visited the great St. Sophia Church , they thought they had entered the Kingdom of God. If the tale were true, Vasiliev thoughts turned to Rabbi Meier and his daughters, what would Russia be like if Vladimir had chosen to adopt Judaism? The idea was fantastic, and yet...

He hesitated for a moment about following the man, and then glanced at his watch. It would soon be time to meet Szymanski. He walked back to the main road and hailed a droshky.

By the time he arrived at the Hotel d'Europe his mood had changed. He ordered a bottle of whiskey and two glasses to be sent

Statue of St. Vladimir

to the private room he had already reserved. He mounted the stairs, entered the room, and stood by the window, watching the traffic. At exactly five o'clock there was a discreet knock on the door. Szymanski came in, dressed in a stylish frock coat. He bowed. Vasiliev took a few steps, extending his hand. He noticed at once that the Baron appeared to be nervous.

"I have the feeling this meeting may change our lives," Vasiliev said.

"Most certainly yours, Inspector."

"Please, let us drink to success," Vasiliev said, pouring the whiskey.

"Ah, Inspector, you anticipate me. I too had ordered a libation. It should arrive soon. But I like your toast. Too often, Russians like to make long speeches at such moments." As they raised their glasses, there was another knock at the door.

"Come in," Vasiliev said.

A waiter appeared with a tray of bottles and *zakuski*.

"My dear Baron, it is I who should be entertaining you. But I forget—traditional Polish courtesy. Shouldn't we finish our business first? I've got a letter for you. It wasn't easy to write. I'm sure you'll make good use of it. You'll see what I mean when you read it." For a moment Szymanski looked puzzled. Vasiliev bowed and Szymanski bowed. Vasiliev bowed again, and reaching into his tunic he pulled out an envelope. Szymanski bowed. Vasiliev wondered how long this bowing might go on. Szymanskii took the letter with trembling fingers and dropped his glass. It shattered on the parquet floor.

How dramatic! thought Vasiliev

The door flew open, and Captain Rudov sprang into the room. Standing behind him on the threshold was the Chief of Police, Novitsky, and two constables who peered over his shoulder.

It was clear that Rudov was running the show. "Gentlemen, I am obliged to arrest you for organizing a conspiracy involving communication with a convict." Rudov extended his hand to Szymanski, who shrank back. "Please, Baron, give me the letter that you have just received from Inspector Vasiliev."

Szymanski seemed to hesitate, and then handed over the letter.

Vasiliev folded his arms and produced his crooked smile. He

seemed to be enjoying himself. A glance at Novitsky assured him that the effect was not lost. The chief suddenly looked bemused.

"Captain Rudov, you surprise me. Convicts? Conspiracy? You seem to be misinformed. Why, to imagine Baron Szymanski involved in something so sordid. This is a personal matter between us. The letter is private. But since you have brought the Kiev police force with you...Well, Baron, do you object to having Captain Rudov read the letter? No? Nor do I. Please read it now, Captain. Out loud."

Vasiliev could hardly keep from laughing in their faces. Rudov's smirk was fading and Novitsky's eyes were dancing. Szymanski looked completely confused. Rudov tore open the envelope, scanned the letter, and flung the paper to the floor.

"Why, Captain, you seem positively disappointed! Baron, if you would be so kind, let the gentlemen in on our secret." Vasiliev picked up the letter and handed it to Szymanski. The Baron looked around like a trapped animal.

"Well, Baron, go ahead—read it, before we all die of curiosity," said Novitsky, who had stepped into the room. He waved his men to follow. "We were promised one kind of entertainment. Now it seems we'll get something quite different."

Szymanski stared at the paper.

"My God!" exclaimed Novitsky, "This must be one hell of a letter. I can hardly wait to hear it."

Szymanski began to read, in a halting voice. Vasiliev noticed that his Polish accent had become pronounced.

Dear Baron,

Here is the information you desire. Since the publication of the *Regulation on Exiles* in 1823 a full statistical record has been kept of all exiles who have crossed the Siberian frontier. The official number of exiles between that date and 1881 is 654,231. They are grouped into four classes: *katorzhniki*, that is hard-labor convicts; *poselentsy* or settlers, *ssylnye*, banished people; and *dobrovolnye*, families of exiled husbands or parents. I was not able in the short time allowed me to compile further statistics from the official records. However, if you apply to the Central Statistical Bureau in

St. Petersburg, they will furnish you with any additional information you desire. My regrets at not having been able to answer all your questions in greater detail.

I remain,

Your obedient servant,

Vasili Vasilievich Vasiliev

Inspector, Moscow City Police; Major, Imperial Russian Army (ret.)

"Apply to the Central Statistical Bureau!" Novitsky's voice rang out. It seemed to Vasiliev that the whiskey glasses were ringing. "That's rich, Captain, you'll have to agree. Six hundred thousand exiles! Baron, let's have the exact figures again." Novitsky slapped his thigh and roared with laughter. He turned to his constables. "Did you hear, boys? Over six hundred thousand we've sent away. You would think Russia would be safe now. Tell me, Vasili Vasilievich, how many of those characters are Poles?" He broke off choking with laughter. Vasiliev poured him a shot of whiskey. Novitsky gulped it down. "Oh God, I can't stand it!" Vasiliev thought he was laying it on rather thick. Suddenly, Novitsky became very serious. "God damn it, Rudov, next time you want to play tricks be sure you have the cards in your hand." He stalked out of the room followed by his two constables.

"What do you think amused Vasili Dementevich, Captain?"

Rudov spun on his heel and strode to the door. "You will have to ask the Baron, Inspector," he said over his shoulder. They heard his spurs jingle down the corridor.

"Don't leave, Baron. I feel I've let you down. Was my answer unsatisfactory? Or perhaps you think I have a second letter for you? Rudov should have stayed around to see. That would have been clever on his part. But he would have been disappointed again. You never received a letter from any Irina, did you? Baron, you are a scoundrel. Do you take that as an insult? Fine, you may send your seconds. I will be happy to accommodate you. Unfortunately, my position and rank forbid me to issue a challenge. Or else I would, even though these romantic gestures are out of fashion. Now get the hell out of my sight, before I thrash you within an inch of your life!"

196

"Listen, Inspector, I'll go of course. But I was forced into this. I had no choice."

"Sorry, Baron, everyone has a choice. It's called the doctrine of free will. What I would like to know, since you wish to excuse yourself, is whether the Governor-General instigated this nasty little plot."

"I can't tell you anything more."

"If you didn't go along with them, they threatened to take away your estate and send you back to Siberia? Well, that isn't much of a choice. But I guess, and I am a great one at guessing—it's a professional disease with me—that you made your choice long ago, when they gave you your pardon and restored your estate. In exchange you agreed to become an agent. Isn't that so? And here you are playing the role of an *agent provocateur*. That is a diseased profession. Please do not bow on your way out."

Szymanski placed Vasiliev's letter on the mantle piece and left the room. Vasiliev silently blessed Ivan for the telegram in his pocket. He thought of Irina and cursed Szymanski.

Chapter Thirty

Kaniever's Inn was beginning to fill up. Mendel held David's eyes for a moment. Then he got up, and crossed the room to the table where his gang was sitting. He spoke a few words to them before coming back to David.

"All right Davy, the night is yours. We had nothing on that can't wait until tomorrow. So I'll listen and believe."

David told him his story, from the time he and Aaron shadowed the Rabbi until he and Rebecca found Reb Moishe. Mendel only interrupted once. "So it was you beat the shit out of those five Russian thugs. What a man—a real giant killer!"

"I had help. They damn near killed me."

"Always the modest one. So go on."

"You see the problem, Mendel. We need to find this goy who wore the amulet. He has to be a convict from Siberia."

"Just a minute. Suppose this goy bought the amulet here in Kiev. Merchants from Siberia come through all the time. It's a long shot, Davy."

"Don't you ever take a long shot? We haven't got much else."

"What about these documents? They must be valuable to someone. You've got to find out what was in them."

"Yeah, but where to begin."

"All right, we'll save that one for later. As for the convicts, you may be surprised to know that our Kiev is a nice peaceful city. Or was until the thugs began beating us Jews. What I mean is this. Kiev is not New York or even Paris. Not a lot of killing. Hey, d'you know there are only four or five murders a year in this Mother of Russian Cities? That narrows down the field. Of course, our man might not have killed anyone before this. Chances are that whatever the crime, he got a tenner. More than that and the survival rate goes way down. He might have escaped. But not many make it all the way out. You know why? Because the convoy officers are a smart lot. The prisoners organize themselves into *artels* for protection. The officer tells the boss of the *artel*, 'Brother, you guarantee no escapes, I'll take off the fetters,' or some such deal. See, the prisoners are collectively responsible for one another. They'll betray any poor bastard who plans an escape. Or else they'll take care of him themselves." Mendel drew a finger across his throat. "Otherwise they'll all lose their privileges. Clever, eh? An old Russian trick. 'Travelers at state expense,' that's what they call the exiles out there. Great humor these Russians have. Well, the 'travelers' who make a break — against the odds, you understand — usually get picked up fast when they get to a big city. Just yesterday we heard about it happening here, in Kiev. They picked up a political. Hey! She made it all the way from Tiumen. A real exploit. But an unhappy ending. They picked her up in the bazaar after a week, sent her back." Mendel looked at his hands. "I hear someone ratted on her." He turned to the bar. "Hey, Rachel, another lager. We're dying of thirst here."

Mendel waited until the lager appeared. He emptied half the glass.

"So I'll bet this goy of yours got a tenner. That means he was bound over in '71 or maybe '70. That's before my time. Hell, you and I were still in school then. But there are some old timers around, like Shmuel the Horse Thief. He isn't here tonight. But he'll drift in one of these days. He'll know if anyone does. "

"Thanks Mendel."

"Listen old friend, you and I go back a long way."

"Yes. But what happened to you? I never understood why you disappeared."

"No big mystery. We were fierce competitors, you and me. Remember how we used to jump out of our seats in school? We'd wave our hands in the teacher's face. Shout the answers! We were great at maths, too. Always trying to figure out new solutions to the problem. Drove all the teachers crazy! They couldn't follow us." Mendel tipped back his chair and laughed. "Same thing in gymnasium, though we learned to stay in our seats. The rest couldn't keep up with us. Fast as Mercury we were. Remember the day we got accepted to gymnasium? What a day that was! Sure you remember. We even got a bit tipsy on ritual wine. I was always just a step behind you. Just a step. But in the end it was like miles."

"You kept me up there, Mendel. I was so afraid you'd catch me I killed myself studying."

"Great, Davy! I never would have caught you. But I never got the chance. So what happened to me? One day I was a smart Jew on his way to the university. The next day I was gone. You never knew? They found out papa was living illegally in Kiev. He'd been here for years. He thought he was safe. But they found out, and kicked him out. I went with him. Back to the wretched *shtetl* where he was born. What a hole that was! So what was I supposed to do — come to you and say, 'nice going, Davy? My life is finished, but I'm going to be a good boy and become a shop assistant.' Where does a smart Jew go when he's closed out? Into smuggling of course, or money lending. But our family was poor. No capital. Oh, I forgot, I could have become a revolutionary. But they're truly crazy. Become a smuggler, someone benefits. Money is made, goods change hands, trade increases, the government doesn't grab everything. But revolutionaries? They want justice? Let me tell you, from what I've seen what they want is power. And what about the students who turn that way? Crazier than the rest. They get the chance of a lifetime and piss it away."

David decided not to argue. Besides, what would he say? He looked up at the ceiling beam. "One more thing, Mendel. Just curious. What are the names and dates up there carved in the wood?"

"An appropriate question, David. The revolutionaries have their pantheon of martyrs, isn't that so? Well that's *our* pantheon. The names are the great thieves, and the dates are the record of their greatest exploits. Nice, eh? And the police haven't a clue. Too stupid to figure it out."

Mendel finished his lager and pulled out a silver pocket watch. "Bought with illegal proceeds, but it keeps perfect time. Got to go! Next time you can tell me about the University. I think I can stand hearing about it, but just." He slapped David on the back and walked out of the tavern. David noticed that Mendel had acquired a bit of a swagger. Not good for a smuggler, he thought.

Chapter
Thirty-One

Rebecca found Ruth still sitting where Vasiliev had left her. Later, she would recall how flushed and excited Ruth appeared. Rebecca was not accustomed to concern herself with her sister's inner life. Later, when she thought back on it all, Rebecca felt pangs of guilt. She never thought her sister even had an inner life. Her mind was filled with Aaron's plan as David had relayed it. But she wanted to put Ruth in the right frame of mind.

"Your dress becomes you, Ruth. I always liked you in that color. And it shows off your assets." Ruth giggled and arched her back thrusting out her breasts. She felt like making a bold gesture.

"That Detective Inspector was here," she said, not trusting herself to pronounce Vasiliev's name.

"What did you tell him?"

Ruth looked directly at Rebecca for the first time since she came into the room. Why should she share every delicious moment with her sister, who could think of nothing but her revolutionary mission?

"Nothing he didn't already know. How is Aaron? Did you visit him?"

"No, I had a meeting at the University. But David told me a specialist is going to operate on him. There's still a chance to save his eye."

"Let God be merciful."

"I say, let the surgeon be good."

Ruth began to assemble the tea cups.

"Don't leave just yet, Ruth. We...I have a favor. Listen, you remember that David and Aaron found that funny object..."

"...the amulet."

"Yes, right, the amulet. Well, it turns out that Aaron spotted its twin. A woman in the hospital was wearing it. It's a long story. The details aren't important. But we...I think that she must be connected, maybe even related to the killer."

"You should tell the Inspector."

"What's this with the Inspector? Listen, Ruth, Vasiliev may be a decent sort. But he was sent to Kiev on an official mission to investigate the pogroms. Good for him. He did Reb Ben-Zion a favor. I don't know why. The old man can be persuasive. God knows. I remember how he tried to teach me. So, Vasiliev promised to help. But his assistant is practically crippled. And he doesn't seem to know what to do next. He comes over here to interview you..."

"How do you know that was so useless?"

"Come on, Ruth. You just told me he didn't find out anything he didn't know. Maybe he just wanted another look at you. I can't blame him for that."

Ruth noisily piled the glass jam dishes on the copper tray. She rang a little silver bell. A servant appeared, and Ruth gestured at the samovar and the tray, a bit imperiously, thought Rebecca. Not like her. But the thought died.

"The point is we...I need your help."

"What's this 'we' business? Which is it—you, my sister, or the revolutionary conspiracy?"

"Ruth! We're trying to hunt down father's killer, not touch off a revolution. It's just that I'm not used to asking favors for myself. Sure, David and Aaron are with me on this. And you should be too, even more so."

"All right, Rebecca, don't be angry. What d'you want me to do?"

"We want you to find out who the woman is. You know, the woman wearing the amulet. We want to know whether she can lead us to the...to the man who owns the other one. Now, doesn't that prove we value and trust you as a friend and ally?"

Ruth raised her hand to her mouth.

"Don't be frightened. There is no risk No one will suspect you. You have a wonderful way with people. You can pretend to befriend her. Get her to tell you about the amulet."

"What happened to her? Why is she in the hospital?"

"She was in an accident. Pretty awful, they say. A runaway cab on the Andrei Descent. She's lucky to be alive. We don't know how badly she's hurt. It may take a while to get her to talk to you. But you should begin to try as soon as possible. And there are just a couple of other things. If she is who we think she is, then she is not going to open up to a Jewess. So you'll have to take on a new identity. How about posing as an Armenian? They have the same coloring we do. You don't have any characteristic Semitic features. Ruth, I have to ask you this. Would you be willing to wear a Christian cross around your neck?"

"You ask too much, Rebecca."

"Even to catch father's killer? We could get a ruling from Reb Ben-Zion. He could interpret some passage in the Talmud to absolve you."

"It's not a matter of the Law, Rebecca. I would just feel it burning a mark in my throat, my chest. I can't explain it. I know it must seem irrational to you."

"Never mind. You can wear a high-necked blouse. Not too much jewelry. Your hair is perfect. This woman is in the Military Hospital. Aaron found out one thing. Nobody's been able to identify her. You can say you're a friend or a neighbor. Tell them you want to see the woman wearing an amulet. Describe it. That should convince them that you know her. It's so important, Ruth."

The two sisters stood simultaneously. Rebecca surprised Ruth by embracing her. That had not happened in a long time.

The Esteemed Person was a firm believer in lucky and unlucky days. He made a record of them every evening. Just like his account books. Life was made up of the rational and the irrational, he liked to say. In the long run things balanced out. You had to prepare yourself for a bit of both. To believe too much in one or the other was to court ruin. In his youth he had sought answers to life in numerology. Like Pierre Bezhukov in Tolstoy's *War and Peace*—a book he had never read, but had heard about—he discovered there was no mathematical system to life. Yet there was a pattern, much as on the Persian rugs that hung in his bedroom. An interweaving of lines and motifs, never perfectly symmetrical, but recognizable to the trained eye. He was just about to complete a lucky day. He was sure of it. In the morning he had found a sixteenth century icon in a dirty stall run by a Tatar in the bazaar. The poor fool. What did he know about icons? Still, it was smart to bargain with him. The Esteemed Person chuckled to himself. He got it at a ridiculously cheap price, half of what the Tatar had first asked for it. He bent over the warped wood. It had to be cleaned, but he felt sure no damage had been done to the image.

He looked up from his work at the sound of Pavel's knock, announcing his next visitor. He quickly slid the icon into his desk drawer. He glanced at his watch. His man was right on time. He had been so absorbed he hadn't noticed.

"Yes, come in Dimitri! You are most welcome."

"Good evening."

"Yes, Dimitri, a good evening it is. There will be more of it coming from you. I'm sure of it. Sit down my good fellow." Dimitri walked over to a straight back wooden chair and sat down.

My goodness, thought the Esteemed Person, he still keeps the habits of an exile. Not like our old friend Stepan, who was easily seduced by comfort.

"Now, what have you come to tell me?"

Dimitri ran his fingers along the edge of his threadbare jacket. It was not easy to understand the sounds coming through his broken teeth.

"Well, I were there, waitin' at the curve o' the Descent, like yuh said. And pretty soon the coach comes slippin' and slidin' down like a drunk sailor. The wheel skips off. The nag is screamin'. Her legs give way. She's tangled in the reigns and such. The whole mess slams into a wall. Breaks up. The nag's broke her neck. The coach's smashed up like firewood. And the woman's crushed. No one could'a lived through that'n."

"Ah, Dimitri, you would be surprised to see what women can live through. Did you make sure she was dead?"

"Make sure? I goes over and looks at her, or the part o' her sticken out. And there's blood over her and she's not breathin'. So how sure was I to be?"

"But you waited until the medical people arrived. Didn't you?"

"The Cossacks git there first. An' they're likey to know my mug. So I leaves."

"Good work, Dimitri. Here's your money and a third class ticket to Rostov, as we agreed." The Esteemed Person did not offer Dimitri any refreshment. Dimitri counted the rubles before he shuffled out. The Esteemed Person glared at a painting of Jupiter enthroned. Stupid of me. I made a mistake. If only I'd had Pavel on the spot. But he had already done his job. Jumped off the coach at the top of the Descent, and Ivan was following Vasiliev. I shouldn't allow myself to be caught short of men like that. But where can one find reliable persons these days? He asked himself. A shadow had fallen on his lucky day. He rang for Pavel.

Ruth ran her fingers lightly over the dresses hanging in her wardrobe. She was giving careful thought to what she should wear. Something subdued, but not black. No need to look older than she was. She took down her mother's dark-red dress with the tight sleeves and pinched waist, with padding on the hips. It was long out of style. But it was respectable, and she had a pair of low-heeled shoes to match. Not too much jewelry, Rebecca had said. That was right. She was supposed to be an Armenian, not a wealthy *rebbetsin*. Just the simple gold earrings.

She had ordered a cab, but she told no one where she was going. It rode along the road to the Military Hospital like a skiff in a storm on the Black Sea up and down the hills of Kiev. But she scarcely noticed the swaying of the cab. She kept plucking at the folds in her long skirt. Only her ankles showed, but she worried that her breasts were too prominent. She rehearsed her Armenian name a dozen times. Her heart was pounding as she entered the hospital and began to ask directions. She was bewildered by the separate sections, each with its own staircase. She never knew which of the long corridors to follow. She tried to stop nurses, but they were all in a hurry. Finally she found the woman's ward. But no one seemed to have heard of a victim of a runaway cab accident. She had the impression that people regarded her with alarm or hostility. But wasn't this just her imagination? She clutched a small bouquet of spring flowers she had picked from the garden. They were already beginning to wilt from the pressure of her fingers. On the threshold of a large room with many windows a nurse accosted her. She blurted out her story. She said she was the employer of a woman who had been injured in an accident. When asked her name she said, "But surely you know about her, the incident is famous! She survived by a miracle."

"Oh, that one! Bed number four."

Ruth stared at the bandaged head for several minutes, trying to control her trembling. She came closer, and dropped the flowers on a small table next to the bed. A few of them fell to the floor. She took no notice. The words she had rehearsed flew out of her head.

Vera opened her eyes and saw a vision. The Angel of Death appeared before her, hovering over her, calling to her to join the heavenly host. Her lips were so parched she found it hard to answer. She felt pain and numbness in her entire body. She could not move. Surely the Angel would gather her up and carry her away.

"You have come for me." She could not recognize her own voice. It was like the croaking of a frog.

The Angel bent over her. Vera smelled the freshness of spring.

"I've come to help relieve your suffering. You must tell me your name."

"Will you take me to Stepan?" Vera asked. "I am Vera Evgrafovna."

"Yes. Vera Evgrafovna. Do you still have the amulet?" The Angel asked.

Vera could not raise her arm but she could feel that the amulet was no longer lying on her chest.

"No. Must I have it to join him?"

"Wait." The Angel vanished. Vera closed her eyes in despair.

Ruth went into the corridor. Nurses and orderlies rushed past her. She remembered passing the office of the administrator. She knocked and entered. She felt calm now. "Vera Evgrafovna must have her amulet. Without it she will lose hope and die. You must understand these superstitious women."

Vera had dozed off but woke suddenly as she felt gentle hands around her neck, the familiar feeling at her throat. The amulet had been restored. She tried to smile, but all Ruth saw was a grotesque grimace.

"Will you take me now?"

"No, you'll soon be better."

"You mean my time has not yet come?"

Ruth understood that something strange had passed between them. She groped for an answer. "No, your time has not yet come. Return to the world."

Vera sighed and closed her eyes.

Ruth watched her for a while before tiptoeing out of the ward. Should she have asked Vera more questions? Had she failed in her mission? She was so preoccupied with her thoughts that she almost ran into a man in a white coat. She felt him grasp her arms and took fright.

"Ruth, my dear, how nice to see you! Have you come to visit Aaron? What a kindness. But only to be expected from you."

She was gazing into the eyes of Dr. Margulies.

"Oh, no—I mean yes."

"What is it my dear? Yes or no?" His smile was broad and friendly.

"I mean I didn't come to see him but..." she hesitated for an instant, "...but to learn about the operation."

"Of course. It's too early to say. My colleague assures me that the operation was a success. In medical terms this means that everything went well in the operating theater. But the results...well, we'll have to wait a few days."

Suddenly Ruth felt relieved that she had not worn a cross.

"You must have gotten lost. Aaron is in bloc B. I think he will be happy to see you."

Ruth took his arm. They turned in the opposite direction from where she had been heading. She stared straight ahead, fearing she might betray her inner state. As they approached the stairwell she suddenly gasped and cried out. She squeezed Margulies' arm so hard that he winced. "Dr. Margulies, that man!" she pointed to a tall, thin figure mounting the stairs from below. The man heard her cry and looked startled. He threw up his arm to cover his face, whirled around, and vaulted down the stairs, disappearing from sight.

"What is it?"

"That man, coming up the stairs. He is the one! Oh, my God!" She was shaking as she clung to him. "Please, we must do something. He is the thin man who came to the house. I told Inspector Vasiliev. We must get hold of Inspector Vasiliev."

Chapter
Thirty-Two

Later the same day Serov found Vasiliev in the safe room clipping newspapers and creating files just as he did in Moscow.

"There doesn't seem to be any pattern to the pogroms. It all looks chaotic. I think I'm missing something, but what is it? Sergeant, tell me the truth so I can sleep peacefully. Has the underworld given up its secrets?"

"Not sure they have any. Meanin' about these riots, pogroms. Whatever they call 'em. Talk a plenty about 'men from the North'. You'd think Kiev was full of angels. Except for the smugglers and such. And the smugglers are all Jews, I hear tell. Their hangout's called Kaniever's. It's a tavern. I hung around in the street outside. They chased me away. None too politely, you understand. Beggars aren't wanted. They looked me over. Just like I was a piece of goods. 'Goy beggars especially' is what they said."

Vasiliev pushed aside the newspapers and lit a cigar. "If the killer was an outsider from the North, we don't have much chance of finding him. Let me bring you up to date. Captain Rudov and the Pole, Szymanski, tried to set me up. The message from Irina was a fake. Rudov must have gotten a description of Irina from his Gendarme friends in Piter or the Tiumen Prison. What puzzles me is how they knew about Irina and me. It wasn't common knowledge."

"Except you went visitin' her the once." Serov couldn't help blurting it out.

Vasiliev looked hard at him. "How did you know?"

Serov rubbed his chin. "If I found out without tryin', others wouldn't have much trouble findin' out too. Isn't that right, Vasili Vasilievich?"

Vasiliev thought for a moment. He'd been foolish not to confide in Serov from the beginning. He took a few puffs on his cigar. "Right enough, Serov, right enough." He placed the cigar on the edge of the table. He watched the gray ash lengthen and fall to the floor.

"Yes, I was being naïve. You know, Serov, where women are concerned I lack discretion." He thought to add, and I lack trust in my friends. But he didn't want to embarrass Serov.

"Let's see now, where was I? About Szymanski's role in the plot. He knew enough from his years of exile to paint a pretty horrific picture of conditions at Tiumen. I admit he scared the hell out of me. Rudov must have notified the police chief, Novitsky. Told him I was suspected of being in touch with a convict. Who knows what else they made up? They could have invented a big conspiracy. If I had written a letter to Irina, I wouldn't be sitting here now. One thing I'm not sure of. Was Drenteln involved? Some evidence suggests he was. The only reason their little plan failed was this." Vasiliev waved the telegram in front of Serov. "Ivan checked on conditions in Tiumen, bless him. He got back to me quickly. Irina has been assigned as a nurse. You remember Letchik, the young medical student who was arrested with her? He was recruited right away by the warden to be a medical assistant. Brought Irina with him into the prison hospital. It's not paradise. But she's not in immediate danger. That gives us some time."

Serov accompanied Vasiliev's account with grunts and whistles. At the end he smacked his lips. "Vasili Vasilievich. We've been through somethin' like this once before. The boys in blue just don't like you."

"That's pretty clear, Serov. But I don't understand what's getting their back up now. What are they worried about?"

"They're not a forgettin' type. Not forgivin' either. They keep sayin' the same. You made it up, the part about one of them plottin' to kill the Tsar. They hate you."

"But there has to be something else. I have a hunch it has to do with what's happening here in Kiev. One good thing seems to have come out of it. Novitsky enjoyed seeing Rudov with mud on his face. He's even invited me to tea. Imagine! Before I forget, Serov. How would you like a new assignment? Following me, or rather following my tail."

"Not again! Just like Moscow. What's it this time, one of them amateurs or a professional?"

"Hard to say. I just caught a glimpse of him. But I would guess, since I spotted him, he's an amateur. With the Gendarmes you usually don't see them. Always two or three men working at the same time."

On his way to Police Headquarters Vasiliev stopped at the Hotel d'Europe to pick up messages. As soon as he entered the lobby Ruth rushed up to him, her face flushed. A jumble of words poured out of her. He couldn't make any sense out of what she was saying. He felt an impulse to shake her by the shoulders to stop her from babbling. But he was afraid to touch her. A figure appeared behind her. He recognized Dr. Margulies.

"Ruth, listen! You promised not to get so excited. Vasili Vasilievich, Ruth has had a nasty shock. We were in the hospital. Something happened there that I don't understand. I agreed to come with her, but I have to get back to surgery. Ruth, please get yourself under control." He took her hand and pressed it. Bowing to Vasiliev, he hurried out of the lobby.

"Come, let's sit over here out of the way. You can tell me what happened." She took his arm, pressing her breast against him.

"Inspector, I'm so sorry to have made a scene. I was just so happy to see you. Now I'm all right. I think I found out how you can trace the murderer. I even think I saw him in the hospital. Oh, I'm still babbling. Let me start with Rebecca, or better Aaron."

"Ruth, it might be easier if I asked you a few questions."

"No, Inspector, I'm going to get it right this time. Aaron was admitted to the Military Hospital to have an eye operation. Dr. Margulies arranged it. While he was lying in the admissions room, they brought in a woman who had been in an accident. She was wearing an amulet. It was an exact duplicate of the one the boys found near papa's body. Aaron told David who told Rebecca, my sister. Rebecca asked me to go to the hospital and find out as much as I could about this woman. Rebecca thought she might lead us to the murderer. I wanted to talk to you first, but Rebecca is a very stubborn girl. I've never been able to resist her when she asks me to do something. I went and found the woman. She's badly injured. She thought I was some kind of…I don't know what. A ghost? She told me her name was Vera Evgrafovna. The man who wore the other amulet, her husband, I guess, was named Stepan."

"You are sure of that?"

"Oh yes! She thought I was going to bring her to him. She must have been confused, maybe delirious. I should have asked her for her family name. But I was afraid she might be frightened by too many questions."

"You did the right thing."

Ruth smiled for the first time.

"Did she tell you where she lives?"

"No. I'm sorry." The smile faded. "I didn't think to ask. I'm afraid, Inspector. I should have come to you first, you know, for advice. But Rebecca wanted to do this by herself."

"Do you know why?"

Ruth bit her lip. She felt she could trust Vasiliev, but she hesitated to betray her sister's confidence.

"Rebecca has a passion for finding things out."

Vasiliev realized this line of inquiry was not going to get him very far.

"Please go on, Ruth. What else happened?"

"The worst thing happened after I left Vera's room. I ran into Dr. Margulies—I mean that wasn't the worst thing. My goodness, I'm all flustered. We were going to find Aaron when I saw him, I mean the tall thin man I told you about, the man who may have stolen the documents. He was coming up the stairwell in the hospital when he saw me. He turned around and ran. He must have recognized me. I was very frightened. I am so happy that Dr. Margulies was with me."

"Ruth, you've got to be careful! You're getting involved in something that's very dangerous. I'm going to ask you not to tell Rebecca what you found out. I'm afraid that she is not only headstrong, but also a bit reckless. I worry that she might try to go after the murderer by herself, or with David's help. Your sister may be very courageous and intelligent. But she is no match for a professional criminal. He's probably done time in prison, and won't hesitate to kill again. You've given me a good lead. Now let me follow it up. I don't want Rebecca competing with me. You need a professional detective to catch a professional killer. Do you understand? I'm going to get police protection for Vera just in case the tall thin man returns. He probably won't. But we can't take any chances. I don't think you should go back to the hospital." Vasiliev heard himself speaking to her as if she were a child. But she looked frightened and vulnerable.

Ruth nodded. "I understand. But I don't know how I can lie to Rebecca. She'll know right away that I'm not telling her the truth. If she sees Dr. Margulies, he'll tell her how frightened I was and then…"

"Listen, you can tell her that you found the woman and she told you her name. You can describe how badly she's injured. But you must *not* mention Stepan's name. Above all, say nothing about the appearance of the tall, thin man. As for Dr. Margulies, I'll make sure that he keeps quiet about it. Can you do this for me?"

The intensity of her gaze startled him. He wondered if at that moment his face also betrayed his thoughts. He felt drawn to her almost irresistibly. Ruth reached out and seized his arm. "I will promise you…" a slight pause that he would always remember… "whatever you wish!" she gasped.

Chapter
Thirty-Three

When Vasiliev arrived at police headquarters the following morning, Novitsky was signing letters. The Chief stood up when Vasiliev entered and walked around his desk to greet him.

"Congratulations, Vasili Vasilievich! Ah, you look puzzled. There is no mystery. Perhaps only a miracle. You have survived over two weeks in Kiev."

"How dangerous was it for me?"

"You may never know. Sit down, my good fellow. You've something to report?" Novitsky went back to his desk.

"I was on my way to see you when your message arrived."

"What a coincidence."

"More like a congruence."

"Ah, lovely! A man who appreciates words and can distinguish between close meanings. Do you write poetry, Vasili Vasilievich?"

"No, I only write about poets. You know how we detectives are—more critics than creators. The criminal is the artist."

"What a unique perspective." Novitsky rubbed his chin. He seemed to have reached the limit of his own cleverness. "So, a report," he said.

"First something else. An urgent matter. I need your help. There is a woman in the Military Hospital. The victim of a runaway cab accident, if it was an accident. She may have the key to the murder of Rabbi Meier. I'm convinced her life is in danger. Could you put a guard in the ward, immediately?"

"An urgent matter. I don't doubt you. But perhaps you could give me a few more details? Surely a few more minutes' delay won't matter."

"One detail should persuade you. The woman is linked to the murderer by the amulet of Siberian origin."

"Ah, the amulet! I have learned more since you first informed me about it."

"But you have never seen it."

"True, but Professor Antonovich has examined it carefully. A student brought an amulet to him with some story or other. Not very convincing. The student is known to have associations with radical circles. Antonovich took him to a colleague, a specialist in the ethnography of the Northern tribes. He identified it. Antonovich thought the incident was worth relating to me over one of our Friday lunches together. These are strange times. In addition to being a great archaeologist, Antonovich is a friend of mine. He is a reasonable man for a Ukrainian. You see, Vasili Vasilievich, there is a movement of Ukrainian nationalists who have been agitating for some kind of separation from Russia. But sensible men like Antonovich are willing to work with us, if we treat them decently. It's too complicated to go into right now. It takes me too far afield. But I have to educate you, you know."

Novitsky laughed, but was soon serious again. Every inch the professional policeman, thought Vasiliev.

"So, a guard you say. I can hardly spare a man, unless you think it's absolutely necessary. But of course you think it absolutely necessary. Or else you wouldn't have asked. I can assign a constable. But for how long?"

"I don't know—a few days perhaps. The woman is in bad shape, so we'll have to wait to question her. I have the feeling she knows a great deal."

"What has she told you so far?"

"That's what I have come to report. But first, Vasili Dementevich, please send over one of your men. The woman's name is Vera Evgrafovna. She is in Ward No. 19. The danger comes from a tall thin man. He was already seen looking for her."

"Good heavens, what a vague description. Tall and thin, but no measurements." He smiled again, then frowned, his thick eyebrows almost meeting, leaving Vasiliev to wonder at his quick mood-shifts. "Yes, well, all right!" Novitsky rang the silver bell and scribbled a note, which he handed to an orderly.

"I do worry about you, Vasili Vasilievich. This business about the amulet. Perhaps your source is also this radical student. No? And then there is Rudov's and Szymanski's clumsy attempt to involve you with a revolutionary convict. You cleverly evaded the trap. But they had grounds for setting it up. No? We have all heard of your unusual methods, Vasili Vasilievich. They have given good results in the past. But this is not Moscow, or Petersburg. Kiev is a different place altogether."

"Perhaps I should have consulted you from the beginning."

Novitsky cocked his head and shook his finger at Vasiliev. "There is no need for repentance; I am not a priest. Let me be frank. I am a Russian, a loyal servant of the Tsar. But I try to understand local politics. Take this matter of the Ukrainians and their language. I'm not convinced we should continue to forbid the publications in Ukrainian. To forbid subversive literature is a duty. But outlaw a language? I obey. I order publishing houses to close down. When I do it, I get a gnawing feeling in my gut. In the villages everyone speaks Ukrainian. And every year more villagers come into Kiev. Let me tell you, they don't start speaking Russian. They want to read in their own language. If we don't let them do it legally, they'll read illegal propaganda. Not an ideal situation.

"Why do I tell you this? Because I want you to be aware of the many lines that get entangled here in Kiev. The Ukrainians have their lines, the Jews theirs, the Poles theirs and we Russians have our own. You must never lose track of any one of them. You want to get to the bottom of a massive crime, the pogroms. You want to solve the murder of an individual. To do this you will have to tap into all the lines. Let me show you something."

Novitsky got up from his desk and moved to the wall, where a large map of the Ukrainian provinces was displayed. Vasiliev followed him. "So, what do you think of my skill as a cartographer?"

Vasiliev studied the map. What he saw were different colored threads tied to pins scattered throughout several provinces.

"What do you make of it? Do you see a pattern to the threads?" Novitsky rubbed his chin again.

"You have to explain the significance of the colors. Perhaps then."

"Of course. The green pins represent the towns and villages

where the pogroms began from April 16 to April 21. The green threads show the links between these places. So you see that there are 39 green pins and the threads that link them are all to the south of us, in Kherson province, except for one in Bessarabia. Then a period of calm, from April 21 to April 26. No riots reported. The red pins show where there were renewed outbreaks from April 26 to April 30. Notice how the riots continue in Kherson. Mainly in one district. They cross over into Kiev province for the first time on April 26, and appear in Chernigov as well. You see how the red pins and threads make a cluster? On May 1 there is another jump to Ekaterinoslav—these are represented by yellow pins and threads— while Kherson remains troubled. But Kiev province is quiet on May first, second and third. Then a rash of outbreaks in our province on May fourth. They end abruptly on the same day. This is indicated by the white pins and threads. Nothing has happened in the few days since then. But I fear things will spread again. Look here. I have a reserve of brown pins and threads just in case. Well what do you think? I ask you again. Do you see a pattern?" Novitsky stepped back, reminding Vasiliev of an artist contemplating the finishing touches to an all but completed canvas.

"I understand now. An ingenious way of portraying things, Vasili Dementevich! You seem to have found some regularities. But do they add up to a pattern, and does the pattern suggest a conspiracy?"

Novitsky took another step back and squinted. He seemed not to have heard Vasiliev. "You see, these are only the main currents, so to speak. There are eddies and cross-currents so to speak." He paused and sighed. "Still, I'll be damned if I can explain what it all means."

"Perhaps you are trying to fit it all into a single pattern. There may be spontaneous elements mixed in with—what shall we call it—planning?"

"What do you mean?"

"Let's look at it this way. Assume, for the moment, that these riots are clues. Each set of colored threads represents a step leading to a premeditated murder. You know as well as I that no matter how carefully a crime is planned, something unexpected is bound to occur. The more elaborate the plan, the greater the chance of something going wrong. Or look at it another way. A crime does not happen in a vacuum. Life goes on around it. People who are not implicated are somehow drawn into the investigation. Their lives are exposed often with surprising results."

"All that is true. But I don't see what that has to do with all this." Novitsky waved at the map.

"Suppose that the pogroms this year broke out spontaneously in these two districts of Kherson. Here look at your map. It's happened before in Russia. Remember Odessa in '71? In the past the pogroms were localized. Now there's a difference. They spread like the plague. Why and how do they move out of Kherson? Why do they crop up again, first in Kiev? The pogroms may not have been planned at the outset. But what if a plan was inserted *after* they had broken out? And what if this plan was confined to one or two places, like Kiev? The plan is carried through, but the riots don't stop. Instead, they spread spontaneously once again to other provinces. Perhaps they have nothing to do with the planned riots in Kiev. You see my meaning. This might explain why the pogroms in Kiev shut down so quickly while they continued to rage elsewhere."

Novitsky turned from the map. "My God, I hadn't thought of it!"

"Now, let's look at it from another angle. Assume for the sake of argument that someone, or a group of men, saw an opportunity to incite a pogrom in Kiev as if it were a natural result of what was happening in Kherson. But they were very clever. They decided to spread the riots outside Kiev in order to disguise their conspiracy in Kiev. As a result, the pogroms in Kiev look no different than those in any of the other cities. Can you see anything in your data that would confirm this hypothesis?"

Novitsky appeared stunned for a moment. Then he rushed to his desk, rummaged in a drawer, and pulled out a sheaf of papers. He kept muttering to himself, turning the pages so rapidly that several of them flew off the desk and fell to the floor. He extracted a chart and slammed it down on the desk. "See here! At the same time that the riots began in Kiev, a whole series broke out in forty-eight villages in a circle around the city. Then three days after we suppressed the Kiev riot, disturbances broke out along a quadrilateral formed by four rail lines. Just a moment, there is more! He pulled out another drawer, but failed to find what he wanted. He frantically rang the silver bell. An orderly appeared immediately.

"Where are the statistics on the arrested rioters?"

"They're in the materials we prepared for Count Kutaisov, Your Honor."

"Well get them for me, at once!" Novitsky shouted. The orderly went white. "They may have been dispatched already." He could barely get the words out of his mouth.

Novitsky broke into a series of curses. The orderly began to tremble like a pine swaying in a high wind. Vasiliev was afraid he might break apart somewhere between his knees and his ankles.

"Get them back, and I don't care how you do it!" The orderly turned and fled.

Chapter Thirty-Four

The next evening David returned to Kaniever's. He could hardly believe it was the same place. Three musicians were playing sentimental Cossack melodies on stringed instruments the likes of which he had never seen before. There were no women in the room, no old men hunched over their soup bowls. Most of the tables were occupied by one or two men, all of whom looked to David like horse thieves, with their shaved heads and long drooping moustaches. They certainly did not look like Jews—more like characters out of Gogol's *Taras Bulba*. Kaniever himself came over to David's table and set down in front of him a bowl of sorrel *shchav* with green garlic. Although no one looked at him, David felt like a freak in a circus side-show. Kaniever discouraged new customers who appeared at the door, waving at the tables to indicate that the place was full. There were empty seats, but newcomers quickly got the message. Private business was going to be transacted. There was no room for kibitzers. Kaniever cleared away David's empty bowl and set a bottle of vodka on the table with two glasses. A few moments later a man entered the room, making straight for David's table. He stood for a moment looking down at him, and then pulled out a chair. He poured two glasses of vodka, and raised his in a silent toast. David swallowed, bringing tears to his eyes. For a moment the man's face seemed to dissolve in front of him. David focused on his high forehead and thick mane of silver hair.

"So, Mendel vouched for you. That means a lot," the man said, pouring another glass. David shook his head. The man shrugged. "Not very sociable are you?" he said, waving the bottle in front of David's face.

"Sorry, no insult intended. I'm just not used to it. Students can't afford vodka."

"One good reason not to be a student." The man tossed back a glass and filled it again.

"I don't give out free information. Since you have no money, it will have to be a favor. Are you a trader."

"What do you want?"

"I haven't decided yet. I'll let you know."

"I don't like signing a blank promissory note."

"A man after my own heart. Don't worry, I promised Mendel I wouldn't sweat you. It may just be a piece of information like the one I give you. Agreed?"

David nodded, feeling the effect of the vodka. He could always refuse, he thought. Then he looked around the room at the men seated at all the tables. He realized that it would not be easy to refuse.

The musicians struck up a gypsy melody and someone began to sing quietly. In David's muddled head it sounded like a cantor's voice.

"Tell me what you want to know," the man said. David glanced at the bottle. It was more than half empty. He felt his fingers close over the top of his glass. The music seemed louder.

"I'm looking for a man who was arrested in 1871 and sentenced to ten years in Siberia. He recently returned to Kiev. He wore an amulet from a native tribe around his neck. He did not like Jews."

"Now there's a picture for you! You're a real Rembrandt, you are."

"Sorry, I know it isn't much."

"Well, well. Let's see. Ten years ago. I remember being alive. What else?" The man slowly turned his head and surveyed the room as if, David thought, he could read a message in the faces of the men who sat staring into space. "Ten years," he repeated. David watched the glass fill up and empty again. A sense of despondency crept over him. This was not a good idea. What could a drunken horse thief know or remember? Of course that Rembrandt business did surprise him. But there were cheap prints of European painters for sale in the markets. Perhaps this man had his walls plastered with old masters. Anything was possible with a Jewish horse thief.

The man folded his arms and chuckled. "You really don't think I can help you, do you? It's all a waste of time. A thief full of booze. Well, you're wrong." The man reached over and seized David's arm with ferocious strength. "Listen, student, ten years ago a tough guy dressed up like a domino at a costume ball in the Merchant's Club shot a mark who was into in some shady business. Didn't kill him. They caught the shooter and gave him ten years. He got back a few months ago. His name was Stepan Tikhonov. Yeah, he wore that funny thing around his neck. Said it had some magic. Crazy. Kept cursing the Jews. I heard he got stabbed last week."

"Stabbed! You mean he's dead?"

"Somethin' like that."

"Do you know anything about a woman, maybe his wife?"

"Hey, I was no friend of the family." The man guffawed. Here and there around the room heads moved. The musicians skipped a beat. "Naw, his women I didn't know."

"Who stabbed him?"

"God Almighty, even if I knew I'd sure as hell not let you in on it." The man looked at the empty bottle. "One bottle is the limit. You've got what you wanted, a name." The man got up and walked out of the tavern. He was followed one by one by the rest of the customers. The musicians played a lively march. When the last man had left, the musicians stopped playing. Kaniever offered them a glass. They drank quickly and scurried out, carrying their instruments under their arms. David was left alone. Then the doors opened and a new crowd began to file in, laughing and scolding Kaniever for keeping them waiting. He smiled good-naturedly and held up his hands as if to say, what can I do? David signaled to him for the bill. Kaniever came over and handed him dirty piece of paper with a number scrawled on it. "And the vodka?" David asked, terrified that he did not have enough money. "Mendel's contribution. He said to tell you you're rapidly acquiring debt."

The next morning David met Rebecca in the Botanical Gardens. A week of cloudless skies had forced open the cherry and acacia blossoms. David gulped down the perfumed air, hoping to relieve the pounding in his head. He related everything that had happened at Kaniever's. When he told her that Stepan had been killed, David was shocked to hear her mutter a curse. He had never heard her use coarse language before. "So, he's escaped justice," she added. "But that's not the end of it."

"He's dead, Rebecca. That's as good an end as you can get."

She turned on him. "No, David, don't you see? Stepan was a hired killer. The incident ten years ago—he tried to shoot a man over a business deal. Stepan wasn't a businessman—he was a thug. Now ten years later, he's back and hired again, maybe by the same man. Who knows? But we're going to find out. This is just the beginning."

They entered an *allée* where the cherry blossoms hung thickly. One brushed against David's cheek as he passed. He was surprised at how soft it felt. He glanced at Rebecca. Her brow was furrowed, and for an instant she looked almost ugly. He shook off his impression.

"What if you find the person who hired Stepan, what then?"

"It depends, possibly render revolutionary justice."

"You promised me a treatise on terror. Now's the time, Rebecca. I want to know how you can justify this revolutionary justice. If it means assassination, then how do you justify it?"

"The attack against father was a political act. The symbolism of the wounds makes that clear. This was not a spontaneous outbreak of thuggish violence. It was planned for a purpose and carried out by a professional killer." Her eyes were blazing now.

"You've committed yourself to forming a defense group, right?"

"Yes, defense, meaning we protect ourselves against attack, but we do not seek revenge."

"A fine line, David. You are drawing a fine line. For us Jews revenge may be the only way to protect ourselves against future attacks. Pogroms are counter-revolutionary acts. They are attempts to deflect popular anger from the autocracy to the Jews. We must strike back."

David was about to reply when he saw a familiar figure coming down the hill toward them.

"Look at her!" Rebecca exclaimed. "Just like a Dresden china doll." David could not tell whether this was meant as a compliment or a criticism. But he thought the comparison was apt. A small hat with a short black veil perched on Ruth's elaborate coiffure.

She wore a white blouse with lace cuffs and a long black skirt with matching low-heel pumps. She waved gaily at them. Her silver bracelets tinkled like a bird call.

"Doesn't she make a great conspirator?" muttered Rebecca.

"Well, no one would suspect her, that's for sure."

The sisters embraced hurriedly.

"What's for sure?" asked Ruth.

"Nothing," said Rebecca, "So, keep us in suspense."

Ruth blushed and blurted out her story. She had rehearsed it carefully in hopes of forestalling any questions from Rebecca and getting through the ordeal as fast as possible. She looked into David's soft brown eyes as much as she dared, avoiding Rebecca's penetrating gaze that always seemed to bore into her soul.

David felt sorry for her. She looked like a student hauled up in front of class to recite the lesson of the day. He was relieved to see her relax when Rebecca told her what he had found out at Kaniever's. But he was surprised that Rebecca did not tell her the name of the killer or his fate.

Ruth tried to concentrate on what Rebecca was saying, but she kept worrying that she was not doing the right thing. She wanted to help Vasiliev and save her sister from some folly that she feared was in the making. But she lost her courage in the face of Rebecca's fierce look. She did not ask any of the questions she had prepared, a lapse she later regretted deeply.

"That was good work," said David. He felt the need to diffuse the tension between them. It was always like that when the two sisters discussed anything serious. He sometimes thought of them as two antagonistic female spirits. Sometimes he wondered why he had fallen in love with Rebecca, who could be hard and implacable. He worried too that his choice was fraught with tragedy. Or was he taking Russian literature for life? All those strong women with no men to match them. "You found her", he continued, "learned her name, and gained her confidence. That's all we could expect."

"What now?" Ruth asked, ashamed at hearing how timid she sounded.

"We don't know," said Rebecca as they reached the end of the winding path and turned around. David was not surprised by her answer. Evidently, Ruth was still not to be trusted. "Perhaps you should visit Vera again and find out her address. Now that you know that her husband was killed, you can ask if she suspects anyone." Ruth nodded, and her little veil quivered coquettishly.

Chapter
Thirty-Five

Iakov Galperin was in a feverish state. For a week he felt as though he had fallen seriously ill; perhaps it was typhus? He would wake up in the morning bathed in sweat, remembering confused dreams. The small mirror above his sink reflected the face of a dying man; it was the same haggard look he had seen on his father's face the day he had returned from work, lain down on the divan, and expired. Now Iakov was alone and tortured by the weight of an intolerable burden. He cursed himself for having failed to carry out his promise to Rabbi Meier. His work at the Southwest Railroad Depot no longer absorbed him, as it had in the past. He could not confide in anyone. He had promised the Rabbi complete secrecy, and now he found himself in a moral dilemma. Didn't his duty to the Rabbi's memory outweigh the solemn promise? Every day another document passed into his hands that he knew he should copy for the Rabbi. But Rabbi Meier was no more. For whom could he continue this work? He had only a vague idea of his part in a larger scheme. The Rabbi told him very little. Once he met another clerk in the corridor of the Rabbi's house, and he sensed that they were there for the same purpose. But he hurried away and did not speak to the man. Now he wished he had. Should he go back to the Rabbi's house? What would the daughter, Ruth, think of him? She had always been kind, but that was her way. What about going to Reb Ben-Zion? The trouble was that he was not a man of the world. It seemed to Iakov that every day he went over the same ground in his mind and could not reach a decision. His boss began to comment on errors in his work. He had bought a bottle of whiskey for the first time in his life, and he poured a small glass as soon as he closed the door behind him at night. He found himself praying more intensely, almost angrily, demanding that God show him the way. He was waiting for a sign.

He began daily visits to the Jewish cemetery where his father and Rabbi Meier were buried. It was a long trip to the Ninth District. He walked from grave to grave, studying the stone markers, lit by the morning sun as it rose over the hill of St. Andrei. On Saturday he slept late and arrived at the cemetery when the sun was high in a cloudless sky, celebrating a perfect day for the Sabbath. As he stood by his father's grave, he glanced across the crowd of headstones in the direction of the Rabbi's resting place. He thought he saw a specter, a black figure standing at the exact place where he had so often knelt in prayer. For a moment he felt a wave of fear. Then the figure moved, and he recognized the daughter, Ruth. Was this a sign? He was not sure. She turned and began to leave. He fell into step behind her. When she came to the gate she turned again, and shaded her eyes from the glare of the sun. He kept walking toward her in a daze. She waited until he drew near and then raised her arm in a greeting. He swept off his cap and hurried up to her.

The Jewish Cemetery

"Iakov Iakovlevich! How good to see you. Are you mourning a relative? May God be merciful."

In Iakov's eyes she never looked more beautiful. It was more than that, he felt. Her beauty had not made her haughty, as it did so many women. He felt enveloped by her kindness.

Ruth Moiseevna, good morning. Yes, I come to visit my father, but also your dear father." He heard the words slip through his lips, as though he had no control over them.

He noticed that she did not look surprised, but murmured some words of appreciation. What should he say next?

Ruth was shocked by his appearance. She remembered how neatly he used to dress. His hair was always carefully brushed back and parted in the middle, his face clean shaven. Now he appeared to be ill, or perhaps suffering some deep spiritual wound. She invited him to tea. "I have a cab, and we can be home in a few moments. You haven't visited us in a while."

Seated across from her in the room that was so familiar, he felt a sense of well-being for the first time in weeks.

"Have you been ill?" she asked handing him a plate of honey cookies.

He interpreted her words as something more than a polite inquiry. Her expression told him she must be genuinely concerned.

"Ruth Moiseevna, you are so kind…I'm…my life has become a torture," he blurted out. Her eyebrows shot up. "What has happened? Oh, you can confide in me."

"Please, your father, God rest his soul, was a great man. I wanted to help him. He thought I could…." Iakov stopped, realizing that he was not making sense. He coughed and moved to the edge of his chair. "My story is long and begins a year ago. No, actually even before that. Ever since I first heard the Rabbi deliver a sermon. What a day that was! What eloquence! But you know that wasn't the main thing. I come from a shtetl in Podolia. The rabbis are holy men, but old-fashioned. Your father spoke to us of the problems of our world. I had a little education, and here was a man of learning who understood our needs. He spoke about corruption and temptation, the need to take a stand for justice in this world. He spoke that first time of Count Potocki of Vilna who was burned at the stake on Shavuoth for converting to Judaism, and how to this day the main synagogue in Vilna offers a memorial prayer. He said the righteous convert is a model for us. The Almighty offered the Torah to many nations, but they all refused its six hundred and thirteen precepts all but the truly righteous few, the forefathers of Judaism, and every generation there are such a few. Then, you must believe me; he spoke of the reading of the Book of Ruth. Yes, Ruth the convert must have been one of the descendents of those who wanted to receive the Torah." Tears glistened in Iakov's eyes.

"It is not enough to be born a Jew, I thought. You must prove yourself worthy of the Torah. But how? The Rabbi's sermons kindled an idea. To seek to render justice wherever injustice is to be found."

A soft knock on the door startled Iakov. He sat back in his chair, feeling the wooden crossbar dig into his spine. Reb Ben-Zion's head appeared. "Ruth, a petitioner begs…"

"Please, Reb Ezra, you must take care of it. This is important."

The head vanished and Iakov leaned forward again. "Can they hear us?" he whispered.

Ruth smiled. "The doors are made of solid oak. Father believed every room should be a sanctuary."

"Ah, a sanctuary. Yes, that's good. Rabbi Meier once said 'justice like the truth needs a sanctuary.' So how could a lowly clerk like myself render justice? Many documents cross my desk. I began to read them more carefully, looking for errors. For out of error can come injustice. I noticed that the figures did not always add up. There were errors, but of such magnitude that they could only mean one thing. How can I explain it simply? The reports to the directors of the company did not correspond to the individual receipts. So, cheating was going on. I mentioned the problem to my superior. He said he would make corrections. But one day when he was sick and absent I had to copy one of his reports; he had not made the corrections. I was frightened. I came to the Rabbi and told him my fears. He asked me if there was anyone in the office I could trust. I said no one. He thought a long time, and then asked me if I would be willing to make copies of the errors. I agreed. I made copies and passed on the documents to him. He said I was not the only one to come to him. He would be a repository of errors, he said and then when there was a sufficient collection he would turn them over to a trusted advocate, a Jew, who would render justice but would protect all of us. I came to him at night once a month. And one time I remember meeting a clerk in the corridor of your house, a man from the Kievan office of the Ministry of Finance. I had seen him at Saturday services. We glanced at one another but said nothing, and went our separate ways."

So *these* were the documents, Ruth thought. Had someone killed for them? She forced herself to stay calm.

"You were right to tell me, Iakov Iakovlevich. Father would have approved. You are carrying on his work. Now what shall we do? First, I must ask you whether you have copies of the documents you gave to father."

"No. The Rabbi said it was too dangerous for me to keep them."

"But you remember some of the details?"

"Of course."

"Would you be willing to tell what you know to another trustworthy person?"

"Who would that be?" Ruth noticed how he stiffened in his chair, a hunted look in his face.

"Someone who can render justice."

"Ruth Moiseevna, I am not a brave man. I trusted Rabbi Meier. I trust you. But there ends my trust. When a Jew is right he gets a beating."

Ruth felt at sea. How would papa have reassured him? She doubted that Iakov would talk freely to a policeman, and a goy at that, even though Vasiliev was a just man. Should she tell Rebecca about the documents? She felt as though some alien spirit had settled in her head and was bombarding her with questions that she could not answer.

"I understand. You were right to come to me." She knew she was repeating herself, to gain time. "Yes, you are a righteous man. Now, we know something important. We know there are errors; there is corruption. We know where to look. So I must find a trustworthy person who can conduct an independent investigation, who can find the original documents. But I need one more bit of information, Iakov Iakovlevich. What is your department in the Southwest Railroad Company?"

Iakov told her but begged her not to mention his name.

When Iakov left, Rebecca called for Reb Ben-Zion. "Now I will see the petitioner." She returned to the divan and suddenly remembered the eulogy spoken over her father's grave: "The crown is fallen from our head: woe unto us, we have sinned."

Chapter Thirty-Six

Vasiliev put down the book of poetry. How many times had he sought comfort in Nekrasov. It was always the same. He had to admit the man was not a great poet. But there were verses that were sublime. *Who Can Live Well in Russia?* was a bad poem. Vasiliev was quick to admit it. Except for the last part. Knowing it by heart, he hardly needed to read it, and a passage near the end fit his mood.

Wretched art thou,
Abundant art thou,
Mighty art thou,
Feeble art thou,
O Mother Russia!

He recognized the symptoms. He remembered why he had gone into the regular police. Because he naively believed in the radical difference between good and evil. But he had been forced to get involved in political crimes, and there the differences were blurred. He had come to admire the spirit and talents of the young, who had turned against the government in the name of justice, against the law and order he had sworn to protect. And the defenders of that law and order had all too often turned out to be corrupt and morally despicable. Mother Russia, torn between her dark twins. Which side would he finally come down on? He laid aside the book and turned to his files. Nekrasov was not going to help him answer any of his questions.

He always used to think there would be a moment when a case broke open. Almost like a revelation. The veil would fall, the curtain would part. He had a dozen metaphors for the moment of truth when everything would become clear. But it never worked out that way. He was coming round to another view. Perhaps there were hermetically sealed cases, lacking any connection with the wider world. But this was not one of them. Perhaps there would always be loose ends, unresolved questions of motive and, who knew, in the end justice denied. That was the trouble with the accounts of the great detectives like Holmes and Gaboriau. At the end they explained everything. Or their chroniclers did. He often wondered what the detectives themselves thought. There were hints in Holmes's reaction to Watson's stories that he was not pleased. It was all too neat. And Holmes for all his ratiocination was also a great guesser.

People came to decisions without anyone being able to explain why. He had realized long ago that it was impossible to retrace every step leading to a crime. To say nothing of getting inside the criminal's mind. He knew he would not be able to restore the whole of a crime, any more than a historian could restore the whole of the past. Mysteries were solved, but not all of them. Criminals were caught, but not all of them. Life was like that. Knots remained tied and connections were missed. He would have to guess at what happened, and in many instances he would never know if his guesses were right or not. And there were times when you solved the mystery but did not catch the criminal. Or, he remembered bitterly, when it was more important to prevent the crime than to solve the mystery behind it. That had been the case with the assassination of the Tsar. He had uncovered the conspiracy, identified the conspirators, pursued them, and finally destroyed them. But it had been too late to save the life of the Tsar. His tasks in Kiev were different. He might find the man who ordered the murder and bring him to justice. But behind the killing of Rabbi Meier loomed the terrible crime of the pogroms. It was unsolvable. That, he knew, was the source of his frustration. The motivations of too many people were involved. He would construct a narrative in the form of a report. But Kutaisov, perhaps others too, would reach different conclusions. Who was to judge which one would prove to be correct? No one could fill in all the gaps. He knew in his heart that the ministers would choose to believe what suited their purposes. He had never wanted to get involved in the political game. Now he was in it, again, up to his neck. He thought of the Stanislas medal in his desk drawer. There was room there for others like it.

He sat down at the wooden table and began to jot down a few notes. Would a few more interviews lead him the right way? He had to believe they would.

When Serov returned he noticed Nekrasov's poetry lying next to the files. He liked this about Vasiliev. As for himself, poetry did not stir him, although he liked song. He thought poetry might have the same effect on Vasiliev. Take his mind somewhere else. A better place certainly. But Serov had always resigned himself to the feeling that it was bound to be a short trip.

Vasiliev immediately caught the look of discouragement on Serov's face. "The arm is a real curse," were Serov's first words. "And it's summer too. No hidin' it under a cloak or such." Vasiliev pushed the book to the end of the table, sat back, and folded his arms. He was prepared to wait until Serov settled down, "shake himself out," as Serov liked to put it, as if he were a hunting dog coming in out of a summer downpour. In Serov's case it took the form of grumbling, mumbling and rambling. What he said was not exactly incoherent, Vasiliev had come to realize over the years, but disconnected. If you waited patiently and followed his line of thought instead of your own, he made good sense and often made a difference in a case. Just like when he discovered dirt leaking out of a cheese cart in St. Petersburg. It led them to the mine planted under Sadovaya Street to blow up the Tsar.

"Your man is very good, the one followin' you. But he's no professional." Serov was playing with the charcoal at the base of the samovar. "He was behind you all the way to the Rabbi's house and back. Too bad! Now our safe house isn't safe, no longer. Why did you let 'em do it?" Serov muttered as if to himself. "Then he took off for his own digs. A third rate boardin' house. Smart. He must have picked me up. You see, here am I strollin' along with my arm in a cast. Now, Vasili Vasilievich, I ask you in all humility, how many people in Kiev are walkin' around with an arm in a cast. And it is white! White! Like a flag. Ah, I've had the sense to get a black sling.

But there's no coverin' up the cast. Does he see me or not? Maybe he's been told to keep clear of the puppeteer, the man holdin' the strings. So he goes into this boardin' house and comes out after a time, goes to the local post office and mails somethin'. Now followin' your method, Vasili Vasilievich, we can guess what's in the letter. But I'm not in uniform and can't rush in to the postmaster and ask to see the letter. So, the report goes to the puppeteer. And here we're no wiser for all of it."

Serov handed Vasiliev a glass of tea, without looking at him.

"Good!" said Vasiliev.

"Good?" Serov repeated in a tone Vasiliev knew all too well.

"Look at it this way, Sergeant. The puppeteer, as you call him, thinks he knows where we have disappeared. Now we'll disappear again, and when we reappear he'll be taken off guard."

"So—Queen's gambit," said Serov.

"A move you avoid."

"Too risky."

"Only on a chessboard."

Serov reflected that Vasiliev was better at solving the real problems of life than he was. His only revenge was Ruy Lopez.

Vasiliev left Serov for the Hotel d'Europe. He picked up a note from Ruth, written in a neat schoolgirl's hand, and took a cab to her house. When he entered the library, Reb Ben-Zion rose to greet him. Vasiliev did not know whether to be amused or angry at having a chaperone. Was Ruth protecting herself against her own feelings? He did not consider himself a dangerous character, but perhaps he was in her eyes, sheltered as she had been. That must be it, he concluded. He tried to remember whether he had given her any cause for offense. Nothing came to mind. But perhaps he had given something away by the way he looked at her.

Ruth was seated behind the Rabbi's desk, concealing the lower half of her full figure. Was this also calculated to discourage his interest in her as a woman? Vasiliev appraised the rest of her. She was dressed modestly, even primly. But no dress, Vasiliev mused, perhaps not even a sackcloth one, could conceal all her feminine charms. Damn it! Vasiliev silently cursed. Being aroused by a rabbi's daughter is absurd. Just as suddenly he wondered what difference that made. It sounded in his head like a stupid anti-Semitic remark.

Ruth told him about her meeting with Iakov Iakovlevich. While he listened, he decided to stop trying to read meaning into her every move and expression. He had always been suspicious of detectives who over-interpreted.

Vasiliev was annoyed that Ruth refused to divulge the name of her source. "More anonymous tips," he growled, glaring at Ben-Zion as if he were to blame. "All right, I'll find him no matter what." He was startled at his own vehemence. He saw immediately that he had upset her. What was he snapping at her for? Was she always going to have this effect on him?

"Inspector, you must understand that the Jews are terrified. They cannot even trust the police. I know you are sympathetic to us. Others in authority are not. So please accept what we can offer you within the limits we have to set."

Vasiliev apologized. "Ruth, everything you have told me is very important. It's the beginning of a trail. Up to now we had nothing. But now I need more information. You've brought us close, but I need more, d'you understand?" He watched her expression change. She dabbed her eyes with a handkerchief and turned her smile on him with full force.

Vasiliev tore his eyes away and faced Ben-Zion. "I've learned that the Holy Brotherhood is made up of high ranking men of good character. From what I know they wouldn't do anything to violate the law, to say nothing of getting involved in murderous plots."

Ben-Zion shifted uncomfortably in his chair. "Inspector, the situation is more complicated. Yes, fine men like Witte are members. So, I hear, is Tchaikovsky. But we have been able to place one of our people in the Brotherhood. Do not ask me how we have done this. He tells us that the Brotherhood has been infiltrated by unsavory elements. Even Witte is disturbed by this. Let me tell you a story. I have it on good authority that an agent of the Brotherhood was sent to Paris to assassinate Gartman, the dynamiter. You must know that he was the man behind the bombing of the imperial train on the Moscow-Kursk line several years ago. I do not know what happened in Paris. But the point is clear. I'm afraid there may be people in the Brotherhood who are using it for personal reasons. Such a person may have been involved…"he hesitated and glanced at Ruth…"in the case you are investigating. This does not contradict what Ruth has learned."

Vasiliev recalled Novitsky's words: 'the Jews have their lines, the Poles theirs, and the Ukrainians as well.' "You're saying that a member of the Holy Brotherhood, one of these unsavory elements as you call them, may have been the murderer, or more probably hired a murderer under the cover of the Brotherhood, that he left a telltale mark, and that his motive was to hide corruption of some sort in the Southwest Railroad."

"It's possible. Listen, Vasili Vasilievich, the Holy Brotherhood is organized on conspiratorial principles. Perhaps they've learned something from the revolutionaries of the People's Will. The Brotherhood is made up of groups of five, none of whom know the members of any other group except for the regional chief. I have heard that the chief in Kiev is Witte. But this doesn't necessarily mean he is responsible for everything that is done in its name. All it needs is one corrupt group of five. Such a group might not even belong to the Kiev organization. God forbid that Russia is becoming a land of secret societies, each one determined to destroy the other. It would be God's terrible vengeance for our sins."

Vasiliev was tempted for a moment to give his own opinion about Russia's sins. But he was not sure he should share it with Ben-Zion and Ruth. They had enough to worry about. But he might give them some encouragement about the future. There was little enough of that around since the death of Alexander II.

"Listen, my friends, Russia's salvation will only come with a constitution." Vasiliev was surprised to hear the words tumble out of him. But this was another bond with Irina. It had been her dream too. She had been too impatient, perhaps, and she had paid a terrible price.

"Yes, I believed in the reforms. We had come so close. You see, Tsar Alexander Nikolaevich..."

"Of blessed memory," Ben-Zion interrupted.

"Yes, of blessed memory. Alexander Nikolaevich had just signed a document, hours before his assassination that would have been a first step. Only a first step, but it would have created a Consultative Assembly. If he had lived, he could have rallied the public behind him. It was a gesture, really more than that—a sign of trust in the best people. It was his way of defeating the terror. Now what can I say? The new Tsar seems to have given up this modest dream."

Ben-Zion stared at him in astonishment. For a policeman to express doubts about the Tsar! He did not expect this even from Vasiliev. Ruth's gaze never left Vasiliev's face. Not since she last heard her father's service had she felt so mesmerized. Her expression encouraged Vasiliev to believe that he was the one casting a spell for a change.

Ben-Zion rose to his feet and embraced Vasiliev. "Would that Russia spoke with your voice!"

"May God's blessing go with you," Ruth murmured.

Vasiliev bowed himself out. As he walked down the path to the street he thought about what he had said. At least for the moment politics, which he disliked, had cooled his desire, which he feared.

Chapter
Thirty-Seven

Maria Alexandrovna's invitation came at a good time. Vasiliev felt the need for a diversion from murder and riot. It was to be a private performance of Slavic choral music. Close by too, in Mezer's building on Kreshchatik, just down the street from his hotel. Serov had gone off to find another safe room. Vasiliev enjoyed watching the strollers, who didn't seem to have a care in the world. He wondered if Muscovites were just gloomy by nature. Or were their faces hardened by the cruel winters? He drew in deep breaths of warm air filled with the scent of acacias. A full moon lorded over a sky empty of clouds. For the first time since he arrived in Kiev three weeks ago, he felt a sense of pleasurable anticipation. He climbed the stairs to Apartment 12. A young woman in Ukrainian national costume handed him a program written in the beautiful script of a copyist. Before he had a chance to glance at it, Maria Alexandrovna was at his side.

"Do you know Lysenko's music? Probably not. We have time before the concert begins. Come over here and have a glass of wine. He has a lovely lyrical style. He's done more than anyone to popularize Ukrainian folk songs. But that has landed him in some difficulty, especially with my husband."

"Alexander Romanovich doesn't like lyricism?"

"Oh, Vasili, you will joke at your own funeral! It's his lyrics, not his lyricism that the Governor-General and the censors don't like. You've heard all about the fuss over Ukrainian nationalism. When Lysenko published those two volumes of songs there was no problem. Now they're carping over the third. It's hard to believe.

But they discovered some orthographic changes from the standard Russian. They think it's subversive."

"Sounds like a quarrel from the seventeenth century."

"Exactly! It reminded me too of the dispute with the Old Believers, when different spellings of Jesus' name could lead to exile and worse. But here is Novitsky. He can explain all the politics. I have to check backstage. A problem with the costumes. Oh, by the way, I discovered something else about Captain Rudov. My ladies, you know. It seems he is an inveterate gambler. He's lost heavily in recent months."

Maria Alexandrovna waved to Novitsky who was leaning against a pillar, sizing up the audience. He was not in uniform.

"I feel out of place, Vasili Dementevich, wearing the only uniform in the room."

"Yes, well, *I* shouldn't even be here. But I love this music. Wonderful young singers! I can always explain my presence as a form of surveillance."

"What are you suppose to be surveying?"

Novitsky pointed to the audience. "Right now, *they* are surveying *us*. Let's sit down. At least we can look as if we came here to hear the music. We'll talk at intermission."

Lysensko led a mixed choir in a group of Ukrainian folk songs. Then he played several of his own piano compositions. The music had a freshness and charm that surprised Vasiliev. What did I expect? he thought. Imitations of primitive Little Russian chants?

"Let's go outside for a smoke. Cigar, Vasiliev? Wonderful musicians, aren't they? All students or amateurs. They'll do anything for Lysenko. He is the kindest of men. What a mix-up life is. Here's a real patriot. During the troubles in the Balkans he organized two Slavic Concerts in Kiev. They performed Czech and Serbian patriotic songs. Those days everyone was for the Serbs against the Turks. We were all Slavic brothers, eh? You were in the Turkish war, Vasiliev. You felt it. Why the stupidity of banning the Ukrainian language? Russia loses the chance to unify all the Slavs of the Empire. And now they're thinking of censoring the third volume of folk songs. Did Maria Alexandrovna tell you? Yes, well, I know the censor. Even *he* says we shouldn't prohibit them. It will just cause us more trouble in the future." Novitsky stamped out his half-smoked cigar. "So, here I am, the chief of police, attending a subversive gathering. You saw the youngsters singing. Yes, let them sing for God's sake. Or else in five years they'll be shouting revolutionary slogans. And in Ukrainian!"

"Vasili Dementevich, I understand. I feel the same way. But let me change the subject. Or maybe it's part of the same subject. You were going to find out something for me, remember?"

"Yes, yes. It turns out—yes, the same subject, I see your point— well, it turns out that the rioters on the quadrilateral of railroads were all Russian railroad workers. You know they have passes. They can travel without tickets. Even the men in the repair shops have them. They went from town to town stirring things up. In the old days it wasn't possible. You had a local riot in Odessa. It stayed in Odessa. No longer. What set them off? I'll tell you. Have you ever seen how they live? Before the government took over the Southwest lines and Witte began to run them, the railroad barons squeezed the workers. Listen, Vasiliev, I may be a Ukrainophile but I'm not a socialist. Understand? But it's not right, the way the capitalists squeezed the men. A lot of anger there. But we caught some of the bastards! A certain Paderin, for example. Imagine! He was the head of the Fifth Division of Southwestern Railroads. Witte was furious. It seems this character appeared in the town of Zhmerynka. Whenever there was a lull in the violence he called in his crowd. 'Boys,' he would say, 'you don't work properly. You should have more vodka.' And tanked up with more vodka, the boys ripped up almost a hundred Jewish houses and shops. So we arrest him. He gets a three-month sentence. But Drenteln orders him kicked out of Ukraine, right away. Why? I've no idea. But it's not just the anti-Semites, you know. What about the revolutionaries? Either way the Jews were the target. You know the railroad barons—Bloch, Kronenberg, Poliakov are all Jews."

"Wait a moment, Vasili Dementevich. What about the others? Just as many were not Jews—Gubonin, Kokorev, von Derviz, von Meck."

"You don't have to tell me! But it was easier to hit on the Jews. Do you expect the police to beat the Russians or the Germans to save the Jews? No, it's beat the Jews and save Russia."

"But Rudov beat the Russians."

244

"Ah, the clever Captain Rudov. Always playing games. Yes, after the end of the riot in his town of Smela he ordered flogging. But who got flogged? Everyone in sight—men, women, Russians, Ukrainians—yes, even Jews who tried to protect their property. And who may I ask incited the riots in the first place? A real careerist that Rudov. But you tasted his poison yourself."

They returned to their seats, but Vasiliev did not enjoy the rest of the program.

The next morning when Vasiliev opened the door to the offices of the Southwest Railroad Company, he felt transported into a different world. The place reminded him of a military headquarters, but with a difference. The atmosphere was charged, but people's movements were more fluid, their voices more subdued. Was this the face of the new, capitalist Russia? Many years later when Witte had become Russia's Minister of Finance and the most powerful man in the country, Vasiliev would think back to his first impression. Witte's secretary, a young man with spectacles and the intensity of a coiled spring, asked him politely to wait a moment while he informed the Manager, who was just finishing a meeting. Within minutes Witte emerged from his office in conversation with a small, dark-complexioned man sporting a neatly trimmed goatee. Witte's enormous bulk filled the room—or was it just the energy that appeared to radiate from him?

"Inspector Vasiliev! Please come here and meet my right hand, Engineer Abrahamson. He has whipped the repair section into shape. Ah, perhaps 'whipped' is not the right word these days! No. I should say he has won respect among his subordinates." Abrahamson bowed and exchanged a few words with the secretary before leaving.

Witte took Vasiliev by the elbow and guided him into his office, closing the door behind him. The walls were lined with books on economics and statistics, mainly thick tomes in German and French. The desk was piled high with folders but they were arranged in neat piles. Witte did not seek refuge behind his desk, but placed Vasiliev sitting across from him in one of the large leather armchairs flanking a tile Dutch oven.

"You see how it is with us, Inspector. Abrahamson is a crack engineer, trained in Germany. But now the Minister of Transportation wants to transfer him to the Moscow-Iaroslavl line. Why? Because he is a Jew. Why can a Jew serve as head of repairs on the Moscow-Iaroslavl line and not on the Southwest Line? That is a mystery that I think you can solve quite easily. You know, Inspector—ah, let me call you Vasili Vasilievich—people ask me why there are so many Jews and Poles in my administration? The answer to that mystery is even simpler. These men have been well trained, some in the best European schools. They have mastered the latest techniques. And so what if they pray differently? Aren't they all loyal subjects of his Imperial Majesty? I have no patience with such nonsense. This Paderin fellow—a real swine. Not my appointment. Glad to get rid of him! He disgraced the whole Company. But Abrahamson is altogether different. He has never expressed a political opinion. It would surprise me to learn that he had one. But you are not here to listen to me rant and rave. How can I help you?"

"Sergei Iulevich, you know about my assignment to solve two mysteries. They may be more difficult than yours. There are rumors, and so far they are only rumors, that members of a secret society may have been involved in the murder of Rabbi Meier. I've heard more talk of your Holy Brotherhood. One theory is that rogue members of this society have committed crimes under the guise of defending the monarchy. What do you think?"

Witte began to drum his fingers on the arm of his chair. "Let me tell you a story, Vasili Vasilievich. Recently, I was in Paris, staying at the Grand Hotel, do you know it? A lavish barn. But—to the point. An individual approached me. Gave me the secret sign of the Brotherhood. In a trembling voice he wanted to know if I had come to eliminate him. Imagine! He confessed that he had been sent— but by whom?—well, sent to assassinate Gartman the dynamiter. And he feared that if he failed he would be eliminated. Shocking! I decided then that things had gotten out of hand. But I felt unable to resign. I didn't want to create scandal. So I wrote a letter to my friends. I proposed that we publish the entire membership of the organization and a statement of its purpose in the newspaper of the Ministry of Interior. That would root out the careerists and God knows what other trash. If I don't hear in a month from my friends, I'll resign. That will be the end of it."

"Thanks for being so frank, Sergei Iulevich. It's not a common virtue these days. One more question, and then I shall let you go back to building a new Russia"

Witte smiled. "We really are, you know."

"I'm sorry. I have a bad habit of being ironic. But behind the irony is respect for what you are doing." Witte nodded. "Go on."

"So far I've found a curious pattern in the mystery of the pogroms. It seems that the May riots in the Kiev region spread along a quadrilateral of railroads belonging to the Southwest Company. The rioters were mainly Russian railroad workers. Did you know about this? What do you think it means?"

Witte rose and walked to a wall map of the Southwest rail system. "Show me the pattern." He handed Vasiliev a rubber-tipped wooden pointer.

"Here, from May 7 to 10 the riots took place along the Odessa-Kiev, Elizavetgrad-Kharkov, and Fastov lines. The police reports show that the railroad workers were leading the riots. They traveled from point to point, inciting the local population. Some reports blame revolutionaries for organizing them."

"What do you know about these workers, Vasili Vasilievich?" Witte ran his finger over the lines traced by Vasiliev's pointer.

"Only what I have read or heard. Your name comes up quite often as someone who treats the workers fairly. But the private owners do not come off so well. It seems they were squeezing the workers to increase their profits. What did Herzen say? 'God spare us from the bourgeoisie!' Here's my question. Would you give me your permission to find out for myself who might have been stirring them up? I'd be working among them. In disguise, of course."

Witte snorted. "Excuse me, Vasili Vasilievich, but how is that possible? What do you know of hard physical labor?"

Vasiliev held out his hands. "I am the son of a peasant woman and worked in the fields of my father's estate, although he never knew this. The calluses are long gone, but the strength remains. I know the language of the peasant and his ways. I have had to adopt disguises in the past. I was taught by a master. If I'm exposed, the worst that can happen is a good beating."

"A beating! Good God, man, you are an inspector of police, a..." Witte gasped for words.

Vasiliev smiled his crooked smile. "They call me eccentric. I'm willing to accept the reproach, if that is what it is. Still, I need your permission to go into the yards. If necessary you can deny you ever gave it. But I don't want to act behind your back."

Witte shook his head. "You are one of a kind, Vasili Vasilievich. Well, what can I say? I've always admired entrepreneurship in business. I imagine that you're an entrepreneur in solving crimes. You seem willing to take big risks, to break the old rules. Yes, the entrepreneurial inspector. I like it." Witte smiled broadly and extended his hand.

He sat back and stroked his luxurious black beard.

"But listen for a minute. I don't think you have to act the part of a worker to find out what you want. It would take you too long to gain their confidence, no matter how good your disguise. Remember, the workers' *artels* are organized around home communities. We're hiring now. But the workers suspect anyone coming from the outside. If you don't come from the right village, they won't accept you. It'd be better if you went into the shops as a sanitary inspector. You'll be legitimate. It gives you the right to ask plenty of questions. And you won't be exhausted by working eleven and a half hours a day."

"Perhaps you're right. I hadn't thought of it."

"That's because Southwest is one of the few enterprises that employs sanitary inspectors. If I ever get the chance I'm going to introduce them in all Russian factories. As a sanitary inspector you'll minimize the risks of exposure. But don't worry. If anything goes wrong, I won't deny you like Peter did Christ. There are ways of explaining you if you get caught. Caught! Well, I seem to be using all the wrong words today. So, as they say, go with God!"

Chapter
Thirty-Eight

Vera opened her eyes after a long sleep and saw a man standing over her. He had a large bandage over one eye. She wondered for a moment whether he had been in the same accident. Then she realized how impossible that would be. Her head was not throbbing any longer. There was only a dull ache. How long had she been lying here, suspended between life and death? She closed her eyes, hoping that the Cyclops would go away. Did she fall asleep again? She could not tell for certain. She opened her eyes. He was gone. Had he been a dream like the Angel of Death? Now someone was trying to push something into her mouth. It was hot and tasted like cabbage soup, though different from her recipe, spicier. Suddenly, she felt ravenous and swallowed a mouthful. A woman's voice said, "Very good!" She gulped down the rest. Then she drifted off.

Aaron came back later. He had talked his way past the policeman. Just another patient, he said, hurt in the same accident. He was pleased to see that Vera was breathing more easily. He had thought about what David had told him. Ruth didn't get enough information. Now it was his turn. He whispered her name. She stirred and opened her eyes.

"Don't be frightened. I'm just here like you. Only with me it's the eye. They almost poked it out."

"They almost killed me, like Stepan."

Aaron felt his heart beat faster. Go carefully, take it easy, he said to himself.

"The world is beautiful, isn't it? You wonder why there are evil men to spoil it."

"Yes, evil men." Vera reached for her amulet, and for the first time she could touch it without causing unbearable pain.

"You are fortunate to have a charm to ward off the evil."

"Yes, it saved my life."

"I wish I had something to protect me, but you can't just pick up magic on the streets of Kiev."

"No, it comes from far away."

Out of the corner of his good eye Aaron noticed a figure standing at the door. It was Ruth, the last person he wanted to see. She was holding a bouquet of spring flowers like the ones that were dying in a glass on a table next to Vera's bed. He stepped back. "I'll visit you again." As he passed Ruth he muttered angrily, "You don't know me."

Ruth had been nervous coming to the hospital again. Vasiliev's visit had shaken her. At first he seemed angry, but then he spoke so beautifully. Now Aaron seemed displeased with her. She had no idea why. She noticed that Vera was no longer as pale as death. Perhaps she could answer Rebecca's questions. But what had Vera already told Aaron? Suppose she repeated what he had asked Vera? Would it seem as though they were interrogating her? She did not know what to do.

"Pretty," Vera said.

Ruth realized she was holding the flowers by her side. She busied herself replacing the dead ones. "The last of the spring flowers," she said, not knowing what else to say.

"Tell me about the spring—or is it summer now?"

Ruth described the flowers in the Botanical Garden. But her thoughts were elsewhere. It seemed to her that she was like an actress who had been pushed onto a stage where an unknown play was in progress. Everything she said or did was at odds with what was going on. Suddenly an idea struck her.

"Did you have a garden where you lived with Stepan?"

"Oh no! There weren't even any trees on our street."

"How is that possible? There are trees on every street in Kiev."

"Not on Chernegia Street."

"Didn't you want a garden?"

"Oh yes. Stepan promised me. We were going to find a better place with the money..." Vera stopped short and bit her lip. Ruth held her breath, but it did her no good. "I'm tired now," said Vera and closed her eyes. Ruth went into the corridor where Aaron was waiting.

"Well, what did she tell you?" Aaron's voice rasped. Ruth felt the need to please him and she repeated Vera's words verbatim.

"You got close, Ruth, I'll have to admit. Sorry I lost my patience. I thought she was going to say something important to me when you interrupted. At least now we know where she lived. She as much as admitted that Stepan was a paid killer. You'll have to tell Rebecca. Dr. Margulies will be furious if he sees me wandering around. Next time you'll have to try to press her for the name of the paymaster." He pecked Ruth on both cheeks. Perhaps, she thought, she had found her part in the play after all.

The Esteemed Person was sitting at his desk when Pavel brought in the mail. From the moment he opened his eyes that morning he sensed this was going to be a lucky day. He glanced at several envelopes before selecting one. He used an antique Persian dagger to slit it open. He unfolded the foolscap and read slowly, deciphering the crabbed writing. Automatically he corrected the poor spelling and supplied the absent punctuation. So Dimitri had been spotted. An unlucky development. But he had traced the detectives to their safe house. The Esteemed Person balanced the two events and concluded that the weight came down on the side of good luck. He felt reassured. Only then did he shift his attention to Pavel, who was standing at attention waiting for instructions. The Esteemed Person did not invite Pavel to take a seat. He had become superstitious about the effect of allowing his subordinates to sit in his presence.

"So, Pavel, what have you to report?"

Pavel spoke in a drawling voice that had never lost the accents of the Volga Region. He had thought a great deal about what he would say. He knew it was important to give a good impression. This meant appearing efficient and useful. Even better, indispensable. If he explained how the girl, Ruth, had seen him in the hospital, the Esteemed Person might have dismissed him. Or worse. It had been bad enough to admit that Vera had survived the accident. Fortunately, he had found this out before Dimitri had a chance to report to the Esteemed Person. It made it possible for him to blame

Dimitri for having failed to finish the job. After all, it had been the Esteemed Person's idea to arrange the accident. "We don't want any more murders," he had said. "Now that the pogroms are over, it would look suspicious." Fine, then he had to take the chance that the accident would be botched. The attack on the three Yid students hadn't gone as planned either. Still, from what he had learned from the hospital orderlies, at the cost of a few rubles, the woman, Vera, was in no condition to blurt out the truth. The problem was how to eliminate her without causing more problems. Something would have to be done soon. There were already visits from those Jews. There seemed to be a whole nest of them in the hospital. He had already planted a rumor among the staff about the presence of Jews. They had begun to complain to the policeman on guard, whispering about a conspiracy to kill the woman. People were willing to believe anything these days.

"Well, Your Excellency, I have a plan to take care of the woman, Vera. I have frightened off the Jew, Moishe, who has fled Kiev and will not talk. Vasiliev seems to have made a friend of Novitsky." Feed him information, he loves it, Pavel thought.

"That damn fool! What kind of a policeman is it that loves to hear Little Russian. A dog's language! No, not even a language! God, what is the country coming to?" The Esteemed Person slammed his fist on the desk. In his rage the idea suddenly came to him of writing an anonymous letter to the Minister of Interior denouncing Novitsky. Yes, that was a possibility.

"What about Rudov?"

"He has gone back to Smela."

"A good place for him. Another idiot. At least he carried out his assignment. And we still have him on a hook."

The Esteemed Person opened a drawer of his desk and took out a sheaf of papers. He removed a page covered with his own handwriting. He noticed that there were discolored spots on the paper. He bent close and realized that they were cause by drops of sweat that had fallen from his forehead while he had been writing. The sight brought tears of anger to his eyes. He shaded his eyes with his hand.

"I have been studying the documents you so kindly obtained for me, Pavel. They spell trouble. My notes tell me that a number of our operations have been compromised. I have been able to identify most of the sources of the leaks. This is a list of the people who have been reporting to the Jew, Meier. If they were able to obtain these documents once, they can do it again. Of course, that will take some time. And they may not know what to do with the information now that the Jew Meier is dead. They cannot very well take it to the police, for these materials have been stolen, you understand. They are not organized. It is possible they do not even know one another. The only problem might be if one of them decides that Vasiliev is a different kind of policeman and they go to him. We have already seen that the family has been in touch. That damned fool subordinate of his broke up our little attempt to beat sense into those Jew students. So he became a kind of hero to them."

The Esteemed Person dabbed his eyes with a handkerchief. He didn't want any more spots on the documents. First sweat, and then tears. No, that wouldn't do. The next thing would be drops of blood. He gave a small shudder. Pavel wondered what all that meant. But he said nothing. He was not paid to worry about the spiritual state of the Esteemed Person.

"You see the problem, Pavel. But do you see a solution? No, that is my task, to find solutions. I propose three possibilities. First, we could attempt to frighten the sources, as you did so successfully with that wretch, Moishe. But one of them might resist. Imagine himself a new David against our Goliath. So we balance low risk of action against high risk of failure. Second, we organize another nice little pogrom and make certain that our boys devote special attention to the sources of these leaks. This means eliminating half-a-dozen or so Jews by spontaneous action of the outraged masses. But here there are many chances for mistakes of commission and omission. So we balance high level of action against high risk of failure. Third, we eliminate Vasiliev as the only plausible intermediary between the Jew sources and official Russia. You say we have already tried this?"

Pavel stared silently at the Esteemed Person. His back was beginning to ache.

"Ah, yes, quite right, Pavel, but it was not precisely we who tried. A good point! You would not have failed, like our Polish friend. There would be two ways of accomplishing this task. First, to compromise him. Yes, yes, I know that was tried, but clumsily. The other way is more radical, more dangerous, but easily done. So in both cases we balance low level of action against low risk of failure."

Pavel said nothing. He knew he was paid very well to say nothing. But he would not have reached the same conclusion as the Esteemed Person.

Chapter
Thirty-Nine

It had taken Serov two days of house-hunting to find a new place that fit Vasiliev's imprecise definition of "not too wretched." Serov waved him across the threshold with mock ceremony. Vasiliev took in the new safe room at a glance. It was a further notch down the social scale. "You told me…" Serov began defensively.

"Right, right! Undercover police, like beggars, cannot be choosers." Still, the place seemed cramped to him—or was it just the lower ceiling? He made a rapid inventory. Two wooden chairs, a sagging sofa and a deal table with one leg shorter than the others. A cupboard strewn with the bodies of dead flies. The dead cockroaches had the courtesy to remain on the floor. The wallpaper must have dated from the beginning of the century, although it was so faded and stained that it was hard to tell its vintage. A window looked out on a bare patch of land at the edge of a ravine, but the green glass was so thick that the view was blurred, perhaps mercifully so, he thought. The floorboards seemed not merely to creak but to cry out.

"In a word, a pilgrim's paradise," he said out loud.

"Not exactly, Vasili Vasilievich. The pilgrims are packed six and eight into a room this size."

"I was being ironic, Sergeant."

"That's always lost on me, if you please." Serov had finally found a substitute for 'beggin' your pardon.' It had just the right tone.

"Ah, Sergeant, you are being ironic to disclaim irony. Very nice!"

Serov felt reassured. Vasiliev had accepted his new idiom.

"All we need is a few nails in the wall to hang our things. I propose that we do not bring any food into the room. In any case, you will be spared staying here very long. I am sending you off to Smela to dig up the dirt on Captain Rudov. I suspect it won't be hard to find. He's a heavy gambler. That's what Maria Alexandrovna's circle of intelligence has found out. Perhaps his creditor will help us discover the man behind the sorry charade with Szymanski."

"And you'll have the luxury of this place all to yourself, Vasili Vasilievich."

"In a manner of speaking, yes. Perhaps I can get a bed at the Southwest Railroad offices to stay overnight. A sanitary inspector should rate a few perks. What did you leave at our former digs to deceive whoever has to be deceived?"

"A couple o' spare uniforms, the papers you already clipped, candles, a few cracked dishes I bought at the bazaar. Left 'em around. The place still smells of your cigars."

"Sounds quite homely. The place'll look lived in. I'm thinking about showing up on occasion, just to reinforce the impression. I wonder whether they'll be watching it all the time. Or maybe they've bribed our landlady to make reports." Another thought crossed his mind.

"I'll need to get in touch with Dr. Margulies to find out when he thinks we can question the woman with the amulet. A full agenda for tomorrow, Serov, a full agenda."

When Vasiliev arrived at the Jewish Hospital he was forced to wait for Dr. Margulies who was making his rounds. He had time to reflect on his last meeting with Ruth. An awkwardness had grown up between them, replacing the budding intimacy. Or had he just imagined it? He felt a strong desire to see her again. But he worried that the next meeting would end badly. Things could easily go in one of two ways. They might draw closer, with consequences he was afraid to face. Or the distance between them might widen, which he would also regret. He was also unwilling to accept a complete break. He felt as though he were in a laboratory preparing to combine two chemicals, without knowing what the reaction would be. He was startled out of his reverie by the voice of Dr. Margulies.

The Jewish Hospital in Kiev

"Sorry to make you wait, Inspector. Another busy day. How can I help you? Or do I already know why you are here? I should warn you that Aaron has been dismissed from the Military Hospital, despite my objections. Also my colleagues have hinted that my presence there is no longer desired. Such exquisite delicacy in dealing with Jews."

"So, Ruth is our only contact with our lady of the amulet?"

"I'm afraid so. She visits every day, bringing food. I'm sure no one knows she is Jewish."

"Doctor, can you find out from Ruth whether she has been able to find out anything more?"

"Of course. But I can't spare the time today. Even tomorrow looks impossible. I've had a number of new typhus cases, probably as a result of the warm weather and the influx of pilgrims. But of course we Jews will be blamed."

A nurse's voice could be heard, and then shouting. A man burst into the office, pulling wildly on his beard. "Doctor! My son! Please, come."

"Yes, yes, at once. But you have no right to break in like that. All right, I'm coming. Sorry, Inspector."

Leaving the hospital Vasiliev looked at his watch. He had promised Witte he would show up in Abrahamson's office in his guise as the Sanitary Inspector at 3:00. He ordered the cab to take him to Ruth's house. The door was answered by another unfamiliar face. "Ruth is at the hospital. Would you care to wait for her?"

Vasiliev felt a sense of relief, then annoyance at his reaction. He had ordered the cab to wait. It was a feeble defense, he thought, against staying too long. He climbed back in the cab. There was just enough time to make a change over in the safe room. He wondered whether Serov had arrived in Smela yet.

Ruth was now a familiar figure at St Vladimir Hospital. The nurses had begun to smile at her as she walked down the corridor. She was surprised to see that the constable was no longer sitting outside Ward 19. She looked around for someone to ask why. But this day the staff was rushing about in a state of near panic. She wondered what had happened; it didn't always seem that way. When she entered the ward, Vera was propped up by pillows. She smiled as Ruth approached. Vera no longer thought of Ruth as the Angel of Death, but as an angel nonetheless, a Life-Giver. They began as usual to talk about their childhood. Vera sipped the chicken soup and pronounced it "very tasty." Ruth had taken a chance on preparing a Jewish dish in the hope that Vera had never eaten it. "I have no one to take care of me except you," she said

Vera occasionally felt sharp pains in her head. Her ribs ached too when she ran her fingers over the cloths that bound her tightly. Her face was still badly bruised but no longer dead white. Her nose was packed and she had trouble breathing. But she was convinced that she would live, and have her revenge. Ruth was telling her about her mother, careful to avoid any indication that she was Jewish, when Vera interrupted her. She had given a lot of thought to this moment.

"My friend, I need your help again. This time it's about the future. When I'm able to stand and walk. You see, it was no accident that put me here. Someone was trying to kill me."

Ruth gasped, and felt her heart constrict in fear.

"I am not imagining things. I am not delirious. I can only tell you that a man put me in a cab and drove me to St. Andrei's Descent. At the top of the hill he and the driver jumped off. They'd fastened the doors so that I couldn't get out. The curtains were drawn. No one could hear me scream. I was trapped in a runaway. I can't tell you why they did this. Some day, perhaps. But I had done them no wrong. Perhaps they were afraid I would find out they were criminals. I think they were, but I can't tell the police. Please believe me."

"I do," Ruth whispered. She thought of the tall thin man on the stairwell and the constable who no longer sat in the corridor. Did she dare tell Vera?

"I know who did this. I mean I know who ordered these two men to kill me."

Ruth held tightly to her chair. Was Vera about to tell her who had planned the murder of her father?

"I don't know his name, but I know where he lives. I must destroy him."

There were beads of sweat on Vera's forehead. Ruth took out her handkerchief and gently wiped them away. "So kind," Vera muttered. She felt herself entering the tranquil state that always followed the visit of her angel, the Life Giver. She closed her eyes and fell into a deep sleep.

Chapter Forty

Vasiliev spent the first day in the railroad depot interviewing Abrahamson and his staff. If there was a connection between the Kiev pogroms and the Rabbi's death, this was the place to find it. Ruth had already told him that the Rabbi was receiving information about corruption on the Southwest Railroads. Novitsky's map and charts made it clear that pogroms had been organized in Kiev province around the quadrilateral rail lines. Vasiliev thought there was a strong possibility that the same person or persons who had incited the pogroms to cover up the corruption had murdered the Rabbi for the same reason.

Abrahamson impressed Vasiliev with his mastery of detail and knowledge of every aspect of the rail system. He was not only a good engineer, as Witte had testified, but a shrewd judge of people. Perhaps even Witte may not have fully appreciated him. After their talk Abrahamson invited Vasiliev to his apartment near the depot. The rooms were small but neat, furnished with solid German pieces. Dinner was a family affair with Abrahamson's wife, mother-in-law and two children. Over a meal of lentil soup, cutlets, and home made noodles Abrahamson talked mainly of his life in Germany. His wife and mother-in-law ate little, but kept piling food on the men's plates.

"We do not keep kosher, Inspector, but we still observe some of the dietary restrictions. Tradition dies hard." After a desert of poppy seed cake, the women and children vanished into the kitchen and Abrahamson led Vasiliev into his small study crammed with books, mainly German, on political economy and technical subjects. "I always enjoyed the theater in Leipzig but I never have time here to read much, and in Kiev only the French theater is any good. Too bad I don't understand French. I'm afraid I'm a man of limited culture. We can discuss railroads or more railroads!" He laughed heartily.

"Let's compromise then, and discuss railroads," said Vasiliev. "Tell me what you know about the railroad workers."

"I'd hoped you would ask me about the latest designs in loco-motives. Well, the workers. I don't have much direct contact with them. But when my men talk to me they speak freely. They're a rough lot. Recently, they've not been shy in complaining about their life. I'm sure you know that the crop failure last year hit us badly. Lots of men were laid off in the mills and the rail yards. But here's the interesting thing. The men who kept their jobs were among the most active *pogromchiki*. Who's to blame? Well, you've probably heard of the Southern Russian Workers' Union. I'm told it was organized by the moderate socialists, the group that called itself Partition of the Land."

Vasiliev nodded. He had no reason to tell Abrahamson that he knew plenty about the group. Irina had been a member. Her friends had even tried to help him prevent the assassination of Al-exander II. But he still thought of them as young and naïve. He was surprised that workers and not just students and intellectuals were part of the organization.

"Please smoke if you like," Abrahamson said, lighting a pipe. "Sorry I don't have any other tobacco."

Vasiliev produced a cigar, and they spent a few minutes lighting up. Abrahamson went to his desk, rummaged around, and pulled out a small pamphlet. "This will give you an idea of the kind of stuff they were circulating. One of my staff found this on the shop floor and brought it to me. As you can see it encourages the work-ers to beat Jews 'with discrimination'—I love that part. What they mean, I think, is that the workers should let the poor Jews alone and go after the 'big bellies.' This was printed the second day of the riots in April. So the socialists didn't start things, as I see it. But they jumped aboard and tried to steer it in the right direction, according to their lights."

"So, you're suggesting that the riots might have been incited by someone else? At least, to begin with."

"Yes. Once that happened there was no way to control them. Oh, and I should add something here. My people, I mean the staff, not the workers, from outlying stations. They reported to me when they spotted men who were definitely not workers showing up at railroad shops and stirring up the men against the Jews. Period. No nice distinctions made between rich and poor."

"Did they attack you?"

"No, and that's a strange story. Not to be publicized, if you don't mind. You see, being the central depot, our workers were well organized by the Union. The word went out. Abrahamson is all right. Leave *him* alone. So I owe my skin to the socialists! This doesn't make me one of them. But it shows, I think, the difference between what happened in Kiev and the outer stations. And it shows that the Partition of the Land, at least, meant what it said. There are even rumors, in some cases pretty well substantiated, that there are Jewish members of the Partition. Also some in the more radical wing, what's it called?

"The Peoples Will."

"That's it."

"I must tell you, Inspector, what puzzles me. Of course I'm just a benighted technician. Still, it seems very strange. Some Russians are beating us for being capitalists, and others are denouncing us for being revolutionaries. Of course, we are both, but so are the Christians. So how are we different? And what about people like me, who are neither capitalists nor revolutionaries? Ah well, that's a mystery you will never solve."

Abrahamson tapped down his pipe. Vasiliev put out his cigar. They sat for a few moments in silence.

"Tomorrow I'd like to speak to a few workers in the shops. Would that be possible? Perhaps you could recommend men I could talk to. The ones who are literate and politically active."

"Of course, but I don't know how successful you'll be. It's hard to get them to talk openly about 'the events'. That's what they call the pogroms."

"Possibly not. I'll also need to meet the section chiefs of the administrative and financial departments."

"Could I suggest another way of going about it? You're looking for men who will confide in you. Why not put up an official looking

264

notice. It could announce that the Sanitary Inspector for the South-west Railroads will be in such and such an office during certain hours to meet with individuals who have grievances. Or to accept written statements, which may be anonymous. See what turns up."

"A brilliant idea. Can you find me an office away from the main building, a place that would give me some privacy?"

"I think I know just the place. We can get the notice up by the early afternoon. That way you'll have the morning to make your rounds of the shop." Abrahmson looked at his watch. "Time to turn in. Why don't you stay here the night. I can fix you up a cot in my office."

The following morning Vasiliev had his first meeting with the shop foreman, a German who spoke Russian with a strong accent. "I hef mine instructions. You can hef half an hour with Telegin. He'll gif you an earful."

Telegin was a short, powerfully built man, almost as wide as he was tall, with gaps in his teeth and a torn right ear. He said he was from Viatka in the Urals and had been in Kiev for ten years. Before that he had worked as a barge hauler on the Volga. "Work that kills you slow-like. I shipped down here. Served as an apprentice, a couple of years, that was."

He warmed up a little when Vasiliev told him he used to hunt in the Urals. They swapped stories. Vasiliev asked him about sanitary conditions.

"It's a hell of a lot better since Mr. Abrahamson came aboard. But even so...Well, you don't have to ask the foreman whether you can take a piss now. And the gate stays open after nine o'clock. Used to be they locked the damn thing at the sound of the bell. If you was a minute late, too bad! You lost a day's work. The foreman doesn't curse us now. Not allowed. Well, 'sanitary' you say. It's all a matter of what's healthy and what's not, you know. Hey, Mr. Abrahamson told us productivity was up ten percent since the new rules. So it pays. Before that the Yid Bloch squeezed us dry. If you want to know why all hell broke loose in May, that's the reason."

"But Abrahamson is Jewish. So are a lot of people in Kiev who don't own railroads. Why did the riot turn against the Jews instead of the big capitalists?"

"You sound just like...well, like some in the Union. But you have to remember that some guys came around the night before and told us all about Bloch. Lives like a king in Warsaw, married some rich beauty, goes to Europe all the time. Owns most of the Southwest. What the hell does he care about us. Sucks us dry!"

"You know he converted to Catholicism?"

"What! Oh, hell, once a Jew always a Jew!"

"So, some smartass agitator comes in. Stirs you all up and you fall for it. Go off on a tear beating up Jews. Nice work!"

"What d'you mean? Who the hell are you to tell us? "

"I'll bet you don't even know who sent these guys to trick you."

"Trick, what trick? Bloch he's..."

"Yeah, I know what he is. But you didn't beat up Bloch. You beat up some poor bastards who were just as exploited as you. What did these guys look like? The ones from the outside. Gentlemen they were, weren't they?"

"Christ you're a hard one."

"Well, how were they dressed? Or didn't you notice?"

"Yeah, well, sure as hell they weren't workers."

"And they weren't students either, eh?"

"All right, all right, so they were petty bourgeois trash, but they was telling us the truth about the Yid exploiters."

"What did they look like? No, let me guess. A tall guy, very thin, black hair brushed back, parted up the middle."

"Who the hell *are* you? A police spy? What d'you want?"

"I just got what I wanted, Telegin." Vasiliev waved him back to his lathe and left the shop.

Vasiliev interviewed two other workers from the repair shop. They were surly and uncommunicative. All he could get out of them was that 'outsiders' had showed up in the workers' dormitory on the night of April 25. When he asked them if they had rail passes, they shrugged and turned away.

Vasiliev cornered the German foreman at the break. "The men agree that outside agitators stirred them up. Can you tell me anything more?"

The foreman scratched his chest. His eyes slid away from Vasiliev. He glanced around the shop. Then he muttered under his breath. "Come to the teahouse opposite the burned out synagogue on Malo-Vasilkovsk at eight and we'll talk." The foreman spat on the dirt floor and someone cried "bravo" from the rear of the shop.

Vasiliev returned to Abrahamson's apartment. He asked him for a pair of old trousers, a worn blouse, and a soft cap. He knew it wasn't much of a disguise, but at least he wouldn't be conspicuous in the teahouse. He arrived early and found a seat in the rear, where the light was dim and the smoke heavy. The foreman came in a few minutes after eight and sat down on a bench along the wall. He ordered tea and took his time looking around. When he spotted Vasiliev he gulped down his tea, threw a few coins on the table, got up, and left. Vasiliev waited a few moments and then followed him. Once outside, he could barely see the blackened ruins of the synagogue. All the street lamps had been smashed in the riots. Light from a quarter moon, coming through broken clouds, intermittently illuminated the street, leaving some shadows darker than others. There was no sign of the foreman. Vasiliev pressed up against the door, holding the handle tightly. In a few minutes he went back into the teahouse and resumed his seat. There was something not quite right about the set-up. He didn't like the foreman's shifty look. After a while he got up and made for the back door. He pushed it open and went into the yard, as if to find the toilet. A smell of ordure filled his nostrils. The yard was surrounded by a low wooden fence. He scaled it and dropped into a pile of dirt along the side of the burned-out synagogue. He made his way around the rear of the structure and came out on a street running parallel to Malo-Vasilkovsk. He kept close to the buildings, stopping every few minutes to listen. He cut down a side street that would lead him back to Malo-Vasilkovsk. When he got there he stopped at the corner. He pressed up against the wall of a wooden structure, inching his way along until he felt an opening into a courtyard. He stepped inside and waited.

Perhaps he had been wrong. Still, it always paid to be cautious. He was about to end his vigil when he heard soft footsteps and the voices of several men. There was no mistaking the German accent. The men passed close to him, but it was too dark to make out their features. Vasiliev waited until he could no longer hear them. He made his way back to Abrahamson's by a circuitous route. The engineer was surprised to see Vasiliev, but invited him in and offered tea.

"I've had enough tea for the evening. But I'll join you for a

smoke. I want to ask you about your foreman." Vasiliev studied
Abrahamson's features but decided there was nothing to suggest
his complicity.

"He was hired three years ago, has an excellent work record.
The men seem to get along with him as well as Russian workers
ever get along with a German foreman. I think he goes out of his
way to ingratiate himself with them. That's unusual. Unique in my
experience."

"What did he do during the riots?"

"He stayed at his post. I only had one complaint. His report
greatly underestimated the absenteeism for the three days of the
pogroms. I suspect he was covering up for the men who were on
the rampage. But given my sensitive position, if you now what I
mean, I didn't press the issue. Why do you ask?"

"I need your help again. Are you a good actor? Never mind!
Here's what I want you to do. It's really very simple."

Chapter
Forty-One

The next morning Abrahamson accompanied the foreman to the office he had provided for Vasiliev. A large map of the Southwest rail system dominated the wall. There were no colored pins and threads.

"Please sit down, gentlemen. I have a serious matter to raise with you about the repair shop." Vasiliev noticed that the foreman kept rubbing his palms along the seams of his trousers.

"But first I have to tell you that I am not a sanitary inspector, but another kind of inspector, a police inspector. Here are my papers." He handed his documents to Abrahamson, who glanced at them, and then stood up, facing away from the foreman.

"This is outrageous!" he said. Vasiliev would have given him a 3 out of 5 for acting ability. The foreman went pale. "You come into my shop under false pretenses," Abrahamson continued, as he passed the documents to the foreman.

"Please sit down Mr. Abrahamson. I'll have to report serious problems in your shop. Your foreman and other workers participated in the April riots. People were injured and property destroyed. These were criminal acts. Then last night this man tried to intimidate me."

"But that's not possible!" Abrahamson cried out. Vasiliev thought he was doing a little better this time. "My foreman is one of the most trusted employees and as for the men—"

Vasiliev cut him off. "You have been duped, Mr. Abrahamson. I can only say that you have been duped, but you're not criminally involved. I just wish you to know how things stand in your shop. You may go now."

Abrahamson rose slowly from his seat and, as instructed by Vasiliev, he patted the foreman on the shoulder as he left.

"Now my dear fellow, you have a lot to explain." Vasiliev thought this might be enough to frighten the man, a foreigner who probably knew little about the Russian Code of Criminal Law.

"God as my witness…"

"I'm afraid that God seldom appears as a witness in the Russian court of law. Let's see: conspiracy, incitement to riot, destruction of private property. Well, we can begin with that."

"Please Inspector, I haf *ein* wife und three children. I'm law abiding." His German accent grew stronger with every word.

"I'm afraid your wife and children also cannot be called as witnesses. However, we Russians are not barbarians, as you Europeans seem to think. I'm sure we can work something out. Now listen carefully! I'm not asking you to betray your men. Frankly, I am not interested in their sins, though they have sinned mightily. I believe that they were misled by outside agitators. Isn't that so?"

The German nodded with what Vasiliev interpreted as considerable enthusiasm.

"Still, I have to wonder who gave them access to the workers' dormitory. And I guess that it was you. How much did they offer you?"

"No, no! It vus not dat vay. Oh, *mein Gott*, I vus veak, veak."

"I see—a woman! They set you up and threatened to tell your wife. Oh, dear! What a banal story. So you are not venal, just depraved. And a Prussian too! My, my."

"*Ich bin ein Sachsen.*"

"Does that explain anything? Mr. Abrahamson studied in Leipzig. That too is Saxony. But he does not seem to have made him either corrupt or depraved—and a Jew at that."

The Saxon buried his face in his hands. Vasiliev thought the whole scene was becoming maudlin.

"I assume you stayed around to hear their little speech, these outside agitators. I won't ask you to repeat it. Dreary stuff. But I want to know who gave the speech."

"I don't know his name. He picked me up in a *Kaffeehaus*. Ach, I shouldn't never have gone der. A message from *ein alte freund* to meet him der. Urgent business, he said."

"But your friend never showed up."

The foreman looked up in astonishment.

"How do you know?"

"I read tealeaves. The outsider, then—he wasn't tall and thin with black hair parted down the middle, was he?"

"Jesus, *Almachtig Gott*!"

"That's two out of three. You might need the Holy Spirit as well. But even the full Trinity…Well! You're in too much trouble. So they introduced you to this woman. Really, a man of your experience to fall for such a common trick! All right, where was the teahouse?"

"In ze City Park *bei Sommer* theater. You know ze one. *Zwei, drei tagen spater…*"

"Please, make an effort to speak in Russian. You know the language perfectly well."

"*Ja*, yes. Zo a few days later… a man was *stossen*, ah, stabbed on ze shtreet outside."

Vasiliev experienced the sensation he always described to Serov as 'the tingling.' It usually came when he saw a possible connection between facts that seemed at first to have no relationship to one another. He did not yet fully grasp what the coincidence meant. Stepan, the man wearing the amulet, stabbed outside the teahouse. The same place where the tall thin man had blackmailed the German foreman. The tall thin man had engineered the accident that had nearly killed Stepan's wife. Who was behind him? The same person, it seemed, who had ordered the murder of the Rabbi and planed the outbreak of riots in Kiev to cover up his crime. A man who had brought in Russian workers from the outside on the railroads. Vasiliev caught a whiff of brimstone and fire. Look for a man with horns and a tail! But first he was determined to take his revenge on the foreman.

"One more thing. You made a big mistake last night trying to set a trap for me. What was your plan? Have some of your toughs rough me up so that I would stop snooping?"

"*Was! Nein…*"

"I know, God as your witness. But I'm not a novice, you know. After you left the tearoom I backtracked. An old hunter's ploy. I ended up stalking you. I was waiting for you in a courtyard on Malo-Vasilkovsk. You walked right past me in the darkness. But your accent is unmistakable, even when you are whispering in Russian. Let's stick with Russian now."

The foreman grew pale. "Ve yust vanted to frighten you. Ve vouldn't haf touched you. Yust varned you…no violence…I beg off you."

"Your list of sins keeps growing. Threatening an officer of the law. That'll get you ten years. But we made a deal. I'll keep my end of the bargain. But you'll keep your mouth shut. Not a word to your boys about our little talk. Nothing! You understand! Get back to work. If I hear of any more agitation in the dormitory, I'll come down on you with the full force of the law. Now, get out of my sight."

Chapter
Forty-Two

The Esteemed Person was giddy with excitement. The idea came to him in the middle of the night. At breakfast he could hardly contain himself. He even forgot to let his tea cool, and burned his tongue. On other days that would have been an unlucky sign. Now he ignored it. The point was to be cautious, he reminded himself. It was important not to leave any physical evidence, as the detectives liked to call it. Pavel had his orders. Or to be precise he knew what he had to do. Of course, Pavel had failed before. So, it was necessary to call on reserves. Life was a struggle, say what you will. He had heard speak of a Napoleon of crime. Why go so far as France? Give it a Russian flavor. He was…a Suvorov of crime! He liked the sound of it so much that he found himself giggling. But was it really so ridiculous? Only a genius could have thought of organizing a pogrom to smash his competitors and get rid of the Jew Meier. That hocus-pocus with the sign of the cross. Another stroke of genius. They'd be running after some Christian fanatic, or maybe the Holy Brotherhood. What a joke that would be.

He brushed the crumbs from his waistcoat and rang for the maid. She removed the dishes and left him alone. He folded his hands on his stomach and gazed at his pictures. Yes, he was like a general calling up his reserves. Was there no end to his cleverness, he wondered? His reserves would be the revolutionaries of the Peoples Will. But they would be the unconscious instrument of *his* will. They would destroy Vasiliev without knowing they were merely his pawns. The teahouse in the City Park would be the easiest place to make contact. But it was not wise to go back to the same trough twice. There was always Szymanski. He had contacts with the Polish revolutionaries and through them to the People's Will. But Szymanski too had been tried, and he had failed. The plot about the girl revolutionary — what was her name, Irina? Yes, that was clever. Well, it was true Rudov had helped there, with his contacts in the Gendarmes. Still the outcome was puzzling. How had Vasiliev managed to find out? Or had Szymanski really sold out? Poles, Jews, Ukrainians, what a lot! You couldn't trust them out of your sight. But the good solid Russians of the Peoples Will..." He giggled again. They were his last trumps. But what was he saving them for, if not this? Everything depended on playing this card. Vasiliev was the biggest threat to his current operations. He also stood in the way of plans for the future The Esteemed Person was beginning to think that he had almost amassed enough capital to become a respectable citizen for the rest of his life. He could retire then and make annual trips to Europe like the rich Jew, Bloch.

Boris Zhuk enjoyed thinking of himself as Russia's first triple agent. He was a member in good standing of the People's Will, a police officer in Novitsky's office, and a sometime employee of the Esteemed Person. The morning after the Esteemed Person had burned his tongue, Zhuk found in his office mail a post card with a photograph of the Lavra Monastery and the single word, 'Greetings' scrawled on the reverse side. That afternoon he went to the Baikovo Cemetery, where he knelt by the grave of an official who had died in 1820. Making certain that no one was observing him, he pushed aside a spray of fresh pine branches, uncovering a small packet, which he tucked inside his tunic. He rose and stretched his arms. He turned round slowly to survey the grounds. His inner voice reassured him. "Only us real mourners here." But he was not a man to take chances. He took a circular route back to his apartment in the Old Kiev District, making sure that he was not being followed. He didn't like to think about who might be watching him. So many possibilities! It was just a way of life now. But routine was dangerous, he reminded himself. It could even be fatal. He stepped inside his small apartment with a feeling of relief. He opened a fresh bottle of Starka and downed two glasses before opening the packet. He removed the wad of rubles and read the short message. Every time the handwriting was different. Having memorized the message he burned it in the grate.

The next morning, before reporting for duty at police head-quarters, he passed through the Alexander Bazaar until he came to a shop selling old pianos. The man and woman who ran the shop paid no attention to him. He went to the rear of the shop, examining the instruments. He sat down in front of an Erhardt, adjusted the stool to the height he liked, and played a series of chords. He cocked his head as if listening to the overtones. Then he ran through a piano arrangement of the overture to Glinka's *Life for the Tsar*. He shook his head, as if displeased, closed the piano and left the shop.

That evening he went for a stroll in the open-air garden by the Chateau de Fleurs, mixing with the crowd. He was wearing a visor cap, Russian blouse, black trousers tucked into high boots—the typical outfit of an *artel* worker. He was carrying a parcel of old magazines wrapped in bright yellow paper. For a while he watched the folk dancers on the open-air stage. With a flurry of skirts and stamping of leather boots, the *gopak* came to an end. The crowd began to break up. A young woman took his arm. Together they continued to stroll around the gardens. Zhuk repeated verbatim the words in the written message. The girl laughed and gave him a friendly push. He frowned and turned away, walking back toward the stage. She melted into a group of shop girls.

Chateau de Fleurs

Later that evening the girl entered a brick building on Lukianov Street overlooking the Old Believer Cemetery, where she met five other members of the People's Will. They were discussing the recent losses in the Kiev organization. The police had been active. A handsome, heavily bearded man in his late twenties was arguing in favor of admitting a few Jewish students from the University in order to fill the depleted ranks. Others favored dispersing into the villages until the Gendarmes got tired of snooping around. A gray haze hovered over them. The girl coughed. She hated the stink of the bearded man's cigar. She shot an angry look at him. He ignored her and kept puffing away. She broke into his monologue in her high pitched voice. She might have taken some satisfaction from knowing how much the sound of it annoyed him.

"We have more urgent things to think about. Our source has identified two undercover agents sent from Moscow. They're closing in on the Podol district group. They've collected important documents in a safe room. They have to be taken out. We have the exact location. No problem with security precautions; they haven't taken any. No contact with the city police."

The room fell silent.

"Why didn't the source notify the Podol group?"

"A police agent has already penetrated the group."

"What else did the source say?"

"Nothing. You know he doesn't give advice. He doesn't want to know the details of an operation. If something goes wrong he's in the clear."

"Creep."

"Creep or not, his information has always been accurate."

There was another moment of silence.

"It's true," said the bearded man. "We have no choice. What do you suggest?" He turned to the man on his left who was chain-smoking cigarettes.

"A bomb with a manually controlled detonator. A raid would be too risky. They are probably heavily armed. We'd have to break in. There would be a gun battle. We might lose a comrade. Same problem in the street. If we have to move fast we can't waste time setting up an elaborate surveillance and tracking operation. No, the bomb is best. We can find out easily enough when the room is empty, gain access, plant the bomb, and make sure they're both inside when we detonate. I'll use the new German detonators. Infallible. I have the rest of the material here. I can assemble it tonight."

Not everyone agreed.

"I'd like more time to look things over. We can't afford to be hasty. Our successes have always been the result of careful planning. Besides, what's wrong with shooting them in the street? This is an address in a poor section. No fear of crowds."

"They might leave the room separately and we might have to trail them both. One might get away. No, I'm for the bomb."

"Let's take a vote," said the girl. "Secret ballot." She tore up six slips of paper. "Mark 1 for the bomb, 2 for shooting, 3 for delay."

She gathered the ballots. "Four for the bomb, one for shooting, one for delay."

The chain smoker snuffed out the cigarette between his thumb and forefinger, which were stained yellow. He stuffed the butt into his pocket, rose, and went into the next room."

"I'll check for access," the girl said.

"It's up to me to plant the device," said the bearded man. "I'll just need one man to go with me as a watcher. We'll find a place to keep the place under surveillance. When we see both men enter the room—poof!"

"What about the landlady?"

"It may not be possible to get her out of the way in time. We'll think about it."

Everyone left the room that night knowing that no more thought would be given to the fate of the landlady.

Chapter
Forty-Three

"I have my orders." The head of the administrative and financial department of the Southwest Railroad was speaking to Vasiliev. "The clerks will show up in succession, every half an hour." He turned and left before Vasiliev could offer his hand. A different bird than Abrahamson, thought Vasiliev. He recalled the early morning visit of Abrahamson's young son, who brought him a platter of freshly baked pancakes. The boy looked up at Vasiliev with a serious expression and recited his father's thanks for the Inspector's "acute sensitivity." He had trouble pronouncing the words as if he had spoken them for the first time.

Vasiliev's temporary office was behind the repair shop. It was bare except for a desk, two chairs and, on the wall, a portrait of Tsar Alexander II. Hadn't they had time to replace it? Or was somebody in deep mourning? Vasiliev counted himself among the latter. He kept going back in his mind to the moment of the attack on the Tsar. He had seen the bomber too late. How could the fate of an empire depend upon a few seconds of time? Sometimes at night he would wake up feeling the dying Tsar's head bouncing against his shoulder as the sledge pulled them back to the Winter Palace, leaving a trial of blood for the people to follow. Vasiliev shook himself out of his reverie.

The first three men he interviewed were respectful, holding their caps in their hands. But they seemed to know nothing about irregularities in the company's operations. The fourth clerk who entered the office was Iakov Galperin. From the moment he appeared Vasiliev guessed that he had something to hide. That, or else he had not been fortified with freshly baked pancakes for breakfast. No, Iakov was a frightened man. He seated himself on the edge of the chair as if poised for flight.

Vasiliev glanced down at the papers in front of him. "Galperin, Galperin; it has a familiar sound. So many names to cope with in this business. Still, Galperin is distinctive. I'm trying to recall who mentioned it to me recently, here in Kiev."

Vasiliev almost felt sorry for the man. His face became blotchy and he gripped the edge of the chair, as if indeed it would fly away from him rather than he from it.

"Ah, now I remember! Iakov Iakovlevich Galperin, an excellent worker. Deeply distressed for some reason. Why has your work been suffering lately?"

"Nothing serious, Your Honor," he stammered.

"Nothing serious, you say. My dear fellow, you are a nervous wreck! Let's see here." Vasiliev rummaged in the papers which were outdated technical studies that he had begged from Abrahamson. "Rustling papers does wonders for loosening tongues," he had explained to the engineer. He picked out a sheet and held it up in front of his face, mumbling as if reading to himself, and uttering little cries of astonishment. He wondered how long Galperin could stand the torment.

"My goodness, my goodness," he muttered, laying the paper down." Iakov Iakovlevich, what do you have to say for yourself."

"You must understand," Iakov blurted out, "I'm only interested in justice. I never did anything for personal gain."

"No, of course not. I believe you. Still, there it is in black and white. You can't deny that!" Vasiliev slammed the palm of his hand down on the paper with such force that Iakov jumped, almost losing his precarious balance on the edge of the chair.

"No, I'm not denying it. But you have to understand…"

"Understand? I am an expert in understanding, Iakov Iakovlevich. You have to tell me what I am supposed to understand. Aside, that is, from the evidence I have of your activities. Are you speaking of motive here? Fine, then let us discuss motive."

"I'm an honest man. Please believe me. When I first saw the errors I thought they were mistakes. More and more turned up. Finally I saw a pattern. My superior wasn't interested. I took them to the one man I could trust."

"Rabbi Meier," said Vasiliev.

"You know this?" exclaimed Iakov

"Please continue. And sit back in your chair before you have an accident. I don't want to lose the important information you are about to give me. Don't be too technical. I have my limits. Later we can have the details verified."

Iakov slid back an inch or two on his seat. "The errors revealed that one of the major shareholders in the company was siphoning off large sums of money. It was done through an elaborate scheme involving contractors and suppliers, which he controlled."

"What are large sums?"

"Hundreds of thousands."

"When was this done?"

"Over the past five years."

"And what did you expect Rabbi Meier to do with this information?"

"He said he was collecting data like this. To submit to a lawyer who would start a judicial procedure against the person or persons responsible."

"You mean that he had other sources of information about this operation? Or perhaps there were other operations?"

"I don't know for certain. But I think he was getting information on other operations. I saw another clerk from another government department at the Rabbi's house."

"So you copied the documents with the errors and gave them to Rabbi Meier. Did you tell anyone else about this?"

Iakov hesitated. "At first, my boss, as I told you, but just about a few errors..." Iakov looked down at the floor.

"And then, you told someone else. Who was it Iakov?"

Iakov looked up.

There were tears in his eyes. "I was so alone with my secret."

"Nothing worse. I can't blame you. You must have trusted this other person. But I have to know who it was."

"It was Ruth Moiseevna, the Rabbi's daughter."

Vasiliev felt as though he had been punched in the stomach. He stood up, turned his back on Iakov, and pretended to study the portrait of the Tsar. He spoke without looking at Iakov.

"Where are the suppliers?"

Iakov told him but Vasiliev was hardly listening. He was not aware, at first, that Iakov had stopped talking. The silence grew between them. Iakov began to fidget on his chair.

"So you don't know who the real culprits are?" Vasiliev said, lowering his head.

"No, Your Honor, but I have a list of shareholders in my office."

Vasiliev glanced at his watch. He realized his mistake. Iakov had been in the office for forty-five minutes, too long.

"Good, please give it to me at the end of the day. You will find me in Abrahamson's office. Thank you, Iakov Iakovlevich. You have been of great help to your country." Vasiliev turned around and shook his hand. Iakov backed out of the office, a startled look on his face. Vasiliev called in the next clerk, and interviewed four more before he went to dinner at Abrahamson's. Mrs. Abrahamson apologized for the simple fare—sweet cabbage stew, fresh pickles served with hot potatoes in their jackets, and fresh rolls. Vasiliev was relieved that Abrahamson enjoyed telling stories about his experiences on the Moscow-Iaroslavl Line and did not ask any questions. After dinner they went together to Abrahamson's office. Iakov was waiting for them. He handed Vasiliev a cardboard file. "The information you wanted, Inspector." Vasiliev noted that his face was drawn but he seemed to have lost his nervousness. Vasiliev thanked him. He chatted with Abrahamson for a few minutes and said good night. He had decided to move to a hotel in order to spare Abrahamson any further trouble. Now he was glad that he had done so.

Why had Ruth not told him? He could only imagine that someone had brought pressure to bear on her. That could only be Rebecca. She was playing her own game. Well, if he couldn't beat her at this... Yet, Ruth's silence bothered him. He felt that she had betrayed him. Was that unfair of him? After all, she had to choose between him, a man she hardly knew, and her sister. Again a matter of choice, a hard one. Still...He ordered two hundred grams of vodka for his room. When it arrived, he filled and emptied two glasses in quick succession. He opened the cardboard file and ran his finger down the list of major shareholders. There was only one name that was familiar to him. He closed the file and finished the carafe of vodka. He went downstairs and ordered another two hundred grams. Ten minutes later he left the hotel and walked to the teahouse in the City Park.

Chapter
Forty-Four

On her way back home from the Military Hospital Ruth ordered the driver to stop at the Hotel d'Europe. She left a message for Vasiliev to meet her. During the rest of the ride she debated with herself. Should she tell Rebecca that Vera had confided in her? She was undecided when she entered the study and found Rebecca, David and Aaron waiting for her.

"Aaron, how wonderful! They released you from the hospital."

"Not exactly. But I feel all right, and released myself."

Ruth was about to ask whether this was wise, but Rebecca cut in.

"We think things are coming to a head. We need Aaron for the *dénouement*." David glanced at her. A curious choice of words, he thought. It was too literary, as if they were walking through the script of a play. He wondered what Mendel would say if told that they were planning the *dénouement*. Probably laugh his head off. "We're eager to hear your report, Ruth," said Rebecca.

"Report? Well, I'm not sure that I…"

"Ruth! You're one of us now. You'll have to get use to it. 'Report' is just what we mean."

"Take it easy Rebecca. Ruth has been great with Vera. She's not going to hide anything that might help us," said Aaron, turning his good eye on Ruth.

"Right," said David. "Ruth's our inside person. I've got the impression that you found out something really valuable today. I can see it in your face."

Rebecca folded her arms and remained silent.

Ruth felt her resistance crumble. If only Vasiliev had been at the hotel. He had told her the address of the safe room, but instructed her to get in touch with him there only in case of a real emergency. "A matter of life or death," he'd said. Was this the moment?

"Shouldn't we have tea?" asked Aaron, sensing that Ruth needed a few minutes to collect herself. He went to the door and called for the samovar.

They sat in silence until the servant set down the samovar. She whispered in Ruth's ear. Ruth murmured her thanks and began to prepare the tea.

"There is more bad news," she said. "A new wave of pogroms in Poltava. We are getting the first refugees. Reb Ben-Zion will take care of them."

"My God it keeps spreading! Will there be no end to it?" David exclaimed.

"Not until we strike back," said Rebecca. "Well, Ruth, are you going to do your part?"

The teacups trembled on their saucers as Ruth handed them out. She searched their faces. Rebecca's stony expression, David and Aaron straining to look friendly and encouraging. She put down her cup.

"Vera told me she knew where the paymaster lives." Her own voice sounded strange to her like a distant echo.

David and Aaron clapped their hands in unison. Like children, thought Ruth, who had been told they could go swimming on a hot day. But weren't they jumping into a deep and dark pool. Rebecca leaned forward and asked, "Where is it?"

"She didn't give me an address. I can't keep pressing her too hard, or she'll become suspicious. You have to realize how frightened she is."

Rebecca thanked her, but there was no warmth in her voice. "We'll have to plan carefully. We have a meeting, David. Let's go or we'll be late."

David looked at her in surprise, but did not object. On his way out he kissed Ruth on the crown of her head. She shivered. She dare not ask Rebecca what she was planning. Aaron pressed Ruth's hand. She hardly heard what he said. She waved him back to his seat.

"Listen to me, Aaron. I'm afraid that Rebecca is going to do

something foolish. She'll drag David along with her." She was groping for words now. "We've got to bring this madman to justice. But
not our justice, you understand. Think for a moment. Sergeant Serov saved your life. Isn't that true? Vasiliev has shown his sympathy with our Jewish plight. We can trust them to do the right thing.
I found out all we all need to know. Now we have to tell Vasiliev.
I left him a message to meet me. But he doesn't pick up his mail
regularly. I have no idea what he is doing right now. But he told me
in confidence where he can be reached in case of an emergency. I
think this is one. Here's what I want you to do."

Rebecca led David into the park in front of the Women's Theologi-
cal School where they sat down on a bench facing the façade of St.
Vladimir University. David thought he knew all Rebecca's moods,
but lately he felt she was drifting away from him.
  "What are you thinking, Rebecca?"
  "I am thinking of Vera Zasulich shooting General Trepov three
years ago."
  David felt his stomach turn. He tried to think of something
to say that might calm her. Suddenly it seemed too late for that.
He looked over her head at the massive structure of St. Vladimir
University, painted bright red with black borders, the colors of the

St. Vladimir University

Order of St. Vladimir. But the colors had taken on a different meaning for him. He had been reading Stendhal, *The Red and the Black*—symbols of revolution and reaction. Were there now only those two choices left in Russia? He ran his eyes over the classical façade, as if he had never noticed it before. Eight great columns supporting the pediment. Symbols of strength and stability. That's what they were supposed to represent. From the outside it could be a university building anywhere in Europe. But nowhere else were students inside debating the virtues of revolutionary terror.

"She fired point-blank and only wounded him," he said softly.

"Exactly what I was thinking."

"Let's have the rest of it. I don't want to drag it out of you."

"No question of dragging, David. You can act so superior. The point is that Zasulich, for all her courage, didn't plan carefully. Either she should have learned how to shoot straight, or recruited someone who could. Even better, she should not have acted alone."

"Somehow I can see where this is going."

"I congratulate you on being clairvoyant." They stared at one another. It was always like this when they were children, he recalled. The dare, the challenge, the flash of anger. He knew how it would end. He was the first to lower his eyes.

"What we need to do is to organize an attack that has the least chance of failing. We've got to find out the address. Ruth has to go back and get it. Then we can get to know the daily routine of the target."

He flinched at the word target. Where did she pick it up? Funny how a little thing like that—a word, an expression—could open up a gulf. You've grown up together and think you know someone, and then this alien thing crops up. A human being becomes a target. He felt an inner chill. But Rebecca was forging ahead.

"Next, we'll have a dress rehearsal. I say 'we' because several people have to be involved. One person might lose his nerve or miss or, I don't know, somehow be prevented from carrying out the mission."

"And what about weapons? Are your friends in the People's Will going to supply you with a revolver?"

"It's not that simple, of course. I've been in touch with the Lukianov group. They've accepted me into the organization. But they're not going to hand over a revolver unless the group as a whole agrees. They decide on the importance of the target. I can't ask them to give this one priority."

"Because this one, as you put it, is a target of personal revenge." Well, there. He had used it too, the word devoid of any human quality. Did it close up the gulf?

"Damn it! I've told you that's not the case. It just would take too long to convince them that he's worth the risk. Also, the Lukianov group is lying low for a while. When they act they would prefer to attack a more spectacular target like the Governor-General."

"So you should accept the discipline of the group."

"Your sarcasm is really exasperating. Do I have to beg on my knees for your help?"

"Give me a rational and practical plan. We'll see if it has a chance of working. But I do this solely for you, and against my better judgment and my conscience. Enough about my inner state! What d'you propose?"

"The only possible source for revolvers is the Jewish underworld."

"Rebecca, Rebecca! God Almighty! Mendel and his friends are smugglers not gun runners; I met a horse thief at Kaniever's, not an American bank robber. They are unarmed."

"For the right price I imagine they could buy arms across the border. Then pass them on to you. Isn't that the way Aaron got his revolver?"

David shook his head. "Rebecca, I respect your passion, but these are fantasies. Do you think Mendel and his friends would risk being implicated in a terrorist attack at any price? Aaron bought the gun from a Jewish war veteran who was half-starving. It was a lucky find. Even then the man had only six cartridges to sell. Aaron used three of them to teach himself how to shoot."

"If this is the case—and I'm not sure you are right—then we'll have to resort to other means. Attacks have been mounted before with other means."

"Oh yes! Dynamite, knives, acid. But every means, as you call them, has problems. You have to be trained to use dynamite, and it too is not easy to obtain. A knife? The most unreliable of all. It takes great strength to kill a man with a knife. Acid can disfigure.

But you have to get very close and—well, why go on? I suspect our paymaster has means too. Means of protecting himself. He may be armed, who knows? After the Trepov shooting, men in high positions have learned not to let unknown young ladies come into their presence without taking precautions. Give it up, Rebecca. Turn the information over to Vasiliev."

"Always Vasiliev! You're beginning to sound like Ruth. But wait, David. How d'you expect to arm your self-defense group?"

"That's just the point. We're just beginning to get an organization under way. It's like your People's Will. Once you have an organization you can get a hold of weapons. But Rebecca, *you're* going into battle alone."

"So you're abandoning me."

"I'm trying to make you realize that even the two of us…"

"Aaron makes three."

"Aaron is blind in one eye and not in top form otherwise. As I was saying, even the two of us do not have the resources or the experience to carry out a successful attack. We're still amateurs in this business."

Rebecca fell silent for a few minutes. "Once we have the address, will you at least help me find out the paymaster's daily routine? We need to know when he goes out and where he goes."

"All right! Just to prove I'm not working against you. But understand that even following a man is not a simple matter. The police usually do it in relays. But we can try it, and you can judge for yourself."

Rebecca smiled thinly. David was not convinced that he had persuaded her of anything. He left her sitting on the bench.

Chapter
Forty-Five

When David came out of the University auditorium several hours later, he was surprised to see Ruth and Aaron waiting for him. "Let's go for a stroll," said Aaron. They entered the Park of the Women's Theological School, passing by the bench where he and Rebecca had been sitting. David had a bad feeling. He was sure they were going to ask him to betray her.

Ruth linked arms with both of them. "Aaron and I have been talking. We agree that we should tell Vasiliev what we know. I've been thinking about what Vera said. I'm worried. She's probably going to ask for my help in some terrible plan of revenge. Just like Rebecca. Isn't that what she asked you about when she carried you off a little while ago? I know my sister. She's obsessed! It's almost impossible to say no to her. She turns everything into a test of love or friendship. None of us can stop her. The only way to prevent a tragedy is to get the police involved. Before she has a chance to act! We are not betraying her. We're just as committed to justice as she is. The only thing we're taking away from her is vengeance. Rebecca may think she is a secular Jew, but she has a Biblical sense of revenge."

David had never heard Ruth speak this way. Of course, she too was her father's daughter. Housekeeping and primping in front of a mirror was only a part of her life. The Rabbi had cultivated her mind too. She sounded more reasonable to David than Rebecca. She wanted justice. But she also wanted to save her sister. David knew that's exactly what he too wanted too, and just as badly as Ruth did.

"Aaron?"

"I think Ruth's right on this one. I figure whoever runs an organization like this one is not going to be taken out by a student and a cripple armed with a lead pipe and three cartridges."

"I take exception to the cripple part of it. But you're right. It's not a job for amateurs. I think we should tell Rebecca what we intend to do."

David felt Ruth's arm tighten against him.

"I'm not sure we are strong enough, any one of us, to stand up to her. She'll be furious."

"Well, if we don't, she'll find out sooner or later."

"Yes, she'll curse us. But once we tell Vasiliev it'll be too late for her to do anything else. If we tell her now she might do something desperate, even suicidal."

"I don't think she's that far gone, Ruth!" protested David.

"No, perhaps not. But that's what it would amount to. Listen, if we agree to get in touch with Vasiliev, there's still a problem. He hasn't picked up his mail in several days. He told me about a safe room. He can always be reached there in an emergency. He trusted me in a way my sister doesn't. I'm not sure even you've been entirely honest with me, David. But it doesn't matter. Anyway, the safe room is in a district where I'd look out of place. Besides, I'm scared to go there. Suppose the two of you went there tonight or tomorrow night? You could tell Vasiliev everything we know. Would you do that?"

Aaron and David exchanged glances. They both nodded. "We'll just have a chance to look the place over before it gets dark tonight. To make sure he's there. Then tomorrow we'll drop in on Mr. Inspector Vasiliev," said Aaron.

"Thank you, my friends. Maybe I should try to find out the paymaster's address before you see Vasiliev. I know what I said to Rebecca about pressing too hard. But Vera is more likely to tell me than him. And that way we can hand him the whole package. My goodness, the expressions I'm picking up. I'm beginning to sound like a conspirator myself. So, what do you think?"

Vasiliev wound his way past the crowded tables in the teahouse in the City Park. The large room was thick with smoke and heavy with the sour smell of working men, for whom bathing was a rare event. Vasiliev ordered tea but left it untouched. He asked for the manager. The waiter pointed towards the back of the shop, where a canvas sheet served as a door. Vasiliev knocked on the wooden door-frame. "Police!" He pushed aside the canvas and entered a small office. There were two badly-done watercolors on the wall. A portrait of Alexander II hung over the desk of the manager. God, another mourner, thought Vasiliev. Is nobody happy with the new Tsar? He pulled out his identity papers and handed them to the manager, who took a long time to read them. Longer than was necessary. Vasiliev studied him. Fat, slovenly and badly shaven. But the eyes did not waver when he looked up. He gave back the papers and grunted. Vasiliev sat down without being asked.

"It seems that recently you've had some odd customers," he began.

"There was no need to come from Moscow to tell me that," the manager growled.

"Ah, a man with a sense of humor. Perhaps you belong on the stage instead of in this business. Perhaps you'll end up there, unless you change your tone."

The manager shrugged. "I beg pardon, Your Honor, but the local police have been all over me. There's nothing left to pick on."

"Very nice of you to spare me the trouble of doing my job. But just indulge me for a moment. A man was stabbed on the street outside your premises. This could happen to anyone. But he must have come out of your place, no?"

"I already told the police. I didn't notice him. If you want to talk to the waiters, please go ahead. They'll tell you the same. Who takes notice of a man drops in for a glass of tea?"

"Yes, perhaps the man didn't stand out in a crowd. But another one of your customers is a different sort. Unusually tall and thin man, black hair parted in the middle. Does that ring a bell?"

"Your Honor, do you know how many men pass through my humble place in the course of a week? Now if he stabbed someone, you see, I would notice."

Vasiliev decided to bluff. "So you deny that your place may be the rendezvous for a gang of criminals who use it as a base for their operations?"

"My God, what an accusation! Even the local police didn't go that far." The manager stood up, pulled aside the canvas, and bellowed "Egor, come here."

"This, Inspector, is my most reliable waiter. Ask him your questions. Or let me. Egor! have you noticed a tall, thin man with—what?—dark hair parted down the middle hanging around the teahouse? Have you failed to report to me any suspicious characters. Perhaps a gang plotting some outrage?"

"How tall, how thin? People don't like it if you stare at them like beasts in a cage, Your Honor," Egor said turning to Vasiliev. "But as for plotters, well most fellows here are too tired from work to hold up their heads."

"I can produce several witnesses who will testify that such men were seen here."

"Well, Inspector, if you are able to do this, then we'll have to hire one of those new lawyer types, God spare us. You see, I've heard something about the new legal reforms and such. I read the *Government Messenger* and I know my rights. But please, Inspector, allow me to offer you tea. We have the best assortment in Kiev— Chinese, Persian, even Darjeeling. Then you can see for yourself whether a tall thin man makes his appearance."

Vasiliev realized he was wasting his time. If he had half a dozen men he would have posted them outside the teahouse. But this was not Moscow. Novitsky was always complaining about the lack of manpower. He had only reluctantly assigned a policeman to Vera's ward. Serov was off in Smela. Besides, there was only a remote chance that the tall thin man would show up again soon. The manager could easily send out a warning to stay away. He was a tough nut, and Vasiliev didn't have the time to crack him.

On the way back to the safe room he stopped at the Hotel d'Europe. Two messages were waiting for him. His heart skipped a beat as he read Ruth's note. He glanced at his watch. Was it too late to pay a call? He thought of her as he had first seen her in a black dress of mourning. He ripped open the second envelope. An invitation from Maria Alexandrovna to a reception that evening for Count Kutaisov. He swore quietly and stuffed both notes into his pocket. He couldn't afford to snub the Tsar's special emissary. Perhaps Witte would also be there. He was next on Vasiliev's list to be interviewed. There was just enough time to get back into his full dress uniform. He was beginning to feel like a quick-change artist.

The landlady who had rented the room to Serov was feeling badly. It occurred to her that it must have been the milk. The peasant who was selling door-to-door looked clean enough. But you could never tell. She had never seen him before. Kitty had been the first to throw up after just a few licks from his saucer. She had been next, sick to her stomach all afternoon. By the time darkness settled in she was exhausted, lying down fully clothed on her mattress, the cat stretched out by her side. Surely, she thought, it would be no great sin if she didn't light the kerosene lamp that night. She was paid well to do it. But the men rarely came to the room and no one was there right now. So what did it matter, missing one night. She didn't like staying up so late to begin with. But there was the money. She just had to make sure she turned the lamp off before going to sleep. Tonight she couldn't get up. Forget about staying up. She turned her face toward the icon in the corner and prayed to be forgiven this small transgression. She was unaware that her modest cottage was under intense scrutiny and that her minor transgression was about to become a mortal sin.

David and Aaron took turns walking past the safe house. The windows were dark. "What a wretched hovel!" said David when they met at the end of the street. "But I don't think we have to worry about being seen when we come back to pay our visit."

"Let's come back in an hour and check again. You know what David? I think that if Vasiliev shows up tonight, we ought to go in. What do you think?"

"Now that we're here and have an idea of the layout, it makes sense. But you're right. Just to make sure we don't attract any attention we'll come back later."

Two men were watching them from the second floor of a building on the opposite side of the street. They had rented a room earlier that day, bringing large suitcases with them. The heavily bearded man turned to his companion. "What are we to make of that?" It was clear that he did not expect an answer. "I think we have a long night ahead of us."

Chapter Forty-Six

Little things were beginning to get on Vasiliev's nerves. Every time a cabby drove him to the Governor-General's, he managed to pass by the equestrian statue of Bogdan Khmelitsky, the old Cossack Hetman who had slaughtered the Jews back in the seventeenth century. He knew the government had commissioned the statute to commemorate the union of Ukraine and Russia. But was that the first idea that came into people's minds when they placed a wreath at the foot of the pedestal?

Statue of Bogdan Khmelnitsky

When Vasiliev entered the Governor-General's salon he sensed
the atmosphere had changed. Perhaps it was just his mood. No familiar faces, to begin with. Novitsky, the police chief, was missing;
so were the Pole, Szymanski, Captain Rudov and the merchant,
Lopatkin. Then Witte came in from the garden. He always cast a
long shadow. Maria Alexandrovna greeted Vasiliev warmly. She
pulled him aside before introducing him to Count Kutaisov.

"Has your ladies' network been working overtime? Supply-
ing the Count with information?" He smiled at her revealing his
crooked teeth.

"Something strange has been happening," she lowered her
voice. "Rumors are flying around like mosquitoes on the Dniepr.
But people who generally know something are falling silent."

"You mean your husbands are hiding something from you?"

"Don't mock us, Vasili. But yes, they are. We know that they are
quarreling amongst themselves. I suppose they are a bit frightened
of Count Kutaisov. What he'll report to the Tsar. I've an idea they
are trying to settle on one version of events. So that he'll give them
all good marks. A bit like naughty schoolboys."

"You've spoken to the Count. Have they been successful?"

"Judge for yourself. Come meet him."

It seemed to Vasiliev that Drenteln was ignoring him—or was
he avoiding him? He couldn't be pleased with his wife's attentive-
ness to a lowly police inspector.

"Don't make a fuss, Maria Alexandrovna. I'll just ease my way
into the circle. Perhaps you and I can have a chat later on."

Vasiliev stood in the rear of the group clustered around the
Count. Kutaisov was finishing up a monologue on the pogrom at
Elizavetgrad. It was the fault of the Jews, of course. There were
good reasons for the outbreak of hostility. The press had to share
the blame. They'd stirred things up. And most distressing, Kutaisov
said, his eyes darting from one face to another, was the reaction of
the responsible officials. "How am I to explain the fact that in Kiev
they were uncertain, confused? Sometimes downright passive?"
There was a babble of voices.

"We hadn't enough men, Your Excellency."

"We did our best with what we had. We protected the Arsenal and
the big properties. We couldn't put a man in every Jewish tavern."

"They should have sent us reinforcements from the frontier troops."

Kutaisov raised his hand for silence. "I understand that you are loyal servants of His Majesty. You're not to blame! I've heard the same thing everywhere I've gone. You are only repeating what our good host, the Governor-General, has been telling me ever since I arrived. And I do not doubt that if the entire army had been put at his disposal he could have brought the riots to an end at once. But, gentlemen, we cannot rush the army into our southern provinces as if the British had landed again at Sevastopol." Kutaisov smiled thinly.

There was a ripple of nervous laughter.

Kutaisov lifted his lorgnette and caught Vasiliev's eye.

"Well, now. Let's have the opinion of an outsider, so to say. Major Vasiliev, I believe, has also been conducting an investigation of his own. Or should I say 'officially unofficial.' As I recall, he has a reputation for employing unorthodox methods. Perhaps here in Kiev they have also yielded some interesting results."

"I'm afraid my reputation for unorthodox methods has given rise to some wild stories. I'm told rumors were circulating not long ago among Moscow coachmen. They said I could change my form into any shape I wished. Would you believe it? Some villagers in the Urals, where I used to hunt, swear they'd seen me turn into a bear. I can assure you gentlemen that I am just an ordinary mortal."

Kutaisov led the general laughter. Vasiliev knew the Count was not about to be put off by pleasantries. When the group broke up Kutaisov took Vasiliev's elbow and guided him to the punch bowl.

"Listen, Vasili Vasilievich, I'm a great admirer of your father. I know the story of your exploits in the war. Your heroism in trying to save our late beloved Tsar Alexander Nikolaevich, is legendary. I'm also aware of the interest of our mutual friend, the Iron Colonel, in obtaining an independent estimate of the causes of the disorders. But my appointment comes from our August Master, Alexander Alexandrovich. To do what? To find out why the disorders broke out when and where they did. To make recommendations. To prevent them from happening again. You know all this. I am just repeating myself. For emphasis, as it were. It would not be in the interests of Russia if we found ourselves on different sides of the barricades. Ah, I speak only metaphorically here. But I've often had the impression that Russia is facing a growing crisis. Everywhere you look there are danger signs. Disorders, rioting, the terror. Crazy young people preaching all sorts of nonsense. If the forces of order are not united, we are doomed. Don't you agree?"

"United in defense of the law, yes. And the legal means of changing it. But we have a duty, do we not, Count, to report the truth as we see it. That is, honestly. We are free to draw our own conclusions. Others will decide how to act. We cannot afford to make mistakes. Or else our enemies will destroy us. And mistakes can only be avoided if we discuss these problems openly."

"But my dear fellow, you see what problems this open discussion has created on the Jewish question. We have newspapers that came close to inciting riots. Is this what you want?"

"Of course not! But we can only have open discussion in a society where it is not punished. Remember, Count, how it was impossible to discuss the evils of serfdom while serfdom existed. As long as the Jews are confined to the Pale and they and other peoples are treated as second-class citizens, open discussion can only lead to riots."

"I must disagree with you here. Much as I deplore the riots, I believe that following your ideas would lead to greater disorder. Orthodox Russia has taken under its wing many peoples of different cultures. It we allow them all to mix together, the Empire will lose its Russian character. There will be chaos. I hope that your report will not contribute to that terrible result."

"I think we are both loyal subjects of His Majesty working toward the same ends. I hope that we can continue to respect one another."

Kutaisov smiled coldly and extended two fingers to Vasiliev. "Please remember me to your father," he said and turned away.

Vasiliev saw Witte standing by the French windows to the garden. He was obviously bored by the chatter of dowager wearing a gray ball gown that was a generation out of date. Catching sight of Vasiliev, he made a mute appeal for help. As Vasiliev approached, he heard the tell-tale lisp of a Petersburg lady reciting court stories as old as her dress. Vasiliev interrupted as gallantly as might have been expected of Count Vorontsov's son. He guided Witte outside into the gardens. Vasiliev was reminded of how he had felt when Szymanski had led him down the same path. He felt different now, close to the solution of the murder and to the time when he could leave Kiev and plan his rescue of Irina. Much depended on Witte's willingness to provide answers.

"You have an able man in Abrahamson," he began. "With people like him you'll be able to put a stop to the irregularities on the Southwest line. You'll turn it into a model for Russia's railroads."

"You mean the deficit, don't you?"

"The deficit is a result of embezzlement covered up by murder."

Witte whirled to face Vasiliev, and uttered an exclamation.

Vasiliev hurried on. "There's at least one person who has been milking the line through fraudulent contracts. I suspect the same man of organizing the murder of Rabbi Meier. The Rabbi was collecting information. He had proof of corruption. After he was killed the evidence was stolen. I think the pogroms in Kiev were incited to cover up the crime. Outsiders were brought in on the rail lines. Most other places the pogroms erupted spontaneously. But not here."

"Astounding. I knew nothing of this. Did Abrahamson tell you about this? If so he has lost my confidence. His first duty was to report to me."

"No. I found out by following my own leads. Abrahamson knows the technical side of things inside out. But he knows nothing about the cheating that went on. He has no idea either about the cause of the pogroms. He is loyal to you. Absolutely loyal. If we are to catch the criminal I have to protect my sources. I promise you one thing. I'll give you a full account when I'm certain that I'm right. You will be the first to know who the guilty ones are inside your organization. But I ask you to be patient. It will only be a matter of a few days, I think. Much depends now on whether you are willing to answer a delicate question."

"Well, I must say I'm shocked by what you tell me. Of course, corruption is not unheard of on our railroads. But murder is. Ask your question, Inspector! I'll answer it if it is in my power."

"It concerns a member of the Holy Brotherhood."

"Ah, that is indeed a delicate question. We are sworn to secrecy about our members. As the head of the Kiev branch I feel a special

300

responsibility to keep my word. Yes, Inspector, a delicate question indeed."

"Suppose I were to write a name on a scrap of paper. If you don't react. I'll assume it's my man. Would this ease your conscience?"

Witte laughed and clapped his hand on Vasiliev's shoulder. "A nice touch, Vasili Vasilievich. But you know as well as I do—that would be merely an evasion. Give me some time to think about it."

"Gladly, but I worry about waiting too long. Other lives may be at risk. The Rabbi's murderer has been assassinated and his wife badly injured to protect the man behind all this."

"Good lord! But you should arrest him."

"First, I need to build a strong case. So far, I have only a strong suspicion."

"What good will it do knowing whether he is member of the Holy Brotherhood?"

"It will help to explain the symbolism of the crime."

"Symbolism? What do you mean?"

"The Rabbi was shot in the face six times forming a Latin cross."

"This is monstrous. But the link between this symbolic crime with the Brotherhood seems very tenuous. You would need additional proofs."

"In this case, Sergei Iulevich, I'm trying to spin a web. I want to catch a murderer; all I have now is proofs that he was an embezzler. The rest is still circumstantial. I'm weaving other threads. Membership in the Holy Brotherhood would be another one."

"I don't deny your expert knowledge. I always admire that. And you've already done me a great service by uncovering this corruption. But the whole vast conspiracy seems—well, as you say, circumstantial. At least give me details about the embezzlement of funds. That might help me make up my mind quickly."

"Of course. I'll send the papers to your office tomorrow."

Witte clasped Vasiliev's hand in both of his. He pressed it warmly. "We must work together to build a new Russia. Pure and strong, a great power free of the taint of corruption and favoritism. Thank you for your loyalty."

Vasiliev remained in the garden after Witte left him. He was overcome by feelings of impotence and despair. Witte and men like him had formed the Holy Brotherhood in the belief that they could help protect the Tsar. But like all secret organizations, its original purpose could easily be twisted to become a screen for criminal activities. He continued to feel frustrated that he lacked hard evidence in the case. Witte was right. Inspired guesses are all he had. He had relied on them in the past. They had always—well, almost always—been right. He also knew how hard he was pressing to wrap up the investigation. Perhaps too hard. He had not been completely frank with Witte. It had less to do with saving lives than saving Irina. The longer he spent in Kiev the more she would have to endure the hell of Tiumen. A month had already passed since he had arrived. It was already mid-May. And what about being frank with himself? He did not want to make a fool of himself with Ruth. She was a temptation. And close to hand. How long could he keep driving away the images he had of her? Especially now that she had begun to enter his dreams. And why had she not told him about Iakov?

Maria Alexandrovna had been keeping an eye on Vasiliev all evening. When he came in from the garden, she sensed that he was discouraged. Had his talks with Kutaisov and Witte gone so badly? For an instant she was tempted to tell him everything she knew. But she realized the cost would be too high for her and Drenteln. He had poured out his heart to her just that morning. She could not betray his confidences. Not without destroying their position in Kiev and their marriage. She still did not fully understand his desperation. Why was he willing to play this dangerous game? He hadn't reassured her. What did he say? There were pressures she 'could not as a woman understand.' She still felt a flush of anger when she recalled his remark. But she knew that it was precisely because she was a woman that she was capable of forgiving him.

She would always remember him standing on the threshold of her boudoir, his face ashen, speaking in a hushed voice. "Maria, I have brought us to the edge of an abyss." He had rambled on for an hour. It had taken her some quiet moments to make sense of it all. He had ignored the warnings coming from Petersburg of the coming storm. What was worse, in her mind, was his decision to let it break against "selected targets" as he put it. He had ordered the army to protect the Arsenal and other key buildings as well as the houses of the rich Jewish merchants. But he had held back units from putting down the riots in the popular quarters. It had been a foolish gamble. He wanted to show the government that the Jews were a dangerous element. They exploited the people and they joined the revolutionary movement. Once he had established that, he thought he could snuff out the riots quickly. He had gone out into the streets himself. How shocked he had been when the rioters had turned against him. Things had gotten out of control. Then the army commanders refused to order their men to shoot. Only men like Rudov had taken extreme measures. But he was in on the game. When Drenteln admitted to his wife that he had made a terrible mistake, he almost broke down in front of her. Now Kutaisov and Vasiliev were rooting around. If their reports blamed the authorities, he, the Governor-General, would have to take full responsibility. He would be ruined. He counted on steering Kutaisov away from the truth. This meant getting him to swallow the line that the riots had been spontaneous demonstrations against Jewish exploitation. He would argue that the Jews themselves had circulated false revolutionary proclamations in order to get more protection from the government. Kutaisov might be persuaded to include some critical comments on the incompetence of local officials. It was their failure to influence the Little Russian peasants that had touched off the pogroms in the first place. It might also be possible to shift some of the blame for the violence onto Novitsky. After all, the police chief was circulating his own version of weakness at the top.

"But Vasiliev is another matter," he had said, sinking down on her couch. She had felt her hands clench. She remembered the rest by heart. "He is a stubborn man, I should even say touched with fanaticism. Remember his wild accusations that the Gendarmes were involved in the assassination of the Tsar. He is unpredictable. I tried to neutralize him with the help of Rudov and Szymanski. You know, my dear, that he has had a dangerous liaison with a female revolutionary."

Maria Alexandrovna felt his words strike her heart. She remembered little of her husband's confession after that.

"Invite him tonight," Drenteln had said. "Let Kutaisov work on him. Help him solve his murder case, and let's get him out of here." Then the Governor-General had pulled her close and buried his head in the folds of her gown. She had stroked his head. "No more foolishness, my dear. Leave Vasiliev up to me. He is an honorable man, but too single-minded. Tell me more about how you tried to neutralize him."

Maria Alexandrovna was smiling as she came up to Vasiliev, but she felt as though she were wearing a mask at carnival time. How could he not see through her? His penetrating gaze, his long experience with people who were determined to deceive him. Yet, he showed no signs of suspecting her.

"Why is it that you always look depressed at my parties?" She had not meant to begin this way, but she found it difficult to repress all her affection for him. It had been the same with his father. Now, she felt as though she were cutting the last ties with her youth. But the time for sentimental memories was over.

"My dear Maria Alexandrovna, I wish I could enjoy your parties. But it's this way. Thanks to you I learn a lot from your guests. It isn't your fault that most of what I learn does not raise my spirits."

"Speaking of information, I've found out a few things that might help you. Even if they don't raise your spirits." She led him into the music room, deserted except for a young woman struggling with a Chopin mazurka. She was having difficulty getting the rhythm right. When she saw Vasiliev shake his head, she got up immediately and left.

"I think I have cleared up one mystery. The meeting between the Governor-General, Rudov and Szymanski. It seems Szymanski has been lending money to Rudov to cover his gambling debts. The Governor-General got wind of this. It worried him. After all, a captain in the Gendarmes shouldn't be indebted to a former Polish revolutionary. The Governor-General insisted that Rudov find another moneylender, even if he were a Jew, and pay back Szymanski. Heavens knows what else is going on between those two men. I do not trust Rudov at all. As for the Baron, I thought he was a charming man who had renounced his past. But I guess I was wrong. I shall never invite either man to my house again."

She could scarcely believe she had told these lies looking straight into Vasiliev's eyes. She could not bring herself to say more. Later that night, as she lay in bed unable to sleep, she thought she had been convincing. It would have been a mistake to pile lie upon lie. It wouldn't have done Vasiliev any good to know the truth. He couldn't win in a struggle with a man as powerful as the Governor-General. They would all suffer. Rudov and Szymanski were expendable. No sooner had she given the word to her thought than she shuddered, turned her face into the pillow, and wept.

Chapter
Forty-Seven

Vasiliev left the Governor-General's mansion in a troubled state of mind. He sensed a subtle change in Maria Alexandrovna's attitude towards him. But he could not put his finger on what it was. Had he lost her confidence? He hurried back to the safe room, hoping that Serov had returned from Smela. Walking down the narrow lane to their drab quarters deepened his gloomy mood. The poor neighborhoods in the big cities like Kiev, Moscow and St. Petersburg seemed more wretched to him than the village where he was brought up. Was it just nostalgia for childhood? Or was poverty in the countryside somehow more bearable? Perhaps his father had been an enlightened landowner after all.

He was relieved to see a candle in the window. Serov was back. Vasiliev recalled how many times Serov's down-to-earth view of things had helped him banish the inner demons battling for his *dusha*, his Russian soul, split between village and manor house. He gave the whistle of the night jar to announce his approach. The sound, however mournful it might have sounded to others, cheered him up.

Serov was exercising his hand by squeezing a ball of clay. He had taken off his sling. He was complaining again that the cast was beginning to itch. He was going to get Dr. Margulies to remove it.

"Did you see the sights of Smela?" Vasiliev asked.

"A lot of unhappy people, is what I saw. That Captain Rudov is a mean bastard. But no need to hear about all that. He owes the moneylenders plenty. No joke. No trouble getting the truth out of his coachman. We killed off a bottle or two. A couple of beers might have done, and cost less. Still, with vodka you can be sure. Your Captain Rudov is not beloved by anyone. And the loan shark is your old friend—"

"Baron Szymanski," Vasiliev said, sounding a bit smug.

Serov looked quizzically at him. "Vasili Vasilievich, you know how often you're surprisin' me like that. Sendin' me off to learn somethin' that you end up findin' out for yourself. And gettin' it faster. But this time you're wrong."

Vasiliev's eyebrows shot up, a reaction that Serov enjoyed producing, but rarely saw.

"Now where d'you get that idea?" Serov asked, determined to prolong his little game. Vasiliev knew there was little point in pressing Serov, who was savoring his small victory. Such was the price, he mused, of smugness.

"All right Sergeant, check—but not necessarily mate. My information came from an unimpeachable source." Even as he said the words, Vasiliev felt a small pang. How much had things really changed with Maria Alexandrovna?

"The Governor-General's wife, Maria Alexandrovna. You remember she warned us about Szymanski's attempt to trap me. She told me just today. It was the Baron who loaned Rudov the money. And that fits the picture of an amoral intriguer."

"Well, if we are goin' to count 'em up, them amoral intriguers as you're sayin', who's left out?"

"Don't keep me in suspense too long Sergeant, or I might pull rank."

"No chance of that, Vasili Vasilievich. But what you're sayin' is very interestin'. Now let's compare notes. You see, I was trained by a very good detective, meanin' a man who didn't care for gossip. What did he used to call it, 'second hand stuff'? Words was one thing, he told me, but printed words was better. So after me and the coachman became chummy like, I puts out my bait. 'I'll bet you can't show me real proof of what you says.' This is my gambit. He says he can. We trade a few insults. He says, 'What are you stakin?' I says, 'a bottle'. He says 'you're on.' The next night we settle in at a local tavern in Smela. Run by a Christian. The only one still standin' after the *pogromshchiki* finish burnin' down the Jewish taverns. He has a big smirk on his face. 'Order the bottle,' he says. 'Let's see the proof,' I says. He reaches inside his blouse. Out comes this piece of paper. He slams it down on the table. What do I see? A note, what is it called?"

"A promissory note," Vasiliev said, knowing he had lost the game.

"Right, a note that promises. What does it promise? To repay one thousand rubles—I tell you my eyes popped at the sum—at ten percent per month! My God, I think, this must be a Jewish money lender. Then I catch myself. I think of David and Aaron and Rebecca, crazy kids, but they're against all them kulaks, usurers, capitalists. So why does this have to be a Jew? And it turns out that it isn't."

"Serov, the candle is burning low. It's time to administer the *coup de grâce*. Who was it?"

"As I was sayin', your old friend, the merchant Lopatkin."

The two men congratulated themselves for planning the operation on the night of a full moon. What they hadn't planned on was a clear sky. But they got that too. A soft light fell on the safe house in the Plosk district. It sharpened the shadows. There was no place to hide on either side of the street. The bearded man pressed his forehead against the cool surface of the windowpane. His cigar smoldered on the sill. His mind went back over every step he had taken in setting the dynamite charge. The night before, he had loosened a board in the wooden fence across the street. At dusk the following day, he had slipped through into the patch of dead ground behind the house. His comrade had distracted the old landlady by posing as an itinerant calico salesman. He had crawled through an open rear window. He set the charge under a flimsy wooden table, concealing the wire under the runner that extended the length of the room. He led the wire out the window into the yard attaching it to a detonator placed behind a pile of logs at the edge of the ravine. It was not an ideal setup, but he was convinced it would work. He had timed it carefully, just how long it would take him to get down the stairs, cross the street, push open the loose board, and reach the detonator. By then the targets would have made their way to their room. There was no margin for error. But the alternatives were worse. If he waited outside, squatting behind the pile of logs, he might be seen in the bright moonlight. There was no other cover in the yard. If he crossed over before the targets arrived, he would have to rely on his comrade to signal their approach. Experience had taught him to trust his own eyes and nobody else's on an operation like this one.

The bearded man glanced at his comrade, whose head was already nodding. Three glasses of strong tea seemed to have had little effect on him. So much for a reliable lookout! He turned his attention back to the sky above. A small cloud briefly obstructed the moon. He began to fret; had the wind shifted? He gripped the sill with both hands, as if by an effort of will he could delay the bank of clouds forming on the horizon from drifting over the target area. He lifted his arm and glanced at his watch. It was after midnight. Lowering his eyes, he thought he caught sight of a movement across the street. He reached out to touch the arm of his dozing comrade. He silently pointed out the window. A few whispered words, and the bearded man was on his feet. His arms hung loosely; he forced his muscles to relax; he waited patiently. This was the critical moment. Too many men grew panicky just before they set off their bombs. That's when they made mistakes. He had the reputation of remaining utterly calm. That's the impression he had cultivated to perfection. That and calculating the correct charge.

The shadows took clearer shape. Two men. They disappeared under the eaves of the cabin. He rushed out of the room, scrambled down the stairs, and raced across the street. He pushed through the loose board, stifling a cry as a splinter of wood pierced the palm of his hand. Crouching, he quickly covered the open ground. Ten steps. A shadow passed over him as the bank of clouds began to cut the moonlight. He sank to his knees, groping for the handle of the detonator. He listened for a moment, feeling a trickle of sweat run down his back. There was no warning signal from across the street. He had not been seen. The targets were in the cabin; he could visualize them cross the threshold and enter their room. Should he wait for a light to show? No, they might spot the wire. He'd give them half a minute, no more, not time enough to light a candle. His fingers were twitching. The moon had disappeared from sight. He set his teeth and depressed the plunger. He knew he was dangerously close to the targets. He could easily have perished in the blast, like the assassins of the Tsar. But he'd planned how to save himself; he hurled himself backwards over the edge of the ravine, rolling down the steep incline behind the house. The explosion shook the ground, sending shattered logs and shards of glass flying over his head. As he picked himself up off the ground at the bottom of the hill and hurried away unhurt, he was thrilled with the certainty that it had been a perfect operation.

Chapter
Forty-Eight

When he first became Kiev's chief of police, Novitsky gave orders that he should be notified immediately of any 'extraordinary occurrence' in the city. No matter what time of day or night. His refusal to give a precise definition of the word 'extraordinary' gave rise to heated debates among his subordinates. On early duty the morning of the explosion, Kablukov, 'our Prussian', never hesitated. Within minutes of receiving reports from the district police and fire brigade, he was pounding on the door of Novitsky's apartment. "A bomb outrage, Your Honor!" Novitsky had never seen him so excited. A police cab rushed them to the bombsite. By the time they arrived the flames had been doused. But the chief of the fire brigade warned them that the embers were still smoldering. It would be advisable to wait before examining the wrecked cabin. Kablukov was already knocking on doors and demanding information from the terrified neighbors. Novitsky shouted to him, "Find out who lives here!" He had pulled on a pair of heavy rubber boots and then doused them with water. He wielded a stout oaken stick, and was poking around on the edges of the burned out cabin, calling for firemen with buckets of water to clear a path for him.

The first body he found was that of a woman, terribly burned, steam still rising from the corpse. Novitsky cursed under his breath. "Haul her out before she turns into cinders!" The heat was making him sweat profusely. "Damn it, get some water down here! Give me that bucket!"

"He poured water over his trousers and boots, cursing all the while. He spotted two legs smoldering under a fallen beam. He tried to free the body. The beam was too heavy. "Give me a hand here! Don't you have an ax for the love of God?" The firemen were exhausted and held back. Novitsky called out to his own men who were beginning to arrive. Two officers moved toward him but then fell back, shielding their faces with their cloaks, the heat burning the soles of their shoes. "Is no one prepared for a fire but me? Look at your feet! Did you think this was going to be a parade?" He struck the beam viciously with his stick. It broke into two pieces sending up a shower of sparks and a spurt of flame. "Fire brigade! Water!" He flicked away a cinder that fell on one of his heavy gloves. Using the oak stick as a lever, he pushed the beam to one side, exposing the torso of a man whose clothes were completely burned off. "Get him out of here!" he cried.

A second water wagon had arrived and a fresh brigade was working the pumps. "Don't drown me for the love of Christ! Buckets! I need buckets over here." Men were behind him now with grappling hooks tugging at the body but only succeeding in pulling off the man's charred leg. "Stop, stop! Just turn him over. Has he got a face left?" He heard a fireman retch. The smell of burnt flesh nauseated him. He fought down the bile rising in his throat, and pushed ahead.

"Another one!" he cried out. His eyes smarted, tears were streaming from them. His face felt as though it had been shoved into an oven. "This one has no head at all! Who the hell are these people?" He seized a bucket from a fireman standing beside him and poured it over himself. The men had never seen anything like it. He was like a man possessed, a demon. He lifted his head toward the sky baying like a wolf. "Damn the swine forever more." Then he turned and walked back through the ashes to the cab. He gulped down a cup of water and handed it back to Kablukov. "Another," he croaked. He leaned against the wheel of the cab. "Who blows up a wretched hovel in this district? Eh Kablukov? Answer me that!" Kablukov shrugged and went off to talk to the chief of the second brigade. A fireman had picked up something from the ashes and was holding it at arm's length. Kablukov came back to Novitsky, a charred shred of clothing dangling from his fingers. Two blackened brass buttons were still attached.

"Your Honor, this looks like a piece of a uniform, the uniform of an officer. It's not one of ours."

"Let's see it. God Almighty! How can this be? Listen, Kablukov, what did the neighbors tell you?"

"Just that an old woman owned the place and had rented it out, she said, to 'important guests.' Someone claimed to have seen two men in uniform go into the house a week ago."

"Do you know what this is?" Novitsky waved the rag in front of him. It comes from the uniform of the Moscow city police. Do you know of any other Moscow city police in Kiev except for Vasiliev and his deputy? I do not. God spare me! How could this happen in my city?"

As they came around the corner of the street, just ahead of them an explosion shook the ground, sending wood and glass high into the air. They stopped dead in their tracks, stunned. For an instant they stood rooted to the spot.

"Oh God! It's started again," cried Aaron.

"Was it…their cabin?"

"Let's get out of here, David. The place is an inferno. No one could have survived. We can't help. If the police find us…quick, back this way."

They began to run. In the distance they heard the sound of a hunting horn followed by the thunder of hooves. They flattened themselves against a high wooden fence as a horseman galloped by, wearing a copper helmet and brandishing a long whip. At his heels two heavy wagons drawn by six dappled horses careened down the street. Men clung to the ladders strapped to the side panels. In the center of the wagons two huge cylinders of water held in place by thick hawsers slid backwards and forwards, as if straining to break loose. The clatter was deafening.

David and Aaron turned away from the main thoroughfare and stumbled down a steep incline. The blasts from the horn faded rapidly. Gasping for breath, they barely managed to stay on their feet by grabbing hold of low hanging branches of the closely packed trees.

"I can't go on," Aaron said falling to his knees. "My legs are finished."

"We're safe here. We can rest."

"What do you think happened?"

"Who can tell? Maybe Vasiliev was getting too close to the kill-er."

"First the killing of our Rabbi, then the attacks on us, the wom-an in the hospital, now this. Couldn't all be the work of one person. There must be an organization. Do you think Reb Ben-Zion is right, the Holy Brotherhood is behind this?"

"I don't know. Maybe Rebecca is right. The only defense is a strong organization, and we don't have time to build it from scratch." David felt he was switching positions all the time. Things were happening too fast. He couldn't get his bearings.

Chapter
Forty-Nine

Vera felt herself getting stronger every day. Her body still ached, her head still throbbed. But so long as she did not make an abrupt move, the acute pain no longer tortured her. At night when the ward was asleep, she practiced trying to get up. She swung her legs out of the bed and rested her feet on the floor. At first, the pain came back fiercely. She had to retreat. But gradually she was able to manage it. The next test would be to stand, and then to walk. One thought obsessed her: revenge. She tried to bend her will to dream it. The first night when she was able to stand for a few seconds, she felt a surge of hope and the urge to plan. It was all right to vow revenge. But half crippled as she was, how could she achieve it? This was a new question to obsess her. A vague idea hovered at the edge of her mind. She had a dim memory that kept slipping away from her. One night she dreamed that she and Stepan were back in the cabin. It was after their evening meal. She was washing up. He had gotten up from his seat and moved to the far end of the room. He was fussing about, crouching down, and hammering on the floor. The noise grew louder and louder until she woke with a start. Had she remembered rightly or was it just a dream? When her Angel came with food, Vera asked her about her dreams. Did she ever dream a memory? The Angel thought so. Vera tried that night to fix her mind on what Stepan might have been doing on the floor. In the morning she could not remember whether or not she had dreamed anything at all.

The next night she took her first step, holding on to the chair where the Angel normally sat. She felt something crack in her leg.

For an instant she feared she had broken something. But no, must have been a bone grinding back into place. She realized how little she knew about her own body. That night she dreamed again. Or was she half awake? Now she could see what Stepan was doing on the floor. He had pried up one of the floorboards and was now replacing it. What could he have been doing there? She knew he would never conceal money or jewelry, not from her. What else would be so valuable, so precious and yet so—what, dangerous?—that he had to hide it? Then she remembered a conversation they had had not long after he had returned from Siberia. He had said something about never going back. "They will never take me again." Those were his very words. "If they come, I have a surprise for them."

This could mean only one thing. Stepan had hidden a weapon under the floorboard. He would not have carried it when he visited the Esteemed Person. He did not suspect he would need it. Suddenly, it all became clear, the memory she had suppressed of having found it. She would have her revenge.

She did not share her secret with the Angel. But she needed the Angel to help her. She knew she was not strong enough to get out of the hospital, make her way home, and then continue her journey of revenge to its final destination. Now that she had solved the problem of revenge, she had to work out a solution to another problem. How to escape?

Vera practiced walking a few steps. It was painful but not unbearable. Just so long as she took her time. She was sure she could make it out of the hospital with the Angel's help. The day that the Angel brought her flowers again, she suddenly found the solution. The Angel was sentimental.

"My friend, listen to me now. I need your help. You've been so good to me. Now I have to ask you one more thing. A favor."

Ruth smiled and patted the bed next to Vera's arm.

"What is it?"

"I have a story to tell, and then I'll ask my favor. My story is this. I have a child. He is only two years old. I do not know what's happened to him since I was injured. I took him to the country after Stepan was killed. He's with strangers. They're probably good people, but who knows? I must get him back!"

She watched the Angel carefully. There were already tears in her eyes. Good! She thought. My little story is working.

Vera explained that she did not want to send ahead for fear that the people would refuse to give up her son. They might hide him. She had to get to him in person. Only she, no one else, could find the village and cabin where she'd left him. She needed help to get out of the hospital and get back home. Then she could manage for herself.

"Please my friend, I know I'm asking a lot. But you are my only hope now. The doctors will refuse to let me go. I can't wait any longer. I'm suffering too much."

Ruth felt that having cared for Vera she couldn't now disappoint, still less abandon her. At first she was frightened at the prospect of doing something illegal. But then she thought of how Rebecca would have acted. The more she thought about it, the more she believed that helping Vera would be a noble act. The following day she agreed.

David and Aaron spent most of the rest of the night wandering through parts of the city they hardly knew. They spoke little, their senses dulled by exhaustion and sickly fear. Martial law had ended, but Cossack patrols still roamed the streets. They would not take kindly to finding two Jewish youths walking aimlessly outside their own district. The two friends kept close to the shelter of the buildings. They paused at the cross streets to listen for the telltale sounds of hoof beats and jingling bridles. They moved slowly, the sounds and images of the explosion reverberating in their heads.

Their meandering took them back toward the river, away from the main thoroughfares. They found themselves approaching Askold's Tomb. The same thought occurred to both of them; but David was the first to express it out loud. "Another mythical Russian hero. We're surrounded by them!" Aaron gave a short laugh. "Yes, but somewhere I read that he was really a Khazar warrior. Would that be something! If he was, he might even have been Jewish!"

"Don't let that story get around," said David. "If people came to believe it, Askold's Tomb would suffer the same fate as Vasiliev's safe house. They'd blow it up or burn it down in a flash." Aaron grunted his assent.

Askold's Tomb

As a sliver of silver light appeared in the east, it began to drizzle. Neither one of them took note of the dawn or the rain. They had been following another train of thought. Suddenly, Aaron shook himself out of his reverie. "How are we going to tell Ruth?" he muttered.

"Just what I was thinking," said David, reassured that the long hours of silence had brought them to the same point again. They had long ago recognized their uncanny ability to anticipate one another's thoughts. When they were younger they came to believe that they were really identical twins separated at birth. Now, once more, their thoughts had come together after wandering through the night.

"To the Rabbi's?" asked Aaron when they had emerged onto Bibikov Boulevard.

"No sense waiting any longer," David replied. "But I'm worried about Rebecca's reaction too. Nothing will stop her now. She's hell bent on revenge."

Reb Ben-Zion opened the door to the two bedraggled figures. He was accustomed to see troubled faces. He read theirs as foretelling a catastrophe.

"What has God visited upon us now?"

"Someone blew up the safe house with Vasiliev and Serov inside," Aaron rasped.

Ben-Zion felt as though he had been struck by a terrible force. The responsibility for bringing Vasiliev into the Jewish community had been his alone. By appealing to the detective's conscience he had condemned him to death, as surely as if his own hand had committed the deed. He turned aside to hide the tears rolling down his cheeks. His next thought was that Ruth would suffer this loss differently, but just as painfully. David and Aaron reached out to touch his shoulder as they brushed gently past him.

"There's coffee in the kitchen. I shall waken the sisters." Ben-Zion shuffled down the dark corridor.

David and Aaron sat shivering in the salon. Late May had suddenly turned cooler. The dull light of an overcast morning sky filtered through the lace curtains. Motes of dust were suspended in the motionless air. Outside, the rain was falling in vertical lines.

Ruth and Rebecca came into the room together. A glance at Ben-Zion's face had forewarned them of bad news. Ruth was very pale. Rebecca's jet black curls were a tangled mass, still untamed by the morning routine of brushing.

David told them what they had seen. Ruth swayed in her seat, covering her face with her shawl. Rebecca reached out to grasp her hand. Ben-Zion hovered behind them, twisting his beard in his fingers. Suddenly, he turned and left them. Aaron rubbed his knees nervously.

David had fixed his eyes on Rebecca, marveling at her look of steely determination. She squeezed Ruth's hand once more, and stood up. "So, David, no more hesitation, right? We have to slaughter the beast ourselves. He'll just keep killing unless we stop him. The police are hopeless. If Vasiliev couldn't get him, they certainly won't."

"And we will?" asked Aaron.

"If not we, then me. Ruth will find out where he lives, and the rest will be easy. Aaron, you have your revolver. Yesterday I persuaded the People's Will to supply me with one, and bullets for both of us. David, if you are going to join us I suggest you go back to Mendel. If he can smuggle horses, he can get you a better weapon than your lead pipe. I'm leaving now. I have a duty to perform; so do you!"

Without another word Rebecca swept past them, slamming the door behind her. David sighed and also stood up. He bent over Ruth and kissed her bowed head. Only then did she begin to sob.

The rain had diminished again, giving way to a fine mist. Just wet enough, thought David to make the walk to Kaniever's seem endless. He felt less sure of himself now that Aaron was no longer at his side. A rush of disconnected thoughts passed through his mind. What they were about to do would snap their remaining ties with the world into which they had been born and raised. They would become outlaws. He shivered and walked faster.

Kaniever's looked different again, as if it had been converted into a normal tavern, with a noisy, boisterous crowd. He tried to appear resolute as he strode across the big room, but he felt that the squishing sound of his wet shoes betrayed him. No one seemed to take any notice. He stopped at the bar where Rachel was installed. She appraised him in a single glance before setting down a glass of lager in front of him.

"I'm looking for Mendel," he said.

"That's no surprise. Lucky for you he's back. He might come in tonight and he might not. So be prepared to wait and to be disappointed."

He sat down and sipped his lager. It was warm and bitter. He tried half-heartedly to strike up a conversation with Rachel, but every word sounded forced and artificial to him. She ignored him. I'm no good at this, he thought, remembering that he felt the same during his first visit. But now the feeling seemed worse. What he was planning was worse. Davy the Giant Killer was about to become Davy the Assassin. His mouth seemed to have dried up. The lager only made him more thirsty.

Mendel came in close to midnight. He surveyed the room and seeing David broke into a broad smile. He brushed aside several men who tried to intercept him on his way to the bar.

"Davy the Giant Killer!" He threw his arm around David's neck and kissed him on both cheeks. "Come to repay your debts or to incur still more?" He laughed, and glancing at the half empty glass, exclaimed "Good God! How long have you been nursing that? Let's do some serious drinking. A carafe, Rachel!" He led David over to a table where two men immediately got up, threw down a few coins and left.

Mendel looked exhausted. The sagging pouches under his eyes were dark, almost purple. Dust stirred up by hard riding had seeped into the fine creases in his forehead, giving him the look of a hunted man. Rachel brought the whiskey and two glasses. Mendel kept a faint smile on his face as he raised his glass: "To friendship."

David let the liquid touch his lips, then set down his glass.

"Listen, Mendel, no joke. I need a revolver."

Mendel swallowed his whiskey and stared at the table. He refilled his glass and looked into David's eyes. "To anarchy!" he muttered, "But God spare us from revolution!"

David groaned inwardly. He wanted to get this over quickly. Mendel was obviously in the mood to prolong things. It suddenly occurred to David that Mendel might be desperately lonely. A fine mind surrounded by thieves and whores. Perhaps what he wanted most was someone to share what really mattered to him. David felt anger well up inside him. He silently cursed the men who ran the system, the police and bureaucrats, the imperial family, all those who sat on their necks. The least he could do was to let Mendel unwind.

"If I was a giant killer, you were always clever with an aphorism. But you can't get away so easily. I need an explication. Paint me a big canvas."

Mendel looked startled. He was accustomed to being dismissed as a crank when he sounded off to the gang. Was Davy humoring him? He thought maybe not, maybe the old ties still counted for something.

"Anarchy is the one-way road to freedom, and revolution is a round trip to tyranny"

"It gets better, but it's still an aphorism."

Suddenly, Mendel felt old and worn out. What did it matter anymore, the science of dialectics? Hell! All Davy wanted was a revolver. Was it his business who was going to get shot?

Mendel made a sound like a strangled laugh.

"To go on would be to go downhill. Let the aphorism be: 'Mendel's last stand'." He toyed with the empty glass, spinning it with his fingers. The fine hands of a writer or a musician, thought David, become the hands of a smuggler.

"A revolver. All right, let's deal. Better still let's just set the price."

"How much?"

"Not too fast, Davy. No coin of the realm. Money I don't need right now. Something else. You're going to have to want the revolver very badly."

"Anything within reason."

"There you go, bargaining already! Do you think dealing is in our blood, as the goys keep telling us?"

David felt his stomach churn. First beer, then whiskey. What would he have to swallow next?

"Anything that's unreasonable, then."

"I love it. Now that's a bargaining position as well. Worthy of a Talmudist."

"Come on, spit it out!"

"And now the language of the street urchin. What a repertoire!"

David was annoyed at himself for thinking that Mendel was a tortured soul. The smuggler's life had taken him over.

"Good. That puts us on the same footing." Mendel went on. "Here it is unadorned by explanation or apology. Ready? Not to be bought, but exchanged. A trade in the form of a mutual loan. You get the revolver for a week—enough time? And I get to use your passport for a week. We meet again in seven days to the hour. I get back the revolver and you get back your passport. Let's agree that we keep quiet about how we intend to use them. One thing's for sure. The risk of using them is nothing to be sneezed at. But the risks are about equal. In which case one or even both of us might not make it to the rendezvous, come the end of the week. But I can tell you this much, though it probably won't go far to reassure you. Your document will make a little voyage across the Austrian frontier, to Czernowitz. The jewel of the Crownland of Bukovina. Know it? A charming baroque town full of Jews who suffer no pogroms. Thanks to Austrian enlightened despotism as opposed to the Russian variety, which lacks the enlightened half."

David realized that his old friend wasn't just blabbering. Mendel had his reasons. He was giving David a few moments to ponder the consequences.

"One-time offer," Mendel continued, respecting David's hesitation. "Tonight's bargain. I have the goods, I know you have the equivalent. No Jew would walk around Kiev without his passport. Let me be generous. You have until the carafe is empty to make up your mind."

Mendel poured himself another shot and swallowed it, never taking his eyes off David. There was enough whisky left for one more drink. Mendel lifted the carafe and held it over David's glass. David shook his head. They sat and stared at each other. David had not expected this. His mind raced ahead. What did it matter if he carried a passport or not? If he was arrested in possession of a concealed weapon, they'd give him ten years with or without his passport. But what would Mendel smuggle out or in? Did that matter either? For himself, David calculated, there was a double risk. If Mendel succeeded in crossing the Austrian frontier, he might not make it back. Of course, all this assumed that Mendel would not use the passport for some other more nefarious purpose. What might that be? This is what worried David. On the other hand, Mendel was running much less of a risk. The revolver could not be traced back to him unless David betrayed him. On the other hand, how could Mendel be sure of him? A lot of time had passed. Too many things had happened to separate them. Then Rebecca's last words came back to him: "no more hesitation."

David poured half the remaining whisky into his glass and half into Mendel's. He raised his glass: "To friendship." They clinked glasses and tossed their drinks back in unison. Mendel got to his feet and made his way to the door leading to Kaniever's office. He returned in a few minutes with a package wrapped in oilcloth. He set this down on the table along with an envelope covered with Austrian stamps.

"It's a Smith and Wesson Model 3, Russian infantry revolver, American-made to Russian specifications. Six bullets. You need more? No, you're not going into battle. Or are you? Nice firing action. I had a hell of a time getting it. But there are a few Jewish war veterans around who are in tough straits. Take care of it!"

David slipped the package into his lap. He inserted his passport into the envelope and passed it across to Mendel, who picked up the envelope and examined the stamps. Two philatelists trading over an empty carafe.

It was still misty when David left Kaniever's. He still could not shake off his anger. Along with it was a sense of something done irrevocably. He felt he and his friends were entering a twilight world where Mendel had already taken up his abode. He knew he was not a fighter by nature. Giant killer indeed! He had to laugh to himself. Just because he had beaten up another boy, a bully, many years ago. They had been still in elementary school. But the other boy had grown into a muscle-bound giant a few years later, becoming a circus strong man. And David had beaten him. So the legend was created. After the story went around, he was never bothered by any of the street toughs. He could protect others like Aaron and once, Mendel too. Now the legend was going to be tested in the real world. He feared he would not measure up to his reputation.

He hardly noticed where he was going. His fingers tightly gripped the package. He had even forgotten to ask how to load the revolver. What an assassin he was turning out to be! The word frightened him. What had driven them to such extremes? The stupidity of the government. Destroying their old way of life but not really letting them build a new one. Keeping them penned up in the Pale like cattle. Sure, it was a big pen, a huge one. But finally you reached the fence. It didn't matter where your travels took you. The smugglers were the exceptions. Or were they? They found holes in the fence and slipped through. But then they had to come back. Back into the pen that was called the Pale of Settlement.

What made Vasiliev different from the others wearing a uniform of the Tsar? David asked himself. A rare bird. He and Serov. Was there such a thing as a philo-Semite? If so, they belonged in the category. A population of two. Even the way Vasiliev talked was different than any other person of authority David had ever met. In a funny way he was like Mendel, mixing popular speech and the accents of the educated upper class. But men like him were never allowed into the government ministries. They said that Witte was also different. But he was only one man and still far from the center of power. This fear and hatred of the Jews would bring ruin to Russia.

Preoccupied with his dark thoughts, David was aware too late of the Cossack mounted patrol that came up behind him. He felt a tremor of fear. He groped for the revolver in his pocket. Was it loaded? Hadn't Mendel said something about a chamber with six bullets? There were six mounted horsemen. An absurd thought crossed his mind. Six Cossacks, six bullets. He sobered up quickly. He was not an American cowboy; could he even have shot one of them? On impulse whirled and raised his hand in greeting.

"Troopers, thank God! Did you see the three thugs who jumped me? Waved their knives at me, they did! When they heard you they ran off in that direction. Looked like they were some crazy Yids. You can probably still catch them."

"Let's go, boys!" the leader shouted, and they galloped off. David slumped against the damp wall of a wooden hut. He felt sick to his stomach. He raised his fist to his mouth and bit hard. Then he ran down a side street and lost himself in a maze of alleys. He stopped, breathless, and vomited in the gutter. A dog was alarmed by the sound and began to bark furiously. David had never felt in greater despair

Serov had awoken that morning with a sharp pain in his forearm. Doctor Margulies had warned him that this would happen from time to time, especially during damp weather. Serov told him he did not relish being turned into a barometer. The spasms would diminish over time but might last for years, perhaps all his life. Serov accepted this. He once heard a man, a professor friend of Vasiliev's, hold forth about "the stoicism that was the fate and the refuge of the Russian peasant." He thought it worth while to memorize the phrase. It amused him.

A little pain was a small price to pay for escaping a hellish life. What would have been his fate had Vasiliev not saved him from the life of a peasant? He reminded himself from time to time of the emancipation settlement, the small plots of land they handed out in '61 when they freed the serfs. When they got finished wrestling in the dust that first time, he and Vasya had sat together by a small stream, washing off and telling one another their life stories. It didn't take much time for Serov to finish. At the end he had confided to Vasya: "If you was willin' to take the cut off, what they called the hunger plot, you got it for free. If you wanted enough land to live on, you paid for forty- nine years." He had always wondered whether this is what was meant by this 'stoicism' thing. Still, he considered himself lucky. Vasiliev had lifted him out of the dirt and ignorance of the village.

The last time he had felt pain like this he had almost died. It was during a mass fistfight. How the merchants loved to organize them, then sit around and watch the peasants knock themselves silly. There must have been a hundred fighters that one time. Mostly young peasants. A few old timers. They were the toughest of the lot. The merchants had invited their friends and wives, like it was a horserace or cockfight. Set them up in easy chairs on a hillside. He and the others had had to drag the chairs from the nearest town for all of them. Hot summer, dusty field, men struggling barefoot and stripped to the waist, no rules, beating one another mercilessly. He had learned enough on the village streets about fighting dirty. Vasiliev had given him boxing lessons after he came back from the first year at the Corps de Pages. It had been a fair trade. When they were still children he taught Vasiliev the art of village wrestling. In return, Vasiliev had let him in on all the secrets of the professionals. How to feint, bob, and weave. In a one-on-one his clumsy opponents could scarcely touch him. "Save your strength and your punches. Wait for an opening, then go for the soft places." Serov never forgot the advice. But with so much milling and stumbling around in a mass fight he couldn't guard his back. Even Vasiliev couldn't teach him that trick. He never knew who hit him from behind. Knocked him down. You could be crippled or die if you got trampled or kicked. That's when he felt the terrible pain. He thought it was all over. But a fellow villager had pulled him to his feet. Saved his life. Always wanted to return the favor. But his friend never came back from the war.

He said nothing about the pain to Vasiliev when he went off to buy provisions. At the food store he heard a strange story that made him forget the pain. When Serov got back and was dumping his parcels on the table, Vasiliev was ready to leave, saying he was going to visit Witte again. Serov thought the strange story might change his mind. Serov flexed his arm.

"Still giving you trouble?"

"No more than your ribs. The real trouble is comin' from another direction."

Vasiliev was swinging his cape over his shoulders, but he let it fall, hearing the particular tone in Serov's voice that always got his attention. He folded his arms and waited for the explanation. With Serov it could often take a while, even without the mantra of 'beggin your pardon.' This time there were no preliminaries; Serov came right to the point.

"Rumor is goin' around about an explosion and fire on Bolotna Street. Last night it was. Wrecked a cabin. Killed the people inside. A kid who'd passed by it told me the story. Said the place was still smokin'. Looks like they blew up our safe house."

Vasiliev swore under his breath. "The people inside, how many?"

"They're sayin' maybe three. But the strangest thing is what's comin' from the police. Just tellin' you what I heard. Might be gossip. Can't be sure about it. For what it's worth, the story goes this way. They dug out two bodies, supposed to be police agents from Moscow. Pretty badly burned they were"

Vasiliev thought for a moment. "It makes sense. They must have found bits and pieces of the uniforms we left hanging up. If the bodies were so badly burned, they must have been unrecognizable. But who the hell was in there, and what were they doing there?"

Serov shrugged. "Will you go to Novitsky?"

"No. Listen, Sergeant, I feel sorry for the poor devils who were burned up. But the bombing may be a blessing in disguise. It makes us invisible. Better than the most ingenious disguise. You understand? We no longer exist. It's foolproof protection. The killer, whoever he is, has written us out of the picture."

One thought bothered Vasiliev, one he did not share with Serov. The only person who knew about the safe house, except for the man who had followed him, was Ruth. Was it possible that she had confided in her friends, David and Aaron? Were they trying to get in touch with him? And were they the two men whose bodies had been found? His only thought now was how to get in touch with Ruth.

Vasiliev picked up his cape and headed for the door. A noise at the window startled him.

"Only the wind!" said Serov.

"Damn it! I hate to get jumpy."

"It's shiftin' to the east, clearin' up it looks like." Serov was sweeping off the shelves and arranging his purchases.

Vasiliev looked outside. The rain was streaking the windows in long diagonals. "East wind from Siberia," he muttered. Did everything have to remind him of Irina living out her youth in exile? Serov looked up, but said nothing.

Things are not going well, Vasiliev thought. Irina gone, one of many good people lost to Russia. All over county the police under attack. Violence of every sort was on the rise. The war with the revolutionaries was one thing. But the pogroms were something new. Then the Rabbi's murder, and now this. Who would blow up a miserable log cabin in a poor district of Kiev? He couldn't see any connection with the Rabbi's death, or even with the pogroms. Possibly there wasn't any, but an inner voice warned him not to be sanguine.

There were still too many questions troubling him. Was there a political motive behind the killing of Rabbi Meier? Sure, he had been collecting material on corruption. Not just on the railroads, it seemed, but throughout the whole city administration. He had intended to turn it over to a lawyer. His assassin had made it look like the work of a Christian fanatic. Now he knew that the man was a hired killer; a former convict from Siberia had been the shooter. Then he had been murdered and his wife, Vera, crippled—presumably by the same man who planned the assassination of Meier. What had Serov called him, the puppeteer? Was it this puppeteer who had the assassin killed? Or was his death a random event?

The documents had been stolen. Reb Moishe had been scared off from identifying the man who stole the documents. The tall thin man again! Another creature of the puppeteer. He must have engineered the fake accident that had crippled Vera. Had she known who killed her husband? If so, why not notify the police? She had to be eliminated. That was clear. The thin man had shown up at the hospital to finish her off. Something had aroused the suspicion of the puppeteer. He had put a tail on Vasiliev and located the safe house. But how to explain the explosion and the bodies of the two men inside? Bombs were the weapon of the revolutionaries. Was the puppeteer trying to unload the blame on them? Who were the victims?

Vasiliev was certain he had almost enough circumstantial evidence to arrest the merchant Lopatkin. He had loaned the money to Rudov. In return he had blackmailed the Captain into destroying the record of Stepan's arrest ten years back. Had Lopatkin been behind the plot to discredit Vasiliev with the help of Szymanski? The Pole also seemed to be completely under his thumb. But what about the Governor-General, Drenteln? Was he also in on this plot and if so why? Nagging questions.

Thanks to Abrahamson he had found out that the railroad workers had been stirred up by the tall thin man. And Lopatkin's name had also shown up on the list of the board of the Southwest Railroad. That made two points in a triangle of guilt. The third must be membership in the Holy Brotherhood. That would be insurance for Lopatkin. It would be taken as a sign of his loyalty to the throne. Suddenly, a terrible thought struck him. Lopatkin might even claim that the Rabbi was part of a conspiratorial organization to which his daughter Rebecca belonged. God only knew how deeply she was involved with revolutionaries. If she were, that might explain Lopatkin's attempt to link him with Irina. It could all be made to appear part of what people liked to call 'the revolutionary contagion.' His contacts with the Meier family could be interpreted as evidence that he was part of a Jewish conspiracy.

Vasiliev recalled Witte's story of Gartman, the dynamiter, in Paris. Russia was ready to believe anything these days. Worst of all, the fear spread by the pogroms allowed criminals, like Lopatkin, to hide their activities. He would make one last attempt to convince Witte to give him Lopatkin's name. But would his triangle of proof withstand a clever lawyer? He was beginning to wonder. If not, he would have to force a confession out of Lopatkin. What worried him most of all was the passion for revenge of Rebecca and her friends. Could he persuade them that his brand of justice would work? Theirs could only lead to greater catastrophes. He thought how he had failed to convince Irina. She was now paying the price in Siberia. He had to succeed this time.

Chapter Fifty

Vera swung her legs over the edge of the bed. She sat still for a long time. She listened to the other inmates of the ward breathing, snoring and moaning. Each one emitted a peculiar noise at night. She had come to recognize them all. She forced herself to stand up. This was the third night in a row she had managed it. The pain was still so great that she almost fainted with the effort. She touched her forehead; it was wet with perspiration. She felt her hospital gown clinging to her body like a shroud. She shivered despite the heat of a summer night. She had trained herself to shallow breathing. It lessened the pain in her ribs. Today, she thought, I'll ask my Angel to help me escape. The idea gave her comfort. She took a few steps alongside her bed, holding on to the frame. Then, she sank back, exhausted. She will help me, Vera repeated, clutching her amulet. She managed to lift her legs back onto the bed without groaning. Another first. Progress, she thought, sinking into a deep sleep.

The next morning when Ruth arrived she was surprised to see Vera smiling. Ruth fed her some soup and was pleased to see Vera was recovering her appetite. "Listen, my dear," said Vera after she had swallowed the last of her soup. "I cannot bear to lie here any longer. The poor sick people around me give me no rest. I must get my strength back at home. You will help me, for the sake of my son, won't you? Help me dress and leave here. I beg you to save me from going mad."

Ruth stroked Vera's arm. "Of course, I shall help you. But I'm afraid you aren't strong enough." Ruth knew that her promise did not spring from her heart. It was tainted with calculation. Vera would lead them to the puppeteer. If only Vasiliev would get in touch. She felt a spasm in her throat. If only Vasiliev were still alive. Strange, Ruth thought, how devious I have become. Would Reb Ben-Zion approve? And what of father? Hadn't he too been devious, hiding his documents? Was it all for a noble cause? Ruth was not sure. She was not sure of many things now. Life had become a maze. She had never before felt ashamed of her own motives.

"Perhaps we should wait a day or two," she said hoping she could settle her conscience.

"Lying here, I might be worse in a day or two."

Suddenly, Ruth remembered the thin man coming up the stairs. How easy it would be for him to slip into the ward now that there was no policeman on duty. She felt she had to get Vera out of danger. She looked around the ward. Some of the patients seemed to have gotten worse. The smell of decay was stronger. Yes, she decided, we must get Vera home.

"What about the nurses? Won't they try to stop us?"

"No, no! You'll come tonight before the night shift takes over. Pretend to leave. When they put out the lights, come back. If you help me dress and let me lean on you, I can walk out. I've been practicing getting up by myself. We can do it, my Angel!"

Ruth was trembling when she left the hospital. She managed to calm herself before meeting David and Aaron at home. She hardly noticed how pale David looked. He was not about to tell Ruth about Mendel and Kaniever's. The whole episode would terrify her. He listened to what she had to say, and after glancing at Aaron, nodded his agreement. Aaron proposed to go with her. He had been a patient in the hospital. His being there would not arouse suspicion. Ruth might not be able to manage Vera by herself. Ruth was reassured. She and Aaron talked it over. "At least, we won't have to worry about running into Dr. Margulies, since they kicked him out of the hospital!" said Aaron caustically.

Ruth had watched the nurses make their night rounds. There was a period of about half an hour when there was no one in the corridor outside ward 19. But Ruth wanted to make sure that she would not be intercepted. She decided to take a chance and bribe the night nurse when the shift changed.

Ruth showed up at St. Vladimir Hospital at dusk, wrapped in a black cloak, hatless and without her jewelry. She had hardly recognized herself in the mirror. Was this what they meant by a disguise? She had to smile at the thought. She felt strangely calm as she approached the night nurse.

"Listen, my dear," she said. "I'm going to help my friend go home tonight. I don't want any fuss. They'll be upset in the morning. But they won't think you're to blame. So here is something for your trouble. Just make sure that you are busy at the other end of the corridor between 10 and 11 tonight." The woman looked frightened, but took the money and nodded her head.

Aaron located the Jewish cabman who had often taken Rabbi Meier to the synagogue and could be trusted. He told Ruth she looked terrific, just right for the part. She squeezed his arm gratefully. As they approached the hospital Ruth gave her instructions. Aaron was to drop her off and then drive around for half an hour. That would give Ruth time to dress Vera. Aaron would then come up to help. "She's still weak," said Ruth. "I'm not sure I can handle her by myself." They would bring her out together. "Do you understand?"

Ruth was surprised at herself. Giving orders to Aaron, who meekly accepted them. When had that ever happened? She felt she had changed in the few weeks since her father had been killed. Life had become more interesting, but more frightening too. The thought of Vasiliev gave her courage.

Ruth carried a small traveling case into the hospital. She found Vera sitting up, holding on to the metal bed frame. Ruth had packed a voluminous robe that belonged to her father, and his slippers too. They would easily fit Vera. She bundled Vera's old clothes in the case. She helped Vera take off the hospital gown. Vera gritted her teeth. A soft moan escaped her lips. Ruth wiped Vera's brow with her handkerchief and wrapped the robe around her as gently as possible. She was shocked by the sight of Vera's thin body, marked with the red scars of the operation. She bent down and put on the slippers, gently lifting Vera's feet. She felt Vera shaking. Ruth held her for a moment, whispering encouragement in her ear. She helped her to sit down. "Rest for a moment," she said. Ruth sat beside her until she heard a soft footfall in the corridor. For an instant she felt fear sweep over her. Suppose it wasn't Aaron but the thin man. She said a quick prayer.

It was dim in the ward. Light came from a small candle burning under the icon in the corner. A tall figure entered the room and she gasped. Aaron's voice came to her like a blessing from heaven.

"Ready?"

They lifted Vera to her feet and held her as she swayed from side to side.

"Can you put your arms around our waists and hold onto our belts?"

Vera shook her head. "Hold me under the arms," she whispered. She felt paralyzed and afraid she might fall.

"We'll have to carry her," said Aaron. He felt angry and embarrassed that he was still too weak to lift her by himself. Vera was quietly whimpering now. They half carried, half walked her out of the ward and down the stairs. The corridor was empty. They waited at the bottom of the stairwell to make sure that the night nurse would keep her word. When they came out on the porch of the hospital, the cab was waiting. The cabby jumped down and helped them lift Vera inside. She was half-conscious. She was muttering something that sounded like The "steamed person." It didn't make sense to them. They drove off. Within half an hour they had arrived at Vera's cabin.

Witte had left his office and was about to step into his cab when a man dressed like a merchant accosted him. "Sergei Iulevich! Don't be startled! This is Vasiliev in deep disguise," Vasiliev's tone was ironic. "Rumors about my death are much exaggerated. Not an original thought, but appropriate under the circumstances. I have to speak with you while I am still being mourned." Witte shook his head in disbelief. "Vasiliev, I have heard about your disguises, but I didn't realize that you also mastered the art of resurrection. Well, come on—climb in, and tell me how you escaped a terrorist bombing. There must be a story! I may find the information useful some day."

"Of course. But first, may I ask you two small favors and one big one? The small ones are to keep my 'resurrection', as you call it, a secret for the moment, and then to order your cabman to drive us around while I ask the big favor. Once I have your answer I'll melt away into the darkness."

"The first two favors are readily granted, but only if you then tell me your secrets as an escape artist. As for the big favor, I fear I know it already. But ask away."

"We have an agreement then. My escape was not an escape at all. I simply was not in the cabin when the bomb went off. I have no idea who was there. Strange as that may seem. As for my big favor, you already know what it is. But this time I'm going to press you harder. You see, the bomb was intended to kill me. No doubt about it. I'm pretty certain I know who ordered the attack. But he always operates at a distance. I have no proofs. My circumstantial evidence would be a lot stronger if I knew for certain that he was a member of the Holy Brotherhood. I told you my reasons. Now things have gotten personal. I'd like to arrest him before he tries to kill me again. You can appreciate that. I'm hoping that you might share my concern, although perhaps not so keenly."

Witte laughed heartily. "My dear fellow, you have the most charming way of putting things. You'll be happy to know that I'm about to resign as head of the Kiev section of the Brotherhood. Things are not turning out the way I expected. So I'll find out what you want to know. But first, I want you to tell me everything you found out about corruption in the Southwest Railroad Line. A fair trade?"

Vasiliev hesitated a fraction of an instant. He would have to risk exposing Galperin, even if he did not name him. But what was the alternative?

"Of course. I'll need a few days to pull it all together."

"Good! By that time my resignation form the Brotherhood will be official."

"A shorter cab ride than I expected. I am very grateful, Sergei Iulevich."

They shook hands. "Listen, Vasiliev, if you ever decide to leave the force, I can always find a place for you in my department. Whenever, now or in the future." Witte signaled the cab to stop. Vasiliev climbed out and bowed his farewell. He never saw Witte again, but read a great deal about him. He accomplished much, but never really succeeded in saving Russia from the dark forces gathering around him. For that, Vasiliev thought many years later, he would have had to have been Tsar.

Chapter
Fifty-One

Baron Szymanski left the Polish Club shaken to the core. The rain had stopped, leaving the city oppressively hot, with steam rising from the cobblestones on the main thoroughfares, and rivulets wearing gulleys in the dirt streets and alleys of the outskirts. Walking down Kreshchatik he picked his way fastidiously around the puddles that had collected on the uneven pavement. He needed to clear his head. Unsavory rumors were circulating, his friends had warned him. All lies. He was supposed to have some kind of hold over a certain captain of the Gendarmes. Blackmailing him. Was this Rudov? According to another version he was a double agent of the Russian government and a Polish émigré organization in Paris. Also lies! Who was spreading these stories? He suspected Lopatkin. The Governor-General would never betray him. He only wanted to get Vasiliev off his back. That was the reason for the clumsy plot to discredit the detective from Moscow. Well, it was true that Vasiliev probably had relations with that woman revolutionary, Irina. That's what Rudov claimed, in any case. He should know! But no one could prove it. He remembered his conversation with Vasiliev in the garden. The man had been shaken by the story that Irina was in trouble. His whole manner betrayed him. What had gone wrong? Someone had warned Vasiliev it was a trick. Maybe Lopatkin was behind that too, informing Vasiliev on the sly, trying to ingratiate himself. The merchant repelled him. Now he was trying to cheat on the latest grain deliveries. That wasn't the worst of it either. But what could he do? The police needed an informer among the Poles and he was it. Better than rotting in Siberian exile.

And Lopatkin had been his contact, the man from whom the government had bought back his estate, the wholesaler for his grain, the mailbox for his reports. The devil only knew what Lopatkin did with the information before turning it over to the Gendarmes. Szymanski wondered whether he used it to blackmail some of his Polish competitors. He felt as though he was sinking deeper into filth. There was no one to turn to. The Governor-General was Lopatkin's protector, and Novitsky no longer respected him—if he ever had. Perhaps he could make it up with Vasiliev. He stopped and looked around him at the strollers, groups of young women in their light-colored summer frocks, chatting and laughing. And he felt like an alien surrounded by invisible demons bent on his destruction.

Szymanski found himself on Aleksandrov Street walking toward the Jewish district of Podol. Suddenly, an inspiration struck him. Had it come from the tower of the Kiev Catholic Cathedral? He caught sight of its silhouette outlined against the late afternoon sky, far in the distance. He hurried toward it, sensing that a sign or message was waiting for him there. Entering the sanctuary, he felt a strange presentiment. He dipped his fingers into the holy water, crossed himself, and bent his knee in the direction of the altar. He walked down the side aisle and turned into a small chapel dedicated to St. George. He lit a candle, knelt, and prayed. He felt at peace. But God did not speak to him. Should he seek solace and redemption in confession? Something held him back. He glanced around him. There was no one in sight. He looked up at the stained glass window. His eyes were drawn to the saint's lance buried deeply in the flesh of the dragon. An idea seemed to explode in his head. To slay the dragon! But how? He would not risk killing him outright. He knew he had lost his nerve in Siberia. The heroism of his youth had died in the frozen wastes. As if to remind him of those days, he felt the cold from the stone floor seep into his arthritic knees. He did not get up. The pain would force him to concentrate his thoughts. Where was Lopatkin most vulnerable? He cheated on the grain shipments. But there was no proof. He was embezzling funds from the railroad. He liked to boast about that, privately. But again, no proof. And there was the darkest secret of all. But how to tie Lopatkin to murder? The police would not believe him. They would dismiss what he said as hearsay. Perhaps the time had come to play his last trump. He crossed himself again and rose to his feet. His legs almost buckled under him. He seized hold of the small altar. The candles wavered but did not go out. As a sign from heaven it was the best he could hope for.

Lopatkin sat at his desk staring at the small Murillo on the opposite wall. He had reservations about its authenticity, but he had bought it anyway. The price was right. He prided himself on being an enlightened merchant. There weren't many in Kiev. He likened himself to Tretiakov and the others in Moscow. Merchant art collectors, men of taste and refinement. He had built up his collection in the hope someday of establishing a museum in Kiev, which would bear his name. Just like Tretiakov had done in Moscow. It would make him immortal. But building a collection required money and trips to Europe, and the little railroad deals were beginning to dry up. He had nipped off the threat to his income by getting rid of the Jew Meier. Vasiliev had been eliminated as well. But now there was Witte, who had ambitions to run the railroads his own way. To build a big career rather than a big fortune. Perhaps it was time to move back into the grain business. He had started to squeeze Szymanski. Soon he would start building grain elevators, charging for storage, securing a monopoly on the grain market in the southwest. The plans were good, but it would cost something to square the right people.

A small annoyance kept interrupting his plans for the future. He took the picture postcard from his desk drawer showing the Hotel d'Europe and re-read the laconic message "Your room has been vacated." It was not signed, but in the lower left-hand corner a small insect had been drawn. Lopatkin thought it was a bit too clever. Vasiliev's hotel, the empty room and the bug (*zhuk*) as Boris' signature. But the meaning was clear. Vasiliev had been eliminated. But where was Pavel to report in person? Lopatkin wanted details. Just as important, he felt uneasy without a bodyguard. The maid servant and cook took care of his daily needs. But a man in his position needed some protection. Perhaps he had been too quick to send the others away. But Pavel was the most reliable. He could only imagine that there had been some difficulty, and Pavel had gone to ground. He would turn up as he always did. Lopatkin carried the postcard to the grate, lit a match, touched the flame to the edge, and let it drop.

Chapter
Fifty-Two

Szymanski had slept soundly for the first time in weeks. He felt exultant as he sat on a bench under a leafy chestnut tree in the Palace Park across the street from Lopatkin's house. The midday visitors, young women mostly with children, preferred the other end of the park, where the paths were flooded with sunlight and the white acacias were in full bloom. In a far corner in the shadow of the Church of Alexander Nevsky, two gardeners were planting bushes. An old man walking his dog sat down briefly on a nearby bench. He soon got up, and continued his bird like passage across the park, resting every once in a while, and finally perching on a bench in the full sun.

Szymanski expected that Lydia would be alone. Not like the day before, linked arm in arm with her stupid friend. At least she had seen him and was smart enough not to give a sign of recognition. If she remembered anything of what he had taught her, she would be alone this time. He resisted taking out his pocket watch. From time to time he dug a small hole in the dirt with the toe of his boot and then covered it up again. He had given some thought to bringing a book but decided that would look foolish. Why be found reading in the shade? He found it difficult to keep his mind from recalling how he had recruited Lydia. She was a submissive girl. Thank God, he had not tried to seduce her. He had learned enough by that time to avoid emotional attachments. It was enough that he sent money to her mother in Krakow. He asked very little from her in return. Now it was time for her to earn her pay.

When he came back from exile, it had not been easy to place

trusted people in important households. He could only be sure of Poles. The trouble was that families of Russian officials were reluctant to hire them, preferring Little Russian girls from the countryside. Lydia's Polish mother raised her as a patriotic Catholic. Her father had wisely kept his Russian name after he had converted to the Uniate Church. Being bi-lingual, Lydia was indistinguishable from a Russian, a perfect disguise. In any normal society she might have become something. Not in Russia, and she knew it. Lopatkin had been happy to hire her as a maid. She was pleasant, modest, and plain, and carried the recommendation of the Baron in the days when his relations with the merchant were still good. Szymanski watched her approach along the path. She was alone and carried a small bunch of flowers. He stood up and greeted her with a bow. In his eyes it was an ironic gesture, in hers a mark of gallantry.

After a few polite inquiries about her mother, he quickly came to the point. "Lydia, my dear girl, I have to ask you for a small favor. It should not cause you any inconvenience. No, and no trouble either. You are a very observant young lady." He liked that touch—no obvious flattery. She would like the "lady" part. "And I need to know something about your employer's habits."

She looked at him and nodded. Such an innocent gaze. He attributed it to her country-bred naiveté.

"He is a man of exact habits, no?" She nodded again. "And he's very careful about money, no?" As long as he kept her nodding he felt on firm ground. "He pays you regularly, no? And I imagine that he asks you to sign a receipt." He gave a short laugh to reassure her. She smiled in return. "I imagine that he must record every household expense. Yes, I can see him accounting for every kopek. A real businessman." She nodded again. Now the problem is, he thought, how to move her from nodding to speaking.

"You know, I should learn from him. I'm careless about money. How he must have trained himself over the years. Discipline, that's the answer. Did you ever see him write down his expenses? I would love to know how he keeps his accounts. A real professional, I'll wager. But I'm too shy to ask him. He would just laugh at me."

"He writes everything in a big book."

"Well, of course, a big book. I can buy a big book too. But it wouldn't help me."

"I've seen him writing. But he doesn't like it when I do. Last time he scolded me. 'You shouldn't come in the room without knocking!' is what he said."

Szymanski was astonished that she was speaking whole sentences, a veritable flood of words. But why be sarcastic, even in his thoughts? This is what he was angling for.

"Now why would that be?" He looked off in the distance as if seeking the answer from anyone but her. The old man had shifted his perch again pursuing the warmth of the sun. A child's ball rolled toward the gardeners. Once of them stood up and kicked it smartly back. A normal scene in the park.

"It's like he had a secret. He writes it all in the big book, and then locks the book in his desk."

"And you saw him do this?"

"Yes. That's when he scolded me." A woman appeared along the path, walking her dachshund. What a stupid dog! he thought. Only Germans have them. He caught himself. I can't let these little things keep distracting me. It's hard to shake the old habits, the habits of an exile. Always daydreaming there. It was the only way to forget where you were. Suddenly, he sensed that Lydia was staring at him. She quickly lowered her head and stared at the ground. Szymanski wondered whether he had covered up the hole he had dug in the sand. Nonsense! How would she know he was nervous? It was another bad habit of his. But she wouldn't understand. The dachshund sniffed at his boots. Szymanski had the sudden urge to kick it. But the lady pulled it away. They were silent, he and Lydia—just like two conspirators, thought Szymanski.

The woman passed them without a word. A few of Lydia's flowers had slipped out of her fingers and fallen to the ground. The Baron picked them up. "For the master?" he asked.

"No, for Nadya, the cook."

"Of course. It would be too forward of you to give them to the master. So, a book locked in a desk. My, my!"

"Yes, and he keeps the key on a chain around his neck."

Oh dear, that's going to be a problem: Szymanski's mind was racing ahead. Too bad Lydia is so plain. How absurd. Even the thought of getting her to seduce him would be out of the question. What am I thinking? Reading too many French romances. Szymanski felt stymied. What else could he ask? He realized, with a sinking heart, that there was only one thing left to do now.

"Lydia, I said I needed a favor. This is it. I want you to go to your mother's for a few days. Isn't that simple? Here's the money I usually send her plus something extra. You deserve a vacation." It sounded foolish when he put it into words. He couldn't think of anything better. Besides, a complex plan would only confuse her.

"I don't know whether I can leave. Pavel isn't around. Master will be alone except for Nadya."

Szymanski could hardly contain himself. "What do you mean? Pavel is always around."

"Master is very angry. He says Pavel has deserted him. He said he has no one to rely on, now."

"Listen, Lydia. That's not your fault. Besides, I asked you as a small favor. You can't deny me. We can even arrange to have a message delivered to you from your mother asking you to come, begging you. It would be something urgent, you understand?"

"But…" Lydia wanted to know why, but she was too shy to ask. She thought for a moment.

"Master might be angry at me then. He might dismiss me."

"No. He isn't that cruel. If he does I'll find you another job, a better one. You can trust me. Didn't I find you this job? And don't I help you with your mother?" He tried to keep his voice steady. He didn't want to seem like a bully. But there was too much at stake. If he had to bully her, he would.

Lydia lowered her head again. Would she cry? He wondered. Someone was calling to the children. Suddenly, the park was deserted except for the gardeners.

"Listen, Lydia. He's too dependent on you to dismiss you. Then he would have no one. You can tell him it's only for a few days. He might be angry. But you can stand it for my sake, can't you?"

Lydia nodded. She dropped more flowers, but this time the Baron did not bend to pick them up.

Chapter
Fifty-Three

Lopatkin was annoyed with Lydia for going off to the countryside. But the poor girl seemed to be so upset about her mother
that he didn't have the heart to say no. He thought the scolding he
gave her was mild enough. But she burst into tears. She promised
to be back in a few days. That could mean anything. These country bumpkins had no sense of time. That's why the Jews enslaved
them. A clever people, the Jews. They knew that time was counted
in rubles. Lopatkin let her go. "Mind, a few days, no longer!" he
shouted at her back. What good that would do he didn't know, but
it made him feel better.

That same night Szymanski ate a frugal meal and then sat for
a long time in the dark. He rehearsed his plan, recalling what he
had learned in the Tiumen Forwarding Prison, also on dark nights,
where he had spent many hours talking to criminals. He had discovered quickly that they, not the guards, were the ones who really
ran things in the prison. You have to treat them with respect, especially the thieves, a Polish friend of his had advised him. When the
going gets rough they'll give you some protection. Then, curiosity
had taken hold. He asked them about their trade. He learned a lot.
He never imagined that his technical education, as he thought of it,
would come in handy some day. It was just something to pass the
time, to avoid the grinding boredom. Unexpectedly, the moment
had come to put it to use. The first lesson they taught him was to be
daring. "Do the unexpected!" they kept saying. He wondered why
they'd been caught if daring was the key to success. They had gone
to the well too often, they told him. It was impossible to stop. The

urge became irresistible. But, suppose you could pull off something really big just the one time, he had argued with them. They laughed at him. "Go ahead, try, but don't blame us if you catch the fever." The difference was, he thought, that they had nothing else to live for. He did, and he knew he could stop. He would be daring, but only once.

Their second lesson was to plan everything down to the smallest detail. "Never break into a place with people inside. Equip yourself with the tools to open any lock." He asked for instructions. They were amused. Teaching a Polish *Pan* how to crack locks. The story got around. He couldn't have asked for better instructors. The cream of the crop. "Be careful," they joked, "we might ask for a cut."

Szymanski knew the merchant's daily routine and that of the cook, Nadya. In the morning he let the excitement that he had held in check take over. A raid in daylight. That was the unexpected part. And an empty house. Last, but most important, he thought, were the tools he had bought. He held them in his hands and remembered what he had been taught.

It was mid-morning when Lopatkin left for his club. Nadya was off on a shopping expedition. Szymanski waited until a postal messenger had passed, leaving the street deserted. He walked up the path to the back door. In a few moments he had it open, and went straight to Lopatkin's study. The desk lock was child's play. He lifted the book reverentially and stuffed it into his waistband. There was some money in the drawer, and he took that as well. Then he pulled out all the other drawers and scattered their contents. He moved to the bedroom, where he created as much disorder as he could in a few minutes. He stripped the bed and ripped open the mattress with a knife. He emptied the wardrobe and drawers onto the floor. It took him no longer than ten minutes. He left by the back door and marched with his soldier's step straight to the police station. Szymanski could hardly resist rubbing his hands together. Unexpected indeed! He chuckled to himself.

Szymanski's thief friends had warned him to look around after a burglary as well as before. He forgot that simple lesson. He did not notice a gardener had quit work and was trailing along behind him. It was one of the men who had been planting bushes when he had been sitting with Lydia on the bench in the shade.

Szymanski entered the station, asked for the officer in charge and introduced himself. "I've just come from the house of my friend, the merchant Lopatkin. It looks like the place has been burgled."

Chapter Fifty-Four

Members of the Polish Club were surprised to see Baron Szymanski appear in the middle of the day. He made for his favorite leather armchair. It had been placed opposite the painting of the charge of the Polish lancers under Sobieski that repelled the Turks besieging Vienna. He slumped down without speaking a single word of greeting. He waved away a servant who asked to take his order. They all agreed his behavior was quite out of the ordinary. In whispered conversation they attributed it to the fall in grain prices.

Szymanski stared at the painting, the last moment of Polish glory. After that, a long decline. Now his plans lay in ruins. The police had believed him well enough. He might be Polish, but no one was going to suspect him of being a common thief. A traitor perhaps, but never a thief. And he had avoided a meeting with Lopatkin. They had simply taken his statement and sent off an officer to survey the damage. Lopatkin would be furious, but that he expected. Would he suspect the real reason for the break-in? It didn't matter. It had all been in vain.

Novitsky had insisted on seeing him. He told him that Vasiliev was dead, blown up by some wretched terrorists. Szymanski clutched the arms of his chair. The worst of it was that he had left the notebook at the Hotel d'Europe, wrapped in a package. An anonymous note to Vasiliev. Strange! The clerk didn't know about his death. All those incriminating figures and dates and names sitting there in Vasiliev's postal box. How could he have known that Vasiliev would never pick it up? The clerk had told him only that

Vasiliev came by from time to time to check his mail, but had no fixed schedule.

Szymanski convinced himself it would be too risky to try to get it back. What story could he invent? He couldn't even prove it was he who had left it. The clerk hardly paid him any attention. People came in and out all the time. There might even be another clerk on duty. The manager might be called. Too many complications! His only hope was that the police would recover it. But they wouldn't know what to make of it. Only Vasiliev would have been able to puzzle it out.

Szymanski ran his forefinger along the side of his nose, a nervous habit from his days in exile. He thought about Vasiliev and his girl—what was her name? Yes, Irina! He remembered every moment of the meeting in the Governor-General's garden. Vasiliev's startled look. His powerful grip. The expression of dread as he took in the horrors of the Tiumen prison. So he was in love with a revolutionary. He'd never imagined a Russian police inspector could have fallen for a nihilist. It was actually touching. Reminded him of his idealistic youth. But Vasiliev was no starry-eyed adolescent. This was the real thing. Amazing! But now he was dead. His girl would grow old and perish in that wilderness. He groaned involuntarily, turning a few heads in his direction. Suddenly he was angry. He silently cursed the terrorists. It was one thing to assassinate tyrants. But indiscriminant attacks like this one were inexcusable. Why did they do it? Sounded like the People's Will. Dynamite, and all that. He wondered whether there was something else to it. He might try to find out. He had contacts. What was he thinking of, avenging Vasiliev? A crazy idea. But wait! It might win him some credit with the police. God knows he needed it. And he could redeem his honor. Perhaps he owed Vasiliev that.

Szymanski took another look at the painting, Sobieski at the head of his troops. A mighty force. Good lads behind him. The Lancers. Hell, they were still fighting a century later, at the side of Napoleon against the Russians. The heroes of his youth. Suddenly he sat bolt upright. Why not? He leaped to his feet and strode boldly out of the Club, turning more startled heads and eliciting more whispers. Had the Baron gone mad? "No", someone said, "it's the Lancers. They always have that effect on him." Szymanski headed down Kreshchatik and entered the Catholic Cathedral. He waited until there was no one in sight and then stuffed Lopatkin's money into a box for contributions to the local orphanage. He paid his respects to St. George, another lancer. Then he marched out of the cathedral on his mission. He didn't care any more if it was his last.

Lopatkin was in a rage. He had returned home to find a police cab standing at the curb. When he rushed into the house, the first sound he heard was the histrionic lamentations of the cook, Nadya. She was in the kitchen blubbering out her tale of woe to a constable, who was trying to calm her and at the same time scribbling a few lines in his notebook. He later confessed to Novitsky that he couldn't make head or tail out of what she was saying, or his notes for that matter. Between the cook's blubbering and Lopatkin's shouting, he had finally given up, snapped shut his notebook, and advised the merchant to visit headquarters. He would be treated with respect and understanding. After he left, Lopatkin continued to shout at Nadya, reducing her to total incoherence. He ran out of the kitchen and into his study. A glance at his desk told him the worst. He felt a surge of panic and staggered against the wall, dislodging the suspicious Murillo. The painting crashed to the floor, breaking the frame and revealing at the edge of the canvas a signature and date at variance with its attribution. Rage again took hold of him. He kicked the painting across the room. This did nothing to calm him. He sank to his knees, scrambling along the floor in a vain search for the missing notebook. When Nadya peeked into the room she saw him sitting on the floor, his back against the wall. He was holding an unframed painting in his hands. As she watched, he carefully tore the canvas in half.

Who would want it? He asked himself. Who even knew about it? Without looking up he mumbled, "Where were you?"

"At the market, master!" she gasped.

Lopatkin rolled his head against the wall. Where the hell was Pavel, he wondered, not for the first time. And what about the maid? He couldn't even remember her name for the moment. Why had she left just when she did? What was Szymanski doing here? Unanswered questions. Then the panic gripped him again.

He dragged himself to his feet and made the rounds of the

house. Perhaps it was just an ordinary thief. He might have grabbed the book without knowing what it was, just in case it had some value. A glimmer of hope. He bathed his face in cold water and ordered a cab.

At police headquarters he tried to remain calm, talking to Novitsky. The chief did not appreciate histrionics. Lopatkin demanded protection. Novitsky was surprised Lopatkin didn't blame the theft on the Jews. He asked for a complete list of missing items. Lopatkin sat at a table and wrote what he could remember. He thought of putting down a valuable Murillo. Then he thought better of it. He read over what he had written. Everything else was there, except the notebook. If they found it fine; he would tell them it was so unimportant that he forgot to mention it. If they never found it, even better.

Novitsky quietly fumed. What was happening to Kiev? Murders, robbery in broad daylight. The city was falling to pieces. Now here was Lopatkin demanding protection. The damage had been done. What was left to protect? Damn it, let him have Kablukov. That'd teach him to demand protection. Kablukov would turn his life into a misery. Super protection! Wonderful. Lopatkin wouldn't be able to make a move without Kablukov, who would stick to him like tar.

Speak of the devil, thought Novitsky. Kablukov had knocked and entered the office. He passed over a telegram, spun on his heel, and vanished before Novitsky had a chance to speak. It was from Petersburg, not something that happened every day. He hesitated a moment. Evil comes in threes. He remembered his mother's warning. He tore open the envelope, read the message, and crumpled it in his fist. He heard Lopatkin's voice in the next room, demanding something or other. Damn him, damn them all! He sat dazed for a few moments before recalling the words of the telegram. It had come from Ivan, the Iron Colonel, Vasiliev's oldest friend and what was worse, a very highly placed official with numerous contacts and mysterious influence at court. It was a reply to Novitsky's official report to the Ministry on Vasiliev's death. He had expected an expression of displeasure, perhaps even a reprimand. It would have been unfair. But this was worse. They had sent a copy of his report to Vasiliev's natural father, Count Vorontsov. The old man had suffered a heart attack, fallen into a coma, and died shortly afterwards. The implication was clear. He, Novitsky, was to be saddled with the moral responsibility for the death of one of Russia's greatest noblemen and a legendary soldier to boot; as chief of police, he, Novitsky, had failed to protect the man's only son. Christ! Would the disasters never end?

Novitsky rang his bell furiously. Kablukov appeared at once. "You are being assigned to protect the merchant Lopatkin. You'll begin at once and stay until I relieve you. You will be his shadow. However much he protests, you will not leave his side. If necessary you will tell him that I have given you orders to that effect and that you dare not disobey. Is that understood?" Kablukov saluted and clicked his heels in his best Prussian style.

Chapter Fifty-Five

The postal messenger had taken a seat in the rear of the Kolo Teahouse. A man in rough workman's clothing, his trousers stained green at the knees, sat down at an adjoining table. After a few minutes the two men fell to conversing about the new plantings in the park. One by one the other customers paid and left. The waiters went into the back room for a snack. A fly ricocheted off the window behind them. In the distance, the hum of street traffic. A lazy summer morning in Kiev.

"There isn't much to tell," said the postal messenger. "The cook leaves for the market. He goes to his club. I'm behind him all the way. Stays for an hour. Walks back home. He's all alone. The cook gets back first. He's next. Not a minute goes by. The door bangs open. He shoots out. Runs—well, I don't know what you'd call it. He moves his body as fast as he can. Heads straight for the police station. I'm missin' all the real action. What happened?"

"Szymanski waited until you got round the corner. He came out of the park and walked up the path to the back door. He was in and out in ten minutes. I could see something bulky tucked into his waistband under his jacket. Could have been a book or a sheaf of paper bound together. I watched him go to the police station."

"Whaaat?"

"Wait. More surprises to come. The Baron spent a few minutes inside, then walked to our hotel and entered the lobby. Again he didn't stay long. I couldn't see what he was up to."

"You couldn't go in lookin' like that."

"Right. Not dressed for the occasion, as they say. When he came out he stood on the porch for a minute. I wish I had been alive, as it were, to greet him. You see, he didn't seem to have the package with him. The bulge under his jacket was gone."

"So he's handin' out gifts. The documents, you think?"

"Possibly. He went on to the Polish Club. That's where I left him. We may have outsmarted ourselves, Serov. Don't you see? We don't know who thinks we are dead. The hotel management? If so, then our Polish friend also knows. They would have told him. If he knew, why would he leave a package for us? Suppose they don't know that we are officially dead. We show up for the package. Fine. Then the news comes that we were killed. The hotel says, oh no, we just saw them. Novitsky concludes, Vasiliev's been playing games again. A lot of important people would be mad as hell at us. Drenteln would be the first to complain. He could use it as an excuse to get me recalled. Is the package worth it? I don't know."

Vasiliev rubbed his side absentmindedly. He stopped when he saw Serov watching him. "Bad habit. A dead giveaway. People remember such things. I have to stop it."

There was another pause. "What do you think, Sergeant—time for some diversionary tactics?" Serov grinned in approval.

They spent the rest of the day rummaging among the piles of used clothes in the Bessarab Bazaar. Then late that night, rigged out as artisans, they slipped in the delivery entrance at the back of the Hotel d'Europe. A few minutes later, the night clerk was alarmed by shouts and curses coming from the dark end of the lobby. He rang for the doorman who doubled as the security man. He was nowhere in sight. It turned out he had been called to the fifth floor to investigate a break-in. He only succeeded in embarrassing an official who was visiting the room of someone else's wife. The clerk then left his desk to call the constable on the corner. The constable was also not at his post. He had been called away some minutes before to investigate a robbery. But that too proved to be a false alarm. The clerk later told the police that when he returned to his post, he noticed that the cash drawer had been forced open. No money was missing. What he didn't notice was that Vasiliev's mail slot was empty. The package was gone.

Vasiliev spent the rest of the night studying the accounts of Lopatkin. The title page of the book showed only a roman numeral, XI. Each following page was ruled into four columns. First came a date, then initials, followed by what appeared to be sums of money. In the last column there were numbers ranging from one to five, like grades in a teacher's copybook. Perhaps that's what it was, thought Vasiliev. Lopatkin was recording his successes and failures. There were lots of fives. The highest grade. The dates began with the New Year. On the first of every month Sz received an identical sum. Irregular payments were made to P on the dates corresponding to the outbreak of pogroms. The initial S appeared only once, a large sum paid the day after the assassination of the Rabbi. P was awarded a five the day the documents disappeared from the Rabbi's desk. The initial ZH appeared only once, the day after the bomb attack on the safe house. This too like the others was given a grade of five. The last entry for the same day was incomplete. The initial P had been entered but no payment had been made and no grade had been given.

The next morning Vasiliev woke up late having recalled, only vaguely, a dream about searching for amulets among the Ostiaks in Siberia. He decided to clear his head by taking a long walk. It was Sunday and the streets were already crowded with strollers. When he turned down a side street, he heard music coming from open windows. Violins seemed to predominate, but he could hear oboes and clarinets as well. It seemed that a whole orchestra was tuning up. What a strange city! Young girls in summer frocks gaily promenading, amateur musicians practicing in almost every apartment. Yet a few kilometers away the burned-out district of Podol still smoldered. He stopped at a bakery and picked up fresh rolls. What an assortment of breads! Hadn't someone told him there were more than seventy ways of preparing bread in Kiev? He bought more folders and returned to his room.

Serov had gone out on his "wanderin's," as he like to call it. He was part of the city now. Had absorbed it into his blood. He knew it better than the pilgrims or the prostitutes, who tended to gather in the same old places. He felt at home dropping in on cheap cafes and teahouses, gossiping with the locals. Only Kaniever's held out. It was made clear that he was not wanted there. He was picking up some new stories. It gave him an idea. He would try it out on Vasiliev later. He would have to choose the right moment.

Vasiliev began to re-arrange his clippings and notes, putting them into newly labeled folders. Sometimes he thought he might have been happier as an archivist. Did he enjoy dealing with paper more than with real people, he wondered? He kept looking for connections, patterns that might give him a way of putting together his report to Ivan. As for the murder of Rabbi Meier, he was certain he had found the man behind it. If he could figure out the notebook, he might have the proof necessary to sentence Lopatkin to ten years. Too bad he couldn't find a political motive. Then he wouldn't need a trial. With Ivan's backing he could send Lopatkin off to administrative exile. Russia's crazy laws weren't always so crazy.

He kept hearing in his head a strange melody on the violin. It was leading him somewhere. He sat back and thought about the next step. Then it came to him, just as Serov returned.

A quick glance was enough. They both saw the same excited expression, as if reflected in a mirror. "You first!" said Vasiliev.

Serov had judged the moment right. He had learned something about Lopatkin. The merchant was in the habit of hiring tough-looking men from the North, Russians it looked like, to do things for him. Then he paid them, gave them railroad tickets, and told them to disappear. Serov thought it might be a good idea to get himself hired. He had almost full use of his arm and felt like a normal person again. He could present himself to Lopatkin as a man in need of work, any kind of work. The merchant might pick him for an illegal job. They could set a trap. What did Vasiliev think?

Vasiliev was non-committal. He had his own plan.

"I've been a little slow on this case. Too many distractions. I missed an opening. We've been trying to solve the wrong crime. Or rather we have solved it. But the killer is dead and there's no way to tie him to Lopatkin. We only have these initials in his account book. Not good enough. But he committed another crime. At least, *I'm* convinced of it. He is the only person who had a motive for having us eliminated. The bombers who blew up our safe house left a signature behind. This was the work of terrorists. No one else goes about things the way they do. So who are they? My guess, and it's a good one, is they're members of a local organization of the People's Will. Now, I ask you, Sergeant. How does a respectable merchant go about hiring terrorists to blow up his enemies?"

Serov shook his head. When Vasiliev was like this, he was like a man on fire, he thought. He knew it was futile to try to keep up. This was not a chess game.

Chapter
Fifty-Six

The Ukrainian owner of the house opposite the blackened ruins was puzzled. She thought her new renter seemed to be respectable enough for an artisan. His clothes were neatly pressed and his bag of tools looked as though they were kept in good condition. His hair was pomaded, but not greasy, and he had an honest look. That counted heavily for the old woman. The last bunch that rented the room did not inspire confidence. Still, it was strange that he wanted the front room, with that terrible sight right in front of his eyes. The other room in the back overlooking the garden had such an attractive view. A bit more expensive. Well, the man was obviously from the North. Maybe he hadn't found work yet. Had to count his kopeks. He said there were two of them. Well, that was all right too. As long as the other man was respectable. She would reserve judgment. This one was a shrewd bargainer. So, she let it go cheaply. After all, she had despaired of ever renting the front room again for a long time. Later that day the second man came. Older, gray hair and a slight limp. But he passed inspection too. They said they would be out most of the day, looking for odd jobs. But if she happened to hear of anything…In the meantime they paid her a week in advance.

As soon as the gray-haired man with the limp crossed the threshold, he signaled his companion to cover the left-hand side of the room. They both went down on their knees and slowly worked their way across the floor. They were using small brushes with fine horse-hairs to sweep up dust and particles of dirt. When Vasiliev reached the window he let out a small gasp. Serov didn't look up for fear of losing his place on the floorboards. Vasiliev took a small envelope out of his pocket and gently brushed a gray ash into it. He sat against the wall, waiting for Serov to finish his sweep.

When Serov flopped down beside him, Vasiliev had separated the ash into two portions on a small block of highly polished wood. He took a small reticule out of his bag, allowed a drop of the liquid it contained to fall on one portion, and watched the reaction.

"Perhaps you remember, Sergeant, what I used to say about the English detective, Holmes." Serov recognized the voice of Vasiliev, the lecturer. Good, he thought, he's found something important.

"I've always been a bit critical of him. But I have to give him his due. He's been preparing a monograph on different kinds of cigar, cigarette, and pipe tobacco ash. Last I heard, he had almost a hundred samples. He was kind enough to share his findings with my uncle in London. Thought it might help us catch some terrorists. Well, he may have been right. I think I recognize this sample. It's unusual. But I really need a lab to check. Witte can't refuse me on this one." Vasiliev chuckled. They waited until it was dark and then left. The old woman never saw them again. They must have found a job in another part of the city, she concluded. Still, to give up a week's rent! Strange people these Russians. "Spendthrifts, after all," she told the neighbors.

Vasiliev sent his sample with Serov to Witte's office. He was not disappointed with the results. They confirmed his initial analysis. The tobacco was a rare blend of Turkish made for a cigar. "Not many places in the city will be selling this," said the lab technician. "'The game's a-foot', as the master says," Vasiliev quipped, to Serov's puzzled look.

Vasiliev assumed his merchant's disguise while Serov spruced himself up a bit to look as if he could afford Turkish tobacco. Witte's assistant had provided them with a short list of fine tobacconists. They visited them all. At the end of the day they had located three who sold the brand they were looking for. Only one of them remembered a recent customer.

"I'm getting low on the supply. Ever since the war deliveries have been irregular. If you buy me out, my steady customer will be unhappy."

"Well, I wouldn't want to do that," said Vasiliev. "Tell you what. I'll leave two boxes. When did you say he comes in? Usually the tenth of the month, regular like, you say? Good that's two days hence. I'd like to meet the man. After all we share an unusual taste, don't you see?"

"But he might not want to meet you," said Serov who stood by looking meek. "Right! Well, listen," Vasiliev said turning to the tobacconist, "I don't want to embarrass you. Some people like their privacy. Still, I'd just like to see him. Maybe I could strike up an acquaintance after he leaves, accidental like, don't you see? Here's what we'll do. I'll hang around the shop, day after tomorrow. Morning, he comes, eh? All right, I have nothing doing then. And you just give me a signal. Ask me if I'd like some Cuban cigars when he comes in. Then I'll leave and no more worries for you." Vasiliev winked, and the agreement was sealed with a handshake.

It took the Baron several days to run down his old Polish comrade from the time of the rebellion. He knew him only by his *nom de guerre*, Bor. He had gone underground in '64 when Szymanski had been taken prisoner. Now he was living in a shack on the outskirts of Kiev, in the village of Demievka near the sugar-refining factory. He had some kind of job as a watchman. They hired anyone, these capitalists, thought Szymanski as he made his way along the narrow, dusty lanes of the village. Bor hardly remembered him. But Szymanski had brought along a bottle. After a while their memories began to mesh. Bor knew another Pole who kept in touch with the People's Will. He served as a courier, crossing the frontier with messages to the exiles in Switzerland. Like any decent Pole he spoke fluent French. It was dangerous work. But you took what you could get. Maybe it was better than being a watchman in a sugar factory. Bor became expansive. He gave Szymanski an address where a message could be left. At the end they were singing old songs of the Polish legionnaires.

A teahouse in the Podol district served as a message box. The owner was a Ukrainian Uniate, who observed the Old Slavonic rituals but recognized the authority of the Pope. It was as close as you could get to being a Pole, thought Szymanski. Still, it was necessary to couch the message in Aesopian language, like any good conspirator. When he came back the following day, there was an answer setting up a meeting in the City Meadows at the edge of Lukianov district. A wide open space. No chance for concealment. Szymanski arrived on the spot early. No one was in sight. Far to the west he could hear the sound of trumpets. The main army base was located there. It was a cool day. Lucky for him he thought. No shade here. He waited for a long time. At last, he saw a small figure crossing the field from the direction of the last houses on Dachnaia Street. The man was carrying a telescope. So he had been under observation all that time. Good! He was dealing with people who knew their business.

It was a short conversation. Practically a monologue. No names were used. Szymanski had prepared a good story. He spoke confidently, looking the man straight in the eye. He had been working as a double agent. That part of his story was true. They could check it out. But the truth stopped there. He said he'd been gathering information for the Polish committee in Paris, the Hotel Lambert. At the same time, he was giving the Russians garbage. Stuff that was out of date. Or just false. But he had lost confidence in the Poles. They weren't doing a damn thing. He said he didn't particularly like Russians—that was a nice touch, he thought. But the People's Will were at least genuine revolutionaries. He didn't care who toppled the Tsars. Poland would rise from the ruins. He struck a patriotic pose. It was easy for him. He was willing to prove his value. He knew for sure the identity of an agent who had penetrated the People's Will in the Kiev organization. In return he wanted a real assignment. He could use his contacts with the police. Hell, he was a guest at the Governor-General's. But he wanted a face to face with a member of the People's Will. No intermediaries. The man listened. They would be in touch. Same message box.

Szymanski returned to his apartment. How many times had he rehearsed his story? It was complex. But he could find no holes in it. The next day he felt feverish. It was a recurrence of the malaria he had caught in Siberia. People in Kiev could hardly believe it. But they had never seen the swarms of mosquitoes rising from the Siberia swamps in the spring. He dosed himself with quinine. He was light-headed when he picked up the message. Another meeting. This time, he read, "with a member of the firm." Complicated instructions. All very familiar. A series of pick ups, one message leading to the next. He'd be under constant surveillance.

He ended up boarding a small riverboat from a deserted dock off the City Hayfields on Trukhanov Island. They sailed up the Starik Channel. The captain, a helmsman and a young woman. She had those stern features he knew so well. "We know all about the penetration of the Podol organization," she said before he could open his mouth. "You've nothing for us."

"It's not the Podol Organization I've come about." He caught the flicker in her eyes. Why would they send a child up against me? All the better, he thought.

He spun his tale. The way he had put it together—ingenious! He should have been a detective. He could have taught Vasiliev thing or two. He had known for a long time that Lopatkin had his very own agent working in the police and for the revolutionaries. The merchant couldn't help boasting. Bits and pieces. But never the whole picture. Then he had a lucky break. The burned card in the grate. He'd seen it when he was robbing Lopatkin. The left-hand side was charred. He couldn't read the message. But there was a small symbol visible in the lower corner. And the cancelled stamp bore a date. It was the day after the bombing of Vasiliev and his sergeant. He checked the entry in the account book. ZH had been paid off the same day. The symbol. A bug—*zhuk* in Russian. He had made inquiries at Police Headquarters. Sure enough, an Igor Zhuk was an officer. Put it all together and *voila*! Zhuk was Lopatkin's agent. He had arranged for the assassination of the policemen from Moscow. Of course, Zhuk hadn't betrayed the People's Will, the men who had carried it out. Not yet, at least. But they were vulnerable; how long could they trust a double agent? He would hand them Zhuk, Szymanski told the girl.

Once he had proven himself, he was sure the People's Will would take him, Baron Szymanski a true Lancer, into the organization. He would destroy them, avenge Vasiliev, ruin Lopatkin and endear himself to Novitsky—forever.

The girl listened. No more twitches or flutters. She was good. But not perfect. He timed it perfectly, reaching in his pocket and producing the burned postcard. He pointed to the bug symbol and the date. He told her about the account book. He should have ripped out the page. But he had wanted Vasiliev to see the evidence. Would she swallow it all? He thought so. She asked for the card. He smiled and shook his head.

"We'll see what they say." She tried to look nonchalant. He was not fooled. She had gone for it. Could she persuade the others? The best he could hope for was another meeting. With the top people. That was all right. Little by little. He had learned patience in exile. When he returned to his rooms, he fell on the bed. He was sweating profusely. "No victory is unsullied," he quoted. Who said it? He couldn't remember. He took some quinine and fell asleep.

Chapter
Fifty-Seven

The bearded man showed up at the tobacco shop as the owner had predicted. A man of regular habits. Always a mistake for a revolutionary, thought Vasiliev. He caught himself from rubbing his side. Any habit is a mistake. Now was the tricky part. Trailing him. He and Serov had long ago worked out the routine. They both carried small bags stuffed with hats, wigs, false moustaches. They wore light jackets that could be reversed. A quick turn down a side street and a new man could emerge within seconds. Varying their distances. Walking alternate sides of the street. They had practiced it many times. They knew that the revolutionaries had also practiced the art of discovery. A game, then.

Fortunately for the hunters, the streets were crowded. The man they were trailing, already conspicuous in Kiev with his full beard—another curious lapse, thought Vasiliev—would know not to turn around too often. That would attract attention. As they approached Old Zhitomir Street the man headed for a tram stop. Vasiliev signaled Serov to join him. He hailed a cab and persuaded the coachman to let Serov share the driver's seat. "Follow the tram, slowly," he ordered.

They were soon caught in heavy traffic. With its right of way, the tram pulled ahead. Serov watched helplessly as the man descended from the tram and hastened down a side street. By the time the cab got there, the man had disappeared.

"It's a long block. I don't think he could have made it to the end without our seeing him." Vasiliev searched the facades. Nothing spoke to him. There was a teahouse about mid-way down the street. They headed for it. Two tables were set outside on the pavement. "Thank God for the influence of Paris," Vasiliev muttered as they sat down. They were on their third cup of tea when Vasiliev got up. "Too much liquid!" he said. He went into the teahouse and out into the courtyard. Back in five minutes he saw Serov staring down the street. His rigid posture gave him away. He had seen someone or something.

Vasiliev sat down next to him, looking in the same direction. Nothing unusual. A yardman sweeping the pavement in front of a three-story brick house. A woman walking a dog. He waited for Serov to break the silence.

"What d'you think, Vasili Vasilievich? Am I a person likely to be imaginin' things? Do I have good eyes still? No need for them new fangled spectacles."

"Spectacles have been around for a long time, Serov. They are not new-fangled."

Serov turned to him for the first time. "You're a patient man, Vasili Vasilievich, a patient man. But your call of nature came at a bad time. Lucky you have a second pair of eyes. I'm sittin' here waitin' for my fourth cup to cool. The street is quiet, like now. From a distance comes this figure. Something familiar about it. Slowly, slowly it's comin', lookin' for an address maybe. Or a sign. Close enough now to be sure. It's a young woman with piles of black curls. No mistake. It's Rebecca, the Rabbi's daughter. No mistakin' her. She's carryin' a big handbag. She stops by that brick house. Asks the yardman something. He points to his place. She nods and goes in. She's still there."

"And the yardman?"

"Sure enough, he goes back to sweepin'. But he's not sweepin', if you get my meaning. He's lookin' up and down the street with every turn of the broom. Then he goes in the house and comes out with a stool. There he is, sittin' in front, whittlin' a piece of wood. And he'll have to sweep up after. So he's got a good reason to be out there a long time. On guard, we can say."

"Check the rear, Serov. These streets have alleys behind them. If she comes out that way keep her in sight. She may be with someone. Follow and stick with her if they separate. I'll cover the front. Try to keep in touch. You know the way. Damn it! Here we are again. Not enough men, no weapons and presumably dead. This is not a commanding position."

Serov moved away quickly without giving the impression of a man in a hurry. Vasiliev was reminded how well he had trained him. He sat back and wondered what he would do if several unknown people began to leave the building at short intervals. That might signal the beginning of an operation. There were too many combinations. Like playing on a three-dimensional chess-board.

Patient he might be. But he worried about what to do next. He had just stopped himself from rubbing his side, when Rebecca came out alone, still holding—or was she clutching?—her handbag. She didn't bother to look around. Vasiliev had his note ready. He called over the boy clearing tables. With his flaxen hair standing on end and his clear blue eyes, he looked like he had just arrived from the countryside. "Here's a ruble. Take this paper to the man behind the brick house. Ask him if he's a pillar. You understand Russian, don't you? A *stolb*. He'll know what you mean. Run!"

Vasiliev paid and added a few coins. "He's running an errand for me. He'll be back in five minutes. Don't scold him," he said to the waiter.

Rebecca was walking briskly. Vasiliev followed at a distance. She never even cast a glance over her shoulder. As she turned down Dorogozhits Street, Serov rounded the corner. Vasiliev pointed her out. "Stay with her. Keep her away from Lopatkin at all costs. I'm back to the teahouse." Serov nodded and disappeared in the crowded thoroughfare. Vasiliev retraced his steps. He was suddenly worried he might look suspicious going back to the teahouse. Had the yardman noticed him leave? And what about the proprietor? Was he one of them too? The only other shop on the street was selling flowers. How long could he shelter there? He went in and made a show of putting in a large order for his daughter's wedding. He took notes and asked about different arrangements. He managed to get the florist to sit down with his back to the big picture window, giving Vasiliev a clear view of the brick building across the street. He had begun to run out of questions and small talk, when a cab drew up in front of the brick building. The yardman stopped whittling. He stood up and took a few steps toward the cab, glancing up and down the street. He put his hand on the handle but did not try to open the cab door. No one emerged for several minutes. The florist was asking Vasiliev about dates. Vasiliev mentioned several. The florist looked at him quizzically. "But that's Ascension Day. Surely not that day." Vasiliev stood up and moved toward the door.

"I'm sorry, Your Honor. I meant no harm. I just..." the florist fumbled for words. What was wrong about what he had said?

The girl came out of the cab first. She also looked up and down the street while pretending to disentangle her scarf from the cab door handle. A man followed. He seemed dazzled by the bright sunlight and shaded his eyes. She took his arm and led him into the house. The yardman said a few words to the coachman, who then drove off. Vasiliev stood by the door. The florist thought his customer was about to be ill. Vasiliev had never seen the girl before. The man was Baron Szymanski.

Chapter
Fifty-Eight

It had been the usual stuff of conspiracy. The successive messages and the meeting in an open space. Szymanski was consoled by the thought that the girl was the same. But there was a new twist. A cab and a blindfold. He settled back in the cab, content to count the time and try to memorize the turns. He knew it would be hopeless. It didn't matter. She was taking him where he wanted to go. When they stopped she took off the blindfold. She had trouble with the knot. It took a few minutes. Then he was out of the cab, in full sun. He shaded his eyes. She hustled him into a building. The only thing he noticed was that it was brick. He wondered why they had chosen a brick building. They were rather conspicuous in a town that was still mainly wooden.

It all seemed so familiar. The creaking stairs, the bad odors, the furtive faces. It had been a long time. But it all came back to him in a rush. Even the code, a series of knocks on the door. Suddenly, he felt dispirited. That was it, his spirit had deserted him. He ought to be back on his estate. Living in comfort. So, let Lopatkin rob and kill. He didn't give a shit about the Russian Empire. It was only Polish pride that would get him through this, he thought as the door swung open.

Vasiliev liked to think that his intuition generally took him in the right direction. He once calculated the success rate. It had been high enough so that he felt encouraged to follow it again. It propelled him out of the flower shop, down the street, around the corner, and into the back alley where Serov had been stationed. He took cover behind the small wooden fence along the edge of the City Meadow. About an hour passed. He heard the cab before he saw it come down the alley. It drew up by the rear entrance of the brick building, facing away from him. He rushed it from behind, wrenched open the door and vaulted inside, rocking the carriage. The windows were sealed. The coachman shouted at him. "Not free. Get out!" Vasiliev swore at him. The coachman jumped down, brandishing his whip. Vasiliev flung open the door so that it struck the coachman full in the face. He grunted in pain and dropped his whip. Vasiliev hit him twice, very hard. The man slumped to the ground. Vasiliev dragged the body behind the wooden fence. He pulled off the cabbie's cloak, retrieved his cap and whip. He stuffed a handkerchief in the cabbies mouth, tore his blouse into strips, and bound him. He threw the cloak over his own shoulders, jammed the cap on his head, and swung up on the box. He hunched over, adopting the classic pose of the long suffering coachman. If someone, perhaps the same girl, was leading a blindfolded Szymanski back, he might escape notice. If not he would have to try something else.

Within a few minutes he heard the rear door of the building creak open. He did not turn his head. A woman's voice whispered. "Step up, and mind your head." He felt two people climb in the cab. The woman leaned out the door. "Take us back the same way!"

Vasiliev flicked the reins, and the cab moved off down the alley. He needed reinforcements. It was time to resurrect himself for good. Novitsky would be surprised, possibly angry as well. It couldn't be helped. He drove around the city at random. With the windows sealed the woman would have no better sense of where they were heading than the man, presumably Szymanski, who must have been blindfolded. If she became suspicious, he was in trouble. He had to assume that the girl was not armed. Certainly not—too risky in the event they were stopped, a distinct possibility. A sealed coach was liable to attract attention. The police were on edge. Cossack patrols looking for anything that might be unusual.

Vasiliev didn't want to overdo it. The last thing he needed was to get lost. He pulled up in front of Police Headquarters. Several plainclothesmen and constables in uniform were coming down the steps. He jumped down. Tossing away his cap, he wrenched open the door of the cab.

"Baron Szymanski! You are at Police Headquarters. Get out, please! You are under arrest. So is your companion. We will soon find out who she is." Vasiliev seized Szymanski by the arm and dragged him out of the coach. The woman jumped out the other side just as a troika was passing at full trot. She crashed into the flank horse and was hurled to the pavement.

Novitsky heard the commotion below and hurried to the window of his office. His men had surrounded the cab. He stared in astonishment. He recognized Vasiliev, who was strangely dressed but bareheaded. He was gripping the arm of Baron Szymanski, who had torn off his blindfold. Two constables lifted the limp body of a woman off the street and carried her into Headquarters. A troika had stopped in the middle of the street, and a constable was questioning the driver. Novitsky shook his head in disbelief. He rang his silver bell and gave his orders. "Bring the two men up here separately. Put the man holding the blindfold in the outer office. The other one, in that ridiculous cape. Bring him to me. Get a doctor for the woman." Novitsky was relieved to have a few minutes to collect himself. Later on he found it impossible to recall his emotions. He sat down behind his desk and folded his hands.

Vasiliev came in, with the cape slung over one shoulder. He was dressed like a merchant. Suddenly, Novitsky felt a surge of anger. He tried to put it into his voice. "I expect a very good story," he rasped.

Vasiliev nodded. He had planned his explanation carefully. "The story is a good one, Vasili Dementevich. But something else is more important. If you act quickly you have a chance to roll up a group of the People's Will. Right now they are holed up in a brick building on Belogorsk Street. I say brick building because it's a potential fortress. That's why they chose it. Two entrances, a look out in front, but not in the rear alley. The woman is one of the gang. I think, knowing their habits, they'll become suspicious when she doesn't return. Then they'll barricade themselves in or get out fast. Don't force me to tell my story now. Believe me! If we get going we'll avoid a bloody fight and stop them from escaping. Your choice."

"Just one question, then. Is the Baron one of them?"

"I don't know. I doubt it. It'll take too long to find out. He too will have a good story."

Novitsky strapped on his holster, opened his desk drawer, and handed Vasiliev a revolver. "Too bad Kablukov isn't around. I'll take as many men as I can round up. Most of them just left. Trouble in Podol again. Always the same damn thing. Not enough men."

"Cossacks?"

"Not a chance. Not under my command. Take hours to get an authorization. Even longer for the army. You see what we face?"

They passed Szymanski sitting under guard. He called out to them. "Good hunting! Just don't take Zhuk along. He's working with them." Novitsky hesitated a fraction of an instant. He plunged down the stairs, Vasiliev at his heels. Novitsky turned to Vasiliev as two police cabs drew up. "God damn it! Zhuk was standing out there on the steps when you arrived. He saw it all. If he's…he could be there now warning them. About the girl and you."

Vasiliev grabbed his arm before he could climb into the cab. "Listen! That changes everything. If they haven't already scattered, we need a different plan." Vasiliev glanced at the sky. The late afternoon sun was covered with clouds. It would soon be dusk. "I've got an idea. A long shot but worth trying. We'll only lose five minutes. Tell the woman warden to strip the girl and bring me my bag."

Zhuk was badly shaken. Once out of sight of Headquarters, he begged off his assignment, pleading a sick stomach. Well, he thought, that's not much of a lie. The girl was his contact. How far could he trust her to keep quiet? Should he worry? He wasn't even sure that she was still alive. That collision with the troika. How badly was she injured? He couldn't stick around to find out. The point now was to save himself. There was no question of warning her comrades. He didn't even know how to get in touch. She was the only contact. Besides, hell, he owed them nothing. As he hurried back to his apartment he kept checking behind him. It was automatic. Why would anyone be following him? Suddenly he stopped in his tracks. How stupid! No need to take any chances. They might be closing in on his apartment right now. He dodged into a teahouse and sat in a corner. He had anticipated this might happen, but his preparations to get out of the country weren't complete. Too bad. Still, he had stashed away enough money. No one would guess where it was, the hiding place. Once he had picked it up he would get the passport. He'd paid plenty for it. They'd promised it would be ready for him this week.

He paid without finishing his tea. He took trams, changing twice. Never drop your guard! The truism had served him well. He walked the last two kilometers to the Baikovo Cemetery. He remembered to buy a spray of flowers from a street seller just outside the cemetery gates. He went straight to the grave of the official, deceased 1820. He knelt down and placed the flowers by the worn gravestone. This section of the cemetery was always deserted. These people had died long ago. There were no mourners left. Just him. He took out a long thick knife from his boot and worked the blade around the edge of the gravestone. He lifted it up, uncovering a metal box. He pried it open and removed a large bag of silver rubles and a smaller bag of Austrian schillings. He replaced the stone and arranged the flowers around the edges to conceal the broken earth. "Goodbye my old friend. May you rest in peace."

It was a long way to Kaniever's. He took two cabs. He waited outside until he made sure that no one was loitering in the vicinity. He whispered a few words to the doorman and pressed a silver ruble in his hand. Kaniever's was almost deserted. He went up to Rachel, the bar girl. "I've an urgent message for Mendel. Tell him the load for Czernowitz is ready." He handed her a silver ruble. Rachel nodded. "The dispatcher will be here at midnight," she said. He wondered how he would spend the next six hours.

Serov was waiting in a courtyard about a hundred meters from the Meier house. He was debating with himself. Rebecca had been inside for at least fifteen minutes. He couldn't stay in place much longer. *Stolb* or not, he had no excuse for being there. Any moment a yardman or a neighbor would spot him. People were nervous these days, especially those living in the vicinity of the Rabbi's house. Strangers aroused suspicion. For an instant he had the idea of baiting the bear in its den. It was almost funny to think of Rebecca as a bear. More like a she-wolf. He had respect for wolves. Smart, tough, loyal to the pack. Yes, that was Rebecca. But then what? He couldn't tie her down.

Just then the door opened and Rebecca came out with Aaron. They were talking—excitedly, it seemed, and began walking fast. Serov fell into step a discreet distance behind them. He had used the few minutes standing in the courtyard to dig into his small bag.

Within a minute he had pasted on a moustache, donned a pair of clear glass spectacles and jammed on a crumpled hat. He hunched his shoulders and changed his gait. Not much of a disguise, but in the growing twilight it would do, if he kept at a distance. They had a lot to learn, these kids, he thought, if they were going to go in for revolution. He amused himself by thinking up the lessons he could teach them. He'd start with the simple things. Always wear dark clothing. Aaron's white blouse made it easy to keep them in sight. They were not headed for Lopatkin's, so he felt safe letting the distance lengthen between them.

There was only one moment of danger. At the head of the Kadet Boulevard, they came to a stop and waited for a tram. Serov held back. He considered retracing his steps and putting Lopatkin's under surveillance. He could intercept them there, if that was their next move. As he thought about it, a small crowd gathered at the tram stop. When he saw the approaching tram had two cars, he decided to take the risk of sticking close to them. He waited to jump into the rear car at the last minute.

They got out at the last stop and crossed the tracks into the Kadet Woods. Serov was puzzled. They were cousins, not lovers. What the hell were they doing there? It was almost dark. They followed a twisting path. The full foliage of early summer concealed them most of the time. But Serov caught glimpses of the white blouse. Yes, friends, you have much to learn. They stopped in a small glade. Serov watched in amazement. Rebecca took an object out of her big purse. Aaron stood behind her and raised her two arms, bringing her hands together. The first shot sounded to Serov like a clap of thunder, but he knew the dense underbrush would muffle it. Aaron said something. He was probably telling her to squeeze off the rounds, thought Serov. Then he realized he was witnessing the training of an assassin.

Chapter
Fifty-Nine

Belogorsk Street was already in shadow when a cab drove up to the brick building. A woman's figure darted out and rushed across the threshold. The yardman, watching from his basement room, climbed up to the street only to catch a glimpse of her long white skirt, swaying behind her as she made for the stairwell. He stepped outside and shot a glance down the street. The coachman's back was a dark mass as the cab sped out of sight. The yardman scratched his head. Something struck him as not quite right. He turned back into the building. In the dark corridor he glimpsed a white blur before he felt a hand clapped over his mouth and the muzzle of a revolver pressed against his temple.

"No sound. I'll kill you if you move. Where are the comrades? Which room? How many? Code? Short answers. Try crying out and you're gone."

Vasiliev lifted his hand.

"First floor. Number 5. Three men. Two quick knocks, two slow."

Vasiliev hit him in the neck with his open hand. The yardman fell to the floor without uttering a sound. The rear door swung open and Novitsky came in with two constables. They silently followed Vasiliev up the stairs. Novitsky tapped his shoulder and winked. Good. They'd found the cabbie trussed up behind the fence. There had been no alarm. The three men stood to the side as Vasiliev examined the door frame, ran his fingers over the hinges. Then he knocked, two fast, two slow. A rustling inside. As soon as he saw the handle turn, Vasiliev threw his full weight against the door, breaking it down. He fell into the room crushing one of the revolutionaries under the spintered door. Novitsky fired over him and leaped into the room, shouting and cursing. His men tumbled in after him. Vasiliev was on his feet in a instant, his wig askew, his dress torn, pointing his revolver into the astonished face of the bearded man. The terrorists offered no resistance. It was over in a few seconds.

Vasiliev had made sure Novitsky would bring along his uniform; he had no wish to enter Police Headquarters swathed in a white linen dress. While he changed in the police, cab, he told Novitsky his good story.

"There's still a lot I don't know. Perhaps Szymanski can fill us in. I doubt the revolutionaries will open up. I know them. But you've got them on a murder charge, even though we don't know who they killed. What a strange case! It's usually the victim we know and not the murderer."

They found Szymanski where they had left him. He was staring at his boots, a sheepish look on his face. He needed no encouragement to tell them everything, from the burglary to the negotiations with the terrorists. He produced the burnt post card. "I figured out it was Zhuk. I wanted to make sure. I offered to work with them. A vengeful Pole, you know. I don't think I entirely convinced them. I thought I could turn them all over to you, Vasili Dementevich. But they kept me blindfolded most of the time. I had no idea where I was. I couldn't have led you to them. I feel quite foolish."

"Rightly so, Baron!" Vasiliev turned to Novitsky. "Burnt post cards," he groaned. "What next? More circumstantial evidence?"

"Now, now Vasiliev. You can't have it all. We've got you back. You've taken out the People's Will for us. And that wasn't even your assignment." Novitsky gazed at his map. He was pondering how to break the news to Vasiliev about his father. Perhaps this was not the time.

"I have a few more questions for the Baron," said Vasiliev. "Then we can let him go. Don't you agree, Vasili Dementevich?"

"Of course. Foolish man, but not a criminal. That's my verdict. Be happy you're not in the dock, Baron." Novitsky was eager to interview the terrorists, already preparing questions in his head. No, this was not the time to tell Vasiliev. He forgot to mention that

Kablukov had been assigned to Lopatkin. Later he would bitterly regret his lapse. He shook hands with Vasiliev, and dismissed Szymanski with a wave.

Novitsky rang his silver bell. An orderly appeared at once. "I want a description of Zhuk sent to all the frontier posts. And don't forget the ports. The bastard is probably making a run for it."

Vasiliev questioned Szymanski on the way out. There wasn't much more to learn from him. The Baron confirmed that Lopatkin had been involved in the plot to compromise Vasiliev. But aside from the notebook he couldn't provide any information about the murder of the Rabbi. Vasiliev left him looking utterly deflated. Later he learned that Szymanski had gone abroad. Another defeated Polish exile. Where would it end? Vasiliev knew he had one more vital thing left to do.

Chapter Sixty

A few minutes after midnight, Mendel walked into Kaniever's, accompanied by two men. He saw Zhuk right away. He spoke a few words to the others. They sat down at tables flanking the door. Mendel sauntered over to Zhuk, his hands stuck in his pockets. There were some people he did not like to touch. He greeted Zhuk with a curt nod and signaled him to sit down. Rachel brought them two lagers.

"You have the silver, right? Yes, well, here's your passport and a skull cap to go with it. You're Jewish now, remember. You don't need a prayer shawl. But the cap will distract from your goyish mug."

Zhuk handed over his bag of silver coins. Mendel peered inside, and hefted it in the palm of his hand. "Feels right," he said. "You'll go across with Sholem the Horse Thief. He's been over the route a hundred times. Only one difference this time. It'll be a legitimate trip. Selling horses for the Austrian cavalry. He's got a license. Papers are in order. No need to worry. Nobody can track you this way. Once you're over the border you'll hand back the passport. From then on you're on your own."

Zhuk took the passport and stuffed it in his jacket. He fingered the skullcap. "You think...is this necessary?"

"Christ, man! It's not going to convert you. You're lucky we didn't circumcise you."

Zhuk flushed and stood up.

"You'll leave in an hour. So sit down and have another lager. You'll be drinking alone." Mendel walked away without another word. One of his friends went into the street and looked around. The other kept his eyes on Zhuk as he followed Mendel out the door. The three of them disappeared into the night. It was twelve fifteen.

Serov turned back along the path leading through the Kadet Woods. He heard two more shots before he came out on the Boulevard. A tram was waiting. He got on, and rode back into town, heading for Lopatkin's house. He wondered whether they would make straight for it, or wait until it was light. "Don't let her get near Lopatkin," had been Vasiliev's parting words. He took up his post in a grove of trees in the Palace Park opposite Lopatkin's house, adopting the classic position of a *stolb*. He resigned himself to standing there throughout the night, if necessary. There was still a light in a corner room of the house. He wished he had stopped for tea on the way. No matter. He had stayed awake for longer periods. The light went out in the corner room. To the east he saw lightning. "That too," he grumbled to himself. He couldn't see his watch. But he reckoned it was one o'clock.

Vasiliev took a police cab from Police Headquarters to the Jewish Hospital. That's where they had taken the girl. A strange choice.

Palace Park

But perhaps the police equated Jews and revolutionaries. Both enemies of the state. Was this Novitsky's doing? He found it hard to believe. It must have been a subordinate. When he arrived the place was like a madhouse. He questioned a medical orderly who was hurrying past him. "More victims of the pogroms. They're bringing them in from the south again."

Vasiliev made his way to the administrator. Standing in front of the office, surrounded by a cluster of nurses and young doctors, Dr. Margulies was the center of attention. He was calmly giving orders, receiving reports. He looked exhausted. He acknowledged Vasiliev with a nod. Vasiliev pushed through the group. "Sorry, Doctor, an emergency police matter. Where did they send the girl from Police Headquarters?"

Margulies did not seem to understand. A nurse whispered to him. He looked annoyed and gestured abruptly. The nurse signaled Vasiliev to follow her. The corridors were lined with cots. People lying on them. Bandages, splints and blood. Outside a crowded ward a cot had been pushed into a narrow space under the staircase. A policeman sat on the stairs. Vasiliev identified himself. "She's mumbling about something," said the constable. "I can't understand a word."

Vasiliev squatted down beside her; she was lying on a blood-stained sheet. "I'm Vasiliev. Your boys tried to take me out. Who ordered it?"

The girl's eyes fluttered. She tried to focus. "Water!" she gasped. Vasiliev told the constable to fetch a glass. He wet his handkerchief and moistened her lips. "I don't know how badly you're hurt. Maybe internal injuries. So just a drop. He wiped her forehead.

"My ribs. They feel caved in," she muttered. Vasiliev touched his side. "Yes, I know how it feels. I'll try to get a doctor to look at you. But they're trying to patch up their own people."

"It might help…" she swallowed hard and winced…"to tell… I'm…was Jewish."

"So, you took a chance with Rebecca."

She opened her eyes wide.

"Listen, I know all about her. All except one thing. What is she planning?"

The girl tried to lick her lips. Vasiliev squeezed a few drops of water from his handkerchief into her open mouth.

"Try not to swallow. Just absorb it."

The girl was silent for a few minutes. Vasiliev was afraid he had lost her. She began to speak quietly. "I'm going to die. Isn't that so?"

"Tell me about Rebecca."

"She joined us. We…I trusted her."

"Did you give her a weapon?"

"Yes."

"All right. Next question. The last. Then I'll get the doctor. Who gave you orders to take me out?"

"No orders. Zhuk was our contact. No names. Only knew you were getting close…" she coughed, spitting blood, "…close to us."

"Not true. I didn't know anything about your organization in Kiev. Someone used you to get rid of me. Who was it?"

"Don't know. His information was always good."

Vasiliev swore under his breath. He stood up and went back down the corridor. Margulies was still standing in the same place. There were fewer people around him. Vasiliev waited until the last one had been sent off.

"Doctor Margulies. The girl. A revolutionary, but Jewish. Take a look. I think it'll take two minutes. I promised her. She is probably dying."

Margulies followed him, stopping every few meters to check a patient, speak a word of encouragement, give an instruction. They came to the staircase.

Margulies bent over her. Vasiliev thought of Irina. Same color hair, same age, only…"

"She's gone," said Margulies and covered her face with the sheet.

For some reason, Vasiliev looked at his watch. It was two o'clock in the morning. He could hear the dull rumble of thunder.

Vera was happy to wake up in her own bed. Still dark. It was her third night at home. She thought she wouldn't be able sleep for excitement. She groped for the revolver under her pillow. She had taken it out of its hiding place the day before. She kept worrying about it. She had never fired a gun. She had examined it carefully. Just point it and pull the trigger. Was that all there was to it? She had no one to ask. The Angel would have been terrified if she knew. The owner of the teahouse could not be trusted, but he surely could tell her how it worked. She thought about trying it out. But where? It would make a lot of noise. People would come running. Unless. She remembered the clouds gathering at sunset. A humid day. Suppose…She turned her face toward the icon, before falling asleep again. The noise woke her with a start. Her prayers had been answered. A loud clap of thunder. The sudden drumming of rain on the roof. She imagined it sounded just like gunfire. And the thunder. Wasn't it heavy artillery? She almost laughed out loud.

She crawled out of bed and lit a candle. The gun seemed very heavy. She held it with two hands and pointed it at the far wall. She touched the trigger. Nothing happened. She pulled it harder. Still nothing. The day before she had broken open the chamber. There were six bullets. No more would fit in. What was wrong? A roll of thunder. Was the storm getting weaker? She took the gun closer to the candle. She found the safety catch and released it. She pointed the gun again and squeezed the trigger. The explosion was deafening. The recoil knocked her down on the bed. Such power! I have to hold it tighter. Arms closer to my body. Once more. She timed the second shot with a loud peal of thunder. She felt the shock go through her arm and body. But she remained standing. She felt exultant. No more practice. Only four bullets left. That should be enough. She slipped the gun back under her pillow. She opened the door to let the smoke out and the rain felt good on her face. She could see the sky beginning to lighten in the east. A few hours and it would be daybreak. Her day. The Angel was going to bring food early in the morning. Then, together, they would go to the house of the Esteemed Person. It was all working out.

Mendel had given strict instruction to Sholem. "Don't let him slip away with the passport. I'm honor bound to get it back."

"So how's that to be done."

"Christ! Do I have to think of everything? I don't know. Loosen his saddle girths. If he tries to ride off he'll fall on his ass."

Sholem chuckled. "Mendel the genius."

Mendel turned away. "Genius," he muttered under his breath. "Yeah, I should have been a professor." He left Sholem. There was business to attend to in Kiev.

At daybreak after the storm, Sholem and his gang were crossing a stream. They had ridden all night and were close to the Austrian border. The rain had let up. Half the horses were across when Sholem saw the riders. "Shit! Bandits!" he exclaimed. Only Zhuk heard him. The one time I'm legal the bastards show up. A hundred horses. My whole capital. They'll not crucify me too. "Hey," he shouted to his men. "*Oprishniki* coming up fast. Beat it to hell. Scatter the horses!" His outriders were unarmed. Without guns it was hard to stampede the horses. Despite their shouts only a few mounts broke away. The men galloped off. Zhuk was riding with Sholem. He savagely spurred his roan mare. She shot forward and he felt the saddle sliding off her back. He fell heavily, but clung to the reins, trying to check her flight. She dragged him in the mud until he thought his arms would be yanked out of their sockets. He was forced to let go. He staggered to his feet. A rider came up and leaned over to peer into his face.

"A Jew horseman," he laughed. "Can't even stay in the saddle."

Zhuk wiped his face. "No, no. A Christian!" he shouted. Suddenly he remembered the skullcap. He reached up and snatched it from his head. "No, no!" he repeated. "A mistake. Look, I'll prove it." He began to loosen his trousers.

"Mother of God, keep your dick to yourself." The rider took out his pistol and shot Zhuk in the forehead. He fell backward clutching his skullcap, his trousers sliding down. The rider dismounted and ripped open Zhuk's blouse. He pulled out the passport. "David Pressman!" He screamed with laughter. "A good Christian name. And he wants to show me his dick." He swung back in the saddle, tossing the passport on Zhuk's chest and rode off.

Vasiliev found Serov standing under a leafy chestnut tree. It gave little protection from the heavy downpour. Serov was soaked. He told Vasiliev what had happened. Vasiliev nodded. "They'll not try anything until it's light. Let's get some rest. We need to dry out, too. Now that we're officially alive again we can go back to the Hotel. On the way I'll bring you up to date. We've run out of things to detect. I'll squeeze the truth out of Lopatkin, if necessary. I've got the book and the documents. He'll break, I'm sure of it! One way or the other he'll break." They stopped at the hotel buffet. A sleepy waiter served them tea. They gulped it down and went to their rooms. "We'll get up at dawn. A few hours. We just need a few hours," Vasiliev said.

Chapter
Sixty-One

Ruth was startled to wake up with Rebecca standing in the doorway to her room. "You always look so pretty asleep," said Rebecca. "Some man will see you every morning that way." Ruth blushed. Rebecca ordered coffee and brushed Ruth's hair. Ruth couldn't remember when she had last done that.

"So how is your patient? You certainly take good care of her."

"She can walk around her room now. She's still weak. But what a change. I never thought I'd see her looking like this."

"That's wonderful. She owes you a lot. Will she show you the paymaster's house soon."

Ruth felt a strange sensation, as if her heart were swelling inside her. "Today," she said.

Rebecca did not miss a stroke as she continued to brush out Ruth's curls.

"When I finish it'll be your turn to do me." Rebecca smiled at her sister.

After breakfast Rebecca asked Ruth when she was going out. "You'll be sure to make a note of the address won't you? I'm going to meet David at the University. I'll be back late."

Ruth watched Rebecca leave the house and walk down the street. The pavement was still wet from the rain. Some of the trees were dripping, as if in mourning, Ruth thought. But for whom she wondered? She sat at the window for a long time. Then she began to dress. She selected a high neck, black dress, and underneath she wore around her neck a gold chain and Star of David, a present from her father on her last birthday. She adjusted the black cloak around her shoulders. She felt the somber color matched her mood. She told Reb Ben-Zion she was going out for the day. He was to be in charge.

Ruth arrived at Vera's at nine o'clock. Vera was dressed and waiting. She looked gaunt. But she seemed happy, if a little nervous. Ruth took her arm and helped her down to the waiting cab. They drove off down the muddy, rutted street. Vera felt the cab rattle and her heart constricted. "No hills, please!" she muttered to Ruth.

David and Aaron had been sitting in a cab at the end of Vera's street. They had already hired the same Jewish cabby who had driven Ruth and Aaron to the hospital and helped to bring out Vera. They told him some story about needing to follow Ruth without alarming her. They said they were protecting her from harm. They waited until the cab with Ruth and Vera passed. Then David signaled the cabby to keep close behind them.

Vasiliev and Serov woke up refreshed after four hours sleep in their old rooms at the Hotel d'Europe. Serov had gone out for his favorite rolls. He brought back plum jam as well. "Almost as good as mama's" He was grinning. They discussed their plan over the samovar.

"I don't want any surprises. You'll cover the back entrance. I'll stay in front. If they don't show up by ten o'clock, my guess is they won't be coming today. At ten I'll go in, and you'll come to the front. Just in case." Serov wanted to ask why they didn't just arrest Lopatkin and question him at Police Headquarters. He thought he knew. Lopatkin had powerful protectors. A message to the Governor-General would end it right then and there. Serov never questioned Vasiliev's judgment. Except during the end game of a chess match. Perhaps, Vasiliev had decided he would have to use methods that wouldn't work, or else wouldn't be permitted at Headquarters. Serov had listened carefully when Vasiliev said he would break Lopatkin. He felt Vasiliev was right. But he also knew that Vasiliev was in a hurry now. And he was angry. And why not? After all, Lopatkin had tried to kill them. And Irina was waiting for them.

They took an ordinary cab and ordered the cabbie to drop them off at the opposite end of the Park. As they made their way along the path they went over their preparations. Had they anticipated all the eventualities? Vasiliev thought so. They stood together for a moment behind a screen of bushes across from Lopatkin's mansion.Vasiliev glanced at his watch It was 7.30. The street was quiet and empty; no one was strolling in the park. The only sound was the twittering of birds. Looking for worms in the moist soil, Serov thought idly, and then drove such thoughts out of his head. The rain had cooled things off. Clouds still covered half the city, but the other half was in full sunlight. The sky was stubbornly divided into two nearly equal parts. Serov felt a twinge in his arm. So what's it to be, he wondered, clear and no pain or darkness and pain? He waited for Vasiliev's signal, a brief nod, and then made his way by a circular route to the back of the house. The sun was winning its battle against the clouds and Serov felt the pain recede. This was going to be a beautiful, sunlight day, he decided.

Vasiliev felt uneasy for all his brave words about breaking Lopatkin. That would be the easy part. He was more worried about how to handle Rebecca. She was strong-minded, vengeful and armed, a dangerous combination. But he didn't want her to get hurt. That's why he had been reluctant to bring in Novitsky. Perhaps it would have been better to go into Lopatkin's mansion and wait for her there. But that could lead to further complications. No telling how Lopatkin would react. He thought he had a better chance to head her off outside, where there would be less chance of someone getting hurt by accident. He thought briefly of Ruth. He would soon be saying goodbye to her. Perhaps that was for the best.

He watched the cook go out for provisions and return. Governesses and their wards were beginning to show up for their morning stroll through the park. They smiled at the officer in uniform; nothing odd these days about police standing guard. Reassuring in fact. It was close to ten o'clock when a cab drew up in front of Lopatkin's. At first, no one emerged. The sun flashed off the cab window facing the park. Vasiliev couldn't make out the features of the passengers, but he was sure they were both women. He had started forward but then he stopped. The cab door had opened on the far side. He caught a glimpse of the two women getting out. He was taken by surprise; this was something he had not anticipated. The cab remained stationary blocking his view. It was only when they mounted the steps that he recognized one of the figures. He was stunned. What was Ruth doing here? The other woman was leaning on her heavily. It could only have been Stepan's wife. The maid let them in. Vasiliev hesitated, a moment he would regret all his life. On impulse he started forward again. At the sound of shots he broke into a run. A sequence of reports—first one, a short pause, then two almost simultaneously. Had it been like this for David and Aaron? He half expected more shots, three more. But only silence greeted him as he pushed open the door, which had been left ajar, and entered the house.

Vasiliev was already inside when a second cab hurtled down the street, coming to an abrupt stop in front of Lopatkin's. Three people vaulted out of the cab. Aaron was running toward the back of the house, while Rebecca and David charged the open front door.

Vasiliev cautiously made his way down the corridor lined with brass fittings. He had drawn his revolver. The smell of cordite grew stronger. He heard a sound like a child whimpering. He came into a big room lined with paintings. What he saw horrified him. For many years after a recurrent nightmare would haunt him. He would be standing at the entrance to a room of dying people, writhing on the floor, reaching out to him, and his legs would not move. His whole body would be paralyzed with fear.

Lopatkin was cringing behind his desk, blood all over his face. The whimpering sounds came from his lips, grotesquely twisted into a monstrous rictus. There was a bullet hole in the wall high over his head. The desk was scarred where another bullet had ripped a long scar on the surface spraying splinters of wood in all directions and cutting Lopatkin's face into a dozen bleeding wounds. He had wrapped his arms around his chest as if to protect himself, but in that first quick glance, Vasiliev could not see any other signs that he had been shot.

Two women were sprawled on the floor, pools of blood forming around them. Kneeling over them was a policeman. The man lifted his tear stained face to Vasiliev. It was Kablukov. "I had to shoot," he gasped. Vasiliev saw two guns lying near the bodies. He recognized Kablukov's gun, a Smith-Wesson Model 3. The other gun was an old fashioned Colt. Where did it come from? Only later, was Vasiliev able to puzzle out what had happened. At least most of what had happened. Always the little gaps would remain. For the moment he had no time to reflect. He too was on his knees cradling Ruth in his arms. A bullet had passed through her cheek, pierced her brain, and exited at the side of her skull. No one could have survived that wound for more than a split second; she must have died instantly. Her eyes were starring wildly, as if pleading with him. The body of Vera was sprawled beside her, her arm outstretched as if in supplication. Blood was pouring out of her neck. Vasiliev felt the tears rolling down his cheeks. "How could you have killed her?" he murmured, not raising his eyes from Ruth's once beautiful face now destroyed by the bullet that had taken her life. Kablukov had no time to respond.

He and Vasiliev turned at the same time toward the entrance to the room, hearing the front door slam behind them and the hurried approach of muffled steps down the long carpeted corridor. Suddenly, Rebecca was in the room, screaming, David right behind her. She rushed past them straight at Lopatkin. Pulling a revolver from her bag, she began firing even before she got to the desk. The first few bullets tore into his chest; then, at point blank range, she emptied the chamber into his sagging body. Vasiliev automatically registered six shots. Kablukov fumbled for his gun he had dropped on the floor next to him. Vasiliev shouted at him, "No!" Kablukov looked at him in astonishment and turned his gun on Rebecca. David shot him in the shoulder. Kablukov fell back; his gun skittered across the floor. There was a commotion at the rear of the house. Serov, his weapon drawn, burst into the room, dragging Aaron by the arm. For an instant no one moved.

"Sergeant, get a bandage from the maid! Anything rag will do. A tourniquet for Kablukov." Vasiliev gently laid Ruth down; an aureole of hair spread around her head. The front of his tunic was stained crimson.

When Novitsky arrived Vasiliev had his story ready. The maid, Lydia, had told him enough to begin with. She had let the two women in without announcing them. "The one looked so weak and helpless. The other was so beautiful. Master was angry. He shouted at them. 'What are you doing here?' I got frightened and ran looking for the constable. I didn't mean no harm." She was sobbing as the cook led her away into the kitchen.

Kablukov had regained consciousness after a few minutes. "What happened?" he asked.

"No, constable. That's my question," said Vasiliev, not recognizing his own voice.

Serov loosened the tourniquet and then tightened it again. Kablukov grunted.

"I heard Lydia cry out. The Chief ordered me...I was suppose to protect him." His voice was hoarse, hardly rising above a whisper. "The woman with the gun, the cripple, had the gun pointed at Lopatkin. The other one looked terrified. I drew my revolver and ordered her to drop hers. She fired, hitting the desk. Lopatkin screamed. I aimed for her gun hand. But the other one, the beauty, grabbed her arm and spun her around. Her second shot went wild. I fired at the same time, just as she spun around. But you understand what happened, Vasili Vasilievich. The other one, the beauty, was trying...Oh God! If only she hadn't tried..." There was a catch in his voice. "My shot caught the cripple in the neck and then...It must have gone clean through and struck the other one, the beautiful one, in the face." He sobbed. "I've never missed my target before."

"Well, Vasili Vasilievich. A Shakespearian climax. Whose blood is that all over you? Never mind. It seems Kablukov owes you his life. But, tell me, how did you let them go?" Novitsky had perched on Lopatkin's desk. The room had been cleared. Lydia was scrubbing the floor.

"My God, girl, haven't you something else to do?" Lydia ran out, crying.

Vasiliev was sitting in Stepan's chair. Serov stood behind him. Vasiliev went over the details. All but the final scene of the last act; that's the way he would always think of it.

Novitsky listened intently. "You'll write it up for me, won't you? Strange, though. The great detective and his valiant assistant immobilized by three young revolutionaries with—what, one loaded gun among them? Hardly seems like the same man who crashed into the nest of the People's Will."

"But then I had you backing me up, Vasili Dementevich."

Novitsky laughed grimly. As they left the house Novitsky

thought to himself: let someone else tell him about his father's death.

Kaniever's was having a slow night. Rachel leaned on the bar, thinking about the coming High Holy Days. It was always like this, quiet, the week before. About midnight Mendel walked in. She wondered idly why he was alone. But never ask Mendel anything, it was the wisest course. She'd learned that over the years. He greeted her with a curt nod. That too was not his usual style. Mendel depressed? Was he too thinking of the High Holy Days? Unlikely! She doubted that Mendel ever gave a moment's thought to atonement. He sat down in his usual place. At least that was something to rejoice about. He signaled to her—a lager. Better and better. Pretty soon he'd be kicking up his heels. He kept staring at the door.

Kaniever poked his head around the corner, saw Mendel and withdrew. The plot thickens, thought Rachel.

Time passed slowly. Rachel never thought of it otherwise. Someone was expected, she guessed. And maybe he—or was it she?—isn't going to come. But Rachel was wrong for once. The door opened, and Davy the Giant Killer appeared. Yes, she thought, appeared is the right word. Just like he dropped from the clouds. But not, she decided, from heaven. Tonight no one was looking normal. She felt a shiver go through her.

David stood over Mendel, holding out both hands.

"I wasn't sure. Not after everything."

"A promise is a promise."

"There are more sacred things."

"All right, honor then."

"Sit."

Rachel was already drawing a lager. She brought it over.

David looked up and thanked her. She saw pain written all over his face. She noticed the package for the first time. She went back to the bar and began polishing glasses that were already sparkling clean. There were a few smugglers drinking in a corner. They kept their eyes fixed on the tops of their shoes.

David placed the package on the table and slid it across to Mendel. Mendel pulled the passport out of his pocket and handed it to David. He opened the package on his lap and examined the revolver.

"One spent cartridge. Courtesy of Davy the Giant Killer, now Dead Eye Davy. He doesn't miss." Mendel forced a smile, but his heart wasn't in it.

David looked at his passport. The top edges were stained. He opened it. The stain had seeped down a few centimeters into each page. There were no visa stamps.

"Sorry for the damaged goods."

"Smugglers don't need passports, do they? So—what...?" David snapped off the end of his thought. There were no questions to be asked. It had been agreed.

David ignored his lager. "Thanks, Mendel. Funny isn't it? I have the feeling neither of us got much out of this exchange."

They got up together and shook hands. After a brief hesitation they embraced. David left without a backward glance. Mendel sat down and finished his lager. Then he raised David's glass to the ceiling where the exploits of great thieves were immortalized. He swallowed it in one gulp. He thought about what David had said. He had heard about the rest. The catastrophe. Ruth was dead. What would David and Rebecca do now? Go underground or leave the country. There was no other choice. As for him he had handed over Zhuk's bag of silver to Sholem the Horse Thief who had lost all his capital to bandits. After all, Sholem had gone back to get the passport. Fair trade.

Finally, it was Maria Alexandrovna who broke the news to Vasiliev. They mourned the old Count together. Vasiliev and Serov attended Ruth's funeral, Vasiliev wearing a black band on his arm. It seemed as if half of Jewish Kiev was there. She was buried next to her father. Reb Ben-Zion recited the prayers. Novitsky posted several men discreetly outside the gates of the cemetery. But Rebecca, Aaron, and David did not show up. They seemed to have vanished completely. Years later Vasiliev heard they had gone to America. A few days later Vasiliev and Serov left Kiev for Moscow. Vasiliev submitted his report to Ivan. Maria Alexandrovna's last words still rang in his ears. "Don't be hard on him. He was only doing his duty." He was hard on Drenteln. But it didn't matter. The Tsar approved Kutaisov's report. In less than a year, the law of May 3, 1882 forbade Jews from settling outside the cities and towns of the Pale. No Jew could live within fifty kilometers of the frontier unless he had been enrolled before October 1857 in a local community.

In the fall of 1881 Vasiliev rode out with Serov to *Nettles* to take over his inheritance. Vasiliev could tell that Serov felt uneasy about staying at the manor house. He was even reluctant to join Vasiliev for dinner the first night in the old Count's formal dining room. Vasiliev insisted. They almost quarreled. But in the end Serov preferred to eat in the kitchen. The cook had befriended his mother and he had known the scullery maid when she was a child.

Vasiliev sat alone at the table covered with a spotless but faded linen cloth dating from the early years of the century and richly embroidered along the edges by some dutiful house serf of his father's. He ate as quickly as possible, and then called to the kitchen for Serov to join him for a brandy and a smoke on the veranda. Serov appeared, smiling, and tossed a remark over his shoulder that Vasiliev couldn't quite catch. He heard laughter in the kitchen. This was not going to be easy, Vasiliev thought. Or perhaps it wouldn't work at all.

He had been thinking how they would work together to improve the place—perhaps hire a German manager, restore the old orchard and introduce a three field system with new strains of rye and oats. All plans aimed at raising enough cash to campaign for Irina's release and a free life in Siberia. But as he sat there quietly gazing over the fields, with the sounds of evening starting up, the distant croaking of frogs in the small ponds by the woods, and the plaintive calls of the nightjar, he wondered how he would manage to become a landlord.

He rose from his chair and dismissed the servants. When he returned Serov was gone. Then he heard the sound of hoof beats, and he knew Serov was riding back to the village. He crushed the rest of his cigar on the railing and went down to the ponds. The croaking had reached a climax. He looked back at the manor house, where a single light burned in the upstairs, the old Count's bedroom and now his. No, he decided, it would not work.

That night he dreamed of Kiev. Rachel was skipping down a path in the Botanical Gardens, her small veiled hat slipping off her head, falling to the ground. He wanted to call out to her, but the trees were closing in, cutting her off. Her heard her cry out, and he woke suddenly, drench in sweat.

The next morning Serov returned and glanced sheepishly at Vasiliev when he joined him for breakfast on the veranda

"So, Sergeant, did you make sure that all was well in the village?" Serov smiled and shook his head.

"Sorry, Vasili Vasilievich. You know what they say; 'Trust in God but don't make a mistake.'"

"We won't make a mistake, my friend. Look, let's agree. You know you're welcome here, but you'll live where you want. I need your help for a while, let's say a month to get a few things sorted out. I'll hire a German manager and we'll go back to our own business in Moscow. As soon as we can arrange it, we'll make off for Siberia, you and I. We'll find Irina. Another life! What do you say?"

Serov rubbed his chin. "Well, Vasili Vasilievich, you know you're always welcome in the village, but you'll live where you want."

Vasiliev burst out laughing. He clasped Serov's hand.

Epilogue

Early in 1882 in New York at a meeting of the American Geographical Society a journalist for *The Century Magazine* delivered an address on the Siberian exile system. He was already well acquainted with the region, having travelled there for two and a half years and written his impressions in a book, *Tent Life in Siberia*. In his talk he proposed to return and interview the exiled revolutionaries who had been involved in the various conspiracies against the Tsar culminating in his assassination. He had obtained permission from the Minister of Interior. Together with a young artist, Mr. Frost, he planned to set out for the adventure of his life. His name was George Kennan.

The Russian consul in New York reported to Petersburg that Kennan had expressed the view in his address that Russian exiles abroad had misrepresented the exile system, painting it in lurid colors. The consul had reason to believe that Kennan thought the nihilists were wrong-headed fanatics. When Kennan's request was received in the Ministry, a man known as the Iron Colonel had been instructed to find a reliable officer to accompany Kennan in order to facilitate his trip.

A telegram from Ivan was delivered to Vasiliev a few days after he and Serov had returned to duty at Moscow Police Headquarters. When Serov handed it to him, he had a strange expression on his face.

"It's marked 'urgent.'"

Vasiliev hesitated a moment before reading it. Ivan's urgent telegrams, he reflected, had a habit of leading to disaster. The first one involved him in the Ushakova case and the assassination of Alexander II; the second had plunged him into the killing fields of Kiev. He placed it on his desk, and asked Serov to prepare the samovar.

Serov handed him a glass of strong tea with two cubes of sugar on the saucer and stood at attention, waiting for the summons.

When Vasiliev finally opened the telegram, his face broke into the crooked smile Serov knew so well. But this time Vasiliev's face seemed almost radiant.

"We're ordered to Siberia, Serov. Ordered!" he exclaimed.

THE REAL AND THE IMAGINARY

In April 1881, a month after the assassination of Tsar Alexander II by terrorists of the People's Will, anti-Jewish riots, or pogroms, broke out in Ukraine. Beginning in the province of Kherson, they spread to other provinces and to major cities, including Kiev. What caused them remains a matter of dispute among historians. Contemporary accounts by journalists, officials and foreign observers offered a variety of explanations. Were they spontaneous outbreaks by Ukrainians—still called Little Russians by many—and Russians, reacting to rumors that the Jews had killed the Tsar, or to alleged exploitation by Jewish capitalists, estate managers, tavern owners and money lenders? Or were they incited by the surviving members of the People's Will, hoping to recover from the widespread arrests following the assassination of the Tsar by creating chaos and a breakdown of public order leading to a social revolution? Were they the work of outside agitators or local groups? Or were they organized by unknown forces working in secret for hidden aims? Variations on these themes circulated widely, but no definitive conclusions were reached at the time or since then. Part of the confusion arose from the ambivalent reaction of the forces of public order and up to and including the Tsar himself, Alexander III, the son of the assassinated Alexander II. The Tsar was known to share anti-Semitic feelings with many of his top officials including the Governor-General, Drenteln and the Minister of Interior, Ignatiev. But these men also deplored the breakdown in public order, and they sought to bring the disorders under control. Drenteln's initial, confusing orders to the army, his delayed "peace ride" on the day following the outbreak of the disorders in Kiev, and his subsequent shifts in reporting the causes of the pogroms reveal the mixed motives of Russia's leading administrators. Kiev, called the "mother of Russian cities", picturesquely located on the bluffs overlooking the Dniepr River, was an ethnic mosaic of Ukrainians, Russians, Jews, Poles and smaller numbers of Germans, Tatars and other nationalities. The struggle for cultural supremacy between the Poles, who held the city for several hundred years until the mid-seventeenth century, and the Russians had been largely resolved following the repression of the Polish rising in 1863-64 and the exile of many rebels. But within a generation a new phase of the struggle had begun. Ukrainian nationalist intellectuals asserted their right to use their own language in the face of a growing russification, which had been aimed originally at Polish influence. The Jews, who had been confined to live in the Pale of Settlement since the time of Catherine II "the Great", were caught in the middle of these ethnic and religious conflicts. The official investigation of Count Kutaisov into the causes of the pogroms led to further restrictions on the movement of the Jews and other discriminatory measures, including the first quotas on their admission to universities. These, in turn, sparked increased Jewish participation in oppositionist political movements from Zionism to Marxism. In the end, Russia was the loser.

CAST of CHARACTERS

Several historical characters are mentioned but do not appear in person, including Alexander III, Princess Yurovskaya, the morganatic wife of Alexander II, Nikolai Ignatiev, Minister of Interior under Alexander III, Petr Vannovsky, Minister of War, St. Vladimir, Kievan prince who introduced Christianity to Russia, Bogdan Khmelnitsky, seventeenth century Cossack Hetman, Lt-General Loris-Melikov, Minister of Interior under Alexander II, Mykola Lysenko, Ukrainian composer, Professor Antonovich, Ukrainian archeologist, A.I.Brodsky, other capitalists and revolutionaries of the People's Will.

Historical figures who make an appearance are as follows:

Alexander Romanovich Drenteln, Governor General of Kiev
Maria Alexandrovna Drentelna, his wife
Vasili Dementevich Novitsky, Kiev Chief of Police
Sergei Iulevich Witte (later Count and Minister of Finance)
Count Pavel Ippolitovich Kutaisov
Alter Kaniever, the tavern owner
Engineer Abrahamson
Captain Rudov of the Gendarmes

Imaginary characters

Major, Inspector Vasili Vasilievich Vasiliev
Sergeant Serov
Ivan, the Iron Colonel
Irina Davydova (Swan)
Rabbi Meier

Rebecca Moiseevna Meier, his elder daughter
Ruth Moiseevna Meier, his younger daughter
Aaron Meier, their cousin
David Pressman
Mendel "the Smuggler" Bornstein
Ezra Ben-Zion
Dr. Mikhail Borisovich Margulies
Iakov Iakovlevich Galperin
Lev Ivanovich Lopatkin
Baron Jan Szymanski
Stepan Tikhonov
Vera Tikhonova
Count Vorontsov (a real name but here a fictional person)
Constable Kablukov, "our Prussian"
Boris Zhuk

All the minor characters are also imagined.

Readers who wish to pursue an interest in the pogroms might begin with I. Michael Aronson, *Troubled Waters: The Origins of the 1881 Anti-Jewish Pogroms in Russia* (Pittsburgh, University of Pittsburgh Press, 1990).

www.ingramcontent.com/pod-product-compliance
Lightning Source LLC
Chambersburg PA
CBHW030351030726
47497CB00002B/287